I0588745

LESSONS FROM MY MOTHER

Bessie Le Couteur

BOOK ONE
ASTON FAMILY SERIES

Copyright © 2025 by Bessie Le Couteur

All rights reserved. This book, or parts thereof,

may not be reproduced in any form without permission.

Independently published v.6

Cover art Copyright © 2025 BESSIE LE COUTEUR

ISBN: 9780646720517 (Paperback)

ISBN: 9780646720524 (EPub)

This is a work of fiction. The events described here are imaginary: The names, settings, places, and characters are fictitious and not intended to represent specific places or persons, living or dead. Any resemblance to actual events or persons is entirely coincidental.

prologue

SCROLL, SCROLL, SCROLL. PAUSE. Interesting. Scroll, scroll, scroll, scroll, scroll. Scroll. Pause. Double tap. Scroll, scroll, scroll.

Exhaling the tension in her body nervously and flicking her wrist, she flung her phone to the other side of the backseat. Silence didn't just make her uncomfortable; it made her anxious. She stole a look at her driver, who held the ever so professionally rigid stance of facing the road, and the road only unless called upon by his client. Not every driver was like Joseph—she reminded herself.

Dear Joe.

A familiar sense of anger rose in her chest, the memory of his sudden departure from his role as their long-standing family driver resurfacing.

She vehemently asked for an explanation from her father why he got rid of one of the remaining people who made it easier to deal with the slowly dissipating memories of her. Joe told stories of the conversations Iylah's mother shared with him, conversations filled with the banter and wit her mother was known for, filled in with her infectious laugh.

Her heart warmed whenever she got a chance to chat with Joe—always rather short-lived though. When confronted about his abrupt decision to fire Joe, her father shook his head and walked off into whatever room his newly acquired wife laid herself out in. There was never a forthcoming answer from him.

Too much time passed since the driver picked her up from LaGuardia Airport—nine minutes to be exact—for her to begin a conversation filled with small talk now?

Another sigh escaped—its hot air passing through her nostrils. Resigning to keep her words to herself, she turned her gaze upon the rather colorful red-mud-brick houses lining the streets of East Elmhurst, passing by. The colorfulness of the neighbourhood displayed in the diversity of people she witnessed trekking along the streets, minding their business.

People fascinated her. Particularly those who called New York City home.

Resting her chin on the knuckles of her hand, she honed her attention in on the surroundings the town car blitzed through. Anything to get her mind off the dull thudding heartbeat encompassing her ears. A hard swallow and another sigh couldn't settle the pulsing energy threatening to take over her body.

When is the peak of anxiety going to slope downwards? That's what Imelda said it would do.

She released her pent-up breath, faintly trying to grasp the words of her psychologist.

Her psychologist. Ha. It felt strange to take ownership of the few sessions she'd attended. When she first started, it was under the instruction of her lawyer and Lena—her sister, forever the dutiful caretaker—then it turned into a voluntary, rather timid basis.

No one likes to admit a weakness that can halt their day immediately. At least not her.

The town car came to a gradual, and timed stop.

"We're here, Miss Dawson. Your residence."

Oh, he speaks? Only to announce the obvious. So useful.

She softened her features, aware that her thoughts towards her driver were strewn across her face.

That plane ride and drive have made me mean. I need a cigarette.

Before she could gather her discarded phone, he pulled himself out of the driver's seat, holding her door open astutely.

Eager to please, are we?

A sense of remorse for her harsh unspoken words came over her as she stepped out into the spring air of Manhattan.

"Thank you." Her full, plump lips moved to give a gracious smile. "Sorry, I don't think I asked for your name?"

But she was also profoundly sure that he gave his name upon their introduction—she hadn't cared to listen. She paused briefly as her middle-aged driver granted her the courtesy of not being offended.

"Nick, ma'am. My name is Nick." He smiled, not too much, just polite enough.

He must have read her disdain and slight off-handed attitude. She seemed to wear it like an unwanted scarf around the neck.

"And I will be your driver for the duration of your stay, as directed by your father."

Not because you find me charming? I need a cigarette.

Tucking a stray lock of dark curl behind her ear, Iylah opened her mouth to apologize for her ways.

Nick, as efficient as ever, unloaded her travel bags from the back of the car before her words could make themselves known. She would make an effort—her mother taught her manners that she would not betray.

"I apologize for my mood, Nick. Long flights are a close second to my most hated." She spoke the truth, sliding one arm through the strap of her rucksack, looking to relieve Nick of the rest of her luggage.

"No need to apologize, Miss—"

"Please, just call me Iylah."

He nodded still with a polite smile, not saying a word. Probably against their code of ethics. Iylah was adamant there was a handbook for all drivers to abide and swear by lest they disgrace the class of distinguished drivers.

Now is not the best time to tell him I don't need his polite smile chauffeuring me around New York. How do I say that without sounding like a complete–

"Will that be all for today, Miss Dawson?" Nick stood, hands clasped around his front.

"Iylah." She would insist on not being made to feel older than she was. "Yes, actually, Nick, how about I call you when I need you? How does that sound?"

That came out better than she expected. Her mouth always caused trouble, rather the lack of control over it sometimes.

"Certainly." His right hand disappeared inside the breast of his intensely black suit jacket to reveal a business card.

For a New Yorker, there wasn't much New York about him—his lack of the twang and his polished demeanor gave it away.

So efficient, Nick.

Iylah reached out to receive the extended business card holding all of Nick's contact information. "Thanks, Nick. I'll give you a buzz."

He was off to his driver's seat with a quick nod, leaving Iylah to face her new residence. All courtesy of her dearest, hands off don't ask, don't tell, father.

Iylah's eyes darted across the brownstone facade of her Manhattan townhouse.

"So this is home."

All four stories of it. She inhaled the scent of Callery Pear trees lining the street with quick regret. She shook off a memory triggered by the smell, swallowing fast and rapidly to take the metallic taste with it.

Germany was far away now—no longer a cause of insecurity or concern. Prison had a way of keeping rotten people there - right? For her sake, she hoped so!

I need a cigarette!

one

WITH A LONG AND purposeful drag on her cigarette, held between her index and thumb, Iylah caught the smoke in her mouth, holding it there for a second longer. She inhaled the smoke pensively, imagining the traces of its contents filling her lungs, telling her body to chill out for five minutes.

One day she would have to answer for this. One day, but not right now.

Using her other hand, she took a swig of her now warm double shot espresso, courtesy of her new favorite coffee dealer, York Avenue.

Upon arriving in Manhattan, it took her weeks to sample the local gold nectar that is coffee in the area. Three months in, the winner according to her seasoned taste buds and caffeine-craving body was York Avenue. Although if she admitted honestly, this morning's coffee hit could have been better done. The barista appeared quite distracted and puffy-eyed. Late night? Or a bitter end to a relationship?

Her new favorite hobby of sorts—watching the figures that roamed the streets of this city and trying to figure out each story based on nothing more than a glance and a willful imagination.

True or not, this coffee lacked its intensity and tongue-tantalizing richness. But of course, she would drink it to its end—it would still do the job.

All she ever desired was for things to do their job in her life, even if the effort sat at the bare minimum.

Flicking her cigarette to the pavement, Iylah inched up the leg of her wide-legged caramel-colored trousers, avoiding getting remnants of any curb-side delicacy on them. Sticking out a clog-clad foot, she disintegrated the rest of the lit cigarette to its death.

Alright. Another day in paradise.

She flung the door to the entrance open, immediately hit with a stale wave of air-conditioning that somehow made her prefer the hot, industrial air outside. True to its original form, the building, once a Gothic Revival monument, held pockets where it trapped old recycled air. The first pocket welcomed anyone who entered the School's prestigious yet unassuming singular door. The rest of the building showed off its detailed carvings of gargoyles and creatures of the like—majestic windows lining the front allowing the light of day to pour in.

Instinctively, Iylah pushed her arms through the sleeves of her trusty light pullover jumper. With the changing season, she'd learned that the School preferred to keep its students awake by freezing them past the cooling relief from a hot summer's day.

Half pulling the jumper over her head, she gave a quick smile of acknowledgement to the security guard standing where he always stood each morning and every hour without fail. He was good at his job if all he had to do was watch every person who set foot through the School of Arts front door. He did the polite thing and smiled back at her, as he always had over the last three months.

Like many others in this building, they acknowledged her existence with politeness and a curiosity mild enough not to intrude, but interested enough to keep watching her minor efforts to fit in. Her take on it all was simply to keep them guessing.

Adjusting the strap of her rucksack on her shoulder, she ascended the four flights of stairs leading to the wide hallways. Students spilled over the dark wood floors, in a hurry to get to class, and some paying no concern to the consequences of tardiness—most of them mature enough to know better.

Iylah pulled her I.D. lanyard from her back pocket, carefully throwing it over her head. She adjusted any wandering strands of her curls that may have been casualties of her haste attire, adding them back into her messy bun. Her class didn't begin for another two hours, but this new pace of life had her wanting to put her best foot forward, going over her lesson plans for the day. Imelda would approve of this hard-fought new attitude.

Whether she ever admitted it to her father, he was right.

He did not want to continue sponsoring a twenty-nine-year-old woman who could not hold down a steady job in what seemed to be accumulating years. Short of being entirely financially cut off from his amassed fortune via the family trust, she wanted little contribution from him in the future. Apart from the townhouse he bought for her, of course, and the trust fund she could pull from at her desire until she became another man's problem.

Her father's accountant kept a rather persistent eye on her spending. She didn't need to be reminded of how well everyone else in the family was doing, as if that ever encouraged a single person to do better. Her mother would ever patiently come to her rescue with warm, sweet words to keep her father's commentary on her life appeased—

'She will find her feet, Freddy. You will find your feet, dear'.

Iylah remembered the certainty in her mother's eyes every time she said this. Each time she found herself unexpectedly but frequently flat on her face, those words and that look would stir her to return to her feet gingerly.

Being in New York felt like that—gingerly.

She swallowed away the choking companionship of grief in her throat. Missing her mother never a manageable task, and her absence became more complex as Iylah grew older.

The anger and all attempts to forget the grief had subsided. Running away from it led to many unsavory and hazardous arms that belonged behind bars.

Iylah's phone vibrated in her rucksack, her feet crossed the threshold of the faculty lounge. As usual, the few faces that were not held up in teaching a class decorated the perimeter of the lounge. Most faces were stuck to their phone screens, but a select few gazed up from their affairs to watch her entrance. No greetings came forth from them.

As usual, Iylah wouldn't let their demeanor dictate hers.

"Good morning." Her voice shattered the silence, offending the intentional lack of acknowledgement.

She wasn't sure how she had gained the disdain of half the faculty upon being hired. Whatever it was, they sure made up their minds about her. Yes, without even knowing her.

Two, no wait, three half-mumbled responses back.

Iylah decided to tip the rest of her rather pathetic coffee down the sink, disposing of its empty cup in the half-full rubbish bin next to the fridge—

An odd place to put it.

With the confidence of a baby elephant, imposing her presence and wobbling ahead anyway, she calmly weathered a smile, making eye contact with every pair of eyes available—simultaneously watching her walk across the room to grab a complimentary bottle of water from the stocked fridge.

All eyes except those of the same one person, who didn't pay her too much attention but always said hello and meant it.

She retrieved her phone, blindly rummaging through her rucksack. Finally, Lena's name popped up on her screen, along with a brief yet heartwarming message.

Lena Big Boss

Visit soon? The girls miss you xx P.S. I've forwarded all your mail to your new place. Love you xx

Iylah's smile grew genuine at the thought of her nieces, who fawned over her constantly.

If she counted properly, her last visit was close to two years ago since she last physically saw them. She held off on a visit to see her sister since her arrival back in the country because Lena knew how to draw unspoken things out of Iylah, much like their mother used to do. And she wasn't ready to talk just yet. If the twisting knots in her stomach were anything to go by, it could be awhile before she mentioned Germany to her father.

The magnificent thing she missed most about Europeans was their slight disdain for Americans. No one batted an eyelid under the knowledge of who her father was—one of America's self-made multi-millionaires. Or maybe billionaire? His current financial standing not something she tracked even remotely.

On cue, her smile disappeared just as quickly as the turning in her stomach began. If only time could hurry and bring distance to all the memories Germany embedded in her mind.

It appeared brutally obvious that she was not even close to being done talking, reliving, or healing from the ever-growing torrential downpour she constantly ran away from. One day she would learn—hopefully, one day.

Iylah's index finger hovered over the mouse-pad of her laptop, eyes scanning the screen, searching for the best flight out of New York to Washington, D.C.

For most of the late morning, she couldn't shake the idea of seeing familiar faces again. Lena's message made her miss having familiar bodies, friendly laughter, and familiar experiences around her.

Her welcome to this bustling cultural hub of a city was short-lived—as was her excitement to start over again.

Mistakes were her thing, but if this failed, she fearfully doubted she would have the energy to keep searching for whatever she sought after. Who knew? She certainly didn't.

On a whim—as was customary—she booked flights over the summer to see said familiar faces. If she was honest, she missed her family despite how different and difficult it happened to be when in the same room with half of them. She missed her mother. She wasn't sure if she would ever stop, or if the ache of her absence made a permanent residence in the hull of her ribcage.

She took a reflective slurp of her freshly squeezed juice courtesy of the deli down the street.

At this rate, I may book a private plane. There is nothing here for the next two weeks. Go figure.

Privy to the company her father flew privately with, she was sure they would bend over backward to provide a plane for one of Fredrick Dawson's daughters. Their relationship came in handy every so often and with a lot of perks—if you were into extravagance and fake friends.

Without hesitation, her fingers drifted over the keyboard, typing the company's name. There it was. A knowing smirk curled around the corners of her lips.

The door to the faculty lounge flung open with a robust creak.

Well, there goes my peace.

She didn't bother to look up—whoever it was probably had no words to share with her. She continued on her quest.

Ahuh!

With a gratified smile, she reached for her wallet to pull out her Amex Centurion credit card. Her eyes briefly landed on the individual who entered the room. It was him. Her frequent greeter.

Name? Nope.

She drew a blank.

Think Iylah. Does he teach? No, still nothing.

She watched him move across to the fridge and grab a pre-made salad and what looked like a shake.

Jeb.

The salad gave his name away because of the countless salads she saw in that fridge with the name 'Jeb' on them.

"Sorry, I didn't mean to interrupt whatever you were doing." Jeb was now aware of her watchful gaze, yet his eyes did not fall on her once.

Quick on her feet, Iylah said, "So I've noticed that most of the faculty seem not to like my existence in this place."

He chuckled, amused by her firing statement, positioning himself in the chair across from hers, digging into his all-green leaf salad.

She admired his commitment to eating that stuff. She concluded it to be the reason behind the glow of his slightly tanned skin and the diamond-esque glistening of his stony-gray eyes under those thick hooded things he had for eyebrows. The guy took his health seriously, and it worked in his favor. Though his age wasn't forthcoming from how he looked, Iylah guessed he sat around mid-thirties to late-thirties. His good looks were subtle—built into his features, not forcefully grabbing your attention—but they kept you looking.

"Surely it's not because of my skin color, right?" She motioned to her complexion with its hues reminiscent of golden brown caramel and the very reality of the lack of diversity on faculty. "Because that would be a nightmare for the H.R. department around here."

He held his words a little longer, chewing in no rush to get to them. Finally, he spoke. "Your dad is Fredrick Dawson, yes?"

"I don't see how my father has anything to do with my question—"

He raised a finger to silence her before she continued on.

Hang on a second. Did he just—

"The consensus is that you got the job after a generous donation to our beneficiaries' fund."

"What!" Iylah's eyes widened at this not-so-overt revelation.

If this were true, her father shot her in the foot before she could even begin down this fresh path.

She rested her forehead against the heel of her palm, piecing the unfriendliness together. Gruffly exhaling, searching for self-control to hold in the verbiage not appropriate for her current setting, Iylah glanced back at Jeb. Her voice even and settled so as not to give away the humiliation of her father's hand and the shame of his unbelief in her once again, she responded—

"I didn't know about that."

Never mind that she spent years studying Fine Arts in the foreign prestigious land of Sweden. His interference got her the job?

She didn't say another word, returning to her forgotten quest in haste to depart from this unfolding revelation. All the while, his observant gaze remained on her.

I can't believe he's done it again.

two

SHE PUSHED HER CELINE glasses up the bridge of her nose and over her forehead, resting them on her head. The midday sun beat hotter than she anticipated on her exposed shoulders and arms, courtesy of her sports bra. Bound to get tan lines from her rucksack in tow, she decided it would be well worth it.

Focusing her camera lens on taking in the dips, the rises, the edges, and the depth of the Gorge before her, she marvelled at the colors of a departing spring still hanging around—holding on at the mercy of the looming summer sun.

New York held a handful of natural sights to offer as an escape from gridlock and brutalist skyscrapers—Letchworth State Park being one of them. However, Iylah couldn't help comparing them to the sights her eyes took in on her spontaneous and lengthy travels, trotting the globe.

The red sand dunes of Dubai springing to mind—the grains of sand pelting your skin from an exhilarating buggy ride, ripping through the vast expanse—no, this didn't compare to that.

Regardless, in her bid to ditch the streets of Manhattan for the weekend, she drove in a recently acquired Porsche Panamera, nearly five hours across the state to breathe in New York's version of fresh air. The experience and beauty of the Alpine foothills of Germany were still etched on her eyeballs—still no comparison—and that is where she would leave them for fear all other haunting etchings of the mind would taint such glorious landscapes.

The shutter sound of her camera broke a lingering old memory. One of an old face, she always fought the dangerous urge to miss. Surely now she could classify these memories as old, no matter if it had been a few months. She decided they were old and no one would convince her otherwise.

Iylah continued her trek onwards, slinging the camera underneath her arm, its strap hanging from her shoulder and pulled across her chest.

This is more like it.

Her shoulders rolled back in relief—briefly shutting her eyes, she tilted her head skywards, allowing the sun's rays to dance, permeating her face. She couldn't remember the last time she had felt so at ease, despite the minor heavy breathing and slight tight hamstrings reminding her of how inactive her body indeed was. Nothing beats being surrounded by beautiful sights and—

"S'cuse me." A rushed woman's voice whooshed past her from behind, abruptly causing Iylah's eyes to open away from their solitude of enjoyment.

The audacious sight of neon pink started jogging backward, calling out to whoever it left in its wake, jogging on the spot to allow her fellow joggers to catch up. Unfortunately, her jogging on the spot left nothing much to be desired, with all the motion emphasizing areas a good sports bra should support, white blonde ponytail swinging from side to side, her neon attire strained to provide ample support to her chest area.

Those are not real? Surely not.

In a moment of involuntary comparison, Iylah shot a peek down at her sports bra.

"C'mon, guys!" Neon lady called out, coming to a complete standstill with a quick roll of the eyes. "Tylor! Jeb! Hustle!"

Jeb?

The name too distinct to be thrown around without a specific target.

An inward grimace settling in her throat, Iylah turned her head around to glance at the pair receiving all this hollering of frustrated encouragement. Her eyes fell upon a young boy, likely to be aged ten, with a sandy blonde mop of hair walking alongside—Iylah only assumed—his father. Jeb. Who also had a similar mop of hair, only today it was up in a man bun.

Of course, it's you.

Not one to recoil from awkward instances, Iylah stood her ground, turning her body to fully embrace the situation about to transpire. She drew her shoulders back to exude the confidence she needed to face whatever transpired next.

"Well, if it isn't the salad man himself?" She attempted to hide the sarcasm and soft endearment of her opening remark towards Jeb.

His eyes hidden behind sunglasses, a strained grin across his face told of his recognition of Iylah as he approached her, dressed like the rest for the activity—black mesh gym shorts, a gym tank displaying the dips and carved muscle of his arms.

She forcefully pulled her eyes away from gawking too long. After all, he's a family man.

"You're a long way from home, Iylah."

A common understanding was established between them the week after the exposing of the rumor mill at the School. One involved Iylah clarifying that she actually qualified for the job and Jeb continuing to maintain pleasantries with the odd banter thrown in there. He was the only person interesting enough to talk to there.

One look at him, the unknowing eye would categorize him as your harmless, average, friendly art teacher on the block—but Iylah knew never to let first, second, and third impressions be the base of judging someone. Something more to Jeb lay neatly hidden beneath the well-maintained physique. And this more definitely included a neon-wearing woman, now standing reasonably close to Iylah.

"You two know each other?" The neon blonde removed her imitation Chanel sunglasses to weigh up this sudden interruption to her run—unafraid to let her eyes roam up and down Iylah, showing no signs of friendliness. Just comparison.

"Honey," Jeb began the introductions, clearing his throat, "This is Iylah. We work together at the School. Iylah, this is my wife, Dawn, and my son Tylor."

Tylor stood timidly next to his father, ever the doppelgänger of him, giving Iylah a small wave.

"Hi, Tylor." Iylah turned her attention to Dawn, adjusting her eyes to all the color wrapped around her slim body.

Iylah didn't bother extending a greeting to her, deciding she didn't like her manner.

"My goodness. I would die to have your sun-kissed skin. How long do you tan for, or is this fake tan?" Dawn's brown eyes rose and fell continuously over Iylah.

The snark dripped off her sentence, nothing Iylah hadn't encountered before. Her rigid, pillowy lips proved all Iylah needed to know.

"Um—I'm biracial. My mother was black and my father is white." She tried not to smirk at the silly observation.

She'd gotten used to explaining her looks to people. What she hadn't gotten used to was the assumption that her skin color came from a bottle or sunbed. Nope, that was a first.

"Was?" Jeb was quick to pick up on the small disclosure. His listening intent.

"Yeah, as in, she died."

Was there ever an excellent way to share the premature departure of her mother? The bricks building in her stomach told her no.

Before further comment could be made, she jumped at a new conversation-turner: "I see we all had the same idea for the weekend?" She prompted towards the scene of the Gorge behind them.

Reading her discomfort on the matter, Jeb followed the turn of conversation.

"Yeah, it was Tylor's idea to explore today. Wasn't it, buddy?" He put a fond hand behind Tylor's neck, who nodded lightly. "Are you tired of Manhattan streets already?"

"I just needed something new to paint," Iylah motioned to her camera, "and somehow the townhouse wasn't inspiring enough, so here I am."

"You live in a townhouse? In Manhattan?" Dawn's voice feigned shock, but the necessary parts to communicate this were firmly in place on her face. "Jeb, you never mentioned you have a new friend who lives in Manhattan. How can you afford that on your measly salary from that School? Wow. Look at the size of you! What workout do you do? You could be a model with that frame." Still, none of her compliments rang sincere.

Unsure which question and statement to answer first, not addressing the loaded manner in which Dawn used the term 'friend'—she decided to keep all of this splendid exchange short.

Too much was focused on her.

"Well, I'd better let you guys continue on your way." Leaving no room for any rebuttal, she pedaled backward. "I will see you on Monday for our last week before two months of freedom." She swung her arm in a pirate-esque manner for enthusiasm.

Great—I'm a pirate now. What is wrong with me?

"See you then." Jeb departed with a mild send-off.

Iylah veered off onto a path, hoping it differed from the direction they would continue.

What was that?

Reaching for her phone stashed in the side pocket of her rucksack, she felt oddly thrilled to text Lena about Neon Blonde. She was running out of things to say to her sister. Her life suddenly became quite dull compared to the life Lena was accustomed to her living.

Iylah sensed deep down that dull and ordinary was what she needed right now, even if she fought the impulse daily to up and leave wherever her roots set down. She needed to start over. Properly. She needed a place to call home.

> You would not believe THE most awkward thing happened...

Her fingers navigated the lit-up letters on the small screen rapidly.

∽ ⁄∾

The midnight air stung the skin on her face. Its chill gripped her while she clutched her burning cigarette, the only source of warmth.

The running rhythm of her heartbeat vibrated through her body—showing no signs of slowing down, not easing up no matter how much she tried to breathe her way out of panic.

Being completely honest with herself, a quick puff didn't have the usual calming it used to. It may be time to quit.

She leaned against the railing of the wrap-around porch, her eyes intent on the reflection of the moon shimmering and distorting across the lake's still water before the cozy mid-century cabin she found on Airbnb. Thus far, her brief escape from Manhattan for the weekend panned out differently from her hoped-for escape.

When would she learn memories couldn't be escaped? When would she decide to face those memories? When would she have the stupid courage to get over Stefan and those daunting last few months?

These dreams seemed to always drag her out of bed every so often.

Tonight's nightmare woke her in a crippling, terrified state. A replay of that disastrous night flooded her bed, mind, and body. The ringing gunshots tainted her ears as though it had just happened. Her mind and ears would never forget—try as she might to blink away the sight of the bodies, they confronted her behind the darkness of her shut eyelids.

She recalled how such a scene blinded her from seeing anything else days after. Stefan's eyes seared with rage, the scar on his face—which she once found a thrill in tracing delicately with the tips of her fingers under his left eye down to his jaw—brought the horror of his ways to the forefront, under the seedy lighting of the club. The red flags she ignored in sheer foolishness led to that night—a night that would not leave her alone.

She drew her phone out of the pocket of her oversized hoodie.

12.45AM

A hollow, concaving feeling bore itself in her chest with the reality of being unable to call her mother. If she had known leaving for Sweden at eighteen would trigger a sequence of tragedies, maybe she wouldn't have packed her bags so fast.

The words her mother prayed over her before she jet set away were etched on her heart.

Heavenly father, guide her when the path becomes dark. Hold her when home seems so far away. Comfort her when life does not go the easy route. Protect her from those who wish her harm and all evil that prowls like a lion. May she know Your love for her even when she thinks she does not deserve it.

She hoped her mother's sentiments were heard. The path was dark. Home was far away. Life was not easy. Harm and evil came her way. And this love she spoke of seemed unreal.

With a last puff, Iylah opened her Instagram mindlessly. Her eyes widened at a recent request to follow her from DawnDayAston36. Instinctively she scoured through DawnDayAston36's curated posts of selfies, some tasteful, some going beyond—far beyond. The images painted a picture of a woman who frequented the stretches of nightlife in New York. Not a single sign of Jeb or Tylor with each self-promoting image.

"Oh, this is good." Iylah sneered, her mind diverted and curiosity heightened in her.

Not hesitating to delve deeper, her search for Jeb's Instagram account brought her face to face with a sad reality. She searched his posts and saw friends, Tylor, Dawn, travels, and art. A slight sense of guilt and a sliver of compassion cemented her find.

"Oh, no."

Poor guy.

Flicking her cigarette to the ground, she made a mental note to be friendlier and more approachable toward Jeb.

It was time to quit this. Another mental note.

three

Tentatively sipping from her glass of Catena Zepata 2014 Malbec, Iylah scoped the setting of her chosen dinner spot for her next victim. The Parisian-style restaurant was alight with movement and conversation amidst the soundtrack of romantic French music. The ambience of the warm lighting picked up on the dark wood of the tables and chairs, adding an element of chic coziness. The checkered black-and-white floor, a nod to many French restaurants. And the aroma of various meals wafting past, on their way to their awaiting owners—her stomach grateful for the decadent meal it would receive soon.

Tables were filled with either couples or girlfriends catching up after a hard workday. She was neither half of a couple nor with a girlfriend, but she'd wandered home to the West Village after work—making a quick mental note to take a leisurely stroll through Washington Square Park. The colors of a soon-departing spring lured her out to witness them in bloom. Merely as an observer of those enjoying the beginnings of the summer evening—unsure yet if she arrived at the stage of enjoying anything.

Her trips out to fill her stomach and sketchbook were fast becoming a favorite recent excuse for these excursions—that and her desire or ability to cook were not an atom of existence. No matter how often she hung around her mother in the kitchen, none of her prowess of culinary goodness rubbed off on Iylah. Lena, however, was well acquainted with the ins and outs of the kitchen.

A-ha! Jackpot. I found you.

Drawn in by a stoically postured woman, dressed in a dark-tailored blazer combined with what looked like a leather skirt—Iylah's pencil got to work. Her subject's face set as stone with hard angular features, swallowing any soft femininity she had—uncategorically beautiful—glaring at the screen fixed on her table, fingers dancing erratically across the keyboard of her laptop. Still in work mode. She embodied everything New York portrayed—edginess, no nonsense and brutalist traits.

No one in New York knew how to relax—nor did Iylah. It made her terrible company.

Iylah's 2B pencil hit the paper of her sketchbook, mapping out the contours and shapes highlighted in the face of her unaware live model.

Her trusted set of pencils always travelled with her, tucked neatly and orderly in the leather case housing them. Her sketchbook always nestled among the clutter of contents in her rucksack. They were her daily accomplices in capturing beauty and life wherever the day brought her. An activity of sorts, to keep her skill set sharpened and quick—while exercising her memory each time her oblivious subjects moved and fidgeted their way around the invisible stage Iylah placed them on.

As her pencil did what it was directed to, Iylah gathered her thoughts from the day.

A student of hers drifted to the forefront of her mind—Tameeka. Though Iylah's role was to teach classical painting techniques, she couldn't help but admire this student's constant pushing of the boundaries. Tameeka challenged the rules set before every artist who held a paintbrush as their tool of choice. Something about Tameeka reminded Iylah of herself at twenty. Bold, brash, with no second thoughts about consequences. What wild and carefree days those were for Iylah—on the surface.

Being the lenient and open to anything kind of teacher she was, Iylah welcomed the pushback Tameeka brought to her lessons. Once upon a time, Iylah was much the same with her College professors—testing the boundaries set by dead and gone classical art stewards.

It only occurred to her now, approaching thirty, that she needed to take stock of her ways. She couldn't be tired and weary, drawn out and strung out forever—still unsure how long her stay in New York would last and whether she had the guts to stick it out. The boldness and recklessness she witnessed in Tameeka, Iylah no longer possessed.

As if he was summoned, her father's name splashed across the screen of her phone sitting on the table. Her eyes rolled involuntarily—it tended to be her general response when it came to him. She'd been avoiding his calls since Monday—he made another attempt on this relatively warm Thursday evening.

She swiftly grabbed her phone to get it over and done with, ripping off the metaphorical band-aid, mild agitation already filtering through her.

"Father." Her usual greeting to him.

"She's alive. You could answer my phone calls once in a while." Sounds of commotion played out in his background.

"I've been busy, y'know, working. I have little free time these days." She didn't bother with fake pleasantries.

The anger of his interference with her life stirred anew, simmering and lingering. The embarrassment went unconfronted—she wouldn't let on about her knowledge of his work of blatant daylight bribery.

"How is this new job? That's supposedly keeping you from calling your father."

"It's great—really great. I hate to cut our conversation short—I'm in the middle of something, but what can I do for you?" She fidgeted with the pencil between her fingers, suddenly wishing it was a cigarette.

NO CIGARETTES! Stop this already.

Iylah's concentration darted around the restaurant, finding something to focus on, to endure the phone call.

He chuckled at his daughter's resolve to have minimal contact with him, but he obliged her haste—

"I will be in New York over the weekend for a charity event, and I would like you to accompany me."

"Is Kendra too busy? I thought she would jump at the opportunity to be your arm candy as always?" The snark could never hide in her voice when it came to her father's new wife, fifteen years his junior.

The substance of their marriage didn't account for much, except overly luxurious parties, public appearances and the odd touch of affection. Iylah discreetly hoped her father abstained from creating children with Kendra—for the children's sake, of course.

"Well, is it too much to ask to spend the evening with my daughter? Whom I haven't seen in over two years. Frankly, I didn't think it would be such a hard task."

His patience tore at the seams. The game of empty endearments he always liked to play, coming up short.

"Okay." Iylah cut his plea short. "Get Laurel to call me with the details." The years passed and she hadn't spoken to Laurel in them, her father's trustee assistant. She was fond of Laurel.

"Wonderful!"

Regret seeped into her anxious veins, settling in to make itself at home.

Iylah kicked shut the double-height, black wooden door leading into her townhouse with her left heel—one hand holding onto a bunch of mail, the other flicking the light switch in the foyer. The intricate geometrical chandelier hanging from the double-height ceiling of the entry lit up her way. She stole a quick glance at herself in the black-trim wall mirror that demanded attention with its size.

Well done Iylah. You've managed not to reduce the bags under your eyes another week.

Tossing her keys on the entryway table, expertly placed under the mirror, they dinged the side of the crystal vase holding pastel purple Hydrangeas, sourced from the flower market one vapidly quiet Saturday. She couldn't resist acknowledging their bloom with a quick sniff. Her feet followed the hallway runner lining the retouched Cedar floorboards, leading into her living room.

The living room was adorned with furniture she had not chosen, yet intentionally put together by whatever interior designer her father hired. Not entirely to her taste.

Far too sterile, lacking the lived-in traits she liked. Her apartment in Berlin held treasured items she'd sought after at vintage stores—period pieces with a mid-century flair. All gone and sold the moment the judge allowed her to leave the streets of Berlin.

She squinted her eyes, attempting to decipher all the mail addressed to her, feeling the effects of the multiple glasses of wine she single-handedly downed without restraint. Finally ridding herself of the weight of her rucksack, she threw it on the floor with a thud, flopping her mellowed body onto the creamy beige corner couch. The couch overlooked the tall windows, inviting glimpses of the street beneath—separated by the wood-burning fireplace in the middle, yet to be used. If she stayed long enough to brave the famous winter nights here.

The doughy cushions engulfed her tired limbs.

Nope. I am not opening those.

She launched a couple of uninteresting envelopes across the couch until she got to the one catching her curiosity. It sat on her lap, waiting to be discovered. A small brown box big enough to fit a pair of shoes, delivered via FedEx, no signature required. She examined the box, lifting it to scan its exterior. There were no signs of the sender's details. Its contents light enough to lift without effort but heavy enough to contain more than paper.

"Okay, mystery box, what do you have for me?"

Pulling at the edges of the tape securing its contents, too lazy not to retrieve the mail knife—she concentrated with wonky vision, watching the tape remove without a fight.

"A-huh!" She had it.

Opening the two flaps of the box, her eyes fell upon a package wrapped in soft beige tissue paper.

Ha! Same color as my couch! Someone has put a lot of effort into this wrapping that's ending in the bin.

Her far-reaching fingers played with the tissue paper, slowly drawing it away from the contents wrapped in secrecy. Leather-bound books—

Journals?

—lay stacked in the box, a handwritten note resting on them. Her eyes widened as she took in the words penned on the note.

Darling girl, I thought you should have these. Your father gave them to me upon her
passing, but my heart always knew they belonged with you. Visit soon.

Lots of love,

Aunt Dee xx

Disbelief, with remnants of the ever-residing hole left in her, got caught in Iylah's throat. Memories of seeing the familiar leather covers found their way.

Her mother's journals.

Exhaling with more force than necessary, Iylah's tears gave way. Delicately—almost to make sure what she held wouldn't disappear—she traced the leather with her fingers. She dug further into the package, pulling out one, two, three, four, five journals.

Growing up in her late teens, she witnessed her mother put pen to paper in the quiet nooks of their expansive home, writing her heart out. Iylah would tiptoe in to scare her, and out of curiosity she'd ask what she was writing. Her mother would respond with tender eyes—I'm writing to Jesus. And she would continue, almost in her own little world.

She never pushed religion on Iylah or Lena. Neither did she force them to join her excursions every Sunday to church. But Iylah knew something changed in her mother after she returned from visiting her sister, Deidre, in Georgia. Since then, her mother started writing to Jesus and didn't cease til her breath required her to.

The tears came rushing, and they asked for no permission.

four

'Hide Your face from my sins and blot out all my iniquities.
Create in me a clean and pure heart, O God, and renew
A right spirit within me.'
Psalm 51:10

As shocked as I am, You are not. You knew this mess was in my heart long before I did. Now it is bubbling to the surface. I am convicted, Jesus, remorseful for allowing such things to fester in my heart. The pride, the fear of man, jealousy, all of it! These are not things that glorify You, nor do they make me more like You.

On the contrary, it agitates me and grieves me. I pray that whatever has bled out in how I treat my family and friends, or whoever I may have come in contact with, has not been hurt by my hurt. Again, Jesus, I repent for allowing these things to fester in my heart. I have valued people's measurements of me for far too long. I chased lofty ideas of what the world and money offered instead of humbly being Yours, surrendering my life. I fear that pride would be my downfall. Thank You for the correction. You correct me as Your child father God. Though it dismays me right now, I have the assurance of Your forgiveness and comfort for this heart of mine. Cleanse this heart of mine. And would Your Holy Spirit help me with my blind spots? Teach me to forgive Freddy each

moment, each day, each week, each month – even if it may hurt to do so. Help me, most
wonderful Helper, to allow You to build me in heart, spirit, character, and love.
  Your daughter
  Lillian

As she sat earlier that morning amongst the green lushery of her landscaped
courtyard garden, reading the words her mother penned fourteen years ago—Iylah cherished the softness her mother was known for, now in her written words.
She admitted none of it made sense to her.

   What unspoken hurt was her mother writing about? What man did she fear?
What pride did she face? And who was she jealous of? What did her father need
forgiveness for? All these questions sprung up in Iylah.

   She wanted to know who had hurt her mother, and if that hurt resembled
anything similar to what she felt. She wanted to know who she feared and if, at
this very moment, her mother would empathize with her fears. She wanted to
know if her mother overcame her pride, and if so, how?

   Iylah didn't expect to find the inner workings of her mother's heart so close
to her current inner workings. Nor did she anticipate how open and honest her
mother spoke about the mess within herself and the safety found in her sharing.
A knowing of assured acceptance. These heart yearnings found space in Iylah's
own, where the same sentiments lay. Fourteen years later, her mother put words
to Iylah's messed-up heart, and all it carried.

   Create in me a clean and pure heart.

   The words rummaged around in Iylah's head, her eyes glazed over, swirling
the half-empty cup of coffee in her right hand. Could a person's heart really be
made 'clean'? And what exactly classified it as unclean? Could it really be made
pure? And how does one get to such a point?

   My iniquities.

   Iniquities? A word she needed to look up, and upon its revelation she
meditated on her own immoral and grossly unfair behavior—a few examples
coming to mind.

   Who was it that dictated right and wrong?

   To her mother, it was Jesus—a man who supposedly was God, yet you couldn't
see him. She looked him up too. With all the existential questions having a bit
of an unrestrained tango in her, she didn't notice the extra presence now in the
faculty lounge.

"Can I—" Jeb disturbed Iylah from her moral crisis examination to get his lunch from the fridge, which Iylah leaned against for the last twelve minutes.

She jumped a bit too far out of the way, startled. Jeb noticed the faintest smile materialising.

"Sorry," Iylah mumbled, moving across to an empty armchair. Realizing who it was, the words left her mouth before she could vet them—"So you turn up to work two days before we go on summer break? I thought you guys got lost in Letchworth over the weekend."

"That's nice of you to notice my absence." Even with his face turned away, the sarcasm couldn't be hidden as he tended to yet another salad by the sink.

Iylah noted his shoulders hunched over, messy hair sitting long down the sides of his face, along with his somewhat crinkled shirt. His uniform consisted mainly of casual shirts and a variation of chinos or jeans, ever ironed and straightened to the last stitch. This look, cried desperately of disorder. She chose her next words with a bit more awareness.

"You're the only person who talks to me in this place. So, my week has been uncharacteristically even quieter."

She studied his face, dressed in light faint stubble across his cheeks and jawline, accompanied by evidence of not having a lot of sleep. He didn't say a word, settling himself in an armchair across the room.

She tried again, "And also, since your wife followed me on Insta—"

"Soon-to-be ex-wife. Wait what? She did what?" Jagged lines formed across Jeb's forehead, a sight Iylah had never seen before on him.

Not one to skip past the most crucial detail, Iylah said, "Ex what?"

"Unbelievable!" Jeb shot his head back, his fingers raking through his hair, rather agitated by the piece of information exchanged in their quick conversation.

"You're getting divorced?"

As much as this made sense to Iylah, the element of shock felt quite genuine. Now she could stop wondering how on earth Jeb and his wife were married. She'd heard opposites attract, but surely not like this. There were big gaping holes that Iylah needed to fill. Four days ago, he introduced Dawn as his wife, and now it seemed something had happened in the middle. By Iylah's calculations, that middle would be why Jeb was scarce from work.

Pinching the bridge of his nose, eyes intently shut, Jeb exhaled sharply. "Look, I'm not wanting to go into it with someone whose life is perfect and paid for—"

When he opened his eyes zeroing in on her, anger brimmed in them—yet what struck Iylah and caused the air to get caught in her throat was the sheer distress and hurt hidden behind the anger.

It turns out everyone was hurting these days.

Iylah raised her hand to put a pause to any other jabs he held for her. "I'll stop you right there—"

Withholding whatever sarcastic remark crept to the tip of her tongue, she took stock of what was before her.

He was hurt, in pain, and possibly blindsided by this recent event in his life.

Don't let your mouth speak words from your hurt, Iylah. See his hurt.

The German voice of her therapist presented the truth for her to consider.

"I'm sorry this is happening to you. It sucks. I wouldn't know the first thing about divorce, so I won't pretend to understand. You won't want to hear this, but your ex-wife seemed selfish to me. Who wears that much neon pink?" Her face scowled, remembering the flashing image of iridescent color. "It's like a walking highlighter with fake boobs and a market spray tan—" She stopped her verbal rampage, aware of its rambling commentary of a man's life falling apart. "Are you okay?"

She should have led with that.

In between her ramblings, Jeb tucked away his anger—the hurt couldn't hide, but his face softened.

"I'm sorry, I shouldn't have said that. Thanks for your concern. I've just got a lot to figure out at the moment." He resigned, sinking into the armchair. "But if you do happen to know of any apartments available within the next two days, let me know." His smile came a bit defeated, knowing quite certainly the chances of an apartment popping up in New York—on their neat salary range—were slimmer than slim.

The cogs turned in Iylah's head, and so did something adjacent to it in her heart.

"Where are you staying right now?"

Please don't say the street or a shelter. Also, who is kicking whom out?

Realizing Iylah wasn't one to give up her flurry of questions; he gave in. "I need to move Tylor and me out of our—the house." Aware of Iylah's raised eyebrow loaded with intrigue, he explained further, "I filed for divorce from Dawn." He cast his eyes downward to the salad his fork was toying with. "It was time. And I'm taking full custody of my son. Not that Dawn cares. I haven't seen her since she drove off on us at Letchworth. And I don't want to be around when she returns from whatever bender she's went on."

Iylah braced her jaw shut, fighting the urge for it to fling wide open in disbelief. Benders weren't unfamiliar to her. A few of them were tucked under her belt. Instant shame clamped up in her bones. It appeared a lot in her days. Often taking the place of the constant anxiety plucking at her nerves like an out of tune guitar..

To put the shame in its place, the words tumbled out of her mouth. "If you're looking for a place to stay, I have a few rooms spare at my place. I live by myself, and there's plenty of room for both you and Tylor."

The notion of her life being paid for rang true. She grew embarrassingly aware of it.

"Look, I don't know how to say this without sounding like I'm shoving 'daddy's money' in your face, okay? What I'm trying to say is if you want, you guys can crash at my place until you get your own."

Oh boy.

A momentary silence fell in the room, where surprisingly, no one had walked into since their conversation started. Iylah watched Jeb tentatively, and Jeb studied her the same.

Finally, feeling the need to fill it and clarify her offer, she said, "It doesn't have to be weird." She got up from her seat to throw the remainder of her cold coffee away, nonchalant about offering a stranger access to her house like it was the norm for her—it was not. "You need a roof over your head—I have free rooms."

Three fairly big spare bedrooms. With her back to Jeb, she could feel those nearly marble stony-gray eyes trying to figure out who she was and why she would extend such a gracious hand of generosity.

That townhouse got eerily quiet most nights, and she needed friends here who weren't associated with her family or father.

Even if it turned out to be a late thirty-something year old about to be divorced man with a ten-year-old son.

five

"YOU WHAT? HANG ON, hang on. I need to Insta stalk this guy to ensure you haven't let a se—" Lena's response to Iylah's news could have been more reassuring, stopping short of mentioning in full how terrible Iylah's idea was. "What's his handle?"

"Can you not, please?" Iylah fidgeted, her fingers itching for a cigarette between them, entirely unsure now about letting someone she knew for merely a second into her private space.

What had she done? Experience told her she ought to be more careful. Had she learnt nothing?

"Look, I know he's not a serial killer—"

The same way I knew that about Stefan?

She pushed the comparison aside with aggressive intent. "He's one of the best-liked guys on the faculty at work. He's got a kid too, for goodness' sake. Serial killers don't have kids."

Do they?

Those were solid enough reasons. She attempted to soothe herself by massaging her left earlobe. "Dammit, Lena!" She scolded into her phone, hoping Lena could feel the brunt of her agitation.

Iylah reached for her handbag on the other side of the back seat in search of a trusty cigarette. She sure had them at the ready for someone mildly trying to stop smoking. The notion was there, yet the dedication went noticeably missing.

She glanced forward to meet Nick's eyes in the rearview mirror; she shook her head at him in question. He shook his head back in answer. Exasperated, Iylah threw herself further back into the seat—the promise of momentary calm got shot down. She yielded, retreating the cigarette back to its origins.

"His name is Jeb Aston." She surrendered the piece of information Lena waited for.

"Thank you." In sing-song, Lena's credible investigative work commenced.

"His photos are pretty boring. Lots of his kid and wife, well, ex-wife." Iylah slid her fingers through her freshly straight blown-out hair, letting it fall back into its full-bodied form.

Her mane required taming for tonight after taking up the role of being her father's arm candy for the evening. His compliments about her hair would be first in line. Growing up in her parents' house, her mother's natural hair in all its coily glory, a rare sight to witness. Younger photos of her mother, with hair as high as the clouds, majestic in all its volume, didn't match the prim and proper straight, always freshly colored hair she wore until her dying day. She observed her mother's hair getting straighter as the years went on. At age twenty, Iylah noticed that Lena never wore her natural hair, which was in part identical to hers—only thicker and dense in curly lushness. She did her research, scouring through old photos, and all timelines pointed to one thing. The day her father found himself in these big and important rooms, buying a bigger house and shinier things—became the day something changed in her mother.

And as she read her newly gained journals, she found her mother's desire to return to the woman she once was before life became fancy and frivolous. Iylah wondered what that would have looked like?

"Iylah!" Lena gasped. "How old did you say he was? He is aging like the finest wine of South France. Be careful now—men like this find ways into your bed."

Her protectiveness of Iylah's love life showed itself once again. Given her track record, Iylah didn't blame her.

"No, he will not." A thought she would not entertain.

Her life needed no romantic links or any other male links.

Her bed needed a break from the ever-spiraling cycle of whatever her brief situationships entailed. She hid in those when reality took a soul-crushing toll.

"Besides his crashing at mine is only temporary. I'm just trying this whole not being selfish thing out, okay? Can you support that?"

"Honey, I'll support you any day, you know that. I'm just having fun. What are you wearing tonight?" Reading Iylah's restlessness and remembering her recent tribulations, the subject was changed.

"A black Yves Saint Laurent dress I just picked up." She peered at the white garment bag holding her evening dress. All five thousand dollars of it.

Her last attendance at these events, dripping with money and champagne flowing all night, were very few since the court trial began and ended. Needless to say, her social life took a rather significant blow amidst testifying against Stefan.

"It's a cut-out, one-shoulder kinda vibe."

"Yes girl, put those abs to work. Please drink on my behalf. These kids are driving me crazy!"

"For many reasons, Lena, I will not be doing that with our father around." When it came to her father, she needed her wits sharp and ready to go.

"Solid point."

"Yep—I can't wait to see you and the girls next week. Can we have a girls' weekend? We can rent a place out."

"You know the way to your nieces' hearts, honey."

Iylah could almost feel the rays of Lena's beaming smile over her phone. She'd missed this—spending time with her sister and nieces. Annoyingly on cue, Iylah's insides clammed up at how she allowed such distance and time to keep them apart.

Nick pulled the car up outside the townhouse.

Time to face the reality of her decision—inviting a perfect stranger in.

Since she extended her home to Jeb, her nights were filled with the same recurring dream. One of her opening an arched door as high as the heavens, each time unable to see what lay past its threshold. When awake, it knotted her stomach up in dread—not knowing its meaning and the uncertainty behind such an illusive dream. She couldn't run away from its haunting hold. The morning sun hit her face as she walked to work.

"I have to go, but I'll send you photos of the outfit, and I'll keep a tally of how many men our father tries to palm me off to like a prostitute. Love you."

Iylah racked her brain again—why she had agreed to go—not coming up with a valid answer. Had the years growing up, paraded like a show horse by her father, not ruined her enough to decline such invitations? Her attendance at tonight's gala certainly wasn't from missing such uppity events.

"Give them hell, honey. I love you."

The conversation ended. Iylah reached for her evening attire, pushing the door open to let herself out. But yet again, Nick The Efficient, beat her to it.

"See you at eight, Nick." A wink and smile solidified their progressing demeanor towards each other.

"I'll be here, Miss Dawson." Though he didn't break his code of conduct, his smiles moved out of the professional courtesy zone and into genuine amusement of everything Iylah entailed. "Good luck." He motioned towards the townhouse.

"Mhmm." Iylah pursed her lips together, walking off to face the new members of her household.

She presented Jeb with her spare key yesterday at work, as discreetly as she could so questions would be avoided on his part. Unfortunately, her discretion needed a bit more practice. Before long, mutterings circulated in the hallways of the School. In proper Iylah form, she desired to set the record straight, but the entire story was not hers to tell.

Shutting the front door, she tentatively walked through the foyer, past the living room, and up the stairs to where the owners of the voices she heard upon entering were. In the open plan kitchen, attached to the unused dining room, she set her eyes upon Jeb and Tylor perched on the industrial kitchen stools at the bench—each with a glass of water in their hands. Both their heads swiveled in unison, turning to spot Iylah. It was rather cute.

Jeb looked different in the daylight streaming through her bench-to-ceiling windows. With his dark blonde hair tamed in a bun, the stubble growing and making its presence indeed known in thickness. He didn't dress like your typical New Yorker. His creased linen mud-brown shirt gave him a laid-back look, while his khaki cargos and Converse's brought the street style together.

Lena's South of France remarks came floating back.

Nope. Not touching that one with a ten-foot pole.

With a slight grin, Iylah greeted them. "You made it?"

You made it? Grand entrance, Iylah. Round of applause for our hostess.

"Hey!" Mirroring Iylah's awkwardness and partly blindsided by her new hairstyle, Jeb placed his unfinished glass of water down on the Calcutta gold marble bench top. "Yeah, we did, although Tylor got us lost twice with his bad directions—"

"Hey!" Tylor exclaimed in dispute. "That was all you, Dad."

"Okay, maybe it was me," Jeb smirked, not at Tylor but at Iylah.

"I believe you, Tylor," Iylah said. "Your dad looks like he uses those paper maps, the ones they used to find old dinosaur bones."

Jeb feigned offence on behalf of his generation, a hand clutching at his chest.

This warranted a boisterous laugh from Tylor. "Yeah—you are pretty old, Dad. So what's in the white bag?"

"Tylor, manners."

"Sorry." He recoiled in his enthusiasm.

"Oh no, it's okay. It's just a fancy dress for the boring dinner I have to go to tonight. Lots of dinosaurs will be there." Iylah scrunched up her nose to show her mild but truthful disdain.

She watched as Tylor's brown eyes widened. The boy was evidently a fan of dinosaurs. Well, what boy wasn't? The sarcasm wasn't lost on Jeb, whose amusement danced around the corners of his eyes, causing Iylah to pause her intrigued scanning just there.

"I appreciate what you're doing for us, Iylah—"

Oops, stared too long.

Iylah jumped in before any further thanks could be said. They made her uncomfortable and feel like a fraud who had done little of anything, really.

"You don't have to thank me every two seconds, Jeb. It's honestly okay."

He dropped any further thanks, hands in his pockets, probably willing a less awkward moment to arise.

"C'mon, I'll give you the grand tour." She motioned for them to follow her.

Their bags caught her eye—lying unattended at the top of the stairs, needing a place to temporarily call home.

That cigarette would be great right about now.

∽ ✌

Iylah's Mach & Mach heel-clad foot continued tapping rhythmically, sitting in her usual spot in the backseat, with Nick at the wheel. Every so often, he would check on her in his rearview mirror. She was certain he picked up on her nerves even in the dimly lit car. Heck, anyone who took one glance at her could tell.

Not knowing what to do with her hands, she played around with her side-swept hair in all its volume sitting over her right shoulder, held ever so simply in place by a single Chanel clip. She strangely felt overdressed. Her dress accentuated her slender frame, the cut-out displaying the flat stomach she barely worked for, her exposed shoulder depicting how these events usually made her feel—cold and alone.

Time passed in between swanky, billionaire-filled events, especially with her few years living in countries where such pressures didn't exist. Nothing in her looked forward to her first taste of high society after a much needed hiatus.

Why on earth did I agree to this? You're a grown woman, Iylah. You could have said no.

She reprimanded herself again a little too late.

The car eased itself to a halt outside the Museum of Modern Art.

Before she could talk herself out of it, she elegantly pulled her rigid body out of the door Nick held open for her, grasping his outstretched hand to assist her. On cue, the cameras flickered and clicked away upon her exit from the car. She did what she knew to do. With a quick fixing of her face, the flirty smile many men stumbled over came out to play. She looked good—of that she was most certain . Her father would have no problem trying to attach her to suitors twenty years senior with no interest in her intellect and every desire for her physical attributes.

She navigated down the black carpet until the entrance doors swung open, courtesy of those who handled them. Just like that, she was back in the world she endured her entire life. Her sight blurred, and her breath held. Through the corner of her eye, she noticed a waiter approaching her with a tray of expensively tall champagne flutes.

Oh, thank God.

"Would you like a—" Before the poor young man could say another word, her eagerness for a drink cut him short while she reached for one without hesitation.

"Mhmm." She tipped the glass in the waiter's direction as a thank you. The first sip wet her dry mouth.

Iylah effectively scanned the room filled with the who's who of the financial world and New York's high society elites, dressed in decadent fashion royalty. Seeing no sign of her father, she resolved to find solace in the art strewn across the walls and floor of the museum.

Each time she stretched her leg out in stride, the thigh-high side slit made way for the length of her leg to be seen, the crystal-embedded bow detail on her heels catching the lights overhead. Heads turned—she could feel them do so—of both men and women. Her natural desire to recoil ever present, but with a life and looks like hers, she could never afford that opportunity—she played to their curiosity instead.

Her interest piqued at the Glen Baldridge piece of art titled 'Dream Burner.

Such tortured souls and a dying breed.

The cliché proved to be true.

Taking a second lengthy sip of her champagne, she felt a hand on the middle of her back. Involuntarily, every muscle along her back tensed up.

"If it isn't my little girl." Standing slightly in front of her, making his presence known, he leaned forward and kissed her cheek. "Always the turner of heads. Your hair, just like your mother's."

"father." Her smile strained, effective enough to portray some form of endearment. "It's always how you liked her hair, wasn't it?"

Whether he picked up on her snideness, he didn't let on.

"Is this any good? "He turned his attention to the artwork before them. "I can never tell. Anything is art these days."

"It is a subjective form of media. To him, it is art, and we are to perceive it from the artist's point of view.

Otherwise, at our own inclination, we can add what isn't there." She delights in discussing something on her home turf of knowledge.

"You always did have an eye for these things. Telling your mother and me off for the pieces of art we bought."

"Well—you bought art for money, not for appreciation."

This time he picked up on her snide.

A silence remained where they both stood there. Her father's silence one of calculated measures.

"My darling daughter, it is money you don't seem to have a problem spending." He sipped his Scotch Old-Fashioned. "Let's enjoy the night, shall we? I'm only in town for the evening." He extended his arm for her to link into his.

She did as she was told, and she hated it.

Whatever her mother needed to forgive her father for, Iylah couldn't shake off the sentiment that it had something to do with his arrogance and insensitivity.

The night progressed as she predicted. Being introduced to multiple nearly forty-something- year -old eligible bankers and hedge fund managers interested in a late twenty-something-year-old woman capable of working rooms and saying close to little while they shined.

Affluence almost never courted or married outside of its sphere. Not that marriage was anything she desired—-far from it.

In the whirl of it all, her left hand never remained empty of a drink—the notion of being on her best civil behaviour thrown out, along with her wits.

It appeared immaculately clear to her within the hour—this world no longer accommodated her. All of it smoke and mirrors to no long-lasting consequence, with everyone in the room pretending their lives weren't bland and diminishing by the day, no matter how much they spent fraudulently trying to make their lives appear lustrous and desirable.

"Welcome back."

A hand on her elbow and a whisper in her ear drew her out of a conversation she wasn't sure how she became a part of. The voice was annoyingly familiar, sending the greatest displeasure down to her gut. Roy Tungsten.

"Oh, look. It's the scum of the earth." She didn't bother to turn around, partially due to her concern of losing balance, her head marginally swimming after the sixth champagne.

"Don't be so pleased to see me, Iylah. It's unbecoming of you." His nearness enough to cause her skin to crawl in revulsion.

He moved himself to stand in front of her—not denying his smugness the pleasure of seeing her squirm.

What did she see in this sleek, blonde-haired, hazel-eyed, silver-tongued hedge fund brat? She chalked him up as another one of her blindly made poor decisions. One that lasted all of two months filled with intoxicating splurges that failed to numb their lives and consciences.

How money and privilege were dangerous for a lost soul.

"Especially not from the outcome of Germany."

Her head shot around to see the satisfaction on his face, aware of him being privy to something that many others weren't.

"What are you talking about?" To be sure, she played it coy.

"C'mon, Iylah." He averted his narrow eyes, content with the fear he created in her. "A criminal? You know how to pick them—apart from me, of course." His hushed voice revealed his desire to hold this knowledge as power.

"You know nothing!" She cried out, her body stiff with memories and dread.

Their interaction elicited attention from those nearby.

Roy, taken aback by her reaction, attempted to de-escalate the situation he'd fuelled. "Whoa, easy now."

"Whatever is going on here, now is not the place. Do you hear me?"

She couldn't see his face, but her father's sudden appearance caused her to scurry away from the scene—not before forcefully brushing past Roy to further drive home her fury-ridden intentions toward him.

In a blind and wet haze, she located the bathroom, swinging the heavy door in a hurry—coming face to face with a group of young women in eclectic gear hunched over a white powder substance at one vanity.

"Ugh." She shut herself up in the nearest cubicle, wanting privacy and a quick erasing of the last two minutes.

Her shaking legs barely able to hold her up in the stall, her chest rose and fell in a huff, promising her what happened next could not be avoided. She glanced down at her hands' jittery movements, her whole body engulfed in shakes. The dizziness set in, and her gaze darted toward the closest seat. No where else to sit, she bid farewell to the pristine condition of her dress. Plopping herself onto the closed toilet lid—like she had a choice.

You're safe, Iylah. No one is trying to harm you.

Clutching at her chest, air struggling to reach parts it should, her shoulders rose and plunged in an attempt to regain control.

Breathe. Breathe.

The words repeated in her mind yet remained void of bringing her body into their submission. Her skin prickled with heat.

Through the nose. C'mon. Out of the mouth.

Her vision distorting, she retrieved her phone from her clutch, bypassing a text message from Jeb saying something about a working bar, and searched desperately for Nick's number. Unable to make sense of the letters swirling before her on her phone, she pleaded inwardly for the need to pick her up immediately to be easily deciphered by him.

Okay, okay. Through the nose. Out of the mouth.

"Iylah? Excuse me, girls—"

Iylah's resolve and remaining concentration crumbled at her father's voice calling out to her, his presence now in the ladies' bathroom. Surely if she kept quiet, he would step back out, giving her time to regroup and bluff her way around him.

"I'm not leaving until you come out. Just so you know, my presence is making these girls uncomfortable, so the longer you stay in there—"

Her desperate attempt to regain control collapsed as abruptly as this had all begun.

Flinging her cubicle door open, coming face to face with her father standing arms folded like he waited for ten-year-old Iylah to obey or face the consequences. She watched his mouth tighten at a loss of her current state.

"Iylah, you're having a panic attack." He reached for her.

Everything mingled into a hurried, blurred sequence of events.

six

Jeb

He wiped the remnants of the Brooklyn Pulp IPA off his fingers on the cloth hanging out the back pocket of his jeans, before setting the brimming tall glass on the weathered walnut bar-top for his awaiting customer.

"There you go, buddy." Jeb's voice got sucked in amongst the roaring mixture of mid-evening likely slurred conversations and the thumping tempo of a mic'd up acoustic guitar being slammed as percussion.

Instinctively he spun the card machine dictating how much the customer owed in a bright white light blurring from its tiny screen. A muffled beep registered the payment going through, followed by a monotonous ping to confirm payment received. With a brief and forced small smile Jeb acknowledged the thanks muttered half heartedly from the lips of an already preoccupied patron moving away from the bar.

And onto the next one.

Friday night at The Dead Pony painted the scene of overpriced drinks being downed, laughter so loud it remained hard to tell if the joke truly hit the spot or over compensation to avoid bruised egos was the case. The tall tables were occupied constantly with little room for bar staff and wait staff to effectively keep an eye on the cleanliness of the place. Still, Roger's whip stayed long and ready to use, so the bar remained spotless as best as helped—well downstairs, anyway.

"What can I get for you?" Jeb threw his voice over the atmospheric noise, his attention on two women waiting to be served.

Both looked too young to be with the Wall street crowd who usually frequented the bar. He narrowed it down to them being potential girlfriends of said Wall Street jerks.

Working there three times a week meant he enjoyed the unfortunate privilege of serving whatever entitled scum the Financial District brought in—enjoyed remained a very polite way to describe his tolerance of them. The tips were above average, the crowds barely grazed average but he kept this second job to pay for the life of his son and Dawn's.

Everything about this city cost more than it should—renting their apartment in Greenpoint, a place Tylor called home for most of his childhood, quickly became Jeb's biggest expense each time Dawn lost a job. When one of them couldn't hold down a job, the other got a second—Jeb was the two-job holder for most of their marriage. Four years later, The Dead Pony was a part of the daily fixtures in Jeb's life.

"I will have the New York Rose cocktail." The brunette smacked her lips, observing Jeb through her dark lashes.

Here we go.

"And I will get the—" The red head squinted her eyes, both her friend and Jeb anticipating her order, "Tropical Club."

Jeb nodded, moving around the bar retrieving each ingredient necessary, aware of the lingering stare penetrating through him. Any other day, he could take it, today however—the simmering scratchy feeling in his chest was ever prominent. The feeling consistently lurked around in the background. Since filing for his imminent divorce, it took front seat to every other emotion.

He cleared his throat trying to disrupt the bubbling in him—it never worked.

"Are you single by any chance?"

There is that dumb question again.

Jeb clenched his jaw, the rising tide of irritation showing itself. Placing the two drinks on the bar counter, he managed a tepid smile.

"Are you willing to be a step-mom to my ten-year-old?" He watched the confidence leave her face, satisfying the irritation in him.

No response came from her, just a gaze now dropped.

He motioned for her to pay, "Fifty-six ninety, ladies."

Without another word they paid what they owed and scurried off to some corner of the bar.

"Rebounds not your thing?" Marcus poured a tap IPA next to where Jeb returned the spirits he'd used.

Marcus' reputation of rotating three girls at a time, left Jeb feigning exhaustion at the thought of dividing his attention between three different women. He wondered how Dawn did it. In passing, Jeb confided in Marcus about his current separation from his wife, with the track leading to the end to his marriage. Marcus was neither surprised nor did he bear any form of judgement against Jeb.

"Right now, no. Poor girl deserves someone who is even mildly interested in her." He wiped his workstation clean, "Tell 'em you have a kid, it will knock the flirting right out of them."

I should call Tylor before he goes to bed.

His mind drifted to his son, who begged him to have a sleepover at a friend's house before their trip to Clovis tomorrow. Given the current state of their lives and the guilt sitting right next to the anger in his chest, Jeb obliged.

The last week shacked up in the luxurious part of Manhattan bought him time to find his feet and map out his next move sans divorce. The awkwardness of being taken in by a wealthy twenty-something woman of whom he knew little about, wore off on the fifth day. In its place curiosity reigned. From what he gathered, Iylah's life, despite appearing paid for, consisted mainly of just her. No signs of a boyfriend on the outskirts. No coked up parties held at the house, like he assumed most rich kids in New York lived for. None of that. Just quiet nights at home, with a sketch pad, a glass of wine and classical music sifting tentatively through the townhouse. She proved to be everything he did not expect. So when she said she might pop in for a free drink, he wrote it off as a conversation filler.

"Excuse me—"

Jeb's eyes lifted from his cleaning task to where the voice came from.

"I'm here for my free drink." Her emerald green eyes crinkled in the corners, a hint of teasing behind them.

The corner of his mouth turned upwards amused, relishing the fact she actually turned up to collect. A buzz ruminated across the bar, Jeb noticed. And rightfully so—the floral mini dress she wore exposed her slender shoulders and arms with the thinnest straps—her presence anything but blendable. She was no wallflower. Judging by the murmurs and interest directed her way, the evidence of her striking looks proved unanimous.

"What can I get you?" Jeb leaned against the countertop, to get closer.

"Two shots of your finest Vodka, sir." She demonstrated with her fingers raised.

Jeb shook his head, the smile on his face growing, as he went about preparing the drink of choice.

"Wow! This place is packed. Is it always like this? You must make a killing in tips?" Iylah observed the crowd spending their Friday night in this bar.

"Well, it depends on how many times I get hit on." He poured the Grey Goose in two shot glasses, placing them on the counter in front of her.

She laughed, the raspy hearty sound of it causing the hair on his arms to stand and Marcus's attention beside him to be hooked. Jeb's smile lifted, in its place a puzzled slight frown questioned the elicited reaction her laugh provoked in him.

Unfazed by the change in his demeanor, Iylah reached for a single shot glass. "You're not on Dad duty tonight, so that one right there, is for you." She motioned to the remaining shot glass.

Jeb's longstanding rule of not drinking on the job was being poked up by a five foot seven billboard of good looks and privilege. Yet he reached for the shot glass offered to him. He could sense Marcus's intrigue reaching higher levels, attempting to listen in discreetly and serve the empty glasses that wanted refills.

Jeb raised his shot glass, regretting telling her earlier of Tylor's absence for the night and also which bar he worked at. The way his shoulders were tense, one shot could probably do him good.

She tipped her head with a smirk, raising her own glass to meet his. "To free shots and deadbeat wives."

This time he chuckled, caution torn down by an insensitive but witty toast. And back they threw the shots down their throats. The warmth and sting of it woke him up. The muscles in his cheeks tensed at the searing sensation caused by the Vodka.

"I'll have two more of those, please. Don't worry I'll pay my way from here onwards. Technically my father will, but y'know—same thing." She shrugged her shoulders, handing Jeb the Amex held between her fingers.

"I only said it once and apologised straight after." He attempted to defend himself again from the ill-placed comment said out of anger from a falling apart life.

He took the card from her fingers, aware of the exclusivity needed to have one of these.

"And I will never let you live it down. Forgiveness is for the weak." She leaned against the bar counter, surveying across the bar.

He chortled at her resolute take on forgiveness, handing her two more shots and her card back, not tapping it for payment.

"Yeah well, right now I would agree with you." He didn't entirely agree, but his last few days fueled her notion.

"There you go." She handed him another shot, "C'mon."

"Iylah, I'm getting the impression you're trying to get me drunk." Jeb crossed his arms over his chest, covering the logo of the work t-shirt every bartender next to him wore, amused by her antics.

"You are correct." She didn't digress.

He conceded not taking much to be convinced, throwing back another shot as did she.

"Start me a tab please? And get your friend over there who's been eavesdropping two shots to catch up." She motioned over to Marcus who indeed weaseled closer to their interaction, "I'll have an Old Fashioned please and I'll be sitting right over—" she scanned for an empty slot to occupy, her face lighting up when she found one, "There!" She pointed over to a spot right at the end of the bar counter where an empty bar stool sat.

Effortlessly grinning and with a quick tucking of curls behind her ear, she traipsed off to her designated spot—eyes following her every move.

"Who was that?" Marcus wasn't far behind with the questions he couldn't bite his tongue to ask.

"That is my new housemate. And these are your shots." Jeb handed them to Marcus, promptly wanting to avoid any speculation from him that would probe at Jeb's already wary heart.

"You better be—"

"Careful with her." Jeb finished his sentence, "Believe me, I know." He sighed, pushing down a new surfaced curiosity he didn't have the liberty to indulge in.

He cast a glance at the end of the bar, to find an already occupied Iylah batting her eyelashes at a brave male staking his interest.

The sooner Jeb figured out his next move the better.

∽ ∾

"You know you didn't have to stay till closing?" Jeb paced his steps to allow her to keep in step with him, "I'm a big boy, I could have walked back to the townhouse by myself."

The spicy smell of garbage, industrial fumes and cigarette smoke lined their walk through the Financial District in the late hours of the evening bordering morning.

A tunneled constant stream of billowy smoke from her mouth obscured some of his vision as it blew back in his face for what seemed to be the tenth time since she lit her cigarette.

"I'm a big girl too, but I'm sure one of the many suitors after my attention at that bar is probably a psycho and I don't feel like being a test dummy for the news tonight." She took another drag from the cigarette held in between the tips of her index and thumb.

"Why do you hold your cigarette like that?" Baffled by it, he slowed in step to dip behind Iylah and swap sides, getting away from all the secondhand smoke.

She did a double take at his quick and discrete movement. "Like what?"

"Like you're a seventies mafia boss." He craned his neck up and down the street in search of a taxi, coming up short.

For someone who raked up a bar tab of nearly six hundred dollars, Iylah did a rather impressive job of walking straight. Granted half of those drinks went to the foursome of guys who were enthralled by her for the rest of the night. Not a usual occurrence in the bar—a young woman buying a bunch of salivating dog-like men rounds of drinks.

In between working the bar, he caught glimpses of her lapping it up. It pinged a sore spot in him—the spot Dawn brutally confused for a punching bag and repeatedly took aim at it with each indiscretion, year after year.

Jeb internally wanted Iylah to make her own way home, her presence reminded him of the wound and she was like sandpaper to it. Women like her and Dawn craved the attention, not discriminating against who afforded it to them—as long as it fueled their self absorbed notions. He struggled to believe that to be true of Iylah at the moment. He imagined the times Dawn did exactly what Iylah did tonight and didn't think twice about it.

Involuntarily his teeth dug into each other, his jaw set and unmoving. He toed the line unsure about what he thought of Iylah.

"Every other way I held it felt inauthentic to my inner mafia boss. So this stuck. Do you really get lots of tips from women?" She tossed her cigarette to the pavement, taking a second to snuff its ash out with the toe of her combat boot.

"Yeah."

"Suckers for luscious hair and blue—well gray eyes—we are."

"Iylah can I ask you a question?" He cut her next words short, tugging at the strap across his chest from his satchel. It suddenly felt suffocating on him.

"Shoot."

"What's the appeal in having every living, breathing male fawn over you?" Again, he searched for a taxi.

"Not every male—can you slow down for just a second?" Her hand grabbed at his forearm, making him tense up at contact. She felt it. "Sorry."

Unsure why his body betrayed him in reacting that way, they slowed to a halt. He looked around, avoiding settling on her.

"Thank you. My goodness. Look, I'm sorry for turning up at your bar. If it made you uncomfortable or I crossed a boundary, I get it. I was out so I thought—hey why not?" She threw her hands in the air. "And for the record, those finance bros back there were solely interested in the fact they know who my father is. You get to the daughter, you get to the father, apparently."

His wandering eyes landed on her, the revelation causing guilt to spring up, witnessing her shoulder sink into a slump. The breeze blew the lonesome curls that escaped from her bun, sending them wherever it wanted them to go. An earnestness filled her face and now he felt stupid for letting a festering wound put an innocent person in the firing line off his misplaced rage.

She crossed her arms over her chest, protecting herself against whatever he said next.

"How often does that happen? People coming to you to get to your dad?" He asked with sensitivity to how openly she'd admitted it.

"More often than I care for." She concentrated on nothing else than the sidewalk they stood on. "I'm gonna go get some food—I'm starving. I'll see you at the house," She backed away leaving him standing in his misjudgment, "If I don't get murdered."

He wanted to tell her to stop, but the uncertainty that he wouldn't say anything stupid again told him to let her go. He raked his fingers through his hair, exasperated by more than just this moment.

I really hope she doesn't get murdered.

A taxi drove past him and he let it, watching her walk away and not turning back to see if he came after her.

I guess she's used to people not caring that much.

The guilt heaped itself on some more.

Lylah

She pushed the front door shut with her elbow, leaving it to make the ka-clunk sound, signaling its shutting. The lights in the foyer were still on, while the rest of the house lights were off. From memory, upon her exit earlier in the night she left every light turned off. She wondered if this was the work of Jeb.

Highly unlikely. With the mood he was in—no chance.

Throwing her keys where she always did, her tired eyes gravitated to a piece of paper carefully placed on the tabletop under the mirror. She narrowed her eyes, picking the paper up to examine the barely legible words written on it. It was a note. Drawing the paper further and closer to her face, in an attempt to read it properly, she settled for halfway.

"In case I've fallen asleep by the time you get here—" she read the penned words in an inaudible murmur, "I'm sorry for my insensitive words. I appreciate the effort you made to come to the bar. Marcus (eavesdropping guy) believes me now that you exist. Ha! I'll see you when I get back, if you'll still have us here. Signed, The Jerk from before, Jeb." Her brows furrowed, followed by a bubbling up in her stomach, pushing Lucky's Double Dog's she ate up and out as a deep hearty burp.

"I am sorry—"

A yelp escaped halfway through her burp, hands flying to cover her mouth, accompanied with a startled jump at the sound of his hidden voice. Her head turned from side to side, trying to identify his whereabouts in the dark living room.

"Oh, my gosh! Why would you do that?" She moved towards the entrance of the living room, flicking the light switch to illuminate his half asleep body sprawled out on one of the pillowy couches. "Why aren't you asleep? It's like three in the morning."

Jeb pushed himself up out of the couch gingerly, rubbing his sleep ridden eyes, dressed in gray sweatpants and a black t-shirt. His hair was damp and loose, obviously from the shower he took when he got home.

"Sorry—had to make sure you didn't actually get murdered. Solid burp by the way." He stood up stretching his arms over his head causing his t-shirt to ride up a little, revealing hints of slightly tanned skin.

Iylah purposed her eyes to look anywhere but there, instilling her own boundaries. She didn't need her wandering eyes rewarded right now. A throat punching hiccup shook her body.

"Great. Now I have—"Another came causing her body to jolt with it. "Fantastic."

They just kept coming.

Jeb laughed to himself, sleep keeping his eyes half closed as he did so. "Sorry for scaring you, for the hiccups and for being an insecure jerk." The insecurity showed in the way his hands found the depths of his pockets and in the small shrug of his shoulders. "I've got a lot to figure out and it's daunting, I guess it's made me mean. Is forgiveness still for the weak? 'Cause I need yours."

Despite the relentless hiccups bouncing her body, something internally cracked. It deepened the crease between her brows. Was it sympathy she felt for him or pity? The two were easily confused yet not the same.

"Lucky for you—" she cleared her throat from the residue of her hiccups. Or was it the residue of something else? "I'm well versed in dealing with insecure men." A half smile revealed itself on her face, "Hey—um—take the town car to the airport. And to pick up Tylor if you need."

"You don't have to do that—" He began a protest.

"Don't deprive me of testing out what forgiveness looks like." She joked.

Jeb studied her for what felt like an eternally long five seconds, unsure of what to make of her. It made a wave of uneasiness ride in through her gut. She deduced that to the hotdogs she ate.

"Thanks, Iylah." His face softened, those gray eyes revealing the curiosity in them. "I should get some proper sleep."

He made his way out of the living room, heading towards the stairs. He paused at her side, forcing their weary gazes to meet.

"For what it's worth, I hope one day you find the one guy that's secure enough not to care who your father is and just sees you."

The air shallower in her throat, willing herself to look away but failing miserably. "Goodnight Jeb." Her words came out softer and more timid than she intended.

"Goodnight Iylah." He dropped his head, continuing his trek upstairs.

Leaving her winded from whatever that was, unaware of her breath holding and the note still in her grasp.

Get a grip Iylah.

Sleep called sooner than getting a grip did. Maybe sleep could solve the formed crack in one of her walls. She'd find out in the morning.

seven

JOURNAL ENTRY DATED: 01/15/2005

'Come to me all who are weary and burdened, and I will give you rest. Take my yoke upon you.

And learn from me, for I am gentle and humble in heart, and you will find rest for your souls.

For my yoke is easy and my burden is light.'

Matthew 11:28

My Jesus, how thankful I am to be Yours. I am grateful to be known amid all of life's travails. When all seems too hard to bear and when my body threatens to fail me—yet I remain known by name by You. I remain sheltered in Your arms, from despair and from hope abandoning me. It is all too much to bear in this season. So much has come against me in thought and flesh. The scars I had long viewed as healed, have begun to show their presence again. It has taken all I can muster Lord but to throw in my last punch and resign to defeat. The words spoken over me by hurt hearts have caused my heart to weigh heavy. The treatment I have received at the hands of those near me has made my body ache, not from sickness alone, but from a heaviness, I cannot describe. I am tired from this fight, my Lord. I am worn down and care not to war against my husband, who does not acknowledge the hurt caused by him and those he allows into our marriage.

Shall I smile longer and bear it, Lord? When shall it end, that my heart and mind would know peace? Forgive me any bitterness that lay hidden in the crevices of my heart. Your good Word tells me to come. And here I come, Jesus, seeking the rest You give—where my mind can breathe, my heart can heal, and your gentleness confronts my jagged edges. Where the exchange takes the place of my weighed down shoulders for your easy yoke and light burden. Only You give such a deep rest and whole love. May I learn of You all things as I surrender and submit to You alone?

Your daughter

Lillian

Iylah

Iylah set her steaming cup of coffee down against her stomach, missing the accompaniment of a cigarette—she didn't trust herself not to get ash on her mother's journals.

Hues of pink sorbet streaked through the morning sky, with a hint of the incoming sun peaking through the neatly trimmed shrubs growing atop the stone wall separating this yard from the next. Washington D.C air held a distinct pungent summer smell to it that rivalled inner Manhattan's.

She'd been still long enough to notice the scent of summer upon her arrival last night. She stretched her slipper-clad legs, her back sinking into the cream-colored cushion of her sister's outdoor armchair.

The house was quiet, with little snores that could be heard as she passed each bedroom down the annoyingly long hallway. The creaking of the stairs, three dozen of them, broke the silence of slumber upon her descent to the kitchen in search of some morning nectar.

Her eyes fell upon the half-empty cup in one hand and the leather-bound journal in the other.

She didn't know yet what to make of the journal entries her mother penned. After browsing through them a few weeks ago, she dared not scour their pages again. Namely, because it left her with many unanswered questions and caused her to feel as if she were missing out on a secret way of life her mother abided by. She found the vulnerability in her mothers' words made her ache to put words to her own unspoken inner conflicts.

The fear always hung around though—the fear of not being able to contain it all once it found an outlet.

How long do you plan on running Iylah?

The memory of her latest panic attack appeared at the forefront of her mind. Involuntarily she winced at the weakness she'd shown that night. What struck her odd was the form of care her father displayed.

She couldn't recall a moment in her childhood or adulthood where she knew her father to instill a sense of calm upon her. He sat with her on the curb, hand on her back, his Gucci suit blazer hung across her shoulders while she shook in the middle of a swirling wind of emotions.

A horrendously timed photo of this episode appeared on one of the high society Instagram gossip pages. Whoever ran it surely worked overtime and needed to be commended for such efficiency.

Her father confided that Iylah's mother used to have panic attacks. But search, as she did, she could not find a single instance where she witnessed her mother in a similar state. She decided the morning after to commit to reading through the journals gifted to her. Though her mother could not give her comforting embraces, her heart poured out on the pages, one of the many comforts that allowed Iylah to start to not feel alone.

If her mother were here, Iylah got the sense she would understand. And if she were here, the possibility of Iylah's decade-long galavanting being a reality would be slim.

And here I come Jesus, seeking the rest You give—where my mind can breathe and my heart can heal, where Your gentleness confronts my jagged edges. Where the exchange takes the place of my weighed down shoulders, for Your easy yoke and light burden.

Only You who gives such a deep rest and whole love.

The words found a crack in Iylah's heart where they would remain until she found space to give in to what they meant for her.

"I see you're still chasing sunrises?" Lena's presence swooped Iylah out of the pits of her internalizing, sitting herself down in the chair next to Iylah with her own cup of leftover coffee from Iylah's pour.

"Hey, what do you know about our mother being a Christian?" Being the oldest of them, Iylah assumed Lena was privy to some insight she didn't have about their departed mother.

Lena's eyes widened over the rim of the cup she swigged from. "Wow—okay—can you at least hit me with some easier questions this early?" Then, recognizing the need for the question to be answered, she obliged. "Not much, just that she was very different in those last years. She had fewer panic attacks and seemed at peace with everything and everyone, including Dad. So there's that." She tilted her head before contemplatively returning to her cup.

"You knew about her panic attacks? It feels like I didn't get to witness that side of her. I mean the vulnerable side—" She motioned to the journal in hand, "I feel like she would—"

"Understand you now?"

Lena could read her little big sister better than the law books she'd memorised during her college years. She was aware the last nine months sent Iylah reaching for the nearest exit off this ride of life. Lena dared not tell her how often she lost sleep over Iylah's safety and well-being. In a way, the role of Iylah's protector and counsel fell on her since their mother died.

Iylah nodded, unsure she trusted her mouth to speak, "Maybe." Her expression closed up in response.

Lena could see the fragility eating away at Iylah. It caused a lump of worry in her throat.

"You need to stop running from what happened, Iylah." She leaned forward, addressing her green almond-shaped eyes. "Accept it and move on with your life. Don't let it rob you any more of your hours. Are you still having nightmares?"

Iylah tore away from her sister's searching light brown eyes, a solitaire tear escaping hot down her left cheek. "Sometimes." One-word responses were all she could manage right now.

With a steady hand, Lena reached over to grasp hers. "I think you should book in to see Imelda again. She can take you as an out-of-town client over FaceTime or something similar. You need to talk this through."

Iylah couldn't deny the truth in Lena's advice—she didn't have it in her to seek the help she needed. She silently wondered what her mother found in Jesus. And whether it was magic enough to erase the past. That's what Iylah needed.

The past gone.

❧ ❧

Iylah sucked the back of her teeth, perusing intentionally across each item strewn across the racks of this eclectic little boutique store. Her browsing not for want of buying, but rather time wasting between picking up the girls from horse riding, after promising Lena she wouldn't forget. She roamed the storefronts of DuPont Circle in no rush, with no agenda but simply being a passerby.

Lena's annoying observation proved to be true—it had been a fair while since Iylah's last visit to see them. Not much changed, apart from her towering nieces—Chloe and Monica. Lena still did Lena things, like being Iylah's replacement carer—not that she'd assigned her that role. She'd taken it upon herself. And for that, Iylah struggled to find the words to thank Lena for her unmerited care.

Ooh—that's nice!

Iylah's eyes perked up, seeking out the appropriate gift to thank her big sister. Never mind that Lena lacked nothing, the way Justin showered her with gifts was admirable but also hard work. Despite all her good traits, Lena's high-maintenance upkeep was hard to miss. Something their father taught them both very well.

A striking red silk top, channeling the romantic era with ruffled sleeves, pulled Iylah's gaze in.

Oh yes, sister, this is for you!

Pulling the garment out of its position on the rack, Iylah didn't bother with the price tag, simply pushing it aside to take in the stunning top more.

Marie Saint Pierre, you do not disappoint.

Lena did like to dabble in vivid colors to wear for work. Never one to be a prude, displaying her strength, grace, and approach-me-at-your-own-detriment demeanor—every bit the world-class woman and lawyer she was.

A fond smile of appreciation drew itself on Iylah's face.

Surprised by her find, Iylah's intrigue truly captured, she began sifting enthusiastically through the garments hung up elegantly. As she did so, she became aware of three sets of eyes studiously taking in her every move. In her usual casual yet intentional manner, she turned herself around to face the culprits—two of which instantly averted their hawking stares back to whatever work they were doing—while one older and more assertive woman, presented herself forward with the thinnest red line of lipstick covering what it could in a professionally tight smile.

"Can I help you?" White-haired, pristine-clothed, slender store lady approached Iylah, looking her over once, twice, three times. Implying exactly what she meant with her eyes.

Here we go.

Heat filled Iylah's chest, meandering its way through her body, finally landing in the walls of her throat. A familiar feeling for her whenever these moments presented themselves. She experienced them most as an early teen growing up whenever her mother and her walked into whatever generic luxury store caught their well-trained eyes.

The look on this woman's face the same look her mother always endured and addressed with great measured words. Once or thrice, Iylah navigated these encounters by herself as the adult woman she appeared to be, but never with the same grace of her mother's.

"Thank you for finally coming o—" Iylah's well planned words were cut short by the ringing of her phone.

A laced smug smile, and a finger held up to pause the exchange taking place, Iylah gave the store lady the option to either desist or persist.

"Excuse me—" she persisted.

Firmly, Iylah placed her finger again, this time a mere few inches away from the store lady's face. A shallow gasp of offense came from her.

Iylah reached for her phone undeterred. The agitated heat rising in Iylah's body turned to a sudden chill—Xavier's name scrolled past numerous times across the screen on her phone. Her lawyer. In what felt like a slowed down motion, she answered.

"Hey Xavier," Her greeting came through tensed throat muscles, along with her now raised shoulders—store lady forgotten in the not so distant background.

The small talk that followed may as well have been said underwater—Xavier relaying the reason for his phone call. Of this she was certain, the words 'he's out of prison Iylah', were one's Xavier definitely said.

The sound of the gorgeous red blouse slipping from Iylah's hand and hitting the speckled concrete floor of the store seemed distant. The murmurings of a further disapproving store lady even more irrelevant to the distressingly obvious state of Iylah's world splintering at the already thin hems it hung on by.

He was out of prison.

eight

Jeb

His keys clinked and rattled atop of the gold vein marble countertop.

His mind still swirling with the thoughts from the day—he winced at the sound of the keys landing, remembering the price of such a kitchen countertop. Down to the cent, he'd researched how much a countertop like this could set one back financially. The gray and gold veining that set it apart, would empty a wallet by a nice round and heavy sum of nearly a thousand dollars by the square meter.

Dawn would find all this extravagance to be right in her ball-park. A ball-park Jeb never signed up for. He needed to get her out of his overloaded system.

The fleeting reminder of his soon to be ex-wife brought the dull throb back across his shoulders. He rolled them back in a pitiful attempt to calm the tension that came in persistent waves across his back.

He sighed, the day suddenly weighing heavy on him.

Flicking his wrist, he glanced down at his humble Casio, pondering if time slipped him for a run. His watch confirmed it did. 11.30PM. But not too late to call Tylor. It was the only reason Jeb opted for the earlier shifts at the bar over this summer—it made space for nightly calls to Clovis. The three hour time difference meant he could catch Tylor before bed.

Another dull ache showed up in his chest.

Did I do the right thing?

He shifted his bodyweight against the bevelled edge of the countertop—leaning forward against it while his arms braced his body on either side of him. In between fielding calls from Dawn, this probing worry kept him busy.

Summer in Clovis for Tylor didn't sound like a bad idea a week and a half ago. Jeb's parents certainly welcomed their grandchild with more than comforting arms, and without saying the words he assumed they were thinking. They considered the elimination of Dawn to be one for everyone's good—Jeb's in particular.

Amid his body telling him he needed to destress, he heard the faint sound of classical music playing through the house speakers—Fredric Chopin, perhaps. He must have missed it upon entering. Iylah was home.

His stomach nosedived in knowing her presence was here. It did that often with her around. It had been like that since her return a few days ago. From where? Jeb could only guess where the life of a trust funded single woman led.

He knew two—no three—things about Iylah; she came from a family of money; she cooked little, and painting turned out to be an outlet of sorts for her. He found this out over the recent days. It was all she did. The appearance of paint smudges and traces across her hands, splashed haphazardly across her chin gave it away.

Amusement dressed his lips, remembering the glint of embarrassment that ran so quickly across her face when he pointed out a passion caused streak. He was yet to see any of her work. She painted in the room on the third floor and being a guest he didn't feel the right to venture there, though curiosity always dared him to.

Despite their growing rapport with one another, he still couldn't quite place her generosity towards him—particularly with the many stupid things he tended to say when the sour taste of his life sprung up to remind him of the sins done against him.

He moved with intention towards the sleek-looking Swiss branded fridge. Tonight might be the night his curiosity won. Scanning the always richly stocked fridge, his eyes fell on remnants of some New York City Pastrami in a brown grocery bag. His intrusion would be met lightly if he came bearing a sandwich. Food always makes people comfortable. Exercising the familiarity he'd gained of his surroundings, he worked his way around the kitchen to produce what he considered stellar pieces of two sandwiches—after all he also had to eat.

Armed with his peace offerings, he beelined for the third floor, trotting up the grand staircase. Another track of Chopin filtered through the house, passing room by room, in the long dark hallway leading to the artist's den.

The door was marginally open. He presumed if he knocked there would be no chance of being heard above the symphony cutting through the air the only way it could—with great skill. Taking great care and restraint not to startle her, Jeb nudged the door revealing Iylah's back to it, perched on a wooden stool in front of a broad canvas where he could see the strokes of her brush displayed expertly.

Stepping into the room and immersing himself in Iylah's world of art, he discovered a wonderful surprise. Displayed everywhere across the room—on the floor, alongside the walls, next to the tall frameless uncurtained windows that overlooked the tree tops lining the street beneath—her hours and days were displayed in the magnificent works of the subject matters she put her brush wielding hand to paint. Each subject matter more alive than the previous. She was an exceptional artist, well trained and meticulous in her work.

The dip in his stomach surfaced again.

"You okay?"

Unaware of the symphony of strings dulling down, and his presence being known, Jeb found himself caught out with his mouth somewhat ajar at what lay before him. He bet he looked odd, with two plates in hand and two bottles of water standing still in the middle of the room.

Collecting himself, he stepped forward gesturing to the gifts of comfort he brought.

"Figured you might need a midnight bite to go with your Chopin."

"Oh, my gosh—is it midnight already?" The straining of her eyes told him time took a toll on her.

She spun to her left where a paint cloth lay on a smaller stool. Reaching for it, Iylah cleaned the paintbrush in hand before plopping it in a mason jar of color murky water at her feet. Her hair pulled up in a ponytail of curls, framing her oval face, emphasising the sharpness of her jaw. It sat comfortably in a messy bun often—except for that one night, the one he swore he heard muffled sobbing, but a fresh faced Iylah the next morning made him question if indeed he had.

It was the night where it became painfully obvious they lived in two different worlds, despite sharing a roof. Her all done up in a dress that made him look away—him currently homeless with his ten-year-old son, trying to figure out how he wound up there with an estranged wife. Soon to be ex-wife.

Tonight though, she donned baggy overalls with a white tank top. The slight edge of nervousness still provoked his insides.

"How long have you been at this?" By this he meant the portrait taking shape before her.

From what he could tell, a resemblance stood out in the eyes between the subject matter and Iylah—though their skin tones were two shades different. He placed her plated sandwich on a long wooden table top, covered in fragments of past artworks and hand-drawn sketches.

"Six hours, give or take." She let out a breathy response, approaching him from behind, "Is this for me? Wow! Can't remember the last time I ate a homemade sandwich. My mother was probably the last person to make me a sandwich."

Turning around to face her, Jeb said, "Now I really hope it doesn't disappoint. Had I known about your lack of experience in having homemade sandwiches, I would have thought twice about making you one." He teased, running his fingers through his lengthy hair.

A haircut for him was past due, but in between everything going on it could wait.

"Well, give me about five seconds and I will tell you where my disappointment lays."

Her eyes sparkled with mischief, the brown specks floating along the edge of their green made prominent. Jeb witnessed how easily she could have anyone eating out of her palm.

He resisted the urge of instructing her to wash her hands before she took a bite. A force of habit that came from telling a certain ten-year-old boy to do so constantly. A ten-year-old he intended to call before he dozed off into restless sleep. Pushing past it, he walked over to take in the acrylic painting she'd been working on.

"Is this your mother?" His knowledge of classical painting technique ran in the unknown range—his eye for art telling him this was not an amateur attempt.

"Mhmm." Iylah sounded with a mouthful of what might not be a disappointing sandwich.

"This is incredible, Iylah." He stood closer to it, taking in the texture of the layers of paint gone into it so far.

You could easily tell how much an artist cared for their subject matter by the details they emphasized from knowing the intricacies of them. Jeb saw the laugh lines Iylah's brush shone on, they were like her own.

Iylah migrated to his side, standing shoulder to shoulder separated by a mere inches. Close enough for Jeb to catch a hint of the Pastrami on her breath. The pit in his stomach deepened.

Why did she make him this nervous?

"Thanks." She examined the work of her hands, and heart, unmoving next to him. "Your sandwich is pretty incredible too. Thanks for sharing your own artistry with me. Y'know, I still don't actually know what you teach at the School? For all I know you could be the janitor. Not that it would matter. At least your father didn't bribe his way into getting you a job there."

Jeb let out a cordial laugh in appreciation of her long-winded compliment to his sandwich making skills. She wasn't used to getting complimented about her work, and though he laughed it off, he was grateful to catch a glimpse of a flaw beyond her perfectly symmetrical face.

"I teach drawing—anatomy and life drawing specifically. No brooms or mops required." He inspected Iylah's profile, mapping it out in sections the way he would on paper—before he worked the delicate details out.

Starting with her strong jawline, emphasising itself as it curved to form the tip of her chin. The rich dark caramel skin where her chin and the jutting bow of full bottom lip met, looked almost airbrushed and poreless. The cupid's bow of her upper lip crumbed with traces of his sandwich mid chew. Before he could get any further in searching out the details that made her face a sketcher's dream, the sound of her voice pulled him out of his gawking.

"Where did you study?" She didn't look at him as she spoke, and it seemed intentional.

Jeb remained transfixed by her. "I didn't—didn't go to college. Mostly self-taught."

Iylah turned, out of further curiosity at this man she allowed into her home and the mild manner in which he divulged this massive revelation.

In past times, when Jeb shared his lack of a college education the conversations usually took a distractingly odd turn—people apologizing for his 'missing' out on education, or suddenly finding another conversation to join. It happened frequently.

She said nothing, so Jeb filled the silent space with an explanation, which he never usually did. He saw the questions swirling around in her weary eyes that appeared darker under the standing light next to her canvas.

"My mom and dad are pastors of a church in Clovis—used to be missionary pastors. After I graduated from high school, I convinced them to let me opt out of college and continue doing missionary work with them. That lasted about a year." He scoffed at the innocence of youth he used to possess.

He remembered those days. They were the days he felt most himself. Whether he was walking miles to go fix a water pump in remote Tanzania with his dad. Or if he was sleeping on a mat made from straw on a concrete floor. Somehow though, seeing his parents struggling paycheck to paycheck when they got back States-side, was enough to make him question everything their good works were built on. And that included God.

"Soon enough, I found myself traveling across the world craving those adventures, and boy did they come." He half chuckled to himself, the memories of reckless days chasing adrenaline displayed themselves on the screen of his mind, along with the faces of those he now called dear friends.

"Then you met Dawn, and she wrangled you in?"

"Something like that."

Truth be told it was nothing like that—he didn't desire to get into the details of it all. Not how Dawn got pregnant due to an omission of her sudden halt at taking her contraception, which led to their impromptu wedding and the birth of Tylor. Followed by plentiful affairs held up by lies over and over again. That story he wouldn't share, because he was still living it out waiting for the credits to roll on that chapter. The scorching betrayal of it all more than he could handle in reliving it right now.

And maybe that's why Iylah made him nervous. She bore witness to his life crumbling, and he wanted her to see the parts that were still whole. If only he could find them.

"Goodnight Iylah." He dismissed himself with a gentle smile, "Thank you for sharing your work with me. Your mother was beautiful." He glanced over once more at her mother in progress, "You look a lot like her."

Their eyes met as he backed away to his exit, the pit in his stomach slowly dissipating the further he got away from her.

Crap! I forgot to call Tylor.

The dull throbbing of his shoulders also forgotten. Curiosity definitely won.

nine

JOURNAL ENTRY DATED: 03/18/2005

'The Lord is my light and my salvation; whom shall I fear?
The Lord is the stronghold of my life;
Of whom shall I be afraid?'
Psalm 27:1

You are my salvation Jesus. My saving is not found in what or how I feel. Salvation in You is not flaky nor is it wavering. It is as sure as You, as solid and trustworthy as You are, as steadfast as you are. It will not vanish nor diminish with a singular small thought, otherwise I ought to think I was never carried by grace then at all. Remind me, Holy Spirit, that being saved from the consequence of my ever lurking sin, is not by my own means. You have gifted me this life of freedom in You, Jesus. I have not earned it, nor can I keep it. I lean on and rely on the power of Your Spirit to keep me in You. I need not be afraid of being snatched out from Your hand of safety. And I do not plan on removing myself from it. I have determined in my heart, in my soul to stick with You Jesus—my stronghold and my salvation. Whom would I ever turn to?

Your daughter

Lillian

Lylah

Iylah drew the back of her hand across her forehead, standing back from a now finished work of art. The summer heat found its way through the cooling system of the townhouse, despite her adjusting the temperature of this room to save the paint on her works. Her mother stared back at her, with a wet glisten to her freshly acrylic coated skin.

Iylah swallowed, endeavoring to remove the reminder now taking up space in her throat. Her arms felt like anchors, heavy and unmoving beside her. Her shoulders sullen, consumed and overcome by things she tried to fend off. As it turns out, she wasn't good at pretending fear didn't keep her up at night. No—she was tired of pretending she didn't feel alone, abandoned. Each time she went to call Lena, she came at a loss of how to explain the crumbling of her inner world that started long before the memories of Germany.

When will this end?

Allowing the wetness of a tear to sear down the side of her face, an embittered chuckle escaped her mouth—she threw the paintbrush she had been clinging onto as her lifesaver, into the dirty paint stained water in the mason jar next to her.

Why did she think painting her dead mother would bring her comfort? Nothing could resurrect the dead. What was she expecting to happen? That magically the world would make sense again? Stefan would be back in jail? This dull ache in her core would go away? And she could finally sleep with no more stupid, crippling nightmares?

Whom would I ever turn to?

The words from this morning's journal read looped around in her again.

"Yeah, well, I've got no one to turn to." As she said the words, she knew them to be untrue, yet she didn't have strength to deny how she felt.

Lena had been calling nearly every day since Iylah made the mad dash out of Washington D.C without so much as an explanation—just a lousy 'I've got to go'. She would not drag Lena into this again, she wouldn't. Whatever came—oh it was coming she could feel it—she had to deal with it alone, this included the consequences too.

Hands on her hips, she stood back watching, waiting. Waiting for what exactly, she wasn't sure. Her desperate need of a shower and some fresh air, the only thing she was certain of. The Saturday morning still in its early form, held room for various summer activities and she could do with a coffee.

I should ask Jeb if he wants to grab one with me.

She shook off the thought just as spontaneously as it had come.

Jeb headed to Clovis again this weekend, for a few days to see Tylor, and she wasn't about to impose her sorrowful behind on a man whose own world stood imploding too. Those cards she held in hand, were staying close to her chest, no matter how lonely she felt she would not bring him into her debilitating chaos. Despite somewhat of a friendship budding between them, Iylah didn't trust herself to fully engage in it—even if she wanted to.

The vibrating of her phone in the back pocket of the orange ambre beach pants she wore, reminded her of where she stood. As if notified, Jeb's name appeared scrolling across her phone. She fixed her curls hanging loose across her shoulder and back, held back by a simple silk floral scarf belonging to her mother. She caught herself doing so.

It's a phone call genius. And also—what?

Clearing her throat she answered, "Hey Jeb—"

"Hey Iylah, sorry to interrupt, but um, there's a couple of serious looking men here downstairs asking for you—"

Serious looking men? Before she could anticipate the words coming from her mouth, they burst forth, "Does one of them have a scar on his face?"

"Uh no—sorry where did you say you were from again?" His attention turned to whoever the men were. There were some words exchanged. "Um—they said they're from the FBI's organized crime division—"

Iylah's body tensed, suddenly winded by those few words, a dozen ideas of what was possibly unfolding flailed around in her mind.

"I–I–I'll be right down. Thanks." The phone slid down from her ear and dangled by her side.

In that moment, her breath releasing slow and shallow with panic starting to set in, she spoke the words she'd been mulling over.

"If you are real, can you please be what you were for my mother, to me?" She spoke to no one in particular, another tear escaping. "Please?"

A lingering sob threatened to rise and engulf her in defiance to her strong will striving to keep it away. She swallowed it down like she always did. Mustering up the courage left in her wavering resolve, she swiped the tear away, turning on her heel and put one foot in front of the other tentatively heading downstairs. Jeb was right.

The two men sitting in her living room were rather serious looking. They dealt with what sounded to be rather serious crimes, so what grounds did they have to be less serious? Life for them, she guessed, was probably always serious. Their seriousness the least of Iylah's worries.

Jeb stood across the unused television room, his figure silhouetted by the light of day coming through the ceiling high glass doors, leading to the ground floor courtyard. His arms crossed, accentuating the contours of his biceps, perplexity running across his face and rightly so.

Upon her entrance into the room, all standing men turned their straight-faced gazes to her. Not quite knowing what to do with her hands, she clasped them together in front of her—afraid if she hid them anywhere else it would make her appear guilty and vulnerable.

She was only one of those things, and guilty wasn't it.

"How can I help you, gentlemen?" Her voice carried an air of confidence which she lacked internally. To appear so, she straightened her shoulders.

Jeb noticed, cocking his head slightly to the right trying to put the pieces before him together. "I'll be outside if you need me, Iylah."

Was there a hint of protectiveness she noticed in his tone, in the presence of these two straight edge men before them?

"Actually, it would be in your best interest to stay sir—" The shorter, sturdier guy out of the pair spoke. Halting the rather baffled Jeb from setting his foot out onto the courtyard.

"It's okay—" Iylah responded to the man's instruction, "He knows nothing about this. I'm assuming this is about Stefan Hartmann?"

There was no point mincing words and agenda's.

The second gentleman nodded.

Time in all its structure, ceased to move for Iylah. Looming fears and nightmares being realised in that one small gesture. She exhaled, the breath in her lungs stinging on its way out. Her nervous system itching for a cigarette to calm its alarm bells down.

"Ma'am, we have to inform both you and your partner of this information, as you are both at risk." Back to short and sturdy gentleman.

"Oh, no—we—we're not—" Iylah's resolve diminished, the weight of the last few days since finding out about his prison release, creeping up on her, weakening her knees.

She caught the armrest of the couch, surprised by her body's betrayal. She didn't know how he got there, but Jeb was swiftly by her side. She couldn't see him with everything churning around—she felt his hands guide her down by the elbow to sit.

"Are you okay?" His voice lowered and tender with what sounded like care, his face directly in front of hers.

She nodded, her lips tightly pressed together, afraid of emptying her wound up insides all over him.

"We understand this is quite a distressing time for you Miss Dawson, but the urgency in the matter is extremely important." There was short and sturdy again.

She couldn't recall if they had given their names.

"I'm Eric Mane and this is my colleague, Jackson Shaw—" He didn't miss a beat, "And as your—uh—"

"Jeb—my name is Jeb."

"Thank you. As Jeb mentioned, we are with the Federal Bureau of Investigation." They both held up their respective badges of identification—not that Iylah could see them clearly. "Is Jeb someone we can disclose the nature of this case to? Are you close?"

"Listen—" Again Jeb's voice remained above a whisper just for her to hear, "If you're uncomfortable with me knowing whatever is going on—"

"I don't think they are giving you a choice." Iylah's small voice outed the disappearance of any courage she faked. She looked at his sterling silver eyes taking her in with concern that looked far more genuine than she expected.

"Okay then." His hand hadn't left her elbow, and she was grateful for it.

Embarrassment had long left the room. She nodded for Eric Mane to continue.

"Stefan Hartmann is an organized crime boss in Germany, dealing with the international market. He's a first generation criminal with an extensive network across Europe, Asia, Africa, and now according to the Central Intelligence Agency—is on our home turf of the United States—"

"Couldn't hack it with the Australians could he?" Without restraint the ill-placed joke fell out of her mouth.

Jeb caught on to her desperate need to lighten up what was going on inside of her—cementing it with a lopsided faint smile.

Eric Mane continued undeterred by her attempt at diffusing the severity of the matter.

"Miss Dawson and Stefan were involved in a relationship over eighteen months—" he paused for any interjection Iylah might have. There was none. "Unbeknownst to Miss Dawson, her then boyfriend was the ringleader of a drug and money laundering syndicate. On June the sixteenth of last year, at an exclusive nightclub in Munich, owned by an associate of Hartmann—Miss Dawson was in attendance. A business meeting gone wrong found Hartmann responsible for the death of seven men with Miss Dawson being the only witness alive in the private room. She reported the crime after escaping from Hartmann's home where he held her captive for fourteen days. He went to trial for murder, along with additional charges from an extensive rep sheet he couldn't be nailed on prior. Miss Dawson testified against him leading to him getting a prison sentence of thirty-five years with no parole options. We have now learnt of his release two weeks ago, which is being investigated further by German Intelligence. However, our border alert on him was activated when he landed in Chicago three days ago. We are not sure who his connections are yet, but we are certain he will attempt to go under the radar. Which is where you come in Miss Dawson—"

Her saliva thickened in her mouth. All she could do to keep from completely unraveling, was focus her breathing like Imelda taught her. She couldn't fathom what must be going through the mind of the man next to her, who had not broken his attention on her during Eric Mane's speech.

Aware of the well of tears on the verge of exploding, she averted her glassy eyes, sniffling back the fear they held.

Eric Mane continued, "We're afraid he may try to reach out to you. We don't know what his purpose is coming into the country. The only link we have to him and the United States is you."

"So what can you do?" The protectiveness in his manner entirely evident and unveiled. Jeb stood up, letting go of Iylah's elbow to face the men that seemed to bring a warning to her doorstep.

"Until we gather further intel on his movements, we recommend that Miss Dawson lies low until further notice. Is there anywhere you can go Hartmann may not know you're connected to? Family is out of the question, given the intimate details of your past relationship with him—we don't want to take the chance of a place you may have spoken of to him."

Dread seeped through her bones, filling them and weighing her down like lead.

"I—I don't know." She shrugged. "He knew of my father, my sister—oh god the girls!" Her hand covered her mouth, the terror of anything happening to them becoming all too real. "I don't know where else to go."

"I know of a place." The certainty in Jeb's interjection made Iylah look up at him. "In Clovis—"

She shot up out of her seat in protest, "Jeb no, no, no—" She shook her head vehemently, "I'm not getting your family involved, not you or Tylor—"

"I think it's a little too late to not get me involved." He held her by the shoulders, steadying her with a firmness neither diminishing, nor harsh. It was reassuring.

"I can't ask you to do that. You've already got enough going on—" She pleaded.

"C'mon Iylah," He took a step closer towards her, "It's my turn to help you out. Let me."

He searched her face with an intent focus, taking in her chaotic mess and all he seemed to see was a woman who ran so fast and so hard, she only just realized no one was around her.

Iylah lost the little resolve she had left. The sobs came, her body engulfed with each convulsion, sinking deeper and deeper into the despair that relentlessly hounded her.

Almost instinctively Jeb drew her into himself, his arms being the strength she no longer possessed. Aware of the snot smearing on the shoulder of his cotton t-shirt, Iylah gripped on not trusting her body to keep itself up. He didn't seem to care about the mess she made of his t-shirt, increasing her teariness all the more. The clutching claws of fear set themselves in as catastrophe filled her mind.

The Lord is my light and salvation, whom shall I fear? Be my light and my salvation, I have plenty to fear. Whoever you are—if you're even listening.

She was practically sure no one inclined their ear to listen.

Jeb

Jeb did not expect his journey to Clovis for the next few days would be taken in a private jet. Nor did he expect to be taking the journey with an extra passenger on this seven-hour flight. Yet here he was—sitting in one of the plush cream leather seats—the widest most comfortable plane seats his back ever leaned into. A window seat to be exact. If the circumstances allowed, he would enjoy every bit of this free flight. The circumstances were not ones he would wish upon anyone, let alone Iylah.

Three hours into their flight, she sat slumped across the aisle from him, blindly staring out of her own window with not a single word to exchange. The panic left her worn and despondent. She hadn't said much since the revelation of her past was laid out for Jeb to witness—apart from offering hiring a private jet and a car rental upon arrival. She dove into a pit of silence, and he thought it wise and sensible to give her the space she needed.

How much space was too much space now? He never thrived at this sort of thing. Him frequently being the one who initiated space with Dawn—seldom the one to be on the receiving end of it.

In a short amount of time, everything he presumed about Iylah had been brought into question. The notion of a spoilt, trust funded, woman who always got her way dissipated by the minute.

He peered over at Iylah—her sassy disposition overcome by a more sullen, withdrawn and scared manner in its place. The compulsion to assure her in his arms growing—crying women tugged on the compassion strings ingrained into him by his mom. The earlier memory of her breaking down, leaving evidence of it all over his cotton t-shirt, did something to him. He wasn't sure what yet.

What happened in those fourteen days she was kidnapped? How did she escape? Was she in love with him? Did she really not know anything about his crimes? Was it a bad idea to get Mom and Dad involved? Tylor?

The questions came with no filter to lessen their frequency—he wouldn't dare ask them out loud. The sole flight attendant on the plane appeared with a decently sized mug on a tray, steaming and bobbing with a marshmallow. She handed it to Iylah who flashed her the briefest smile of thanks and made her way over to Jeb.

"Can I get you anything, sir?" She asked in the professional manner they were trained to, for the fifth time since the flight began.

Jeb prepared his response to be the same as the last four times, until Iylah jumped in.

"Don't be shy Jeb." She spoke her vacant stare unmoved from her view out the window, a hoarseness coating her melancholic voice. "Please, get something to eat or drink at least."

She turned to face him, in case he dared to turn her down again. The flight attendant nodded in agreement, with a well-rehearsed smile, her freshly painted face not showing a single imperfection.

"Fine." His mom always said not to rob someone of the joy of being a blessing. "I'll have an espresso double shot thanks."

Relieved—probably that he finally caved—the flight attendant nodded and made a move before he changed his mind.

Taking his chance, Jeb unbuckled his seatbelt to make his way across to Iylah.

"Wait—your seatbelt was on the entire time?" And there she was—a small glimmer of the sass she usually exuded.

He perched next to her, putting this seatbelt on too. "They have them for a reason, I'm just saying."

And that reason cemented the difference between life and death to him. She narrowed her eyes at him unsure what to make of his statement.

He chuckled, "I don't make the rules."

"Mmkay." Iylah turned back to her window, "How's the divorce going?"

Her question came wildly unexpectedly, stunning Jeb back into his own reality.

Was that the purpose of her question?

"That's really the question you want to ask me right now?"

She just stared.

His hands raked through his hair attempting to piece his response together without giving away his own chaotic inner dialogue. "Dawn's been served with the papers, after I finally located her—"

"How'd you find her?" She took a lengthy sip from her hot chocolate, the marshmallow no longer.

"Her Instagram." He sighed agitated by just how long he put up with her. Too long.

"Seriously?" Iylah's bottle green eyes were bewildered by his revelations.

He shifted in his seat, the dip in his stomach resurfacing.

She continued, "Are you okay?"

Was he okay? The question he hadn't really taken the time to ask himself lately. He knew how he had to respond though and he did.

"I will be."

Their eyes still engaged, neither one of them turning away—despite chastising himself inwardly for whatever took place in his swimming gut.

"Do you still love her?" Another unhindered question came from her at such speed, quieter and more timidly—aware of the parts of his heart she pried open. This time Jeb saw something switch in her eyes. He couldn't quite place it.

"You're nailing it on the questions front by the way. She's the mother of my son, I'll always love her for that." His tone matched hers, "But it's a different love. It changed the second time she cheated." And the third, the fourth.

"I'm sorry." Iylah settled her intrigue back on the cup she held in both hands, taking another sip from it.

"Did you love him? Your ex? Sir Crime Lord?" He pried at her own shattered heart.

Drawing the cup away from her face, she turned back to him with a lazy smile, "No," She gazed past Jeb at nothing, "I just didn't enjoy being alone."

There it was. A confession of the loneliness he observed her living in. Was her loneliness the underlying reason she invited a total stranger, into her home without so much as an interrogation?

It seemed the truth suddenly grabbed him by the head so he could see it for what it was. He hoped he hadn't made a mistake. He hoped he was wrong.

ten

Lylah

The smell of bacon filled the room—as did the California sunlight through a crack in the closed curtains, announcing the new day. With her eyes half shut, Iylah held onto the top of the sheet sticking to her sprawled out body, covering half her face. It smelled of yellow roses. Leisurely rubbing her sleepy eyes, they finally opened to take in the quaint bedroom where she had fallen asleep.

Small by her usual standards, but the biggest bedroom in the house according to a rather gruff Jeb—in case she dared to be ungrateful. Which she wasn't.

To be completely honest, she was exhausted. Her growling stomach reminded her of the dinner she excused herself from so she could get some sleep—it was all her body felt like doing. She reached for her phone sitting on the chunky oak wood bedside drawers.

I've been asleep for twelve hours. How on earth did I manage that?

Those sleep-deprived nights caught up with her, and it took leaving Manhattan for her body to get it.

A runaway lazy yawn leaving her mouth, she scanned the room once again. Her two suitcases opened and spilled out in the corner next to a single brown leather armchair. A light wooden dresser with a mirror against the wall at the foot of the Queen-sized bed, an inbuilt wardrobe next to it. The walls were adorned with two strategically placed print paintings of Yosemite and the other of some river brook. The bed took center stage, with its vintage ivory frame—and the colonial glazed windows to the left of it. It was a cozy room and she would accept it with gratitude, no matter her preferences. Jeb's parents were overwhelmingly kind to welcome Iylah into their home, especially given the less than ideal background knowledge Jeb obviously disclosed to them.

A tinge of embarrassment gripped Iylah upon their arrival in the late afternoon, as Jeb's vivacious, frequently embracing mother scooped up Iylah. She lost count of how many hugs she received from Kathy in the space of their introduction. Iylah determined through sheer cheek biting not to fall apart in the warm and genuine hugs.

She'd forgotten what hugs from mothers felt like—all consuming, erasing of life's troubles and a weighty reminder you weren't alone. The ache for her mother's hug bit terribly hard.

Jeb's father, Frank, extended a hand to shake with few words. Tylor, on the other hand, once a fellow Nintendo playing friend, gave a rather disinterested greeting to Iylah. Something had changed in his perspective of her since they last saw each other. Were ten-year-olds usually fickle in friendships? No wonder her middle school memories were nowhere to be found. Jeb corrected him sternly, Iylah brushing it off, saying, 'boys will be boys'. A saying she had never used before.

Throwing her legs over the side of the bed, Iylah thought it best not to linger too long between the covers for fear of falling back asleep. Her feet met the fluffy, sheep's wool rug placed intentionally at her bedside. She forced her mind away from the knowledge of it being imitation sheep's wool. Years of living in cold European climates made her well acquainted with real sheep's wool. She wasn't about to pass judgment in a place that was now her safe haven for who knows how long.

How did I find myself here?

All she heard about Clovis was how undecided it was about whether it belonged in Southern California or Northern California. A place that didn't know where it stood. Much like her. It's summer's known for being brutally close to desert temperatures, rather than the coastal ones she preferred. A county encompassing small-town vibes, depending on which pocket of its cityscape you lived in. Iylah took a rough shot at guessing that Clovis—where the Astons resided—sat on the family centric scale, complete with surprisingly leafy streets and adolescent faces zooming past on bicycles as they drove in from the airport.

Iylah succumbed to a sigh. The uncertainty of what lay ahead felt uncomfortable in her gut, making itself permanent.

Gingerly, she made her way over to the mirror, her entire body rigid with the lumbering baggage she carried. The dark circles under her eyes confirmed what the rest of her body felt. Her hair, in all its volume, hung in a lopsided, unruly bun—basically a nest. Bringing her hands to her face, tracing her cheeks that now held less meat on them by no means of trying. Exhaling, pushing aside the persistent hankering for a cigarette she always woke up with, she resolved not to be a drag around a family who clearly had all the joy and hospitality in the world to take her in. Fiddling around, she attempted to make herself appear more alive and kept.

After a few minutes navigating her hair, she combed IT through with her fingers to separate her curls, leaving them loose in all their untamed glory today. Throwing on a black Off-White t-shirt and a random pair of gray sweatpants—of which she couldn't presently trace their origins—she exited the cozy bedroom to an even cozier hallway, its eggshell painted wall lined with family photographs. Stopping to take them in, she noticed how far back some of them dated, hanging securely framed in their black and white memories showing faces that may not be around anymore. She traveled along the length of the narrow hallway—the photos dictating the timeline of the Aston family until she finally got to a particular face.

A faint smile drew itself on her face. She recognised the young boyish face squinting back at her, standing next to another slightly older-looking boyish face. She could see hints of Tylor in his young features. She imagined the childhood he had lived in this very home. She gathered by the images she saw displayed here, how much joy these walls were observers to, the love that tested unconditional, and the summer activities planned for enjoyment—it was all a far cry from her rigid-fit into-high-society upbringing.

Maybe that's why she rebelled so vehemently against her father. The very thing she saw in these photos is what she craved her entire life. A close-knit family with history and a warm your belly type of charm.

Tension coursed through her body at the thought of her estranged family—a father she avoided at all costs and one sibling whose phone calls she currently dodged.

It wouldn't be long before Lena found out about Iylah's current safety risk—she had a knack for finding out things. Part of the perks of knowing nearly everyone in the legal system of the entire United States. Iylah decidedly was not going to be the one to tell her.

A slamming door ripped Iylah out of her immersion. Some conversation started towards the front of the house, where the kitchen was located. Taking a shallow breath, her timid feet made their way out of the hallway into the open planned living area next to the kitchen. The smell of bacon, now stronger, awakened her stomach as its aroma filled the air. Kathy stood over Tylor at the kitchen table, dishing out an extra helping of bacon accompanied with a smirk and a wink. While Jeb stood at the sink, back from his morning run, nursing a bottle of water, his shoulders visibly rose and fell from his efforts. Iylah couldn't allow her eyes to linger on him, promptly setting them back on Tylor, now aware of her presence.

"Good morning, Iylah. Have yourself a seat, I've got some breakfast ready for you." Kathy flashed her perfect rows of teeth in a hearty smile, scurrying back to the stove where she slaved away. Though her peppy countenance didn't make it look like slaving. Giving Iylah no time to object, she added, "I didn't know what you liked, so I made a bit of a buffet-style breakfast for everyone. There should be something in there you might like, I hope."

Her smoky, curly white hair bobbed with each movement of serving. Her short, sturdy frame crossed each corner of the kitchen—busy with delight.

"Thank you, Kathy." Iylah slinked into a chair two seats away from Tylor, who looked anything but pleased with her. "You didn't have to go to all this trouble, honestly."

What did I do wrong? Relax! He's just ten.

"Nonsense. Can't have you going hungry on my watch." And that was that.

Unsure of where to rest her eyes, trying not to land on Jeb, she peeked down at her fidgeting hands, cracking them at the knuckles—the sound of it more amplified than she would like.

"That's gross!" Tylor made his disdain of the sound known.

"Tylor!" Jeb interjected in a tone that made Iylah sit up. "Finish your food and get dressed, please?"

With a pout and a firm grip on his fork, Tylor did as he was told.

"Sorry." Iylah mumbled, suddenly feeling self-conscious and aware of her imposition. "I think it's from all the painting I was doing."

"Oh, you're a painter?" Kathy placed a well portioned plate of food before Iylah. Scrambled eggs as fluffy as they come, some bacon and two neatly stacked pancakes, with a piece of avocado toast. Normally such a generous helping of food would put Iylah off, but given her lack of home-cooked meals—this was one meal she would finish with gusto.

"Thank you." She gave a feeble smile to Kathy.

"And really good at it too. You should see some of her work, they give some of your pieces here a run for their money." Jeb took another sip of his water. The expression on his face, a foreign one to Iylah, whatever bothered him last night was still at the forefront of his mind.

She didn't respond to him, unsure what was appropriate to say given the way his gaze kept falling away from hers. Regret showed its face.

This was a bad idea. I shouldn't have come here. He's obviously changed his mind.

Her appetite waned, the familiar coldness of shame taking over her stomach.

"I would love to see them. I'm sure you paint just as beautiful as you look." Another wink came from Kathy, setting down her tools of mass breakfast production. "C'mon Tylor, go on and get dressed, sweetie. We should head off soon—actually, Iylah, would you like to join us for church this morning?"

"Mom, I don't think Iylah—"

"I would love to!" Before she could put reason behind her words, Iylah accepted the invitation she'd never received before, cutting Jeb short of yet another interjection.

This time she could read the expression on Jeb's face. It matched the state of her heart. Confused and wanting answers.

Jeh

He wasn't sure exactly how he found himself in these seats again, after what felt like more than a decade.

Everything remained exactly the same as when he left all those years ago. The faces sitting in the surrounding seats were mostly still the same—not including a few new younger faces, even young families. The big black ceiling fans attached to the white high beams still turned the same way—in a rickety fashion enough to make you keep an eye on them. The dark stained wooden floors teenage him always mopped and swept, remained unchanged in its polished and worn appearance. Even the way his dad preached hadn't changed—passionately, clearly and with great conviction.

He always admired the passion and utter assurance in his dad's voice when he spoke about God, whether it was behind that solid pulpit or sipping a cup of coffee with a church member who needed to be reminded of what they believed and trusted. Truly, time stood still here—nothing changed. Nothing, except him.

No longer naïve anymore, he wasn't any better for the life experiences under his belt. On the way to a divorce, about to be a single father, living in someone else's home in a city he definitely couldn't afford to live in. There were a few life decisions he needed to iron out, but he wondered silently if this unravelling life was all part of God's plan—just like his dad preached about this morning.

Ha! Fat chance. You reap what you sow, isn't that the verse?

Then there was Iylah. Sitting next to him, unmoving, intently listening to every word coming out of his dad's mouth. If she felt uncomfortable, she hid it well. Oblivious to the erratic way his nerves responded to her nearness. How he hoped he wouldn't regret this reckless idea of bringing her so deeply into his own personal life. She somehow found a space in his falling apart world, while hers was doing the same.

For someone whose safety slanted heavily towards being at risk, she sat at ease next to him. Her instant acceptance of his mom's invitation earlier surprised him. She didn't strike him to be the religious type—still they both found themselves in church on a routinely hot Sunday morning. Amidst the curious looks, both from longstanding church members who knew Jeb from his eager to please years, to recently attending church members wondering who this new 'couple' was.

Two or more awkward conversations happened, resulting in him explaining in the middle of polite niceties, that he and Iylah were not in fact married and she was not Tylor's mother. When then asked if Tylor's mother would join them, he said a kind no through a tight lipped variation of a smile.

He was aware, however, of the stolen looks Iylah kept getting from some women and the odd male. In her attempt to find something 'churchy' to wear—her words not his—she interestingly landed on the most eye-catching dress. A long, crochet knitted, orange, sleeveless dress that draped well on her frame, revealing her slender shoulders and skin's warm highlights shining under any light. Her hair propped in its natural habitat—a low bun she always pulled off, with two strands of curls escaping on either side of her face.

Was there any wonder they stared?

The rest of the church service continued, ending in song and a prayer of send off. Before Jeb could make a beeline for the exit, he got caught in yet another conversation about his absence. Iylah managed a hasty escape outside, away from nosey eyes and ears. His patience and polite nature started losing its grip after the third conversation, to which he excused himself.

He stepped outside the big arched wooden doors of the church building, met with the dry summer air he grew up loving. It did absolutely nothing to provide a cool reprieve. Head towards the sky, he closed his eyes, bracing his neck with his hands. The tension in his shoulders showed itself, along with the rolling waves of unease, washing through him leaving sandy murky residue.

How did I get here?

Opening his eyes, allowing them to roam around at the congregation streaming out steadily, he spotted a familiar orange dressed woman standing under the tall and broad shade of a Fremont tree. She seemed distracted and unaware of her surroundings, zoning in on nothing in particular on the ground.

Words were barely exchanged between them earlier, on the way to church. Jeb in his thoughts about setting foot in a church after so long, and Iylah out of her comfort zone and general sense of familiarity. Not forgetting the unease of knowing his presence in her life could be a mere way to distract herself from her own jeopardy. He hadn't done a good job at hiding his suspicion.

"Y'know, it was your idea for me to come here." Were the words she greeted Jeb with as he now stood next to her.

Her eyes didn't meet his, remaining cast downwards timidly—a trait he didn't think she possessed.

"What?" Caught off guard by her statement, watching the side of her set face, Jeb asked, "Iylah, what choice did I have? You took Tylor and I in—I wanted to return the favor."

That wasn't the only reason, and he knew it.

At those very words, her head shot around, locking her stunning despaired eyes on him. "Returning the favor? I'd rather you didn't. I'm not a charity case—"

"Oh, and I was?" The uneasiness riddling him finally spewed to the surface. "Why did you invite us to live with you? To make yourself feel less lonely? My life is not a substitute for whatever you lack in yours Iylah!" The bite in his words marked Iylah enough to cause her mouth to gape open.

"Because your life lacks nothing?"

He could see the glistening wet of her eyes staring back at him in disbelief.

"Do I need to remind you, your life is falling apart just as bad as mine—granted your ex isn't a criminal, but at least I can admit I've made a mess of things, instead of pretending it's not there." She bit back.

"I knew this was a terrible idea." Jeb rubbed his face gruffly wanting reality to be anything but this.

He removed his hands from his eyes just in time to watch Iylah's entire face drop. The taste of regret hung on the tip of his tongue, but it didn't stop the flow of his simmering furious rage.

"I have a kid who hates me right now. I'm at the start of what is going to be a long drawn out divorce, because my soon-to-be ex-wife can't stay long enough in one spot to finalize anything. I've brought a stranger whom I've known for less than four months into my parents' home and I'm not even sure why." Again, he recognized the last part to be a lie, but he would not admit that to himself or to Iylah.

She fiddled with the chain of her pint-sized handbag, her face tired and worn barely able to disguise the hurt dug up by his words.

Abruptly Iylah turned on her heels marching off, away from the shade of the tree. Determination to get as far away from Jeb in her steps. If fury didn't cloud him, her storm off would have amused him. Never had he encountered a woman with as much determination cooped up in her lithe frame.

Jeb knew there wasn't far she could go—this town being new to her, held pockets she could get lost in. That didn't seem to deter her though.

"Where are you going?" Jeb called out to her, frustration embedded on his face.

No response from Iylah, who continued onwards, down the steps of the path meandering up to the sidewalk, further down and out of sight beyond the shrubbery that now hid her escape.

Did he care enough to go after her? His unmoved feet showed his own stubbornness—his wringing hands betrayed his heart. Tearing himself away from her direction, now aware of the eyes and ears privy, truly interested in the conversation that transpired. He looked around, eyes averted.

Finally, he beelined back inside to distract himself somehow, with something. Anything.

Iylah

Her vision blurred by the tears clinging onto her lashes—unable to see clearly. Even if she could see clearly, nothing looked remotely familiar.

Where am I going?

She scoffed at the existential probing the question held for her. Her current loss of direction mirrored her life far too accurately.

The strings of anxiety tightened, threatening once again to whirlpool the moments to come. Her insides taut with anticipation of the oncoming panic about to attack her nervous system—even so her body held itself limply, tired from holding on and holding in disarray.

A lonesome tear escaped, sliding down her cheek, taking with it the last of her willpower causing her knees to buckle beneath her.

Finding nowhere else to sit, Iylah sat herself down curbside—a new forced habit. Pulling out her pack of Backwoods, a lighter and her phone—her bottom lip quivered mirroring her shaky breath. Blindly she scrolled through her missed calls, ready to return the one call which could put her at ease.

The phone rang twice on the other end before its recipient answered.

"Iylah! Where are you? Why haven't—"

At the sound of Lena's voice, Iylah's sobs broke forth engulfing her words till nothing else could come out of her mouth.

eleven

JOURNAL ENTRY DATED: 04/24/2005

'Don't let your hearts be troubled. Trust in God, and trust in me. There is more than enough room in my father's house. If this were not so, would I have told you that I am going to prepare a place for you? When everything is ready, I will come and get you so that you will always be where I am. And you know the way to where I am going.'

John 14:1-4

Jesus, in this world You guaranteed we would face trials and tribulations. You guaranteed this life would bring to us paths and doors that would lead to suffering. But in Your mercy You also assured us a safe passage through You overcoming the world. My heart knows this, yet my mind rehearses over Your word with a doubtful lens. Oh, that You would grant me the eyes to see You overcoming my current plight. Grant me the eyes to witness the truth of which You have spoken over Your children. The promise of a place forever with You. A place of peace, of the fullest joy and the nearest love. In the natural everything I see is through wounded eyes and a calloused heart. Heal the parts of me that create a barrier between You and me. May my heart release all its trouble to You, in surrender and bold trust, knowing what You have planned and prepared for me is good. This present trouble does not compare to what is to come with You and I would trade none of this if it draws me to Your ways.

Your daughter

Lillian

Iylah

Your ways? Iylah's finger traced the last words she read from her mother's journal. The dancing shadows of the Sycamore tree she lounged under, displayed themselves on the pages—light cracking through each movement from the gentle afternoon breeze blowing in the Aston's backyard. The more she read the longings her mother penned, the less everything made sense—scrambling her already up heaved life.

Allusions littered the pages of what her mother faced day to day—some hints at a strained relationship with Iylah's father—those parts made sense just from knowing her father, but the rest felt quite cryptic. The god of which she wrote, the Jesus of whom she spoke with such tenderness and affection towards—who was he?

A discomfort of wanting to know more bore its way into Iylah. Moreso now after her morning in what seemed like a sanctuary for many others. She witnessed and had lived enough to see the truth of the matter—not a single life on this earth was perfect.

In church that morning Frank spoke what she now knows to be a sermon—the faces of those sitting around and beside her drank in his sayings like their lives were parched. Everyone, except Jeb who constantly fiddled and squirmed rather restlessly in his seat. She observed him to be miserable in this setting and recalled his own confession of not being overly fond of the God of his parents anymore.

Still, no amount of misery justified his outburst towards her.

She hadn't seen him since navigating her way back to the house, courtesy of her wireless earphones linked to her phone. In hindsight, it was a fifty-minute walk she needed, though her feet spoke a different story now nestled in the brittle off-green grass. It was also the phone call she didn't want to make to Lena, but her options ran out.

Lena needed little updating about the current state of Iylah's life. Through her superb networking skills, Lena was well informed of Stefan's arrival in the country. Iylah never admitted it but Lena's need to be aware of even the smallest hint of danger approaching Iylah troubled her. Who was she to protest now? Evidently she did need a babysitter and a savior.

For most of her walk the conversation tittered around Iylah trying to dissuade Lena from taking matters into her own legal hands, with a stern warning not to trauma bond with a strange man in his parent's home. Her firm warnings resulted in Iylah making multiple promises to Lena if things escalated—like she couldn't be trusted to make up her own mind about it all. Those promises could only hold Lena away for so long.

Iylah's plan forward? Well—it was as clear as how much she understood about Jesus—pretty frigging foggy with Google being no place for answers.

I want to understand.

Growing frustrated with herself, she sank down in the wicker lawn chair, shutting her eyes and allowing a ragged, uneven breath to escape her.

I want to know what she knew. Show me. Somehow, please just show me.

The pleas swirled in her mind, directed to no one in particular. Every single one of her mother's journal entries pointed to a Jesus that heard please and cries. She figured he would be the one to call out to.

"Don't forget to put your wet clothes by the laundry shoot!" Jeb called out to the back of his ten-year-old son racing through the kitchen, probably attempting to avoid any contact with Iylah.

Jeb became increasingly aware of the sudden cold shoulder Iylah received from Tylor. He never behaved in such a manner normally. Jeb couldn't blame him.

Close to two weeks ago both their lives shattered. Regardless of his own disdain towards Dawn, she was Tylor's mother, and that's all Tylor saw and cared about. Jeb suspected Tylor—in his prepubescent brain—blamed Iylah for it all. Earlier today, Jeb misguidedly did the same.

Burning traces of the last conversation between Iylah and him, branded him all day after she stormed off at the church without the faintest clue where she was going. He said enough to push her to find solace in the streets of a place she did not know. When the ever present scorching settled in him, dread took its place. Dread at who he was becoming. A man whose heart resembled an ash heap he kept blowing in people's faces—in Iylah's face.

Once the convicting realization of the irrationality of another one of his blind outbursts set in, he tried to call her in a panic. After all, a crime lord actively searched for her whereabouts. The worry packed on in him when there came no answer to his barrage of calls. Eventually she sent a rather simple blunt message.

> Stop calling me. Needed some air. I'll find my way back.

So he stopped—his worry didn't.

Deciding he couldn't wait around for Iylah to show up, he took a brooding Tylor for a swim at Lost Lake, the local swimming hole—the same one where his own summers were spent. He forgot how much he loved Clovis summers. Long, dry and fire-starting hot summers marked his youth. Those suffocating days spent chasing any slight activity bringing relief from the sun—the breeze from skating down a hill at unsavory speeds; the long hikes searching for the best not so crowded lake spots to swim in with Ezra—created permanent memories.

Dawn's aversion to being anywhere near his parents, made being here seem strange. The odd family holiday hard enough for her to stomach.

Jeb shut his eyes, pushing away the reminder of how much she stole from his life. He continued towel drying his wet hair, sipping on some water attempting to quench something other than a physical thirst. From where he stood by his parents' kitchen sink, taking in the backyard he saw the figure sitting in his mom's lawn chair. Her back to the window and her head thrown against the chair's cushioning, her sleek curls wildly draped over its edge. He imagined what they would feel like for his fingers to stroke through.

The pit in his stomach appeared again.

"Hungry?" The voice of his mom drew him back into the room. "I'm making your favorite tonight, in honor of my prodigal returning." She jabbed him in the back gently, walking past him to get to the fridge.

"Prodigal? Really, Mom?" He turned around to face the woman who knew him so well despite time and distance changing them both.

He chose to take paths that caused her to stay up late in the night praying.

"Well, last time you were here Jeb, Tylor was six—so yes prodigal." She scanned the fridge, searching for the ingredients for the fish pie on her to do list. "Who knew it would take a divorce and something to do with a crime boss to bring you back into my kitchen." Her good natured chuckle, a reminder of how she was never one to take anything too seriously.

"Surely you saw the divorce coming? If I didn't know any better, I would say it was at the top of your ladies group prayer list. And if I recall perfectly, you have had all sorts of troubled characters come through this house—almost every year since I was twelve." He crossed his arms, leaning against the sink.

It all rang true and his mom couldn't pretend it didn't. Troubled characters are what these pastors specialized in—that's what got rid of his hesitation to bring Iylah here.

"Oh, hush." She swiped him with a dishcloth, turning the faucet to wash her hands next to him. "Have you apologized to her yet?"

Word must have gotten back to her about his argument with Iylah. He certainly hadn't told her—it's how it worked around that church. Shaking his head at the hypocrisy of it, he admitted, "No, but I'm going to. You don't have to tell me off for it" He raised his arms in mock surrender.

"Poor thing. Came back tired and even more lost. It won't be long though, these storms are always imminent but so is the sun."

Jeb grinned at her hopeful nature, steadfastly unwavering no matter how bad the scenario—especially when it was in fact pretty bad.

"Such a beautiful girl." She continued on with her dinner prep, "And don't think I haven't noticed how you look at her too, son."

He caught the glint in her eye she always got when she sensed something unspoken. It made him think twice before getting into any mischief growing up. She found out before he'd committed any crimes.

Jeb opened his mouth to defend himself, to bring a swift denial to his mom's astute observation—he came up with nothing. She identified the cause of the pit in his stomach—the cautious wariness brought on by his sudden curious attraction to this woman who plunged into his life unexpectedly. He slicked back the wet strands of his hair with a defeated half chuckle.

Hand on hip and all her attention on him now, Kathy stood shoulder to bicep with her son. "I know you're afraid Jeb," Her tone lowered and tender, "Don't let your heart go where your hurt hasn't been dealt to yet. Heck—I don't think her heart even knows how to beat with life and not fear. To live on the run from so many things has a way of graying our lives."

"I barely know her Mom."

And I'm too old to be getting a stupid crush on someone years my junior.

He knew this to be true in theory. He also knew why he was afraid. She scared him, not in a manner that deterred him but in one that wanted to stick around and figure out why.

"Then make the effort. She needs a friend, not another guy who's heart is all twisted up. Figure yourself out first, son." She pushed herself forward to begin her task at hand, "More importantly, you owe her an apology."

"Yes, ma'am." Taking his marching orders, he kissed his mom on the cheek before making his way out to rectify his wrong.

He'd been tallying up a few apologies to her a lot lately.

The creaking of the fly screen door leading to the backyard, alerting her of his presence, making Iylah jolt upright in her seat, turning back to look at Jeb. Sheepishly he waved, presenting himself on friendly terms. She didn't return the smile, turning forward, focusing ahead on nothing in particular. He deserved that.

Bracing himself for his apology, he made his way across the lawn to occupy the second chair beside her. He noticed her swiftly shut a leather bound journal on her lap as he sat himself down. He didn't take her to be much of a writer—or a reader for that matter. How much did he know about her, anyway?

They sat in a cove of silence for what seemed longer than necessary. Jeb needed to be the one to pave the way for this conversation, he gathered she would not be forthcoming with any small talk.

A nervous chill wedged at the bottom of his spine, hands clasped together steadying the thoughts using his mind as a highway.

"Iylah—" He paused searching for words to frame a sincere apology, "I'm sorry about what I said earlier this morning." The sourness of regret lined his throat. "Truth be told, being back here was not how I saw my summer going. It just brought back a lot of memories I'm uncomfortable with and it made me feel like a failure so I took it out on you." He turned his attention towards the side of her face he'd studied more times than he realised, "I really am sorry." He swallowed the guilt down as the words left his mouth—it just wouldn't go away.

She didn't move, she didn't waver in staring at anything but Jeb. "Why do you feel like a failure?"

He sighed, the hole in his stomach intensifying at the thought of being completely vulnerable and honest, not just with her but with himself.

"Where do I begin? Um—losing ten years to someone who never thought twice about me, becoming a single father. None of those were really on my list of resolutions for this year. I know they don't think this, but being the family screw up isn't something I'm proud of." A self appointed title he wore, fulfilling the prophecy plaguing the middle child. "My brother and sister seem to have life figured out, and I seem to always be taking alternative routes." He scoffed, covering his mouth with a hand, afraid to let her see further into his turmoil.

"It's not your fault, y'know. It's okay to be angry about it."

Iylah still didn't look at him, the calm breeze picking up strands of curl making them dance around her high cheekbone. She let them move with the wind, before tucking them away safely behind her ear—he watched every movement.

"You loved Dawn and wanted to build something with her, unfortunately she was wired a bit differently. That's not your fault."

"Neither is what's happening to you right now—" He flipped the mirror in their conversation for her to see it too.

"Oh but it is." Iylah cut him short, turning her head towards him.

The weariness cemented in her eyes, so did the terror pulsing through to her heart. His chest tightened at the sight of it.

"When you make as many selfish decisions as I have, soon enough you reap it. Thanks for trying to be nice, but I know my life and I know myself." She turned away.

"What bad decisions did you make?" The question fell out of his mouth before he could sift it.

She shifted in her seat, the rawness of where his words hit, clear. When she responded, her willingness to give him a glimpse into her own regrets, noted by him.

"Well, my honorable mentions go to every relationship I have ever been in, or lack of really. Not mourning my mother properly. Not quizzing my father closely—just to name a few."

The revelation of terrible relationships didn't catch him off guard—intrigued him, maybe.

How many crime lords does she have lurking in her past, exactly?

Frankly, his own position didn't make him fit to judge, so he decided wisely not to pursue it.

"Are you close with your dad?" She called him 'father' rather matter-of-fact, instead of endearing. Jeb guessed not.

Shaking her head, she said, "Let's just say he's used money to buy my affection over the years and I have let him. Never really present and when he was, I wished he wasn't. Are you close with your parents?" She flashed the question back on him, her sharp emerald eyes searching parts of him he held as sacred space.

"I love my parents, but if I'm honest my escapades over the years have put distance between us." He played around with a blade of grass he'd torn from the ground absentmindedly. "They found out about my wedding to Dawn three days before it happened." He didn't consider it his finest moment, as it later turned out to be a moment not destined to happen.

Her mouth gaped open, eyes widened with amusement creeping in the corner of their creases, not hiding the sheer shock of his statement. "No way! Why did you do that to Kathy?" Upon realizing her own judgment, Iylah retracted her words, "Sorry, no judgment here. Trying really hard not to, but—"

He smirked, conscious of how easily he did around her. "Oh, that definitely felt like judgment."

Relief set in his body. Upsetting Iylah—again—not something he desired to make a regular occurrence of. This new clear air between them, he welcomed. Deciding to change the subject, he motioned to the journal sitting in her lap.

"Didn't take you for much of a writer."

She considered the shut journal and clasped it with both hands, her fingers delicately tracing its edges. Her demeanor softened.

"It's one of my mother's journals. I've got a stack of them—actually—" She pivoted to face him entirely, curiosity framing her eyes, "I know you grew up around religion and stuff. My mother writes a lot about Jesus and God in all her journals, and this morning watching everyone at your parents church respond similarly—" she shrugged, giving in to the curiosity overtaking her, "Can you tell me anything of this Jesus or God? Whatever he likes to be called. I don't know where to begin searching all of this up."

"Um—" His words left him, dumbfounded by her request.

The conversation traveled further away from his planned destination—a simple apology—not a lesson on another part of his life he didn't want to touch.

"I don't—um—" he cleared his throat, piecing his revolving thoughts together. "Well um—" Jeb watched Iylah's brow rise in question, earnestly searching and he could see it.

He shut his eyes, rubbing his own brow, attempting to tell the tale of what had been embedded in him from such a young age, only to lay deeply hidden now.

The years had gone by. The fire and desire grew dim. His understanding overshadowed by most of life and the decision to pursue a wider road. If his mom was within earshot, her heart would do bounds and leaps at the sound of her prayers being heard and answered.

When Jeb finished laying out all he remembered from his Bible reading days, his eyes opened to face a bewildered Iylah. Her tear ridden eyes set on his. Shock and relief? Unsure of what he identified in them, he drew further to the edge of his seat, not second guessing the hand he placed over hers.

"Hey, hey—are you okay?"

She blinked the tears away from where they hung on the tips of her long dark lashes, causing them to cascade one after the other down those high cheekbones of hers. They kept coming, but not a single sound came from her. She dropped her teary blinking to where their hands lay—on top of her mothers journal.

Becoming all too aware of the breach of personal space he made, his hand retreated to his knee timidly.

How have I become so invested in this woman's life?

"Is it true? Do you believe it? Do you believe this Jesus is real?" She finally spoke, not giving anything away in the manner of her tone—swiping away the individual teardrops lingering behind the others.

Jeb shrugged at the question he spent most of his early twenties asking himself. "What difference does it make if I believe it, Iylah? It's whether you believe it yourself to be true."

He did come to a conclusion a few years ago about it. One he never shared or voiced for fear of betraying what his heart knew.

"I don't know what to believe," She tightened her grasp on the journal, pulling it closer to her chest, as though she willed it to give her assured certainty. "My mother believed it was true. All her journals keep talking about a God who loves, who hears her hurts, who gives her hope and who forgives. And you're saying that God has a son named Jesus who he willingly let die so he could love us, people, properly?"

"I know—it sounds really far fetched."

"It sounds like a beautiful love. One I don't think I have any business being a part of."

Those whispered fears tugged some more at his invested heart, her tears continuing in an earnest flow, accompanied by silent sobs jilting her body.

Again, Jeb forwent the notion of personal space to comfort Iylah without hesitation—along with the begrudging realization that it might be time to revisit a conclusion he book ended a long time ago.

twelve

Lylah

Her wet cascading curls danced up and down on half her head, the other half her locs silky, straight and fresh from a blowout—courtesy of the thermal brush she grabbed on a whim upon packing. The bags under her eyes were leisurely disappearing, not in a hurry, noting the amount of sleep gifted to her over the last few days. A sense of safety bode well for a wrecked sleeping pattern. The freshly showered face glaring back at her through the wooden arched mirror showed signs of a bit more life, a fraction less worry and a dull pulse of—dare she say—glimmers of a foreign hope.

On her own, she couldn't identify this newfound sense within her. Hope—-it sounded expensive and allusive. A word she heard Kathy nearly sing out every morning for the last few days since she took up mornings of Bible reading with her.

Iylah woke up to a Bible placed at the foot of her bedroom door the morning after her insanely vulnerable breakdown in front of Jeb. A pre-owned Bible, unnamed, filled with highlighted pages and underlinings detailing how its previous owner found great solace in reading it. When she went to investigate who it was from, the only person she found in the house was Kathy, sitting out in the backyard. Kathy seemed none the wiser who was responsible for the little drop and run. She smiled in fondness, disclosing the Bible used to belong to Jeb. The culprit was quickly identified.

Although as the days went on, Jeb would not acknowledge it, so Iylah chose not to bring it up—afterall embarrassment remained present.

She could not place what came over her that afternoon, except a yearning to know more stemmed from it. Now the rather uncertain owner of a Bible, she sought Kathy for advice on how to tackle such a lengthy read. For the three days gone by, Iylah did so with a strong cup of coffee for courage and a mind full of questions. None of it was making sense yet, but her intrigue kept her searching, hoping no question was too dumb or obscure for Kathy's knowledge.

Iylah gently tugged her tresses through the thermal brush she rarely used. To add something new to her rather predictable day, she chose to forgo the natural state of her hair. Five days of doing nearly nothing invigorating started to take their toll.

What do people do for fun in this town?

A pang of panic in her chest reminded her she didn't have the luxury of fun at her disposal. Clovis wasn't a holiday—it existed as a place of escape from pending doom in the form of Stefan.

Of course. Silly me. How could I forget the sentence on my life?

An empty and desperate breath left her airways, arm dropping to her side from the finished work of tending to her hair. Setting the brush down, she combed her fingers through her straight dark mane.

Maybe I should color my hair? Pass. Iylah, you're twenty-nine, not fifteen.

She looked herself over in the mirror—hands stuck in the back pocket of her flare-fitted jeans; the stance stressing the slender lines of her shoulders exposed by the asymmetric black halter bodysuit she wore.

Pulling her searching eyes from the image before her, the Bible on the dresser top caught her vision. An internal push and shove fought for space in her cluttered inner world—today didn't feel like another day she wanted to be plagued with more questions. Today she needed something, anything, but that.

Opting for whatever else the morning held, she reached for the handle of her door, the itch for a cigarette beginning.

The house stood in a hushed state, with barely anything stirring apart from household appliances. Sauntering her way into the kitchen, she found Frank standing by the kitchen window, a steaming mug in one hand and an endearing smile on his face.

Apart from dinners and brief chance encounters—like this one—Iylah hadn't gotten the pleasure of a conversation with Frank. And now the moment presented itself. Putting her disdain for father figures aside, she made the effort.

"Good morning, Frank." Iylah pried a cupboard open in search of a mug to pour herself some energy.

"Morning," A quick peer over his shoulder acknowledged her presence before he returned his attention right back out the window. "Did you sleep well?"

She approached the carafe sitting a couple of steps away from him. "Well, the bags under my eyes disappearing is a good sign, I think." She poured the dark nectar to her satisfaction, curiously trying to figure out what exactly Frank stood in awe of.

He chuckled similarly to Jeb—slight crinkling around the eyes, lips shut and spread in a smile and light jogging of the shoulders. "That is definitely always a good sign."

Iylah spotted Kathy sitting in her usual spot in the backyard, where Iylah should be sitting next to her. The internal tug showed itself again.

"We bought this house because she loved that tree." He offered a conversation starter about the woman he leered over so tenderly from the confines of their kitchen. "Mind you, it wasn't as majestic as it is now. That tree barely stood at our shoulders, but Kathy knew what it would grow to be, and that's what she held onto this house for."

Unsure what to add to his reminiscent sentiments, Iylah sipped her coffee, allowing its sharpness to wake the sleeping parts of her. It didn't reach every part.

He shifted, walking around Iylah to get to their single-door fridge. "A bit like God, really. Knows how we're all going to turn out, and he extends himself even with the off chance we might reject him."

"So I hear." She needed something stronger to hose off the niggling in her, now that Frank had poured kerosene over it. "Hey Frank, do you mind if I smoke out front?"

The need to ask for permission came this morning, despite the many times she had never sought it since her arrival.

With an egg carton in hand, he responded, "Go for it. As long as my front lawn stays free from any fires, we're good."

"Got it. No fires. Thanks." She beelined out of the kitchen, through the open planned living room and out the front door.

The dry 7AM heat greeted her as she set foot outside, snatching a gust of air out of her in discomfort. Clovis summers continued to show her the brunt of their worst—nothing like the mild summers she spent in Germany.

Mild summers filled with long hours of glorious daylight—maybe a magical walk during a sun shower to cool you down and remind you life wasn't all that terrible. That is, when she wasn't buried deep in a mosh pit at one of the many music festivals she garnered free access to—courtesy of Stefan's business—illegal as it may be.

Germany presented a different hell of its own this Clovis heat could not match.

Plonking herself down on the curb, she found relief in lighting her cigarette. The reassuring texture against her fingers, paired with the satiating drag engulfing her nerves with every harmful chemical some genius could rattle off. She was no genius—just a victim of perfect marketing and addiction.

Am I an addict? Does this make me one? Does my smoking bother Jeb?

She watched the searing stick she held between her fingers. She'd never attempted quitting this habit—no incentive to do so ever came up.

A memory floated by, making itself known. The day her mother sniffed out the smell of cigarettes on Iylah's clothes, Iylah returned home after school to find her ill mother sitting in their lavishly designed backyard, a tuft of smoke billowing above her. Iylah, with great concern, pulled the cigarette out of her mother's clutches, informing her deteriorating mother how smoking would not aid her in getting better. To which her mother responded, if it's harmless, then it shouldn't affect her healing.

Iylah smirked lazily at the point her mother tried to make. Maybe the time had come to quit.

Taking in the neighboring houses down the quiet street, she pushed aside the prospect of parting with her brutal friend. Houses all fitting the picture of suburbia—white picket fences and rose bushes to match. The yards were a lot smaller than what she grew up accustomed to, as were the houses. She bet the families living in them genuinely enjoyed and loved each other's company though. A wishful concept for her.

The sound of approaching running feet caught her vigilant attention, drawing her squinted eyes to the figure of Jeb making his way up towards her on his morning run.

My gosh! Someone's body clearly benefits from these morning runs.

Averting away from the revelation of Jeb's bare toned torso, she focused excessively on putting her cigarette out on the gravel of the road—no lawn fires to be had. And no other fires, for that matter. She swept her voluminous hair across her back to sit upon one shoulder, by all means using self-control not to peek again the closer Jeb got.

Most people appeared somewhat uncoordinated when they ran—whether it be flailing limbs, an overly bobbing head, sweat running down like little streams of water—not Jeb though. Athletic and poised described his running better—like a well-rehearsed movie scene.

He stopped a couple of feet away from her, walking off his run, chest heaving, t-shirt dangling from the waistband of his running shorts. He hunched over, hands on his knees to catch his breath.

"I don't know why you think it's a good idea to run so early in this heat?" Iylah trod on the remains of her cigarette with the toe of her New Balance sneakers.

"Some people choose a strong cup of coffee and a cigarette to wake up." He motioned to her own choices. "I choose runs." He stretched out his agile body, accentuating muscles Iylah didn't know the human body had.

Clearing her throat, she forced her head away from his direction. "Touché." And tipped her mug of coffee in agreement.

He made his way over to where she sat, inviting himself to occupy the curbside next to her. "You sleep okay?"

A hint of his sweat wafted her way, heat emanating from his overworked body.

Sipping her coffee, words falling short, a simple—"Mhmm"—sufficed. Nodding her head at the same time, causing the liquid in her mug to clumsily lap over her upper lip.

Jeb saw.

With a mouth full of coffee, she stifled an awkward giggle, wiping its remnants off with the back of her hand.

"Easy there." He teased.

She sensed how effortless it would be to allow her usually flirtatious nature to take the driver's seat in their conversation right there, at which she assumed she would have him eating out of her palm. It's always what happens between her and guys. A game she played to see how far she could take it. In this case, the need to play such flirting games with Jeb proved to be childish and ill-placed.

She tucked the coping mechanism away. It left her with nothing to offer.

He noticed the silence on her end and filled it. "Tylor and I are going for a skate after breakfast—"

"You skateboard?" The new piece of information to the puzzle forming Jeb shocked and amused Iylah in half a sentence.

"Why does that come as a shock to you? How old do you think I am, Iylah?" If he was offended, the upturned corner of his lips did a good job of hiding it.

"Forgive me—" She put a hand to her chest, feigning remorse, "You're right. Totally judgmental of me. Sorry, finish your sentence."

"Wow!" He shook his head, with a peal of laughter. "As I was saying before you rudely interrupted—Tylor and I are going skating. Yes, I skateboard, so does Tylor. There's a bike in the garage, so you can ride along with us. Can you ride a bike? I mean, since you're old too—"

"Excuse me! I would push you over, but your armour of sweat gives me reason not to." She drummed her fingers against her knees. "I'll have you know, I used to bike everywhere when I studied in Stockholm. Besides, you never forget how to ride a bike—just like skateboarding."

He narrowed his eyes, the features on his face scrunching up. "I'm—hmm—I'm—not sure it's the same."

"How hard is it to stand on a board and kick your way around?" She shrugged naively.

Jeb stood up from where they sat. "How about you join us so you can test out how hard it is?"

"Done."

"Really? You'll try it?"

Standing up to meet his intrigued face, she suddenly needed space from his nearness.

"If you're a good teacher, I'll be skateboarding by the end of today. Let's find out." Iylah winked and strode away, leaving Jeb amused by her challenge.

How painful might breaking a bone be, anyway?

⌒ ⌒

Jeb

Kids tended to gravitate towards one another, even as perfect strangers. All they needed was one thing in common and you'd be under the impression their new found friendship spanned over years.

Upon making plans to head over to the local skatepark earlier in the morning, Jeb bore no anticipation of it being swarmed by children and the dreaded bigger children alike—teenagers. His original plans didn't have Iylah involved in them either. When he saw her sitting on the curb this morning ending his run, whatever it was compelled him to extend the invite. Maybe the daydreaming look on her face got him. Or the vulnerable chasm they'd both inched open a few days ago—her asking him questions he begrudgingly answered, and him finally putting to words half of what simmered in him.

So much for being careful with her. Marcus would relish in his feeble attempt of caution. His curiosity towards Iylah kept winning in spades over logic.

Jeb watched onwards, Tylor weaving in and out in tandem with his new crew of four boys, roughly his age, over the various speed bumps with the odd struggle at the quarter pipes. The laughter vibrating out of his son's body a missed sound—one Jeb felt relieved to hear.

As the three of them tore through the neighbourhood streets, the crunching sound of asphalt under the wheels of their boards and bike, a distant soundtrack beneath exhilarated whooping shouts of enjoyment. He couldn't remember the last time a sense of liberty filled his lungs, the air rushing through him one kick and push after the other. Older, maybe not wiser Jeb, thanked younger Jeb for sticking with the hobby of skateboarding over the years. Time didn't permit him to do it like he would be inclined to—working two jobs and single parenting mostly, didn't make for an excess of free time. Neither did a straying wife. It all left no space for him to just be.

Jeb adjusted his baseball cap, flipping it backwards and smoothing his dark blond locs before placing it back on firmly. He scanned the skatepark from the bench he lounged on, Iylah coming into view. They were the only two functioning adults here, naturally an air of certain responsibility fell on them.

Which is how Iylah found herself surrounded by a group of preteen girls on bikes and scooters, completely enthralled by her.

Was there any wonder?

Jeb quietly instructed the opening crater threatening to swallow his caution, to behave.

Her erupting laughter did something to him. Its contagious timbre rang through his ears, as they coasted up and down the streets—him cheekily grabbing hold of the back of her bike seat while she pedalled, allowing him to ride alongside her, the wind whipping her temporarily straight hair under the cover of one of his baseball caps she borrowed. She was having fun. He was having fun. Tylor was having fun. So why couldn't he shake the sadness looming over his head like the nuisance of a cloud it was?

Its familiarity told him he lived under it for longer than he noticed. Happiness being a mythical state he only ever saw other people take part in. When was it his turn? Seldom one to be reckless anymore, he threw away the blimp of a desire to chase after a fleeting piece of the happy pie—a transient stupid idea. Even as he acknowledged it as stupid, he couldn't tear his eyes away from Iylah approaching him.

The sun did things to her skin he'd never seen it to do anyone else's—it caused the melanin in it to shimmer. Her face hidden by his cap she wore, only allowing him to see the tip of her slender button nose and her slightly parted full lips. He would be remiss to deny her allure.

"Are you checking me out, Jeb?" Iylah never skirted around saying what she meant, or asking questions in search of honesty.

He liked that.

She placed herself next to him, prying an answer out of him with her playful scrutiny.

He couldn't bring himself to look away, his efforts went into working overtime to calm the deepening gulf in his core. He chose a shrug and a half smile instead.

"Just making sure you don't get pummeled by one of these high octane testosterone jocks trying to impress you." Close to the truth—she had the older boy's attention.

"I bet you were just like them growing up here? Y'know, the whole artsy skater boy Cali vibe?" She stretched her legs out, the simple movement sending the scent she wore in Jeb's path.

Flowery and earthy.

He sniggered at her inaccurate assumption, shaking his head. "When I was fifteen, saving the world seemed more important. I begged my parents to home-school me so I could go do missionary work with them. Eventually they gave in, homeschooled all of us and took us to very remote, sometimes dangerous, undeveloped parts of the world to help the less fortunate." At some point, his parents became America's version of the less fortunate and that became his bone he picked with God. "So no, I didn't spend most of my summers trying to impress grown-up women out of my league at a skatepark."

She adjusted her body to face him, crossing her legs up on the bench, her demeanor turning serious.

"Oh boy. Why do I feel you're about to interrogate me?" He settled further into his seat, preparing for the onslaught her intrigued mind set out to bring.

"'Cause I am. So—" She appeared to be gathering whatever specific questions would bring her the information she needed. "You must have seen a few surreal things then? Do you remember any of it well?"

He rustled the skateboard under his feet, her keen interest in his past bringing a subtle fear accompanied with opening up the remnants of his life some more to her. Still—he obliged. The nearest memory he recalled emerging from the collection of his early life.

One involving a girl—the same age he was at that time, a Brazilian orphanage and a local gang.

Maybe that's where my habit of wanting to save train wrecks started.

"We were in Brazil, in Aquiraz—volunteering at an orphanage through a Baptist Church." Sediment from the memory lined itself in his throat, he readjusted his cap once again, "One child there, a girl, she was fifteen I was sixteen—befriended me. Couldn't speak a word of English, but she always used to follow me around. We had this weird silent friendship."

He watched Iylah's face listening intently, her eyes brimming with anticipation. It eased the nerves in his stomach.

"One night after dinner and the curfew, everyone was in bed—my family and I slept in separate areas from all the kids. For whatever reason I couldn't sleep so I stayed up sketching away outside—"

He retold the story of witnessing the girl sneak out from the orphanage, and him making the naïve decision to follow her into the night, only to wind up at a local gang's headquarters. Iylah hung on to every detail. The girl spent nights sneaking out to go there, a place filled with vile men whose intentions matched the darkness of the night she hid under to escape. Though she never spoke about what happened to her there, that night Jeb got a rude awakening to the life of a fifteen-year-old orphan girl, who craved attention desperately she let grown men use her in exchange for whatever cheap alcohol they offered her to numb the pain of being rejected. When he found out, he hid in the shrubs waiting for her, not willing to leave her alone knowing he couldn't do much of anything and not get killed. The days before his family left, he wouldn't leave her side—even after she slapped him for reporting the matter to the Matron in charge. When he arrived back in America, he spent many nights in tears over the life the majority of orphans endured, while the safety of his room held his vastly different reality.

Iylah lunged for Jeb, her arms trapping his neck in a sudden hug, throwing him off balance—a little stunned.

He laughed sourly, unsure where to place his hands as she held on. "It was a long time ago, Iylah."

"I know." She didn't let go. "This hug is for sixteen-year-old Jeb, who experienced all of that."

He settled his hands in the middle of her back, endeavouring not to fall prey to the comfort it provided to his currently bleak outlook.

Recoiling from their embrace, Iylah remained somewhat close to his frame. Her fingers played around with nothing in particular, head dropped hiding her face beneath the visor of the cap on her head. "You're a good human, Jeb."

The softly spoken statement took him unaware, rendering the tension in his shoulders silent. Heat caught in his chest, he struggled to push past it and breathe.

"I'm not, but thanks for thinking so." Jeb watched his son who lived in the brunt of his grave decisions and misplaced loyalty.

He had no interest in dragging Tylor into something that would only do him more harm.

So Jeb kept up his diligent fight against what he presumed were the beginning trails of interest in Iylah. He hoped she would do the same—for the sake of them both.

thirteen

Lylah

Iylah walked over to her clothes hanging up in the wardrobe. Kathy insisted she stop living out of her suitcases and make her stay here as comfortable as possible. A stay that currently had no end date in sight.

Iylah's instructions were to stay put and be inconspicuous at all costs until further information came. Despite how much Lena tried to pry from the FBI, no movement or progress was gained in her efforts. Lena got one stern warning—by no means should she try to visit Iylah or attempt to pick her up, for fear Stefan watched closely. He was very well aware of Lena through her incessant checking up over the months Iylah and he dated.

Iylah's skin prickled at recalling being close to Stefan. The haunting way his dark eyes burnt possessive holes in her, branding her unfit for anyone else. She mistook it for affection, when in the end all it ever amounted to was a man with a penchant for control, rage and dangerous schemes.

Purveying her clothes, taking cues from the sun streaming its presence through the windows and from the smothering hot days gone by—something light and perfect for air circulation suited her church outfit. She scoffed in amusement, picking out her yellow floral embroidered sleeveless shift minidress, with its cute bow detailing on the shoulders. To think her Sundays now comprised choosing an outfit to go to church in a town she on no occasion would have set foot in of her own accord. Not only that, but to have an eagerness to hear what Frank would share today.

Something was happening, and she wasn't sure what.

After spending fifteen minutes on her hair and make-up, resolving for a minimal effortless dewy look that could withstand the heat—she made her way into the kitchen where Kathy made sure everyone was fed before they all squeezed into her 2010 Buick LaCrosse.

Everyone except Jeb.

"Your dad is not coming today, Tylor?" Iylah asked the ten-year-old version of Jeb, whose friendliness came and went in waves.

Still, she tried. He would meet her halfway one day—she was half sure of it.

He shook his head in a singular response.

Kathy handed her a plate. "Says he's got something better to do. You eat up, dear." She ushered Iylah over to the breakfast spread.

If Jeb's absence bothered Kathy, she sure didn't show it. Kathy continued to be a steady stream of positivity and quiet observance. Iylah caught her a few times watching her interactions with Jeb, and the wink she threw over to Frank every time Jeb laughed at one of Iylah's offhanded snide jokes—or when she cheated her way at every board game they played.

Iylah made a mental note of how she handled herself around Jeb.

Don't trauma bond.

Lena's words rang loud and clear always.

"Thanks, Kathy," Iylah tentatively grinned in appreciation for the care she felt under Kathy.

Scooping some fluffy eggs into her plate, she wondered what exactly kept Jeb busy this morning.

Iylah observed the after service buzz happening from the back of the church, sipping gingerly on the homemade cheek-tingling sweet lemonade.

Shying away from the spotlight, she hastily took off for the refreshment table after the last song. Jeb's absence meant she sat front and centre next to Kathy—the murmurs behind her confirming it to be an issue with some of the older ladies. Upon making a moderate, offhanded examination, she learned the hemline of her summery dress appeared too short for their liking. Eyes looked her up and down from her open-toed clogged feet to her messy curly bun.

Apologizing for anything unnecessary wasn't her usual way of operating—the urge to do so, however, poked at her self-confidence.

The murmurings were reminiscent to the times as a little girl her father used to parade around at the age of ten—her striking features gaining quite the compliments. This time, this parade felt more like a shaming rather than admiration.

In the solitude of her thoughts, she pushed aside the discomfort to focus on the words Frank had spoken this morning.

Iylah didn't know much about Frank except how often he spent time at the church most days—counseling people, tending to the maintenance of the building, meeting up with the various groups involved in the church. Meanwhile, Kathy dutifully drove in with a freshly made lunch and a cool flask of Peach Iced Tea. Jeb disclosed this to Iylah after she asked him how come Frank wasn't home much. Iylah got the impression, this was the way the system ran for the Aston family and Jeb found contention in it—she didn't ask beyond that.

The Good Shepherd. The phrase Frank repeated when he spoke. Jesus, the Good Shepherd. From her dim understanding, Iylah noted that Jesus meant a lot of things to many people. She pondered how anyone ever decided who he really was and not a constructed version of someone's own desires and whims. She pegged the question in her brain to ask Kathy later. This version of Jesus Frank shared, tended to each person's soul, as a real-life shepherd would to helpless sheep. Attentively, gently, intentionally, but with great strength to come to its aid when in trouble.

Sentiments like these resonated with a journal entry her mother wrote. If they were true, then Iylah needed the Good Shepherd. Standing there in the muck of her past, she wasn't sure if he would take her.

"Are you from the area, dear?"

Iylah startled, not at the question, but at the sudden closeness of two older women whose murmurs she'd heard earlier. Both of them stood side by side with their crowning glory of grayed hair—one slightly shorter than the other—both dressed in muted tones, minimal makeup, identical crosses dangling from dainty chains around their necks, Bibles and purses clutched tightly by their sides. Though they bore smiles, Iylah grew up learning not to trust such tightlipped politeness—even if they called you dear.

When Kathy called you dear, she meant it. They did not.

Discreetly flicking off spilled lemonade from her hand, Iylah returned the tight-lipped smile. "No. Just visiting."

"Oh—how did you find out about our precious church?" The shorter one enquired, sounding rather protective of their so-called precious church.

"The Astons." Her answers were short and measured. Iylah understood such nosy intrigue should only and always be met with minimal disclosure of the truth.

"I see." The fascination increased in the eyes of the taller one. "I didn't know Jeb was seeing someone so soon after his divorce proceedings."

How did they know about the affairs in Jeb's life? Iylah figured that if he spent little time in Clovis, his life would have been elusive to the gossip mill that every town has.

"We're work colleagues." Iylah interjected before anything more could be said of that.

"You're from New York?"

"Seattle, actually—"

"Ladies, I see you've met the beautiful Iylah?" Kathy's arm linked in Iylah's at just the right moment—thankfully.

Iylah could already feel the snark rising within herself.

"Isn't she just beautiful?"

The tightlipped smiles between the three unrelenting even in Kathy's presence.

"Linda and Alice here, help me run the women's group. We are just about to start the planning for our annual summer fundraising gala. Aren't we ladies?." Kathy swiftly changed the direction of the conversation to one on her turf.

"We look forward to it every year." Linda showed genuine enthusiasm at the mention of the gala. "Have you attended fundraising galas before?"

Iylah shook her head, her mouth slightly down-turned trying to truly sell the lie, ignoring the pang of guilt for the blatant mistruth in a church. Years of her mother hosting such galas, not information she wanted to willingly part with. She assumed far less drama took place at a church fundraiser.

A sudden appetite for a cigarette appeared. The hankerings started to die down once she started taking the nicotine gum, aided by the past whisperings of her mother's attempts to convince her to stop. Somehow, she found herself desperately in need of one every time she came near this church building.

"I hope you stick around to experience our gala." Alice remained smug-faced, without a hint of the hope she spoke of.

"I hope so too." Another lie came from Iylah.

Jeb

Jeb placed the industrial fan a few paces away from the freshly unpackaged easel, the plastic wrappings sitting at his feet. He doubted for the fifth time in the last hour whether this little corner of his dad's garage would be suitable for what he set up. If he thought too hard about it, the entire project will be aborted, so he persisted with his choice of positioning.

Satisfied with where the industrial fan now stood, he glanced over at the high table laid out with all manner of supplies he gathered from Allard's Art earlier in the week, hoping it sufficed. A quick trip to Walmart this morning brought the finishing touches he needed to life.

Stepping back to take in his work from the last two hours, his toes dug into the new rug he bought to hide the ugliness of the garage's dull gray concrete, immediately overcome with uncertainty.

"What am I doing?" He scratched his head, tucking back strands of hair loose from his high bun.

Returning all the things he bought didn't present itself as an option he wanted to take—he wanted to commit to this project.

The timely disturbance of his phone ringing in one pocket of his cargo shorts cut short the sea of uneasiness surging in him. Fishing it out, he grinned lazily as he saw the name scrolling across his phone.

"Look who decides to call—" Jeb settled down on the stool, bouncing in it before the new leather succumbed to the weight of his body.

"Listen, mate, you know how terrible I am with this time difference thing. You're eating your tea while I'm counting blimmin' sheep to sleep at two in the morning. So this will have to do."

Jeb chuckled at the thickness of Clint's Cockney accent. "How are you, Clint?"

"I should ask you that question. Soon to be a single father—women love that crap. You'll be hot property pretty soon. Is your divorce from that wench completed yet?"

Clint wasn't one to miss a beat in asking the more important questions. Neither was he the sort to hide his distaste for Dawn, despite being the best man at Jeb's wedding and Tylor's godfather.

"I doubt a thirty-eight-year-old man living back with his folks puts me high on the list of eligible bachelors."

"Are you in Clovis? Why on God's green earth would you decide to move back there? I mean—move here to London first before you move back there. What happened to shacking up with that trust fund woman you messaged me 'bout? She kicked you out already?"

There were a few pieces of the puzzle missing for Clint since Jeb had shared his current life status last with him

"Uh—not exactly." Jeb was unsure what parts to tell and what parts to keep hidden for the safety of Iylah. Of course he could trust Clint—it wasn't his story to tell. "She's here in Clovis with me and Tylor." He awaited Clint's shock with pinched shoulders.

"Hang on—am I missing some'in?"

Jeb sighed, "Yeah, there's a lot to it. I'd rather spare you. Before your mind goes there—nothing is going on between her and I. We barely know each other, and we're only just striking up some sort of weird friendship. She's just in a bit of trouble." He still denied all feelings trying to cross the platonic line.

A moment of stagnant silence hung on the other end of the line—Clint's pause an obvious indication of his confusion at what to make of this news his friend shared.

"Must be pretty serious then for you to take her to Clovis. But I can't say I'm surprised—you always know how to pick 'em."

"We're just friends—"

"The only one you're telling porkies to is yourself, mate. I know you, hopeless romantic you are. Just don't go marryin' her."

Jeb rolled his eyes at the inside knowledge Clint possessed of how he operated.

"So you movin' back permanently?"

The question Jeb peddled back and forth in his mind. His life stood at the precipice of change, as did Tylor's. He would be in a world of denial if he thought he could raise Tylor on his own without help. His parents, committed as they were to their way of life, were exemplary parents if perfection wasn't the goal.

"The verdict is still pending on that one. I've gotta think about what's best for Tylor, who currently hates me because he thinks I allowed another woman to break up his mom and me." He rubbed his eyes at the complicated days he found himself in.

"Just say the word and I'll have you both on a plane to London town. Better yet, your lil' sugar-mama can foot the bill. Did a wee bit of research on her, and oh my—her father is in the big leagues. Definitely not shy of a penny."

"What do you mean, big leagues?"

The obvious signs of wealth in Iylah's family were there. The townhouse, her driver, the clothes she wore, the private jet she flew on, the amount she ate out or ordered in during Jeb's brief house sharing experience with her—not to mention the overtly subtle bribe paid to get her the job at the School. Affluence ran in her life—he hadn't bothered to find out how much. Interest piqued the more he got glimpses of Iylah as the days increased.

"I'm talking net worth in the late hundreds of millions, mate. Self-made man is her father. Definitely puts my banker's paycheck to shame. What sorta trouble is she in?"

"Enough to involve the FBI." Jeb paced the short length of the rug. "I can't go into details about it, let's just say money can't always guarantee you safety."

The magnitude of what Iylah faced hit him in the chest again, causing the doubts about this project to dissipate naturally. He wondered how afraid she must be. He recalled her breaking down, feeling unworthy of a pure love—her body overcome by what appeared to be shame.

He looked back at the setup before him, profoundly knowing he'd done the right thing.

fourteen

JOURNAL ENTRY DATE: 03/27/2005

"The Lord is my shepherd,
I shall not want.
He makes me lie down in green pastures;
He leads me beside quiet waters.
He restores my soul;
He guides me in the paths of righteousness
For the sake of His name.
Even though I walk through the valley of the shadow of death,
I will fear no evil,
For your rod and your staff , they comfort me.
You prepare a table before me
in the presence of my enemies.
You anoint my head with oil;
My cup overflows.
Surely goodness and mercy will follow me
All the days of my life,
And I will dwell in the house of the Lord forever."
Psalm 23

Heavenly Father, from you I get all I need. In You, my life is kept and held. You offer so freely refreshment for my weathered soul. My weary soul where life has wrung it dry of peace. Your guiding love causes me to be sure in the steps I take, though it may not make sense to anyone. You directed me to remain with Fredrick despite the hurt his actions have caused me. My assurance is that You are not one to lead me astray, nor one to leave me in the darkest of moments. You protect me when my soul is surrounded by the darkness of the one against me. In You I am hemmed in, surrounded by Your kindness, strength and goodness. I have known no other comforter greater than You; I have no desire to search elsewhere for such care. You know me inside so tenderly; I dare not seek another to trust my hurts with for healing. You withhold nothing and pour out everything so that I may be made whole. Your goodness and mercy are all I need on this earth til I'm face to face with You eternally.

Your daughter
Lillian

Lylah

It rang, and rang, and rang some more.

The late afternoon sun beat down on Iylah's shoulders and the back of her neck. Her dark caramel skin sang in its light, absorbing all it needed to transform it a shade or two darker. A favorite pastime of hers—laying luxuriously out in the summer sun wherever called to her. Be it on the shore of the Amalfi Coast, or on the beach chairs of the Hamptons.

This summer held different luxuries, one of them mainly being safety. Coastal beaches were traded in for lounging on the somewhat green grass of a backyard in Clovis.

Sunday afternoon proposed the problem of not having much to do. Mind you, she knew no one and didn't have the faintest clue what made up entertainment in these parts. She politely declined Kathy's invitation to join her, Frank and

Tylor for a barbecue held by one of their congregation members. Iylah endured her fair share of ogling for the day and answering nosy questions—she couldn't think of anything worse than going through that again. Jeb, still nowhere to be found, Iylah decided on having a solo afternoon in the sun, her legs laid out and the bowties of her dress inched lower down her shoulders for exposure—while her mouth did the work of gnawing away at the peppery nicotine gum in her mouth.

A welcome distraction from the itch of holding a cigarette between her fingers.

Her lounging proved relaxing until racing questions overshadowed the serotonin the sun supplied. Questions about what she'd heard this morning in church, questions about her mother and father, questions about how her life would play out when she could resume her normalcy and if she wanted to—privy of the emptiness it all held.

The only questions she possessed control over concerned her mother and father. Something unspoken transpired between her parents—her mother's journals dictated so. Her father being the sole parent present to ask, she bit the bullet and tackled the one question she could get answered. She ended her attempted call on the tenth ring, tossing the phone to her side, left to deal with the lingering questions.

The familiar creaking sound of the screen door broke her sigh. Unaware of Jeb's presence in the garage, she jumped to her feet, ready to face whomever she was to face.

"Just me." Jeb raised a pacifying hand while the other held the screen door open.

Iylah tried to calm the thumping of the heartbeat in her ears with a measured deep breath.

Aware of how big a fright he caused her, Jeb apologised. "Sorry, I didn't mean to scare you. I've got something to show you—c'mon."

"I didn't think anyone was home." She retrieved her discarded phone. "Have you been here the whole time?"

"Yeah, I've been working on something in the garage." Jeb wore a sprightly expression on his face, holding the screen door open for her to come through.

"What is it?" Suspicion rose in Iylah as she followed the rather smug Jeb through the hallway, past the kitchen and through the mudroom door leading into the garage.

She rarely ventured to this part of the house. Really, she basically lived in the room allocated to her, doom scrolling on Instagram watching everyone's summer parties. Or reading her mother's journal alongside her Bible.

In the garage, a half-covered muscle car Iylah couldn't quite make out sat parked, its rear being the only evidence she could see. The garage, tidy and well kept, housed the norm of tools, bicycles, well used body-boards and in the corner towards the roller door—what looked like a makeshift painting studio.

Iylah caught wind of Kathy's painting hobby, but didn't take it to be more than just that. This makeshift studio held all the fine things of an experienced painter on a budget—an assortment of natural brushes, multiple linen-textured paper pads varied in size, acrylic paint as a substitute for oil paint, given how long it took to dry. All elements of what Iylah saw, she deemed as smart purchases by Kathy—quite similar to what she used in her home studio back in New York, complete with solvents, sketching pencils and sketching pads. Laid out neatly and hardly touched.

Naturally, she gravitated toward the setup, running her fingers over each item—a slight tug at her heart suddenly feeling the urge to create. In the flurry of events, the desire to paint vanished in the last couple of weeks, replaced by a dull, sleepy state—a numbness oddly familiar. Except this time around she chose not to medicate it with nights of alcohol and strangers running away from their own lives. She chose whatever was going on now.

"Wow! Your mom takes her hobbies seriously." She bemused, taking a small step back from it all.

"Mom? She hasn't painted in years." Jeb remained in the background, allowing her to take it all in. "This is for you. It doesn't come close to your studio in New York, but I figured you probably missed having a space to just paint."

Iylah snapped her head around at this revelation to glance at Jeb. "What—what do you mean?" Her almond-shaped eyes widened at what she heard.

His hands in the pockets of his cargo shorts, Jeb nodded sincerely, confirming what her ears heard. A creeping warmth engulfed her, hands clasping her face, the words failing to come out. His simple gesture parted the threatening clouds, allowing the sun—a reminder to her of what lay beneath the sorrow brooding in her. The words may not have come, but in their place a ready well of tears came.

Iylah flung herself at Jeb, arms wrapping around his neck ever so tightly to display her earnestly seeded gratitude. "Thank you." Her gratitude reduced to a whisper.

Their embraces were steadily turning into a rather normal part of this unexpected friendship of sorts. He received it, gradually allowing his arms around her. She didn't let go—he didn't seem to mind. Growing conscious of their closeness, and the strength of his arms, Iylah noted the ease with which the knots in her loosened. She didn't expect the safety his embrace brought.

Promptly retreating, sheepish in demeanor, Iylah apologized. "Sorry. I really never cry this much, I promise."

The back of her hand dabbed away the moisture running down her face. She thought she saw Jeb swallow harder, through her tear-stained lashes.

"Wanna go get a drink and some food with me?" His tone softly did away with her self-consciousness. "Mom and Dad won't be back with Tylor for a while, and I could honestly use a drink." The way his eyes took her in, hastened her to look at anything but him.

She nodded. "I'd like that."

He motioned towards the door with a smile. "C'mon."

She followed.

∽ ∾

The aromatic fumes of a freshly brewed coffee lingering in the air caught Iylah's senses. Eyes half shut, she lifted her head up from the pillow, swiveling it ever so slightly to identify the origins of the smell. There sat the culprit. A beige stone mug next to her phone on the bedside table, steam still weaving its way up into the air.

The sun streamed in through a slight crack in the curtains as it did every morning, inviting her to join yet another day. Most mornings she obliged begrudgingly. However, this morning, even as she turned to lie on her back—a curiosity in her stirred.

Curiosity about what lay ahead today, because as she was finding out certain things were taking place and she wanted to investigate further the meaning of it all. Reaching for her phone instinctively, knowing she slept past her usual wake time, she checked her phone.

9.03 blurred loudly at her from the phone screen, so did a text message notification from Jeb. With bated breath, her finger swiped to access it.

Good morning! Enjoy your coffee, heard you tinkering away in your new studio late last night—thought you might need it. Headed out with Tylor for the day. See u later. Message if u need anything ♡

Reading the message twice over, she caught herself beaming, quickly chastening herself from wearing outwardly what she felt inwardly.

The events of last night resurfaced amidst the morning haze circling her mind. After the initial shock settled from the most generous gesture anyone had ever extended towards her, spreading heat through every inch of her body and causing her to momentarily forget the grief and fear she dwelt in daily—Jeb introduced her to the night scene of Clovis. He added the disclaimer that he himself was not one for it. He'd contently settle for a low-key bar-restaurant with the best beer in town, and that's where he took her.

A bespoke bar, with a hole in the wall aesthetic about it—making you forget you were in the middle of dry California, transporting you to New Orleans. If you were mistaken, you would think it only sat a capacity of twenty people, but as the night went on, Iylah soon learned just how many people it could hold.

Jeb's claim of the best beer in town appeared closely accurate. She tested the beer on tap, much to his astonishment—he witnessed Iylah casually drink through a craft beer or two. Her time in Germany and many Oktoberfests in various parts of Europe trained her taste for it.

Tales were exchanged between the two of them. His detailing of the years of adrenaline-fueled travel and close calls in seedy backpacking hostels—to his near miss of death swimming in the waters of Indonesia, that left him with a gashing scar on his left calf as evidence of survival.

Iylah noted the way his stone-gray eyes animated with a zeal for life from years past. They were fond memories to him. She wondered silently why he settled for a life with Dawn. The question stuck with her, she eventually asked it out loud and watched the animation leave his eyes. She wanted to take back her question there and then—but he obliged her by answering it, revealing his desire to do right by Dawn and their unborn child. Iylah dared not ask another question for fear of bringing both their realities back into the spotlight.

The lighthearted banter soon returned, much to her relief.

When they both realized the indistinct murmur replaced the earlier bustle of the bar, the night swept past them. The remaining patrons beginning to either pay off their tabs or make small chat with the bar staff cleaning up. Under the bar's tainted warm glowing light, Iylah really saw Jeb—without the cloudy fog of her own mindless troubles.

A deliberate pull towards him brewed in the caveats of her wall protected heart—he'd slipped right past the dead bolted armoured door. This sudden revelation initially drew a smirk from her, its settling presence startling her into retreating, suggesting they head back to the Aston's to get some shut eye. He noticed her abrupt change of demeanor, and didn't press for an explanation.

Yet again, he obliged.

Iylah fought to get some sleep last night, resulting in her incessant internet search for anything to do with trauma bonding. Lena's warning still loud and unavoidable. Eventually sleep crept up on her—which led to the second thing.

The dream.

She stood, knee deep in meadow grassland. The grass swaying gently from a cool breeze wrapping itself around her, catching her hair in it. A bright light shone and illuminated the entire grassland so expansively, leaving no part of it untouched. Though the light shone as bright as the sun, it emanated not as the sun did. It felt more fierce, and oddly comforting. Her feet treaded forward along the landscape, her ears harkening to the bubbling water of a brook dividing the grassland in two. Drawn to it, she pursued a path to the brook, kneeling over and drinking from it. Something caught her attention in the reflection of the waters flowing by—her own reflection. Resembling that of a sheep.

A quiet still voice spoke '*I will restore you*'.

Those words piercing her heart, she awoke. Not in a panicked sweat like she was accustomed to—rather encompassed by peace.

When she checked the time, it was 11:45PM and nothing stirred in the house. Nothing, except her heart. Yielding to the unknown sense of urgency, she forwent any further sleep and found herself in the garage—intently mapping out on canvas the scene from her dream with the words spoken ruminating to the depths of her softening soul.

Stumbling back into bed four hours later, resulting in her little sleep in and the coffee steaming by her bedside.

The Good Shepherd.

That's what the painting shall be titled.

Throwing back the covers, she prepared herself for the day to be spent reliving and painting this dream.

Right after she downed this thoughtfully prepared cup filled with morning nectar, of course.

fifteen

Jeb

His throat opened up, making way for the water he now slugged down. Squeezing the emptying bottle, Jeb finished its contents, his shoulders rising and falling attempting to catch his breath. The silence in the house engulfed his panting, amplifying it above the hum of the fridge.

When it became incessantly hard to remain awake laying in bed awaiting the birds to welcome the sunrise, Jeb opted to start his day before anyone had the chance to be met with his relentlessly grouchy demeanor. He made the wise choice to take his morning jog as the light of day approached.

Standing in his mom's kitchen, everyone still asleep, unaware of the promising cracks of sunlight tainting the sky an amber orange. Everyone except Iylah. He observed the slight movements of the back of her head, sitting in the lawn chair, a cup of coffee on the armrest next to her. He wasn't the only one who couldn't stay asleep for long.

Her muffled footsteps past his bedroom door at 2am alerted him to when she'd finally made it to bed, after spending four hours in the garage painting again last night. He'd counted the hours unwittingly more observant of her every movement whenever she was in proximity to him.

He grumbled to himself, the steeping sensation in his stomach returning as he continued to watch her.

Two nights ago, Jeb made the mistake of enjoying her company more than he was prepared to. Her sitting across from him, in a bar humming with Sunday night activity. The orange shade of the lighting in the bar, bringing out the contours of her striking face—the green eyes constantly glimmering when she glanced at him, were illuminated with great delight whilst. She listened to him retell stories of a life he once pursued. Her keen smile engrained itself at the front of his memories, labeling itself more important than the broken heart he nursed. That night he became uncomfortably aware of how easy it would be to allow the curiosity building in him, to lead the way into territory past a platonic relationship with her.

Was that what they had? A platonic friendship?

The rip tide in his gut told him otherwise. He needed to tame its influence, before he got ahead of himself.

Confronted by her fresh faced gaze, as she stood up from the lawn chair—his old Bible in hand, retrieving the cup next to her and catching him in the act of mindlessly staring at her. Heat flushed to his cheeks, only managing to pull a small sheepish smile across his face when her eyes met his. He couldn't look away now, it would only add to his suspicious behaviour—so he moved across the kitchen to pour himself a cup of freshly brewed coffee, willing the squirming in him away.

You really need to get a grip, Jeb.

The screen door creaked open announcing her arrival into the kitchen. Jeb kept his bare back deliberately to her, buying himself time for the heat in his face to settle. He reached over for a cup, shutting the cabinet door where his mom meticulously lined the cups—aware of the silence still lingering in the kitchen. He sensed her presence behind him, even if she didn't utter a single word. It drove the tugging in him deeper down his middle.

"Morning." He broke the incriminating silence, not daring to turn around kicking himself for not putting his t-shirt back on after his run.

"Good morning. How was your run?" She made her way over to his side, extending her mug for a refill as he poured his own.

"Good. Less eyes at this time of the morning." He tended to her cup, avoiding any unnecessary eye contact. He'd already been caught staring for too long.

"Less eyes? Do you have stalkers that watch you run or something?" She didn't move away from where she stood next to him. Her question adding irony to his own stalkerish behaviour.

She cemented her position next to him, turning around and leaning back against the bench-top.

I guess this is turning into a full-blown conversation.

Taking a micro step back, Jeb leaned his shoulder into the fridge door, crossing his free arm across his chest—a mild form of self-protection. "Not quite stalkers, but definitely frequent garden watering at the exact time I run past, every morning." He took a sip from his steaming cup, alluding to the steady appearance of a certain blonde haired woman.

Without fail, around 6.45 when Jeb rounded the corner into his parents' street, a peering gaze came from a white picket fenced yard with barely much of a garden to warrant the forty-something old woman holding a hose to nothing. The flirty waves only started happening the last few days, and it took a lot for Jeb to ignore them and not change his running route. He told Iylah his dilemma.

A burst of laughter erupted from her, delight at his misfortune causing her wide grin.

He couldn't resist zoning his sights to the phenomenon that was her laughter. He rather revelled in being the one to bring her hearty laughter out. He wouldn't admit this to anyone else though.

"You have a fan. And it's clear you have a type." Her laughter settled, her dancing smile remained.

"A type?" He questioned.

"Yeah—blonde and bold." Mischief tinted her expressive face. "Too soon?"

"Wow." He mused at her implication, "Blonde is not my type, Iylah. Besides, hair color doesn't count towards someone's personality."

Her eyes widened with fascination at his confession. "You're a personality kinda guy, huh? Okay, Jeb—so what is your type? I mean you're practically a single man now."

Somehow it didn't sound as bad when she said it. It didn't sound as daunting. The truth of the matter was he'd lived the last seven years as a single parent—not a single man. This new ground yet to be explored, and he wasn't sure he could muster up the know-how or care for what it entailed.

"The divorce isn't finalized." He took a swig from his cup, deciding there and then he felt most comfortable avoiding this subject altogether. "As for my type—" he pushed off against the fridge, the need for a shower and distance making itself known, "I guess I'll find out. I'm gonna grab a shower. Thanks for making this very strong coffee."

She tipped her mug in his direction. "You're welcome. I'm here for strong coffee and dating advice."

He chortled at the shared knowledge that neither one of them was in any position to date or give advice about matters pertaining to the heart. "Noted. Hey, Tylor and I are heading to the Big Fair at the showgrounds this afternoon. Its on every summer and it's kind of big deal in Clovis, did you want to join us?"

"I'll have to check with my overseer. Big crowds and all don't mix well with being hunted down by an ex." The fun in her eyes dimmed, the brash reality she faced confronting them both.

"Right. Let me know what your overseer says." With a slight upturning of the corners of his mouth, Jeb backed out of the kitchen, bothered by the dampening of her playful mood.

What is my type?

A question that also bothered him just as equally.

❧

Lylah

She worked hard at not letting it bother her. Every step her clogged feet took, made her brutally aware of the hunkering two men following fifteen paces behind her. Their attempts at being inconspicuous not entirely convincing. Still, this was the deal she cut with Eric Mane. Two agents monitoring her late afternoon in a place milling with a crowd, here to enjoy the biggest Fair she'd foolishly agreed to go to.

Why did I agree to this? That's right—shirtless Jeb.

The air fizzed with the smell of cotton candy, aromas from varying food trucks mixed with the dry hot air of the day. Everywhere she turned bodies of people surrounded her, swamping her existence amongst them.

Apart from the Aston's residence, the church building and odd trips down the road for walks—this was the furthest out of the suburbia she'd grown used to. A sprouting shoot of panic hummed low in her, wiring her body ready for anything to happen.

She snuck a quick, subtle glare behind her, spotting her designated chaperones. Paying no attention to the oncoming foot traffic headed her way, Iylah found herself grabbed by the elbow and pulled away from the group of rather animated teenage boys plowing past her. She crashed into Jeb's side, his grip still on her elbow, guiding her alongside him.

"You okay?" His voice drew close to her ear, distinct above the commotion and briefly peering down at her, searching for anything pointing to her distress.

She nodded with a tight-lipped smile, striving to reconcile the mild anxiety this place gave her and the calm his attentiveness generated in her—the two emotions at war with each other. The warmth from his touch seeped through the silk blend fabric of her sleeve. The multicolored off the shoulder crop top she wore, no match for it.

His wrinkled brow rendered him unconvinced by her. "Okay, I think it's time for our first ride."

Jeb pointed to a giant boom arm up in the air, rotating full circle swinging its current occupiers up in the air, before plunging them back down at full speed. Their shrieks evidence of the thrill levels this ride gave.

"That is the first ride you want to go on?" Iylah pointed at the harrowing ride, sensing the mild panic winning at Jeb's suggestion.

"Awesome!" Tylor's enthusiasm matched his father's, the grins on both their faces making Iylah conclude that thrill chasing ran deep in their blood.

"What d'ya say, Iylah?" The glint of eagerness in Jeb's eyes a rare sight to witness, "Should we give it a go?"

"Let's do it!" The cotton candy Tylor consumed less than ten minutes ago, appeared in his enthused energy levels, complete with a fist pump.

"Oh, my. I think you've created a thrill seeking sugar hopped up ten-year-old." A matching grin weaseled its way on Iylah's tentative face at his excitement.

"He's been on far worse rides than this." Jeb motioned to the line of people he had unknowingly led them to. "Promise, I won't let you fall."

"Fall?" Iylah's mouth gaped open, rubbing her slightly glistening palms against her flared Levi's. "If I fall to my death, I am going to haunt you."

"I can live with that." His bemused expression struck Iylah in her middle like lightning, forcing her to take notice of the flush it created in her.

What was that?

The slight fluttering she endured around him were increasingly harder to ignore and more tiring to decipher. There couldn't possibly be anything going on between them. This isn't usually how it went with her and men. In fact she endeavoured to do the complete opposite of how she carried on in the past. She put to bed her careless flirting. She didn't call upon the need to parade her body and all her inherited good looks—she'd done none of that. So how on earth did she find herself desiring to see the fondness in his sterling glances every time he stole a look at her. Surely they were friends, right?

"Don't tell me you never went on rides as a kid? I would find that insanely hard to believe." Jeb craned his neck, peering over their shoulders behind them in the line they now stood in.

"As a kid no, as an adult with a hip flask full of vodka, yes." She confessed her secret to courageously setting foot on any carnival ride.

Fairs and carnivals were never a favorite pastime of hers, and that was before she needed two bodyguards to protect her from Stefan. Neither her parents spared the time nor the desire to be seen at such places, preferring to be on a yacht on the water in the middle of her summer breaks. On the rare occasion she'd been bribed to go to one in Stockholm, it was under the premise she'd be able to call upon the assistance of some liquid courage to even contemplate it.

"Seriously?" Jeb's brow rose in disbelief.

"Oh, yeah." She nodded, aware of how close to the front of the line they edged. Her palms weren't getting any drier. She crossed her arms over her chest, involuntarily shielding herself from what was to come. "My family didn't really do fairs and rides growing up. We did yachts and trips to the Mediterranean."

"Iylah, when was the last time you've been to a fair?" The earnest manner in which he asked her, made her attentive to his concern of her lack of enjoyment at said fairs.

She narrowed her inspection of him. "Why do I feel like you're going to judge me if I tell you?"

"Have I ever judged you?" He tilted his head, placing his hand to his chest in mock offense.

"Oh please, you most definitely have. Don't give me that." She quipped, relishing in the lighthearted chuckle he responded with.

Fun looked good on him, even if it was about to be at her expense.

"Wristbands please?"

The ride attendant's less than patient voice recoiled the banter between the two, as he scanned their wristbands. Tylor hopped through the open gate leading to the wide and narrow looking carriage seat, followed by Jeb. Iylah faltered behind him, the saliva thick in her mouth, despite her doing all she could to not let her disdain win. Everything about being strapped in an open air contraption doing unimaginable things against her will, screamed disaster.

Jeb stuck his hand out for her to aid her in bravery.

"I've got you. I promise." The softness in the depth of his gray gaze, made her believe him against her better judgement.

She reached for his hand, following in behind him. She positioned herself next to him, Tylor and her on either side of Jeb while the ride attendant did the necessary safety checks. The safety harness around Iylah's waist not giving enough assurance to calm her heart riding up into her throat.

"My heart is literally in my throat." She snaked her arm around Jeb's bicep, still clutching onto his hand resting on his jean clad knee.

The muscles in his arm rippled with tension at her touch. Loosening her grip, afraid she might cut off the circulation he very much needed to keep her in this carriage, if indeed the threat of falling to her death became real.

"It will be over before you know it." The amusement in his voice made light of the terror running all over her.

Too preoccupied with not sliding out of the carriage, her nearness to Jeb didn't phase her. She counted it as an important part of her survival on this ride. The carriage moved upwards slowly into the air, clunking as it did so, sending Iylah's body cowering into the safety of Jeb's arm. Her face hidden in his shoulder, hanging on to his entire arm for dear life.

This is not good. Terrible idea Iylah.

Squeezing her eyes shut, bracing herself against him, the breeze created from the ride blew Jeb's hair into Iylah's face. The pine and mint scent an oddly comforting distraction. Settling herself in for the duration of the ride, she pulled in a breath, tentatively opening one eye regretting it immediately upon seeing how high they'd got before the ride stopped mid air.

"You ready?" He spoke into her hair, the inflection in his words causing her to peer up.

"It's a bit too late to back out now." She half muttered, the volume of her voice caught in the hinges of her throat. She didn't quite know whether it was from the discomfort she felt being stuck up in the air, or the way Jeb mapped her face as though he needed to remember this moment she clung to him.

The moment extended itself, just before Iylah's stomach dropped rapidly, the carriage plunging them back down—her shriek escaping, Jeb's laughter ringing beside her.

Jeb

A quiet satisfaction hung around in his dad's Bronco, the passing streetlights illuminating the tired bodies sitting side by side. Jeb flicked a quick peek over at the dozing pair next to him—Tylor's head leaning against Iylah's shoulder, while she rested against the window.

Running his hand over the scratch of his stubble, grappling against what permeated in the hull of his chest. Images of the afternoon, painted across his mind pulling the corner of his mouth in a careful smirk, before the bothersome monument of his coiling life poked at him. He slid his hand through his hair, ruffling his loose locs, a restlessness draping over him now.

From the second Iylah clung onto his arm, clawing at his hand, her chest imprinted against his side. To the teasing both her and Tylor heaped on him when he wouldn't go anywhere near the clown act, calling clowns menacing. Inch by persistent inch the interest Iylah stirred in him grew. It wasn't until, with a mouthful of a corn dog he realised whatever his type was, it needed to be something like her. Not for her attractiveness he fought off the urge to address. Neither for the sole reason of the safety she felt around him, expressed in the numerous times they'd exchanged embraces. His type needed to be something like her because of the ease she brought over him, as unfamiliar of a feeling as it was. Her, for every reason the heat of the day didn't compare to how her hand smouldered in his. Her, when Tylor forgot his reasons for not liking her while she met him halfway him none the wiser. Her, mainly because she'd snuck past the iron clad gates formed by a shattered marriage and a despairing heart.

His mom was right. He couldn't go there yet, but boy did he really want to. The task now was to keep such a revelation at arm's length, knowing it would be detrimental to grasp it with both hands.

"Dad, " Tylor roused, sounding worn out and half asleep, "I don't feel so good."

"What's going on, buddy?" Jeb's focus honed in on his writhing boy.

"My stomach hurts, and I feel hot." A raspiness took to Tylor's throat.

Using the back of his hand, Jeb felt Tylor's neck for any sign of a temperature Sure enough, his son's skin felt clammy and warm to touch.

Jeb's mind went back to the corn dogs they both chowed down, despite feeling distinctly uneasy about their texture.

"Tylor, do you need to—"

Before his suspicion could be voiced, the gagging sound coming from Tylor's body showed exactly what was about to happen. Instincts kicking in, Jeb swerved to the far lane looking for a place to park. Not finding one quick enough, Tylor's body concaved releasing the contents of his stomach all over Iylah's unsuspecting front. The sound of it snatching her out of the slumber she nestled in, only to be confronted with the sight of a mixture of cotton candy, corn dogs, a couple of sodas. All stirred and shaken up by at least half a dozen rides.

"Oh, my god! Oh, my god! Pull over!" Iylah's wail filled the car, not before Tylor vomited once more, straight into her lap.

Trying his best not to get them reared into, Jeb found his way over to the side of the road, switching his hazards on—panic festering between all of them.

'Dad." A lethargic Tylor called out to him, while Iylah flung her door open, alarmed at what the dredge drenching her.

"It's okay, buddy. I've got you." Jeb hopped out of the car, going around it, hastily pulling his flannel shirt off his back and over his head, making his way over to Iylah. "Take your clothes off."

"What?" Horror at the state of herself covered her face, mirroring the state of her clothes.

"Change into my shirt."

"Dad."

"Go, go, go." She grabbed the shirt he extended to her, shooing him away to tend to Tylor.

Getting to him, Jeb reached into the car, maneuvering Tylor out past remnants of the puke and into the open air. He bent on his knee to inspect Tylor under the fading light of the sunset—cars honking as they drove past them.

"Shut up!" Iylah retaliated at the attention she'd garnered from stripping down on the side of the road.

"You okay, Tylor? Do you still feel like puking?" Jeb wiped the perspiration from Tylor's forehead that made his hair stick to it.

Tylor weakly shook his head, his eyes drowsy from the effort his body went through to expel whatever it didn't agree with.

"We need to get you home."

Iylah trudged barefooted past them, heading to the passenger side, his shirt swimming over her and nothing else.

"What are you doing?" Jeb stood up quickly, suddenly regretting it, his stomach lurching at the motion. He swallowed it down gingerly, watching Iylah use her clothes to wipe down the residue on the seats, which surprisingly Tylor didn't have a trace of on him.

"Wiping off the seats. We need to get him some water." She called back.

Before Jeb could respond to her instruction—or to the sight of her exposed shapely long legs—the nausea in his stomach increased, threatening a repeat of what they'd just witnessed.

Oh, boy!

Turning around, hunching over, his body doing the rest of the work—the suspected foul play of the corn dogs ripped through Jeb's throat from his dissatisfied gut, spraying all over the patch of dry grass before him. He coughed up the residue clinging to the back of his throat, his frame feeling limp from the shock of it all.

"You too?" Disdain riddled her tone.

The disbelief in Iylah's voice held a chance for comic relief in the midst of a rather sickly situation, had it not been for Tylor joining in a third time, triggered by Jeb's own puking.

"Another reason I hate fairs."

Unable to help himself, Jeb scoffed at the irony of it all, clearing his throat—the burning sensation stinging the length of his throat. Through watery eyes, he glimpsed Iylah soothing Tylor, rubbing his hunched over back. Irony faded, the all too familiar pit replacing it. This time no match for the nausea swirling his insides. Still clear enough for the sight before him to tug at something he yearned for.

Without the puke.

sixteen

Jeb

Using the back of his wrist, Jeb wiped the beaded sweat from his brow. The mid afternoon, late July sun beating down on them void of mercy. He picked up what looked like the wooden leg of a broken chair and hurled it in the back of the trailer. He wasn't timid of hard work, but clearing out the church's storage facility during the summer months remained a longstanding tradition for his dad. Jeb just missed a few years worth.

Not thinking much of it, he volunteered his Thursday afternoon to help his Dad. Jeb's stomach held up sturdier than it did two days ago. The recollection of the rather rancid night of violent, body jerking illness, elicited a slight smile on him. Not from any fondness in seeing Tylor in such a state—but because of Iylah.

The brief image of her dressed in his flannel shirt, roadside as traffic soared past, while she tried to tend to two poorly guys who'd fallen victim to food truck poisoning—that's what pulled the amused expression on his face. As did her incessant check in's through the night. All the while, Jeb tried not to take much notice of his parents watching on with the subtlety of a cactus.

Frank kept many of his opinions to himself on a lot of the matters that involved Iylah, let alone Jeb's corkscrewing life. He didn't chip in often, only when he felt prompted. He left the meddling to his wife. Jeb wasn't here to pick his thoughts on Iylah. He was here to run his up in the air plan past his dad, the strongest and most consistent sounding board in a man he ever did witness. That and Jeb genuinely enjoyed the company of his dad.

"How on earth did you guys get all this stuff?" Jeb lifted an old hand basket half-filled with pot-pourri to emphasize his point.

"A lot of well meaning folk who think the church will take anything they give us. And we do." Frank half chuckled, "Mind you, some of it came in handy over the year. What would really come in handy would be an increased budget, but we make do." He shrugged letting the issue roll off him as quickly as it came up.

"How are you and Mom doing this year?" Jeb's voice took a more serious intonation. It always did when he brought up anything pertaining to his parents' finances.

Earlier years taught him just how frugal they needed to be to continue on as pastors of Living River Church. And his second-hand clothes growing up were a constant reminder of what they were sacrificing. It's how he learnt to make a little go further. Life lessons he carried to this present day—much to Dawn's dismay.

"God provides, I tell ya. We just don't test Him enough in these things. Always trying to figure things out on our own."

"So, what does that mean, Dad?" A personal annoyance of Jeb's—the cryptic manner Frank answered this question. "Are you and mom doing okay? Do you need help money-wise?"

The question not an abnormal one to ask for Jeb. Nor out of the ordinary for him and his siblings to pool money together, making sure that either the Buick and Bronco got fixed. Or something around the house got tended to. Rarely done begrudgingly.

"It means we are fine son." Frank threw layers of styrofoam into the heaping trailer, "I appreciate your concern, but don't you have far more pressing matters to tend to?"

"There's no way of forgetting those matters, believe me." Jeb put his rubber-gloved hands on his hips, taking a moment of rest. He drew a few breaths before allowing his half processed, circulating plans out, "I'm thinking of moving Tylor and I back here, to Clovis."

Jeb watched his sixty-five-year-old father slow his movements to register what he shared. He said nothing, simply tilted his head the way he always did to signal for any of his kids to continue speaking whatever riddled their mind. A learned cue and Jeb took it.

"Once the divorce is finalized—since Dawn surrendered her rights for any form of custody, I figured it would be better if we moved closer to you guys." Jeb cast his eyes downwards, confronted by the truth that followed, "I can't raise him on my own Dad. And I know I haven't—"

"Jeb," His dad stopped the stubborn guilt about to flow out of Jeb's mouth, "This place is your home. Yours and Tylor's. You never have to do this alone. Don't believe that lie for a second. You haven't failed yourself, Tylor or us." Father and son locked eyes. "It's okay." Frank smiled, giving Jeb the reassurance he so desperately needed then.

Jeb nodded, words evading him, the much desired relief rolling over him and the returning knowledge of the constant love of his dad. A man who lived on principles Jeb only hoped to go back to. Maybe this was another chance for him to relight that dead fire. He ran so hard and so far from anything remotely resembling a belief in God. Despite his well-formed reasons, seeing those around him embrace such beliefs made him question his stagnant unbelief. More specifically, seeing Iylah dig into what he once believed, made him hugely uncomfortable—maybe even marginally open to revisiting all he cast off.

"And Iylah?" As if his mind had been read, Frank probed his son.

"What about Iylah?" Jeb returned his attention back to the task at hand, to throw off his dad.

"What happens once all this is over? Because it will be over."

"Not a clue dad," Jeb scoffed, sharing his uncertainty, "I guess she goes back to living her life—whatever that looks like for her." The tip of his tongue soured as he betrayed what he could not ignore.

There needed to be no admitting that the more time he spent with her, the more she fascinated him. She dismantled every notion he held of her, from the day she first appeared in the faculty room at the School. His first impression, much like everyone else's, was rooted in how striking every part of her was—holding the confidence of a well-traveled woman who captured the rooms she found herself in. Her upfront nature some deemed brash and immature, but he learned that in the world she grew up and lived in, people needed to be like that so they weren't taken advantage of or have their time wasted.

His impression of a spoiled woman cracked, falling bit by bit. In its place, he saw a woman who grew up in privilege and knew no other form of life, but didn't despise those who weren't afforded such. He saw a woman desperately trying to catch the pieces of her disintegrating life whilst on the run from a haunting past. He witnessed her resolve strengthen each day, the laughter starting to light up her eyes—her smile coming from a genuine place instead of pretending. Other aspects of her hovered above the surface of his heart. He wouldn't allow them to settle at the present time.

Frank's phone rang, breaking Jeb's train of thought. Removing a glove, Frank fished it from the back pocket of his pants. "Hello dear?"

Jeb continued on with his task, pining for a cold drink to quench the prickling heat in his throat.

"Okay—okay. Calm down, it will be okay. We're on our way." Frank kicked away the remnants left from storage, hanging up the phone. "Jeb, we've gotta go. That was your Mom."

"Have they bought out the entire Walmart again?" Jeb teased his mom and Iylah's frequent Walmart trips together.

"No," Frank's pace increased in a hurry and caused Jeb to pause, "Dawn's turned up at the house."

"What!" The blood drained from his face, a sharp pain shooting across his shoulders—the coursing dread filling his veins instead.

At that moment, the heat of the day became a secondary issue for Jeb.

~ ~

Jeb swung the door of the car open before Frank eased the car to a complete halt.

"Jeb!"

The festering rage, prominently sitting in the centre of his chest, bubbled over as he closed the distance rapidly from the driveway to the front door of the house—reaching and opening the door with great force, the hinges revolted in a deep creak. The scene that met him in the front living room of his parent's house did nothing to cause his anger to subside.

"You lying scumbag!" Dawn's accusation came fast, her wired eyes on him, trying by all means to rise from his mom's couch.

Iylah stood in the middle of the room facing Dawn—her arms crossed, utter disdain etched in her features. An expression Jeb hoped he'd never see again. She stood between a crying Tylor seeking comfort from his mom and a hysterical Dawn rocking from whatever substance coursed through her body. He'd seen this before.

His mind rocketing with many thoughts fuelled by Dawn's presence, Jeb turned his attention to his crying son. "Mom, can you take Tylor into the other room, please?"

"No, he's not going anywhere!" Dawn shrieked, attempting to stand up from her seat—her body failing.

"Dawn, sit down!" Jeb barked, and she took notice, so did Iylah. "Mom, please."

Kathy didn't wait for another instruction, bundling up Tylor and leading him away from whatever transpired next.

When they were out of earshot, he spoke, restraining himself through gritted teeth, his chest rising visibly, the heat of his anger inflating it. "What are you doing here?"

"You lied to me. What is she doing here?" Dawn leaned back on the couch, unable to focus on him or anything for that matter. Her words fall short of being intelligible.

"You don't get to ask the questions! You turned up here unannounced—"

"I wanted to see you guys." The puddles of black trickled down, adding further streaks of mascara in their path. "I miss you."

Exasperated by her state of mind and reasoning, Jeb shoved his fingers through his hair gruffly, familiar with this narrative that played out time and time again in their now dissolving marriage.

"Do you want me to leave the room, Jeb?" Iylah spoke delicately, taking in the volatile scenario playing out.

"I still love you." Dawn wailed, dropping her head into her hands, her body swayed. "I can change, I promise."

Her promises no longer mattered. They were too far gone. And her habit of breaking every single one she uttered did nothing to build confidence in Jeb.

"Keep an eye on her, I'll be back." Instinctively, following a routine of protocol he mastered, Jeb marched down the hallway in search of his parents. He found them in their room, embracing the scared and tired frame of his ten-year-old son. "Dad, is there somewhere I can take her for the night? She's on something, and she needs to sober up. She can't stay here."

"We can take her to the church. She can stay the night there." Frank offered.

"I'll go with her." Jeb's eyes fell on his quietly sobbing son. The lump pushing down in his throat grew unignorable. Weary tears stung the back of his eyes. Not allowing them the option to appear, he swallowed them away.

"I'll get you blankets to use for the night, and I'll organise dinner for later." Kathy left the room, doing what she knew to do best—caring for her son and those who needed it.

Jeb approached Tylor, kneeling in front of him, wiping away the moisture from tears he wished he didn't need to. "I'm so sorry, Tylor. It's gonna be different from now on, okay?"

Tylor threw his arms around Jeb's neck, burying his face in his shoulder. "Just make sure she's okay, Dad."

Jeb squeezed his son, willing the years away of seeing his mother in such a state. It had to be different now.

Please, God, let it be different.

❧ ❧

Jeb picked up on the third ring.

"Hey," his voice was worn out and hollow.

"Hey, I've got dinner. I'm outside the church. Not sure what door to come through." Iylah announced her unexpected arrival.

Jeb assumed his mom would do the dinner delivery like she said—the task now delegated to Iylah. Either that or Iylah took it upon herself. He stole a look over at Dawn lying asleep on the makeshift bed. She lay there without a single movement, only a slight rising and falling of her chest to confirm she was still breathing.

"I'll meet you at the front entrance."

Pushing himself in the chair away from the desk, where he sat avidly re-searching drug and alcohol rehabilitation programs in Phoenix. He dragged his shattered body through the quiet halls of the church building to meet Iylah.

His mind ceased its racing barely an hour ago and frantically settled into the surrounding silence. It allowed him time to process his promise to Tylor—to make sure Dawn would be okay. Guilt overwhelmed him pondering how he should have done this sooner, instead of exposing Tylor to such chaos repeated-ly.

Why didn't I?

His harbored suspicion rang true. Maybe he enabled Dawn in her behaviour. Sure, he didn't hand her the drugs or push her away. Instead, he made it okay for her to keep coming back, when it shouldn't have been. No ultimatum ever worked past two weeks. This time around, Jeb determined to give her one last attempt at help. After that, he hoped she'd find her feet and whatever needed to be fixed within her, by herself.

He swung one of the big wooden arched doors of the entrance open, reveal-ing Iylah standing sincerely with three containers full of homemade food. Jeb chuckled at the sight before him. The first time his mouth moved from a scowl to the costly smile he wore.

"She said when you're stressed, you tend to eat a lot." Iylah meekly explained the feast she carried before her. "I offered to drop it off 'cause Kathy slaved away in the kitchen, and I felt bad because my sous chef skills nearly burnt half the food."

"Yeah, I believe that." He motioned for her to come in. "You drove the Buick?"

The image of Iylah driving a car not one he was familiar with. For the duration of their knowing each other, she persisted in being a passenger in a town car, which appeared precisely when she wanted it to.

"Yep." She continued ahead of Jeb down the aisle of the chapel. "This place is surprisingly eerie when no one is in it." Her head turned, taking in the empty grandeur.

He followed behind her, aware she didn't know where to go but deciding at the last minute to pop herself on the front wooden pew, settling dinner next to her, pulling out two forks.

"Dawn sleeping it off?" She extended a fork towards Jeb.

He received it from her, while she popped open each container, crossing the legs—he'd briefly admired roadside—up on the pew and discreetly tugged at the leg of her shredded denim shorts that looked chewed up and lazily put back together.

"Yeah." He followed suit and placed himself on the other end of the containers his mom filled with food.

Macaroni Cheese; some Chicken Casserole and Zucchini boats stuffed with mushroom, onions and pepper. She really outdid herself and stood correct about stress making Jeb a devourer of food. Today, however, his stomach reminded him it was in recovery and his appetite was stolen by the task at hand. Iylah had already started her way through some of the Macaroni Cheese, beating him to the title.

"You don't want a plate?" Amused, he watched her dig in some more before he picked away at the food.

"Mmm nope. My gosh, your mom knows how to make food taste so good. I'm gonna weigh a few extra pounds by the time I leave." A brief silence followed her enthused statement as they both ate.

No one really knew when that departure date was. For now, it was okay to pretend it didn't loom.

"Are you okay?" Iylah filled the silence, asking the question she drove in the Buick to probe. "It was pretty intense back there."

Intense didn't adequately describe it. Her bearing witness to a snippet of the calamity his life revolved around made him apprehensive.

Jeb peered at her across from him. She continued to eat at a much faster rate than him—his predicted appetite not as robust as assumed. If she was aware of him watching her, she didn't allude to it, her concentration cast down at the food before them. He wanted to tell her that upon her arrival, the tension across relieved itself off his shoulders and the dull headache impending now a mere whisper. But he didn't. He avoided the question altogether, not admitting what it meant

"I'm gonna take her to Phoenix. She's got family there she still talks to—an aunt." He intended to suggest she use money from their joint account to send her to rehab before all of it got divided up in the divorce.

Iylah hesitated, her fork midway to her mouth at his statement. "You really are a better person than most, Jeb. Do you have a middle name?"

He laughed sharply at what he considered to be a lie. He suspected his promise to Tylor kept him in Dawn's life—not the notion of being a good person. Guilt drove his loyalty.

"Can't say I'm a better person. I just made Tylor a promise to make sure his mother would be okay. And no I do not have a middle name. Do you?"

She nodded, her jaw currently occupied with her mouthful of food. "Jane. So, do you have a habit of doing this then? Rescuing various damsels in distress?" She still didn't look up from her endeavor of shoving the food down in the best polite way she could.

"If I'm not mistaken, I was the damsel in our particular situation." He tucked loose hair behind his ear, wincing inwardly at his use of the word 'our'. He didn't want to add a rather intimate air of ownership over it.

"Do you have a habit of taking in strays?"

A question he'd once been itching to ask since those plush seats on her private chartered jet, made him second guess his vocation. The same question that stood at the centre of their fight a couple of weeks ago.

This time she looked up.

The tip of the fork lingered in her mouth. "How long have you been wanting to ask that question?"

"How long have you been wanting to ask me your question?" He set his fork down on one lid from the containers, setting his gaze firmly on hers.

The conversation opened up about intentions, and he hadn't been the one to pursue it. Apprehension washed ashore in his stomach. Despite his plate being metaphorically full with life's unfortunate events, a willingness to partake in whatever discourse followed next, presented itself. He studied her face as she drew the fork away from her lips, allowing it to dangle in her hand. She watched him carefully, darting across his face from one feature to another.

"My sister keeps warning me not to trauma bond with you."

"Well, are you? Are we trauma bonding?"

The term amused him, but he fought the urge to show it because he sensed the nervous alarm in Iylah. Her eyes narrowed to read him.

"I think it's very noble and kind of you and your family to take me in." The fork fidgeted in her grasp, betraying the edge in her body, despite the calm demeanor written across her face. "No one has ever been this wildly charitable as your family has been towards me. And I don't want to take advantage of it—"

"You mean you don't want to take advantage of me?"

"You're an amazing man, Jeb. Dawn definitely doesn't deserve you in any capacity. You deserve—"

"And what do you deserve?" The invasiveness of his question struck her unaware, and he observed the shift in her arms folding across her chest. He didn't need a psychology major to know a defensive posture if he ever saw one.

"Jeb?"

The sound of Dawn's present voice halted their conversation, both their heads shooting across to the direction in which she leaned, next to the classical piano. Her hair in disarray and disheveled tear-streaked makeup added to the look of calamity. A look Jeb witnessed far too frequently.

"I'm gonna go." Iylah placed the fork down, gathered her things and stood up abruptly. "Um—good luck." Her departing words were without any eye contact.

Uncertain of what exactly transpired between them, Jeb concluded he needed more than just luck to work through the maze of his life. For now, his efforts needed to be focused on ensuring the mother of his child remained alive.

seventeen

JOURNAL ENTRY DATED 05/12/2005

"The earth is the Lord's, and everything in it,

The world, and all who live in it;

For he who founded it on the seas

And established it on the waters."

Psalm 24:1

Heavenly Father, if I ever needed the assurance of who it is who is in charge over all, this is it. My heart leaps at this sweet knowledge—You who made the earth and hold it, knows all there is to ever know about us, all who live in it. You not only know of us, but we are known to You. We are Your possession and your desire. Life has a way of being the louder reminder of the lack of control I have, yet it humbles me in submission and admission that there is One far greater and far more capable to orchestrate the days and moments of this life. I am choosing not to scrabble for any control whatever I may try to cling to, as I feel the weakness in my body begin to set in. The earth is Yours Lord, and everything in it, including me. I surrender all my understanding, and confusion, looking onward to You for the path You have laid out for me.

Your daughter

Lillian

Iylah

SEVENTEEN

Iylah's fingers zoomed in on the image displayed on her screen, the mouse pad of her laptop under her touch. Known to be handy for many things, she didn't consider herself a frequent user of Pinterest, until she volunteered her time to help the two sour sisters—Linda and Alice—and the rest of the charming ladies of Living River Church with their summer gala.

Her intentions merely to lend a hand here and there, were to dispense her accumulating free time in between finishing her painting and scouring through pages of ancient Bible text. After the first meeting she found herself being quite the fountain of ideas. Dare she say they came naturally to her, given the years she spent attending fancy soirees with budgets too vivacious compared to Living River's.

In her brief stay as a temporary resident at the Aston's, Iylah witnessed the care and time both Kathy and Frank put into their little community of both attendees and strangers they simply bumped into on random Walmart trips. All recipients of their kindness, her included. She quietly identified how little support they received and how infrequent people cared for them.

Short of leaving an anonymous envelope of cash at Frank's desk, the next best thing she could offer was herself and so she did. The offering of her service meant her Friday afternoon outplayed at Kathy's kitchen table—hiding away from the Clovis heat and scrunching her nose at Pinterest's suggestions.

The 'Garden of Hope' gala theme she'd put forward, came creatively inspired by her fascination of the creation story she read during one of her early morning readings. Aware of Iylah's upbringing, Kathy jumped at Iylah's eager ideas, giving her sole charge of the creative direction for the event. Much to the clear dismay of the Sour Sisters.

The house hummed quietly with the soundtrack of the movie Tylor opted to watch this afternoon, paired with the slight murmurings of the ceiling fan circulating hot air in the open plan living area. Iylah's background soundtrack.

Kathy scurried her busy body out to do another round of groceries to feed the extra welcomed mouths who called her house home for the summer. Iylah insisted on contributing to her stay here, standing stubbornly firm when she came face to face with Kathy's refusal. Kathy, just as stubborn, allowed Jeb to sway her into accepting Iylah's monetary contributions. Iylah made a mental note not to get Kathy suspicious, with her intention of discreetly funding the new creative director role for the gala, bestowed on her.

Iylah pushed away stray curls clinging to the back of her neck, from the light perspiration dotted along it. Her sheer floral print top, tank top and denim shorts were no match once again for this desert mimicking temperature. Still, she'd endured harsher temperatures than this. A rather spontaneous, quick trip to the east coast of Australia, during a Sydney summer reminded her of why air cooling existed.

A trip taken solely for the purpose of being anywhere but home. An acquaintance—Australian by birth—enticed Iylah to the shores of her hometown. She'd collected many acquaintances along the way. Sticking around long enough to make friendships beyond the threshold of acquaintances, not a skill she possessed. One she frequently envied others for having the ability to set roots down in community with others.

Her attention to the task at hand waned, the frailty of her organizational skills beginning to show. Skills she rarely used outside of her class. She deliberated her unspoken dilemma—if she would get to go back to teach at the end of the summer. Beyond today, nothing was assured.

The earth is the Lord's, and everything in it, the world and all who live in it.

The words thrummed in her heart, bringing forward the recent understanding of how everything was subject to God. It certainly seemed that way in what she read. She made small decisions daily whether truth existed in what she poured over in the books of the Bible. Decisions about if she believed the words her mother penned, without knowing Iylah would one day read them. Parts of her started to believe it.

Reaching into the back pocket of her shorts, she tugged out the last remaining tab of nicotine gum. Twiddling with it between her fingers, she suddenly felt the craving for ice cream.

Madagascar Vanilla from Ampersand really should not taste that good.

She skimmed over her shoulder at the ten-year-old boy tapping his foot against the mushroom colored rug. Boredom setting in.

Jeb's absence created a gap truly unfillable for the eight days gone by. Noticed not just by Tylor, but by Iylah too.

Iylah confessed to Lena her abrupt indiscretion of disclosing the warning her sister astutely gave her. Lena found it recklessly amusing, while Iylah found it to be an unfortunate slip of the tongue. Amongst Iylah's other confessions, she disclosed her growing desire to know Jesus, to which Lena shared her own intrigue behind what enticed their mother to religion. A guttural feeling in Iylah, foretold of the journals in her possession not ending in just her hands alone. For now, her mother's words were filling in the gaps she needed answered, simultaneously creating bigger gaps of untold struggles.

Standing up from her ended Pinterest scouring, she joined Tylor in the living room he occupied. His stance towards her softened, with brief conversation strewn in here and there. Her heart felt sad for what he grew up being privy to. It shattered both Tylor and Jeb. Having been in a whirl of her own messy decisions, Iylah learned candidly how there was always more behind what drove a person's life—sometimes off the cliff.

The hull of her stomach filled with a vibrating warmth every time she thought of Jeb. This occurred often, the feeling unfamiliar, as most of the emotions in this life detour were. Some would class the emotions as caring—the pessimist in her inclined to call it, being around the same guy for too long. At least she would stick to telling herself that.

His absence tending to an ex wife, sparked many emotions she couldn't quite explain. All she wanted to know was whether he was okay? Would he be okay? Why did he instruct Kathy to keep up his morning routine of leaving Iylah coffees by her bedside? When would he be back? Would they pick up from their last conversation? Did she care to find out what sort of friendship they had? Did he?

"Hey, do you wanna get some ice-cream when Kathy gets back?" Iylah stood by the entrance of the living room, leaning against its arched doorway.

She figured a ten-year-old like Tylor found sitting around mindless, compared to the nature of activities Jeb and him pursued most days. The swimming, hiking, playing baseball, skateboarding—Iylah couldn't afford any of that in Jeb's vacancy, however an excursion for a treat she could offer.

"Ampersand ice-cream?" The ten-year-old enquired, his head cocked towards Iylah.

"Is there any other ice cream worth having?" Iylah probed, knowing very well Tylor's designated favorite flavor from Ampersand. Chocolate Chip.

"Nope. Okay, I'm in."

With a content smile, Iylah left her ten-year-old friend to his movie watching.

∾ ⁓

"So your favorite band is the Red Hot Chili Peppers? Aren't you a little too young to know who they are?" Iylah shoved another scoopful of her beloved Madagascar Vanilla ice cream, into her expecting mouth.

"Me and Dad listen to them all the time. I learnt how to play Californication on guitar, back at home. I'm not very good at it." Tylor stood leaning against the Buick next to Iylah, Chocolate Chip running down his ice cream cone, no match for the sun angling down on them.

"Impressive." She offered. "Can you play it for me one time?" Tylor shook his head. "C'mon why not?" Iylah teased.

"I'm not very good." Insecurity tinted his boyish face. "Besides, Grandpa and Gammy don't have a guitar."

Iylah caught the words before they rattled out of her mouth, offering to buy him a new guitar to win him over. From her experience gifts or money never forged good relationships.

Her father slipped to the surface of her mind. Still no return of her phone calls and her questions remained resoundingly unanswered, even as she fought the urge to come clean with him about her own secrets.

"I'm sure we could borrow one from the church, but—" she raised her hands feigning surrender, "Only if you want to."

Tylor kicked a loose piece of tar underneath his feet, "What's your favorite band?"

"Well—" Iylah heard the muffled ringing of her phone, "My mother and I used to listen to Nat King Cole—" She retrieved her phone from her vintage leather cross body handbag, "But classical music is more—" Her voice trailed off at the name of one FBI agent, Eric Mane. She held her breath for a beat of a second, allowing herself to feel the beginnings of knots in her chest. "Sorry Tylor, I've just gotta answer this—" She stepped forward creating distance between her and innocence, "Hello Mr Mane?"

"Miss Dawson, I hope I'm not catching you at a bad time?" In all her interactions with him, niceties were not his forte, more of an inconvenience to him.

"Depends on what you're about to tell me." The remains of her ice cream lost its form into a slosh of soup.

"We've been tracking Stefan's movements since his arrival into the country. Our last knowledge of his whereabouts was twenty-four hours ago at a restaurant in the West Village, since then he appears to have gone dark—no trace of him."

"West Village? That's less than half an hour from my house—" Breathing became sufficiently harder, with no intention of resolving.

"We are aware of that, yes. He did in fact go within proximity of your home two days ago—"

"What! Can't you do something about that?" A chill settled in Iylah's spine. "How does he know where I live?"

"Until we have just cause to apprehend him, we have nothing to bring him in on. His only crime is being released out of prison early. If he breaches the restraining order against him as enforced by the court in Germany and the court here, we can bring him in. We are going to locate him and his whereabouts Miss Dawson. For now, remain in Clovis until further notice. You will continue to have surveillance with our two agents stationed where you are."

Her ice cream now hanging low by her side, the enjoyment of it gone, she swallowed away the bitter taste overcoming the sweet traces of ice cream—silently thanking Lena for her swift thinking filing the restraining order. "Okay, I guess I'll stay put."

Any anger that arose from her fear was misplaced.

The only person to be mad at was herself—a particular road that started to get tiresome. She couldn't live in hiding any longer.

eighteen

Jeb

Jeb threw himself back onto his own bed, embracing the comfort of its familiarity. Ten days of sleeping in a less than accommodating three-star hotel took its toll on day five. He had a mission to complete and he wouldn't leave without doing so. The stress of it all rolled through his shoulders and nothing eased it. Almost nothing.

The silence in the house rang loud. Upon his late arrival, everyone slept soundly, unaware of his presence. Jeb crept into Tylor's room to remind himself why it was necessary to do what he did, and what he needed to do going forward. The days of Tylor living in crippling dysfunction were no longer and it would all be final in close to a week according to his small budget lawyer.

With Dawn checked in to Crossroads Rehabilitation, there wasn't much else left to their marriage than the sole being of their son. He wouldn't be a husband to a wife who found more pleasure in the arms of others.

The years ahead felt too far to grasp their hope, though he guessed it might have been the tiredness robbing him the full delight of a different future.

Jeb rubbed his eyes, a yawn fleeing his mouth. Rolling over onto his stomach, an image of Iylah smiling fleeted across his mind. He buried his face into the navy comforter on his bed, his breath making its surface warm.

This was happening a lot.

Random screenshots of Iylah kept lining his imagination. He knew why. They hadn't spoken since he flew out to Phoenix with Dawn. The longing to call or message her incessant and annoying. He stumbled on what to say exactly.

I miss you.

What right did he have to miss her?

I can't stop thinking about you.

Is that what they both really needed right now?

I care about you.

Her presence an unforeseen bloom in his rather beauty deprived life, and he enjoyed the fragrance she brought.

Before he could dissuade himself, Jeb hopped off his bed, his bare feet leading the way out of his room, down the dimly lit hallway, past her bedroom with its door ajar revealing the empty darkness where she was not. He knew where she was and he headed there. The thrashing of his heart made him aware of the truth he fought, with each step he made towards her.

He opened the door next to the mudroom leading to the garage. His breath hitched and suspended in his chest when his eyes fell upon Iylah facing towards him, brush in one hand, a wooden palette smeared with an array of acrylic paint in the other.

She stood her attention now cast upon him away from the canvas before her, dressed in an oversized t-shirt with Sade's face on it, the brightest royal blue sweatpants known to man, and not an ounce of makeup with her curls restrained in her signature messy bun.

A strange sensation of relief filled his gut. A pull unlike any other he'd experienced in her presence. It drove his desire to be in her proximity—intimately.

"Hi." Her voice brought heat to his neck.

"Hey." He stepped into her space of creativity wearing an involuntary smile, closing the door behind him.

"When did you get back?" She to the canvas before her, averting her twinkling eyes. Although her mouth didn't smile, her eyes did.

He swore a gladness spurred in them.

Jeb stuck his hands into the pockets of his loose-fitting pants, making his way towards her side, the unrelenting thumping of his heart matching the cadence of his steps.

"About twenty minutes ago." He caught a hint of the jasmine woody fragrance she always wore. It made the skin along his arms rise in spread goosebumps.

"How was the trip?" She intently focused on where her brush went on the canvas. Maybe a little too intent.

Her painting, one he hadn't seen before. Yellow Ochre and Naples Yellow laid as the backdrop of whatever vision she began.

"Long." That's all he wanted to disclose. Not Dawn's begging for a tenth second chance. Not the kiss she thought would save an already ended marriage. Not the loneliness he suffocated under in that hotel room. Not the silent, short prayers he found himself saying. Long would suffice. "What happened to the pastures painting?"

Her head motioned to the right of them where the finished product sat leaning against a makeshift stand. "All done."

Jeb moved closer to the finished artwork, taking in the crafted image of a meadow grassland, lit golden by a light that couldn't be described as the sun. A glistening brook ran through the meadow grassland and at the top of it a singular sheep drank from it. Something about the image put a still yearning for refreshment in him where it wasn't there before.

"Is this the dream you had?" He recalled her detailing a dream, one sounding awfully similar to what he examined now. He remembered the way her eyes shimmered with the signs of tears when she told him the dream.

Those moments made him aware of something changing in her, a softness beginning to envelope her fearful heart.

"Yeah—" she paused her current painting to take in her finished one. "What do you think?"

"What do I think?" Jeb gibed, "I think you should forget teaching at the School and just do this, Iylah. It's incredible."

He'd seen enough of her works to know the depth of her skill set. Unlike him. He couldn't remember the last time he sketched or drew just from inspiration. A lot left him uninspired in the last few months.

He retrieved a breath in before the resounding admission stumbled out of his mouth, "I'm sorry I didn't call or get in touch while I was away—"

"Jeb, you don't have to apologize. I wasn't expecting you to." Her eyes met his briefly, both trying to read the other.

The presence of all things unsaid between them weighed in the room.

"You've got stuff going on, you don't need to check in on me." She shrugged, "I'm a big girl." A faint smile teased at the corner of her full lips before she turned back to her task at hand.

"I wanted to, you know?" He snuck a look down at the rug beneath his feet. A shade of insecurity caused him to measure how much of his inner dialogue to reveal. "I wanted to call you."

When he glanced up again, he watched her movement slow down in anticipation.

"But not to check up on you. You don't need me to do that." His hands found the lint hidden in the creases of his pockets, eagerness overtaking his stomach. "I wanted to call to hear your voice because I missed you." He tried the words on for size.

Iylah turned her body to face him and immediately her captivating eyes set his heart off on a race it wouldn't win.

"I wanted to call you to tell you that getting to know you has been the better part of this strangely messed up summer for me. That I care for you and I'm realizing just how deeply I do right now as you're looking at me—" his words lingered, leaving room for the quaking reality he expressed to settle between them.

She remained still.

"Look," Jeb tucked some of his hair behind his ear, "I know what our realities are—I'm not oblivious to them. I have a son to consider and take care of. And you've got an ex hot on your heels, so I get our situations are dire and honestly one whirlwind of a story that probably needs time to smooth over. I just wanted to tell you the truth." He chuckled, the nerves doing their erratic dance as he rubbed his chin, not sure what to do with the energy fizzing in him.

"Who gets to take care of you?" The words she finally spoke were not one's Jeb foresaw.

The gentle enquiry of hers tugged at a part of Jeb's heart he forgot needed tending to.

She placed her tools down on the high stool next to her, taking the most timid step towards Jeb. Close enough for him to forget how to swallow.

"I care about how you're doing. I care whether you've gone for your run in the morning because it seems to balance you out and make you breathe easier through the day. I care about protecting you from being taken advantage of. You've experienced the worst in people yet somehow focus so well on their best and not everyone appreciates that. I care about Tylor one day feeling confident enough to play Californication on the guitar." Arms crossed over her chest, she kicked her foot into the ground, shrugging. "I don't know when it happened, but it did. And I can't stop it."

Under the yellow tinged light of his parents' garage, her features became magnified and Jeb wanted to trace the beauty in them with his fingers. But he couldn't and wouldn't for fear of toeing past an invisible line he'd just drawn.

"Are you saying you feel the same? 'Cause my nerves really need reassurance."

She giggled, and it reverberated right through Jeb, as she threw her head back.

"Yes, Jeb." She mirrored his own stance, shoving her hands in the pockets of her sweatpants. "But we can't go there right now."

He knew it to be true.

She stepped forward catching him off guard, her arms wrapping around the middle of his body, pressing her head into his shoulder. Struck by how comfortable it was for her to do so, instinctively his own arms held onto her, his head finding solace in the back of her neck, setting himself on fire by how close they were.

Jeb held on hoping his racing heart didn't betray him with her head close to it. At this point he didn't care, all he wondered was how long he had until these moments weren't frequent anymore.

The future wasn't his to see, but the days to come would be ones he would relish in as long as she was close.

God, it would be great if there was a way.

Another short, simple prayer.

nineteen

JOURNAL ENTRY DATED 06/03/2005

'The Lord himself goes before you and will be with you; he will never leave you nor forsake you. Do not be afraid; do not be discouraged.'

Deuteronomy 31:8

Grant me the courage dear God, to face the things in this life that bring me the most fear. The courage to confess my fear unto you and to grab hold of the strength found in You. All the days of my life, whether or not I have seen You, You have gone before me, keeping Your eye and Your hand over me. What shall I fear then if the One who created the skies and the seas will never forsake me. Whom then shall cause me to cower away in the trenches of fear when you are with me. You cover me and carry me; You sustain me and love me. Take my fear, take my discouragement and give Your boldness and Your strength, for I have none of my own.

Your daughter

Lillian

The Bible lay open in the middle of her crossed legs, as she perched up in the bed, the covers still embracing her. To her left, her mother's journal displayed precious life learned truths.

Iylah's daily morning routine for the last four weeks comprised pouring through her mother's penned words that kept leading Iylah back to the Bible.

This Jesus her mother spoke of, seemed to find Iylah as she searched for him in these pages. Most mornings Iylah spent the early hours in the backyard with Kathy, Bible in hand, but today she needed the space to process. She looked to her right at the cup of coffee now sitting empty at her bedside. The space to process the kind of towering attentive care she felt rising in her for the man who brought her coffee every morning in bed, while she slept.

This morning, however, she rose earlier than normal, the memory from last night not allowing her to sleep. The electrifying heat that coursed through her body when Jeb shared his feelings for her. The glint of excitement in his eyes when he spoke, seeing her essence—maybe even who she was changing into and it made him come alive.

She transformed as the days rolled on—she was beginning to let go of the extra clutter shrouding her heart. Though they hadn't known each other for a length of time, she got the impression Jeb witnessed the traces of anxiety leave her; the shame dissolving into an ash heap, the past still lingering but becoming less loud. It all changed when she did what Kathy suggested one morning.

Kathy called it an exchanging of wills, a changing of natures. When night came, before Iylah closed her eyes, she muttered a timid but daring prayer.

I believe in You Jesus. Exchange my will for Yours, and my natural tendencies for Yours. I'm sorry for the time I wasted, the life I wasted doing things that didn't matter. I'm here now wanting to do things differently with You.

Those few words brought a satisfied clarity of how she wanted her life to be from then on.

She wanted Jeb in it too.

Her heart saw Jeb differently since the night he surprised her with her mini studio. She was nervously aware of the kind of man he is—one who put others far above himself, and would make the effort to show it. His imperfect ways of trying to move forward were endearing—much like her own. The zeal returned in his eyes, emulating the color of the roughest of seas under the noonday sun. His square set jaw always peppered with stubble. The strength is his arms whenever she occasionally found herself in their embrace, engulfed her in safety she hadn't felt in a while. The way his hair played around whichever way he desired to toss it. She relished all of it.

So naturally when he opened up to her last night, she opened herself up too. They'd allowed themselves the space to be honest and boy did it feel good, despite a heavy touch of sadness making itself known to Iylah.

Neither one of them could explore these new waters because the shore from which they both left, still tugged them back to reality. Truthfully she didn't know herself without these clingers of the past, and eagerness to find what life could be without them prodded at her each day. An understanding of her mother's life and faith brought to light Iylah's own need for this life and faith. That and maybe it was time to stop chasing after men—including Jeb.

The last one still had her on the run.

She exhaled, letting the swirling desire of a new life wrap around her. Why could things never be straightforward? Her life constantly on the run, split open an aching longing to plant roots. To have friendships spanning longer than a quick stint in foreign countries. To do something with her life that made her proud.

For crying out loud, thirty approached in age and she still cashed in on her father's workday earnings. There was more to life than she grossly believed and she desperately needed the courage to figure it out. At the upmost top of the list, she wanted this hiding from Stefan business to end.

Reaching for the new black leather bound journal, freshly unwritten in—she opted to follow the suit of her mother. Writing her prayers down.

If it worked for her mother, surely God would pay attention to her written prayers too, right?

∾ ⁓

An empty cup of coffee in hand and the confidence from a fresh shower, Iylah strode the length of the hallway as she did every morning, to find Kathy in the kitchen at her usual station. Once or twice Iylah offered to make breakfast, but Kathy's words of polite yet firm refusal reminded Iylah that she was her guest. Eventually Iylah conceded and made herself useful with cleaning up dishes. Her proficiency in dish duty increased. Prior to her stay at the Aston's, it was pretty abysmal.

The flared skirt of her black ribbed sleeveless dress swished with every step, grazing her ankles. One of her favorite purchases from her time in Berlin. Its scoop neck stressed her collarbone, making it appear sharp, showing off her elegantly long neck. She admitted though; it fit rather snugly in places it never used to. It took a bit of a pull to do up the gold tone buttons around her hips. Gaining weight didn't bother Iylah, simply because she rarely ever gained it. Since her smokefree journey begun, food was never to be passed up—thanks to her sense of taste making a comeback.

"Good morning Kathy," Iylah placed her hand on Kathy's shoulder, walking past her at the gas stove top heading towards the sink.

"Good morning gorgeous girl." Kathy regularly showered Iylah with nothing but compliments, encouragement and some hard truths. The language she spoke daily and Iylah admired her for it.

Her own mother treated her most gently, which would explain how much Iylah got away with.

"Missed ya this morning."

"Sorry, I was up late last night painting and the bed was just too comfortable." It was a half truth and it would do.

"You need all the rest you can get, darling. We've got a big couple of weeks ahead before the gala. I've roped in a couple of helpers to go to the Floral Wholesaler today with you." Kathy swiveled around from the stove to dispense her famous fluffy scrambled eggs onto a serving plate.

Iylah hoped it wasn't those horrid Sour Sisters, who loved to point out her 'lack of experience' in planning such prestigious events like the gala.

"Awesome. Who?" She rinsed out her empty coffee mug under the warm water of the kitchen faucet.

"Me."

She startled at Jeb's voice, water splashing across her middle. Grabbing the nearest dishcloth, she dabbed away at her clumsiness, turning around in time to witness Jeb pull a crisp white t-shirt over his head, displaying his rather well worked out torso. She attempted to look away in time for Jeb not to catch her staring but she failed astonishingly, stumbling across her next words. "Uh—great. Thanks Jeb."

She'd seen him without a shirt a few times before—this instance felt provocatively different.

He smirked, aware of her lingering gaze he tossed his wet hair back causing it to sit like it had been purposefully styled there.

Oh c'mon! This is unfair.

She gathered herself, turning away with her head down, concentrating unnecessarily on drying the mess she made.

"Alright, everybody sit. Breakfast is ready." Kathy chimed, unconcerned with what just happened, she continued serving up her spread.

"Tylor!" Jeb called out to his absent son, much like he did most mornings.

Except this morning it dawned on Iylah the amount of responsibility balancing on Jeb's shoulders to care for his son as a nearly single parent. She wondered silently when his divorce would be final.

Iylah propped herself down next to Kathy, across from Jeb at the kitchen table decked out with a well-prepared breakfast. Once again, Kathy delivered. The pattering of running feet filled the room, Tylor scurried on in to take his place next to his Dad, who ruffled his nearly identical hair. As was customary in the Aston household, thanks for the meal were prayed before anyone dug in.

"I think it might be time to get you a trim young man." Jeb uttered, "How about after we help Iylah, we head down to the barber?" He tossed a couple of pieces of bacon onto a plate and passed it to Tylor.

"Are you going to get a trim too?" Tylor quizzed his father.

"Do I look like I need one?"

"Mom would have told you to get one." The words came out innocently from Tylor's mouth

The adults at the table exchanged gazes. Iylah watched Jeb's face as it remained unchanging, he rubbed his brow slightly.

"I say we put it to a vote." Iylah rode in on the silence to keep the banter going. "All those in favor of Jeb getting his hair trimmed raise your hands."

"Wow. What am I? A dog?" Jeb retorted.

Two hands went up—Kathy and Tylor. Iylah's remained steady on her fork and knife, giving her honest vote. Admittedly, she was a fan of Jeb's nearly shoulder length dark blonde hair. For someone nearly forty, he wore it better than most.

"It's a tie—"

"Hang on, I'm pretty sure your Dad can't vote for himself Tylor." Kathy gave Tylor a wink of solidarity.

"Time for a trim Dad." The ten-year-old wore his victory with a smile.

Iylah shrugged at Jeb, shaking his head amused at the fate of his hair. "I tried."

"Did not expect my hair to have so many opinions on it." He bit into his toast as he playfully glared at Tylor. "Dad already left for the day?"

Kathy nodded mid swallow, "He's got a few house visits to get through today and a couple of hospital visits too."

"Never ending, huh?"

Iylah saw the slight pensive look in Jeb's eyes. There seemed to be an opinion left unsaid there.

"Your father enjoys it, as do I. Don't you say anything else." A pre-warning came from Kathy who seemed to know her son really well.

"I said nothing."

"Your face did." Finished with her meal, Kathy stood up to get to the next portion of her morning. "Oh, and don't forget your sister arrives tonight with the boys."

Iylah's attention perked up at this new piece of information. Jeb didn't really talk about his siblings or allude to them at all. The only evidence Iylah had of him being a middle child were the photographs hung up along the hallway wall of their childhood.

"Got it." Jeb's one worded answer with his gaze cast down at his plate, said enough.

Another opinion left untold again.

"You will love Laura, Iylah. She's about your age with two precious boys, Cruz and Joey." Kathy tinkered away at doing the dishes, Iylah's cue to scoff down the rest of her eggs and make good on dishes duty. "She put up with her brothers and gave them a run for their money." She chuckled.

Iylah placed herself next to Kathy, clearing her own plate, "Sounds like my kinda gal."

She hoped she was. Not every woman welcomed Iylah with open arms—skeptic arms, yes. Iylah turned around to grab some of the used plates from the table, only to glimpse Jeb's discrete stare over her dress and how it draped on her figure. The male gaze and the disturbing remarks that followed, weren't foreign to her. His wandering eyes did not feel like that. This felt safer. She smiled coyly when he recoiled after being found out.

Check mate.

Jeb cleared his throat to speak, "We should probably leave soon for the floral place."

Iylah sensed now with the truth being out in the open, to be detached from these new and growing feelings would prove to be a challenge neither one of them expected. The evidence showed in the racing of her heart.

Reality would set in soon enough right?

❧ ❧

The sound of Iylah's clogs hitting the concrete floor of the warehouse made her regret wearing them. They brought attention to her—unhelpful attention. Jeb and Tylor were close in tow, waiting upon her command for help—Jeb more willingly, Tylor not so much. It made her chuckle a little.

The long running aisles in the warehouse were lined with large white buckets bursting with a sea of blooms in season. A woman who frothed on whatever beauty she could find in the world, Iylah enjoyed this welcome splash of pretty color. She lowered herself down to smell the Zinnia's, picking up two bunches of the mixed in color Zinnia stems with one hand, while the other held onto her trustee sketchbook. In it, pencil drawn sketches of the frame designs she dreamt up to hold the flowers littered a few pages. Her Pinterest scouring hadn't really paid off, so she resolved to conjuring up decor designs with the hope of them materializing to something breathtaking for the gala.

"I'll take those." Jeb and Tylor stood by her side, "They look ridiculously heavy."

He outstretched his hand to receive the Zinnia's from Iylah with a smirk. She obliged, handing them over and choosing to ignore the sarcasm. An air of cheek in him hid underneath his Los Angeles baseball cap, he wore drawn to sit just above his brow. It sent her stomach quivering with butterflies.

He handed one bunch of stems to Tylor, to keep him useful. "What are you planning on doing with these, anyway?"

She straightened herself up to stand, opening her sketchbook to reveal her designs. "This."

He crept in closer to get a better look—near enough for Iylah to take in his scent. A distinct scent, free from cologne exuding a pine earthy clean smell mixed in with his natural body scent.

"I'm going to weld some frames in these shapes to hold maybe about two hundred stems each. They'll be standalone frames giving the illusion of the flowers floating upwards."

He turned the page to reveal more of her designs.

"And these are for the ceiling to hang singular stems from without having to go so high up."

"You can do this?" Genuine awe rode on his voice, he flipped back a page.

"More or less. I did similar frames for my solo exhibition for my fifth year of Fine Arts. And I saw a welding machine in your parents' garage. I just need to test it out on miniature versions first, and that's why we're getting these now." She turned her eyes up to look at Jeb watching her, their faces the smallest distance apart. Unsure what to make of the woman before him.

"Not just a pretty face, huh?" He traced every angle of her face with his eyes, eventually resting on her lips. "Pretty incredible."

For the shortest second Iylah wondered what it would feel like to run her fingers lightly along his stubble ridden jawline.

Don't let your intrusive thoughts win.

Reluctantly turning away she retrieved her sketchbook back from Jeb's hands, the sensation of heat rising to her cheeks. Thankfully, the dark tones of her skin did a dutiful job not to betray any signs of blushing.

"Thanks. Just don't tell Kathy how many flowers I'm planning on buying, otherwise she'll be suspicious." Such an undertaking sat well out of the church's usual budget, but well within hers.

Iylah walked ahead, exhaling subtly at her victory over her intrusive thoughts.

"You know you don't have to do all this." Jeb iterated in behind her.

"Yes, I know." She also knew how indebted she was to Jeb's family for giving her safety in the middle of another one of her life's storms. Particularly a storm of her own making.

She desired to make better decisions, whatever that meant and looked like.

Even if one of the better decisions currently proved too hard to live by.

twenty

Jeb

Jeb readjusted the baseball cap on his head, its sweatband sticking to his forehead from the beads of sweat. The late afternoon sun lasered down on his hands through the windscreen as he held onto the steering wheel, waiting for the green light to allow them through. He flicked his head over at his son, sitting silently staring out of his window—his fresh hair trim making him look older. Or was it the deep set expression of concern on his face that added years to him? His demeanor rather quiet and observant since this morning at the floral warehouse, like he was trying to figure something out. Jeb knew how perceptive kids were, particularly Tylor.

"You okay bud? You've gone quiet on me." The green light came allowing Jeb to press on the accelerator of the Buick.

He probably needed to think about getting his own car. His own place to live. A new job. Enrolling Tylor into a new school. All of it. The phone call from his lawyer while he waited for Tylor's haircut to be done, finalized everything. He was officially divorced as of an hour ago.

"When mom is better, are we going back to New York with her?"

He'd sensed this conversation would come sooner or later, and right now appeared to be its designated time. Jeb sighed, having a hard time himself comprehending his new reality.

Was it over just like that? Years of disappointment, betrayal and being manipulated by a woman with no self control. Empathy had always been his natural response towards Dawn. Not anymore. A rising anger stifled any empathy left for her.

"Tylor, mom won't be joining us. She's getting the help she needs in Phoenix and after that," Jeb turned into his parents' street, "I'm not sure when you will see her next."

"Don't you want her to come back?" Tylor's brown eyes stared back at Jeb. He had her eyes.

"Remember how I mentioned that Mom and Dad were getting divorced?"

"Yeah."

"Well, that means your Mom and I are no longer married and no longer together. We love you, but we can't be together." A preemptive lump formed in Jeb's throat, preparing himself for what might come next.

He'd done his research on how to approach this and what would happen. Most of the articles advised expecting lots of questions and adverse reactions.

"But if she gets better, why don't you want to be with her?"

"It's a bit complicated, but Mom won't get better if I'm around." And neither would he if she hung around.

"Will she visit?" Tylor twiddled with his hands. Jeb detected the apprehension stirring in him.

"We'll see." Jeb pulled up into the driveway, bringing the car to a slow halt—turning it off. He reached over to soothe his son, rubbing the back of his head. "But you and I are going to move closer to Grandpa and Gammy. We won't be going back to New York at the end of the summer—"

"I don't wanna move here!" Tylor's brow tightened and his voice rose.

"Tylor—"

"You promised me you were going to make sure Mom would be okay. How is she going to be okay without us?" The tears of anger and confusion ran down Tylor's cheeks, past his chin and beyond.

"Tylor—" Jeb shifted in his seat to face his distraught son—aware what a brutal blow he dealt him with their new reality.

"You promised me!" Before Jeb could console him further, Tylor yanked his passenger door open, "I hate you for bringing me here!" He screamed, making a dash for it out of the car and up the driveway, bursting through the front door leaving Jeb in the wake of his warranted anger.

A familiar ache took over Jeb's shoulders, along with his chest. He slumped further down in his seat, gruffly yanking the cap off his head and throwing it across the dashboard, slamming his palm against the steering wheel. Through the corner of his eye, he caught the black SUV of the agent's in his rear-view mirror slowing down as it drove past his parents' driveway. Another reminder of the situation at hand. His breathing increased, working hard to disperse oxygen in his lungs—his chest squeezing.

Did I make a bad decision? Is this too much for Tylor? Am I being selfish? Maybe it wasn't that bad? Will he forgive me? Can I forgive Dawn? This is harder than I thought. Am I being punished for something? I can't breathe. I can't breathe.

Jeb clutched at his chest, questions and fears swirling relentlessly, making sure they went unignored. His palms overwhelmingly clammy. Closing his eyes shut, he grimaced, attempting to slow the chaos down. The sensation of his throat closing in caused an avalanche of panic to roll through him, restricting his breathing further. He heard something in the background but couldn't gather himself to register it. A hand forcefully grabbed his, away from his heaving chest.

"It's okay. You're safe. You're safe." Someone joined him in the car. "Focus on holding my hand, Jeb. Focus on my hand and squeeze it."

He did as he was told. Feeling the hand in his with fingers intertwined.

"Let's take deep breaths in and strong breaths out through your nose, okay."

Again he did as he was told.

"Good. Keep going, I'm right here. I'm not going anywhere."

Time took the opportunity to slow right down, not allowing the moment to catapult him out of this misery. After what felt like ten minutes, his racing heart slowed down. He focused again on the hand holding his—eyes still shut, its skin soft. It was Iylah's hand.

Silence enveloped around them, while his internal world returned to a wonky state of normal.

"What's happening to me?" His voice detached from his body, sounding distant and void of strength.

"You're having a panic attack."

Opening his eyes gingerly, trying to trust his body not to freak out on him once more, he glanced down at their entwined fingers. He felt her eyes on him—he wasn't ready to see what they held.

"We can sit here a little longer." She offered gently, not wanting to disturb the return of stability to him.

He nodded silently. She obliged.

The emotions within him still simmering from their explosion. To feel out of control like this, a foreign thing for him—not something he ever wanted to feel again. Had he been holding it in all along? Was this a sign of things to come? He clamped his eyes shut, a penetrating frown revealing the displeasure of having to go through the last twelve minutes in the future.

"Hey, do you want to go for a drive? I'll drive." Iylah must have noticed. "Kathy is with Tylor right now. I think it might help to have some space for a bit."

Again, he nodded with no language to decipher what was going on with him. She obliged.

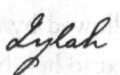

She slid the Buick into the parking lot of Spano Park. A few cars littered the surrounding space. A new pocket of Clovis Iylah hadn't explored before—not that she did a lot of it. Kathy offered it up for a recommendation one afternoon when being in the confines of the house caused her to slug around in a grouch trying really hard not to smoke.

Today was as good a time as any to check it out.

A prolonged hush hung around in the car, the engine tempering down. Not a single word came from Jeb's lips on the fourteen minute drive, and she got it.

How many times after a panic attack did she feel like talking? Scarcely. So she didn't push, she waited.

Observing Jeb next to her, whose eyes remained shut, she resisted the urge to stroke his hair. His shoulders caved in, leaning his head against the window—defeated and vulnerable. She wondered if she contributed to any of his anxious turmoil? Regret tugged at her heart.

The air abruptly thinned in the car, alerting her to the need for space of her own. Iylah opened her door, closing it firmly behind her.

Picnic tables strewn up ahead of the parking lot on the main patch of grass, caught her frazzled attention. Iylah beelined for the furthest unoccupied table.

Being careful not to pull at her dress, she hoisted herself up onto the tabletop, kicking her clogs off and settling herself down to overlook the San Joaquin River. The late afternoon sun caused the water to glisten like tiny diamond particles dancing on its surface. Her arms warmed up quickly under its rays. It wasn't the most majestic view she'd experienced. She reminded herself this wasn't for her—this was for Jeb. Iylah toyed with her hands, remembering how tightly Jeb held onto them at his weakest, like he'd done for her a few times now.

Whether or not they realized it, they found comfort in each other when their worlds were turning upside down. She enjoyed knowing her presence could calm another. In many instances, the presence of others acted as a source of calm for her in the past, but she was seeing their falsities and her ignorance. None of them were invested in her as Jeb's embrace implied.

A car door shut behind her, followed by some gradually approaching footsteps. Jeb warily placed himself next to her. No words needed to be exchanged, and she was comfortable with that. Silence no longer needed to be treated as a space of uncertainty by her.

"My divorce was finalized today."

Iylah faced him, a multitude of questions bouncing around. He did the same. His usually piercing eyes were sullen, tired and riddled with the dark presence of angst. A familiar feeling for her—she hated witnessing it on Jeb. Instinctively, wanting to erase the weight of it all for him, she reached over gently cupping the side of his face with her palm. She couldn't explain how natural it felt to do so. Her thumb tenderly stroked the top of his cheekbone down to his jaw, the bristle of his stubble grazing against it.

"I'm so sorry." She apologized for the turmoil that came with this recent development, and for the years gone by he possibly felt stuck.

He nestled his face into her touch, briefly closing his eyes to experience it. Her stomach fluttered, signaling the rest of her body expelling a silent gasp. Once more she held it together.

He retrieved her hand away from his face, holding onto it. "How is it possible to feel two very different emotions at once?" He sniffled through the emotions. His thumb traced over the top of her hand making her spine light up in tiny fires.

Iylah smiled empathetically, 'Well, what are you feeling?" She hoped her prying wasn't the cause for another panic attack.

"Terrified." He stared out onto the shimmering lake.

Iylah inspected the side of his face while he spoke, completely enamored by him.

"Terrified that I'm blowing up my son's life for selfish reasons and that I made the wrong decision. I'm terrified about this—" he motioned to their entwined hands, "and how I can't seem to turn my feelings for you off. Now I'm also freshly terrified of ever experiencing whatever I've just been going through for the last half an hour." His free hand rubbed away at his face exasperated by it all.

"That's a lot of terror." Iylah found her words despite the violent fluttering overtaking her gut. "Is that the first time you've had one of those?"

"Yeah, at thirty-eight years old." He scoffed, "How pathetic is my life."

"I mean in defense to your panic attack, you look thirty so there's that." She teased with an elbow nudge, "Pathetic is having them nearly every day for almost a year."

It was Jeb's turn to watch her, as she took in the scenery. "Do you still have them?"

Two northern mockingbirds wrestled each other mid air, putting on a display of aerodynamics in front of them.

Iylah shook her head, "Not since I've started reading the Bible."

That was part of the change she became aware of but couldn't quite understand yet. It brought her great peace to read the wisdom and revelation penned thousands of years before her existence, pointing to a God who cared enough to reveal himself in them.

"I should say your Bible, actually." Removing her eyes from the horizon ahead, she placed them back on Jeb intently taking her in. "Why did you give it to me?" A question she always wondered but never asked.

He shrugged, "You were looking for answers."

"Where do you go to find your answers?" Another question flew out unexpectedly.

His eyes narrowed skeptically at Iylah, "Did my Mom put you up to this?"

Amused by his suspicion of her genuine intrigue, a heartfelt laugh as she threw her head back ripped through her body. It felt good to laugh. The days where her humor was dulled with pain were slowly becoming obsolete.

"Kathy did no such thing. That was all me. I'm just curious."

"Right," he played around gently with their entwined fingers. Neither one of them dared to let go. "Iylah?"

"Yes, Jeb?"

The tensing of his hand alerted her of whatever serious statement or question would come next. She braced herself for it.

"What happened with Stefan?"

She hadn't really told him the full story. All he was cognizant of were the bits Eric Mane divulged. She credited him for not asking sooner.

"The whole story?"

He nodded, shifting closer to her until they were knee to knee, thigh to thigh and shoulder to shoulder. The contact awoke her to embrace how she rather enjoyed feeling him close. It came a shining second to wearing his flannel shirt, even beside a busy highway. Inhaling the pine and mint oozing from his skin and onto its fabric, made her ache for more moments like these than she'd been willing to admit.

Taking a breath, she inhaled that same scent for courage.

"After my mom died, I didn't want to stick around because everything reminded me of her—so I hopped from country to country avoiding anything that made me pay attention to the massive hole she left. I did different stints in Europe and I landed in Germany two years ago. We met in some random club in Berlin, owned by one of his friends. He came and introduced himself."

The memories of that particular night remained vague at best.

"He would take me to all these exclusive spots, always knowing someone there. I fell for his charm, his lifestyle matching mine and the edge of danger he danced on, amongst other things."

She didn't want to mention the intimate parts of their relationship for fear of the shame it would spark.

"One night we were in a VIP backroom with people he said he did business with. I never asked what sort of business he did 'cause frankly I know no better businessman than my father so it didn't impress me. I was drinking Cuba Libre."

The scenes laced the front of her mind, feeling recent and near, knotting up the butterflies in her stomach, killing their flight.

"He was sitting next to me having a small argument with one guy over how much he was willing to pay for a business deal. Before I knew it, the argument escalated, he stood up at the table with a gun, and shot away at the guys in front of him—"

A rogue tear slid down her cheek, she quickly wiped it away.

"He didn't stop till he ran out of bullets. I'll never forget the disgusting satisfaction on his face. He enjoyed it. I ran out, but he sent his thugs to get me and I barely made it out of the club before they pounced on me. I smacked my head on the pavement knocking myself out and woke up in his bed with a concussion and IV drip attached to me."

Another tear found its way down the side of her face.

"Iylah, did he—" Jeb's voice caught struggling to get the thought out, he cleared his throat, "Did he hurt you?"

Shaking her head, remembering the fear taunting and gripping her that morning when she woke up naked in his bed. Her bottom lip trembled at the memory of it.

"He kept me holed up there for a couple of weeks. Eventually I escaped through his garbage shoot and contacted the police. We went to trial pretty quickly, and I testified against him. He was supposed to get thirty-five years in prison." She exhaled sharply in a bid to release the induced panic threatening to override her resolve, recognising the terror Stefan rained on her life ever since.

Jeb's attention remained on her.

"I'm sorry I got you and your family into this mess." She searched the piercing eyes looking back at her, asking for forgiveness for the part she played in his world spiraling.

"I'm sorry I got you into mine." He lightly touched his forehead against hers.

Her eyes shut, willing the tears away—not succeeding. She heard him take a measured breath in, before the cushioning of his lips gently met hers. Without second guessing it she reciprocated. Iylah clutched at the fabric of his t-shirt in her hands, drawing her body closer to his—confessing internally how she'd thought about this moment more times than she should have. He held her face in his hands, fanning embers of suppressed longing, relishing the feel of her under his touch. His lips searched hers for whatever his heart yearned for. Gently at first, until neither one of them could deny the new desire consuming them both. Each kiss got firmer and fervent. Caught up in each other until air lacked. Iylah pulled back ever so slightly, breathless, her heart reeling in the euphoria of their shared kiss. A tenderness engulfed his eyes, one she'd never seen before—a tenderness for her. Its presence set her whole body off in goosebumps.

Jeb pulled away, dropping his gaze from hers, just in time for her to see a flash of regret appear. The fire in her belly ceased, replaced with the familiar tendrils of shame.

"Sorry—" He cleared his throat, shifting uncomfortably in place. "I shouldn't have done that." Frowning, he avoided her eyes, shutting his own, clenching his jaw.

The euphoria that once took over her being, subsided faster than she would have liked. Unsure what to do next, Iylah stood, wanting to quicken the pace of the disappointment sinking in so she could be over and done with this scene.

"We should probably head back to the house."

Not waiting for his response, her feet walked away from the crime scene before them, towards the car, her clogs in hand.

The scene where it felt possible to let someone in again. The scene where it scared them both to do so.

Jeb

Jeb opened the zipper of the tent, inspecting it for any sticking. Standing up from the ten minutes he just spent ensuring the boys backyard camping included a secure tent, he rubbed the back of his neck—the knot in his chest begging to be acknowledged. Pushing a long breath out, he slumped himself in one of the lawn chairs. The background noise from inside the house filtered through the night, adding to the buzz emanating in his head.

Clutching at his head with both hands, the recollection of the smooth plumpness of her lips against his, riddled his stomach with a fieriness he couldn't put out. The way she succumbed to his touch, sent his mind wondering what the entirety of her felt like to embrace without space or caution between them. His curiosity led him to do it. No, he couldn't blame his actions on that. She saw him, down to the fear shaking up his core. She comforted him with a care he hadn't known in what felt like accumulating years. The boundary line crossed with no way to forget kissing the woman who crept up on him and knocked on the bolted iron door of his heart.

What have you done, Jeb?

The screen door creaked, alerting him to a new presence in the backyard. He peered over his shoulder, the outdoor garden lights strung overhead dully illuminating his sister's figure as she approached him. A wave of disappointment rode ashore over his shoulders.

Had he been expecting Iylah?

The car ride home held a quiet pensiveness, coupled with a fresh tension that had him grasping onto straws of self control—while Iylah sat at the wheel, avoiding any point of connection with him. She couldn't get further away from him quick enough when they arrived back to a full house and to an awkward introduction to Laura, his little sister.

"Interesting woman you brought back." Laura placed herself next to her older brother. "Did you know she smokes? Having a good ol' puff out the front as we speak."

"She's trying to quit." The knowledge of what happened between them causing a lapse in her resolve to stop smoking, sunk his heart. The peppery taste of her mouth from nicotine gum, coming back to him. "You know, you didn't exactly give her the friendliest welcome? What was that about?"

Jeb addressed the apprehensive coolness Laura extended towards Iylah upon meeting her. Ever protective of her family, Laura held a distrusting front that eventually dissolved once someone proved themselves worthy of her trust. A trait she'd carried since they were children—one she used especially around Jeb's prospective girlfriends. She seemed to do the same here with Iylah.

"Are we forgetting dear brother, that you've been away for four years without so much as a postcard? Then you appeared with a stray woman—"

"She's not a stray woman, Laura—" Jeb grimaced at her description of Iylah, "She just needed a place to go—I'm assuming Mom already told you?"

"She didn't have to. Did my research, thanks to Google." She crossed her legs, settling herself in next to him.

Jeb groaned, preparing himself for the onslaught of questions to come from Laura's supposed research. "You shouldn't believe everything you read on the internet, Laura."

"Never mind her. Jeb—" her hand placed on his forearm, a meekness she rarely possessed made him glance over at his sister's question riddled face. "Where have you been?"

Her delicate question pried at his already falling apart edges, bringing his absence from their lives in the spotlight once again. The last time he'd spoken to his sister via text message was over three months ago, wishing him a happy birthday. Remembering the day wasn't hard—Dawn made sure of it. The day she'd driven off without them, after accusing Jeb of flirting with Iylah when they bumped into her mid-hike. The day enough had become loud enough for him.

His shoulders sank, a swell of disgrace plaguing him, triggering his chest to tighten. He couldn't go through another panic attack again—the threat of it shooting cold chills along his arms. Retreating his arm away from Laura's hand, he fought to not look away from her worried gaze.

"I can't talk about it right now, Laura." His jaw worked hard at keeping the oncoming panic away, stopping a quiver from setting in. "There's just a lot going on. I need time to figure it out."

"I know most of it has a lot to do with Dawn, Jeb—it's pretty obvious. Iylah told Mom that the divorce got finalized today—is this true?" Laura's hazel eyes peered at her brother, the same way their mom's did when she needed to get to the bottom of whatever affair bothered her.

Jeb nodded, his throat coated with the sorrow the last few years delivered at his doorstep.

"Oh, honey—"

"I don't need pity Laura—"

"Jeb, I'm your sister. It's not pity. I've missed you—we all have." Under the dim lights, the glistening of her tears was hard to unsee. It thickened his guilt.

He hadn't considered how his absence created a void in the tight-knit family he grew up in. The dire need to survive the sham of a marriage he'd found himself in, trumped being a part of anything to do with Clovis and the life he ran so far away from. He couldn't explain all that to Laura. Any explanation he offered fell insignificant to the hurt in her eyes.

All he could do at this moment was hang his head—the day's events growing heavier. Laura's arm coiled around his neck embracing him, not asking anything more. He let her, tension coursing through him to keep himself from becoming a blubbering mess. The screen door creaked again signaling another presence in the backyard. Laura didn't let go, holding onto him firmly and quietly. He caught the sweet scent comprising of vanilla notes his mom always wore, just as she positioned herself on the wooden arm of the lawn chair he sat in. Her arms wrapped around her two children—multiple prayers spurning in her. Another presence joined them. Sis dad's familiar hand found a spot on Jeb's back, soothing him with a still firm placement.

Squeezing his eyes shut, the triggered tears clogging up space in his throat, a rousing exhale escaped his body leaving him weak but surrounded by the people he knew he'd miserably failed.

"Welcome back home, son."

twenty-one

Iylah

She pulled at the metal square tubing she measured out, causing it to bend in her direction. One foot stood on the end of the tubing laid on the concrete tiled courtyard, at the back of the church building. Her work-gloved hands pulled the other end up and into an arched bend. One half of the decorative wrought iron arch she was making—the other half, lay flat on the ground. Giving one last tug, she created the desired curve for her arch. Iylah laid it down on top of the other, preparing to measure out some more square tubing for another designed frame.

A wave of faintness hit her. Out of breath, she bent over, putting her hands on her knees, head dropped allowing the wave to pass. Iylah wiped the skin stinging sweat on her brow with the back of her arm. The white tank top she wore under a camo linen shirt came in handy when the heat set in.

The thought to pack for heavy duty work upon leaving New York hadn't really crossed her mind, so her denim shorts and trainers sufficed to get the job done.

Exhaustion gripped at her determination to finish what she started. Silly her thought burying herself, preparing for the gala would take her overthinking mind off her muddled emotions. All it did was wear down her physical ability to rationalize. She blew the threat of tears away, standing back up to resume her work.

Five hours went by since Kathy and the planning committee ladies left—Iylah hadn't stopped. If she stopped, it meant she needed to address the disarrayed desires within her.

The desire to no longer be on the run, to confront her past head on, to live a life of stability. The desire to have Jeb in it past brief moments of impassioned embraces. She wanted more. No longer being on the run meant taking to task the wounds left by death. To confront her past meant getting Stefan back in prison and out of her life for good, the constant need to look back over her shoulder gone. To be with, Jeb meant to be with Tylor too—if that's what he wanted.

The idea of being a mere timely distraction from his own frazzled life, forced her jaw to squeeze. Perhaps they were two broken souls longing for a place to land and they brushed past each other mid journey. That thought brought humiliation, and it weighed her down into a pathetic mess.

Don't be afraid or discouraged, huh? That's turning out fantastic.

She winced at how she handled it all, by doing what she did best. Avoiding everything at all costs including Jeb. So here she hid, sweating it out in the courtyard of a small church in Clovis, California.

Did her avoidance do more harm than good?

She needed to call Lena. Lena would tell her what to do after I told you so's were said.

Iylah dropped the bandsaw onto the makeshift table she made of ingenuity. Reaching for her phone in her back pocket, ready to speed dial Lena, she realized another presence. Her hyper-vigilance kicked in, head rapidly pivoting around and spotting Jeb standing at the entrance of the courtyard.

"My gosh Jeb!" Startled by his silent entry she put her hands to her waist, her ears plagued with her heartbeat. "You scared me."

"Sorry." He looked freshly showered, his hair in a wet low bun, a khaki shirt on, cargo pants and Birkenstocks to top off his always laid back aesthetic.

He really does age like a fine wine from the South of France.

"I assumed you would have heard the creaking door."

Tucking her phone back into her pocket, she cast her eyes back onto the table where her task lay.

"What are you doing here?" The sound of the heartbeat in her ears ceased, but its racing rhythm didn't. This is what he did to her.

He approached her, the closer he got the surge of movement in her stomach increased. "Mom sent me to come get you." He stood beside her, his proximity sprouting a new type of heat over her.

She didn't dare lock eyes with him.

"That and you can't avoid me forever Iylah. There's only so much space in that house."

"I'm not avoiding you." She kept all her focus on the tubing at hand, ready to saw away any excess—til Jeb gently grabbed her hand, halting any chance of distraction.

"Stop. Please." He was close enough for his shampoo to get hold of her sense of smell.

Pine and mint.

She scanned his hand on top of hers and back up at him. His pleading stormy eyes bust open the memory of their kiss two days ago. The way the skin on her face felt the chilling heat from his fingertips when he held it close to his. The brief moment she forgot where they were—his inquisitive lips on hers erased everything else going on. Denying how incredible it felt to share the same breath and yearning, brought the realisation of every kiss she'd ever had holding an echoing emptiness. This was full, real and all consuming.

Until Jeb's regret made her second guess it all.

"I know this is confusing," Jeb sighed, reaching for the right words to say, "The last thing I want is for you to feel uncomfortable. I just—" He looked away and Iylah recognised the same struggle she fought internally written across his face. "Honestly, it's a little hard to think straight when I'm around you."

"Why did you kiss me?" Iylah removed the work glove she donned, unsure where the anger building in her stemmed from.

"I know it was a stupid thing to do." Jeb rubbed his eyes with the heel of his palms. "I wasn't thinking straight—"

"So it was a mistake?" Shame knocked again, making it a concentrated effort for her to breathe.

They surveyed one another, revealing the tenderness in his watching of her. The same emotion she saw after the infamous kiss.

"I wanted to kiss you Iylah. I have since the night at the bar. That's not the stupid part. The stupid part is the awful timing. The absolutely unfortunate timing of when you turned up in my life. I don't regret kissing you." As if compelled by something invisible, he stepped towards her. "I don't think I have anything to offer you right now—I mean—you deserve more than I can give."

Iylah inhaled tentatively, the recognition of the truth in his words resonating with her own dilemma. She didn't have much to give either. All of it still broken, awaiting excavation to find what could be salvaged.

You need to be an adult about this Iylah.

A silence fell between them, filling in the distance separating their tense bodies standing in the courtyard. Iylah aggressively shut down the urge to reach for his hand and to smooth out the crease on his brow from worrying.

"You deserve a lot more than I can give too." She labored to get the words out past the disappointment, playing it close to her chest.

Jeb gave an incredulous laugh, his hand gruffly scratching the stubble around his jaw. "I know neither one of us wants a fling. I don't want to waste your time and I don't want to mess up what you've got going on with—you know? God."

"Why do you think you would mess that up?" She frowned.

"You really want me to spell it out for you?" His words carried the underlying tone she guessed lay in his heart. He shook his head, "Let's just say I don't know how it would work out—look—I think we should just be friends."

Iylah witnessed the cartilage in his throat bob as he swallowed the real reason down.

She detested the words edging their way out of her mouth, yet she knew they had to be said. "Friends it is."

She caught the glaring sadness in his eyes. "This oddly feels like a break-up before we've even had a chance."

She stepped back from him, the weight of what he spoke displaying how much care developed between them. She wanted that chance—she also wanted to not taint it with the things that chased after her.

The pressing of his jaw and yearning in his eyes said far more than his next words.

"C'mon, let's get you back to the house."

In that second Jeb now possessed a piece of her heart and she didn't care to claim it back.

∽ ∾

The drive to the house carried a solemn tension between them. Stuck in their thoughts of the other, not knowing entirely what to say but understanding what needed to be done. Sitting next to Jeb in the car drove Iylah equally sad and equally besotted with no margin in between to explore the last one. The background track to their current misery, a steady stream of unspoken longings the entire twenty-minute ride.

Iylah wondered what was to be said of shattered hopes, because hers remained in such a state.

What if none of this worked out the way she wanted it? What if these brief glimpses of a promised future amounted to nothing? Waking up six months from now still hiding away from a menacing past? And Jeb—was she okay with nothing more happening, despite wanting to show him he too was worth caring for?

When they did eventually arrive, neither one of them moved out of the car, its engine humming to silence. She couldn't move, didn't want to. Mustering the courage, she left. Jeb remained in the car. Iylah said her quick hi's to everyone in the house, including Laura whom she was certain had a profound disdain for her. Iylah didn't care. Being disliked wasn't something new to her. She excused herself from dinner with the measly lie of needing an early night sleep. Thankfully, no one pushed further, the ruckus of the three young boys took up all their attention instead.

Iylah perched herself at the edge of the bed, the day showered off and rinsed, brushing her wet curls, her mustard robe pulled shut tight in an effort to bring a level of cozy comfort. It wasn't working. Her heart kept threatening to sink out of her body.

Am I doing the right thing? I didn't expect this to suck so bad. God, what do I do now? What do I do now? I don't want to live in hiding anymore. I really want to experience that new life I read about.

Deciding that her hair needed a break from getting the brunt of her frustrations, she put the brush down next to her and just sat. Sat staring at the fluffy rug under her feet with more tread in it than when she first arrived. Four weeks and three days since she arrived seeking refuge from her past, now here she was, her past preventing her future. Surely she couldn't just sit around waiting for something to happen? Waiting for Stefan to leave the country for her life to continue, only marginally free until the next time he made his presence known. So much he stole from her with no regard and no remorse. To what end?

A knock at the door shot her up onto her feet and out of a moment of existential thought.

"Only me." Kathy's sing song voice partially shattered Iylah's hope of Jeb being at the bedroom door.

"Come in." Iylah cleared the lump sitting against the walls of her throat, checking her robe to avoid indecency.

"Just coming in to see if there's anything you need?" Kathy walked in with her ever-present smile, closing the door behind her, kindness adorning her eyes.

Iylah pondered if she always wore such a smile—welcoming, warm and full of everything that made life enjoyable.

Iylah shook her head, pushing wet curls behind her ear, "Just some sleep." She attempted a feeble smile. "Sorry, I skipped out on dinner."

"No, no, don't apologize. You and Jeb seem to have the same stomach tonight." Standing before Iylah, Kathy's hands fidgeted with the hem of her peach blouse. "May I?" She motioned to the bed wanting to take a seat.

"Oh, yeah—" Iylah moved her hairbrush out of the way, "Totally."

Kathy sat herself down on the bed and Iylah followed suit, not sure what was going to happen next. Whatever did, she trusted Kathy enough to know it to be worthwhile. She mustered a great magnitude of reservation to not burst into tears under the motherly gaze Kathy held.

With a knowing smile Kathy asked, "Well?"

"I'm sick of hiding, Kathy." Iylah exhaled, the threat of unraveling tears no longer a priority—she let them come. "I want to explore a life free from fear, and past the way I've always lived. I can see it and feel it. I'm changing, the way I'm seeing the world is changing. I'm starting to get excited about living, really living and not merely getting by in between panic attacks—which I haven't had in an entire month by the way. I know Jesus offers me new life in Him and with Him if I believe and turn away from living apart from Him. I believe, I really do. Every time I read the Bible, I start to understand, and it excites me. And these dreams I sometimes have, the pieces are making sense. I just can't seem to shake off this idiot who held my life on ransom for the last nine months." She let it out unafraid of how she sounded, and feeling the relief of wording it out. "That and I'm pretty sure I have feelings for your son." A helpless shrug took over her shoulders, using the sleeve of her robe to remove the residue of her unleashed emotions from her face.

Kathy quietly chuckled at Iylah's last revelation.

"Gorgeous girl, I'm afraid that's the tension you will always feel in this life even as you walk with Jesus. It's a good thing He tells us to give Him our burdens, to let Him iron it out however He sees fit for our good." She placed her hand on Iylah's, "You are changing, you will continue to change and you have to be courageous enough to step into that change, if it means letting go of all the old haggard things, keeping you prisoner and even being bold enough to confront your past. You can't do it on your own steam, but you have a Helper at your disposal. You need to take the next few steps for the rest of your life with Jesus. And as for my son—" She giggled, "Darling, he will be okay. You both will be. There's just some loose ends that need severing."

Iylah swore a sparkle in Kathy's eyes appeared with her last remark. Did she know something?

Without another word, a gentle pat on the hand, Kathy stood up and made her way out, just as swiftly as she came in.

Iylah flung herself back on the bed, overwhelm settling in her chest.

Help me, please. Show me what needs to be done.

twenty-two

"Blessed is the man who walks not in the counsel of the wicked, nor stands in the way of sinners, nor sits in the seat of scoffers; but his delight is in the law of the Lord, and on his law he meditates day and night. He is like a tree planted by streams of water that yields its fruit in its season, and its leaf does not wither. In all that he does, he prospers."

▢ Psalm▢ ▢ 1▢ :▢ 1▢ -▢ 3▢ ▢

Heavenly Father my deepest desire is for the children You've given me on this Earth to know You. Though I struggle and fall short in instructing them in the way they should go, I ask that You would reveal yourself to them. I ask that You walk with my youngest gift, Iylah. She is a free spirit, full of energy and joy. Would You draw near to her in times of trouble? Deliver her from all evil that would set out to harm her. May her life be filled with Your love even when she can't see it clearly. Would You send people to be your love to her? Give her the courage to stand against all fear; grant her wisdom to navigate the paths life would take her on. Lead and plant her On Your paths for the glory of Your name and the testimony of Your goodness. In every season of her life, bless her and cause her to flourish and thrive in all circumstances. I pray for the family she would one day have, the man You would send to be hers and her to be his—would he be a man of honor, a man who You call Yours and one who would love her heart and protect it always. And when she strays, I thank You that You are faithful

to continue pursuing her. Keep her in Your palm. Show Yourself to her, that she may
receive Your gift of salvation. I ask this in Your name, Jesus.

   Your daughter

   Lillian

Jeb

They put the last of the dark wooden pews down, among all the others piled
in the back room. Jeb watched his dad stretch out his back again with no luck.

"Dad, I don't think you should lift anything more." Jeb followed Frank's big
strides out of the backroom, heading to the main chapel where more things
needed to be carried.

"It will be fine," Frank dismissed Jeb with a wave of his hand.

"It won't be if you severely injure yourself."

They entered the general meeting area of the Chapel, where many other
busybodies were moving something or seeking Iylah's guidance. She would
efficiently and graciously prompt them for probably the hundredth time. Jeb
witnessed it happen thrice.

"Nothing God can't fix."

Jeb rolled his eyes at the stubbornness of his father and the notion of leaving
it all up to God. He remained positively sure God valued wisdom too.

"I heard you roll your eyes." Frank called back at him, making his way across
the large Chapel space.

Jeb forgot how vast this space was. High ceilings displayed wooden beams,
arched windows lining the white outer wall, allowing their east facing ways to
stream in sunlight. Light bounced around freely in the Chapel, making it the
heavenly place it meant to mirror. Naturally as a child, spaces like this were
endless grounds to hide and seek—standing there now as an adult, its grandeur
was still clear.

A buzz moved around in anticipation of the gala two days away. It was all
that occupied most everyone's time, including some of his. That is in between
hunting for a new place of residence for him and Tylor, finding a new job,
getting Tylor enrolled into a new school before summer ended, mending his

relationship with said son and gaining a new car. Not to mention navigating the complicated waters between him and Iylah.

Two out of that list were checked off. Tylor had a new school to go to and Jeb the new owner of a gunmetal 2017 Ford Expedition. The other items on the list looked like they required more time.

Hands on his hips, he followed the movement around him, his eyes eventually fixating on the one whom he wanted to give attention to the most. Never mind that nearly two weeks ago his days got brighter and darker at the same time. No amount of processing made it easier being around her.

Iylah stood unaware of his current gandering, with a clipboard in hand, the top of her nose pinched in concentration looking down at the plans she spent a couple of nights drawing up at his Mom's kitchen table. Her curls flowed to her shoulders in continuous circling waves. The red and black crescent-patterned satin dress with thin straps she wore ended by her elegant ankles and opened up to reveal her slender back. She mesmerized him daily.

Since their fairly upfront conversation, they'd maintained a friendship of lighthearted humor, a few minutes spent alone here and there, shielded behind avoidance of allowing any genuine desires to come to the surface. Her time occupied with all things Living River summer gala and a stream of endless phone calls she seemed to get nearly every day. Curiosity got the better of him one night, and he asked her if everything was okay—a simple 'it will be' with a rather temperate smile was the non-reassuring response he got.

Jeb soon discovered he didn't like being kept in the dark by her. A sense of entitlement to her world showed its head, and he worked hard to silence it.

Just as hard as he worked on making his panic attacks nonexistent, after a second one nearly took him out again during his morning run yesterday. No space is safe anymore from the greedy hands of anxiety. This time he confided in his dad, who directed him firstly to prayer and secondly to therapy. He was yet to do the second one; the first one came more naturally to him than he'd anticipated, given his track record with God.

One thing he held great certainty in—God heard every prayer, even from straying souls like himself.

"Pick up your jaw, son." Frank walked past carrying the solid wooden pulpit he used on Sundays, with enough time to give walk-by counsel to Jeb.

"Right." He snapped himself out of his daze and proceeded over to Iylah for further instructions, like everyone else did. "Direct me, please."

"Sure." She took a brief look around. "I think we can now do my favorite part—bringing the frames in." She did a little hop and jig of excitement, extracting a grin from Jeb. "There's that smile."

Seeing the mixed bag of complexities Iylah was, tugged at his desire to know every part of her makeup. To sit and study her until his heart was content in being an expert on how she operated. Though hollowed by a past worth trembling at, she filled in those empty spots as she created and enjoyed the birth of her idea.

It astounded him to watch.

"You're cute." The problem with trying to stifle the heart—your words always betrayed it.

"I try." Becoming aware again, she tore her view back to her clipboard. "Hey, is it okay if I get a ride back to the house with you later?"

"Yeah, sure. Just let me know when." Immediately he looked forward to it. "I'll start getting the frames in."

"Thanks, Jeb." Her eyes met his, accompanied by a sudden gloominess in them despite her smiling lips.

"No problem." A sinking motion rode in heavily through his gut as he turned to walk away.

He didn't like being in the dark when it came to her.

~ ~

She put her leather rucksack at her feet, tugging her passenger door shut. "Phew!" She let her breath out, leaning back into the seat, her eyes shutting. "That was a lot of work."

Jeb started the engine, pulling on his seatbelt. "You're really good at this. Can't say I've ever been to galas, but I am looking forward to seeing everything you designed come together."

He staved off his heightened awareness of her nearness to him. The rapid fire in his stomach was harder to ignore as the scent of Jasmine filled his car.

"Learnt from my mother and many years of her hosting my father's business partners and parties." She did her belt up. "She was fantastic at hosting people, even if she didn't like them."

"I'm sure she'd be proud of you if she saw all the work you put in." He put his car in reverse, pulling out of the narrow driveway that led behind the church, hoping he hadn't pried at an open wound.

Truthfully, he was proud of her.

"I hope so." She spoke quietly. "Do you think those in heaven get to watch us slum it down here? I haven't really wrapped my head around the concept of heaven yet." Her question was laced with genuine innocence.

Jeb focused on the oncoming traffic zipping past before he made a right turn onto the main highway. "Well, I'm pretty sure there's a verse in the Bible that talks about a cloud of witnesses cheering us on." He shrugged, "I could be wrong."

He knew he wasn't. Bible verses were coming back to him at the oddest of times lately. Once upon a time he'd memorized them astutely.

"I like that." She mused.

A lull filled the car between them.

"Can we take a drive to the river?"

He turned his head to watch the side of her face, unsure what to make of her request. "Are we sure that's a good idea?"

The combination of unease and hope drove co-pilot in him.

The river held secrets and a bittersweet experience of what couldn't be. Did they really need to revisit it? The mental whirlwind she spun in him every time he thought of kissing her wore him out enough already.

She chuckled tiredly, peering over at him through her dark lashes. "It will be fine Jeb."

There was that statement again.

She reached down into her rucksack, pulling out a hair band and began mounting her hair up into her infamous bun, revealing her long neck. Jeb shook his head with an unsure, lopsided smile.

He hoped it would be fine.

By the time they got to the river, the sun had set over it. Lighting it up in sherbet orange hues with the ball of fire descending into the horizon. They sat at the same picnic table, in the same positions—with a little more distance between them. Conversation kept coming, and so did the laughter. It was easy for both of them to be this way with each other. Until it wasn't.

Jeb contemplated the woman sitting next to him, taking in the remaining sunset light. "Iylah, you're beautiful." He couldn't help himself. His sentiment and appreciation of her beauty too hard to keep down. He had more to say, but he thought better of it.

She looked at him, a timid smile showing itself in the corners of her lips. The sadness washed over again.

She turned away, attempting to hide it.

"What's going on?" He asked, studying her fiddling hands with her head down.

"I'm going to Seattle on Sunday morning." She raised her head up again to face him.

"I don't understand." A frown creased his forehead.

From his knowledge, Seattle is where she grew up and where her dad lived.

"I've been talking with Eric Mane and Lena for the last couple of weeks about my options to end this whole mess with Stefan. I'm tired of hiding and running, Jeb." Her shoulders sank, the weariness she tried so hard to keep away, evident. "The only way to get Stefan out of the country is to get him deported on criminal charges and banned from ever coming back to the United States."

The density of her revelation turned his stomach. He got the impression there was more to it than what she disclosed. He waited for it with baited breath.

"I'm going to use myself as bait. If he's here for me, he will come find me, and when he does, he can get charged for breaking his restraining order, possibly getting him back in prison in Germany." Even as she said the harrowing plan, her demeanor remained composed—almost too resolute. Her mind was made up.

Jeb's response came out hot and charged. "Are you serious?"

He hopped down from the table, finding himself standing in front of Iylah.

"You can't do that! That's a terrible idea!" His voice raised, blood rushing profusely to his temples. "What if he hurts you? What if he kills you, Iylah? Isn't that why you left New York? So he couldn't get to you?"

"Jeb, I have to do this. I want to have a life out of hiding—" Her voice matched his. "Don't you get it? I've spent most of my adult life running from grief, and now running from this man. I just want a shot at doing life right, and I can't deal with the idea of him searching for me."

"What if he kills you?" What wasn't she understanding? Surely she would see this wasn't an option if he stated the harsh reality.

"I'm still going to have surveillance and protection from the FBI. If he gets that close, they will step in. It's a risk I'm willing to take." She skirted around the blatant reality of his question.

"Iylah! What if he kills you?" He ran his fingers through his hair, giving it a frustrated tussle. "You seem to forget, it's something he enjoys doing."

"There is no other option." She shrugged tearfully. "If there were, don't you think I would take it?"

"For crying out loud!" He threw his hands in the air, exasperated by her oblivion to the sheer magnitude of possibly losing her life. "This is the best one?"

His anger rendered him speechless, a thousand scenarios running through his mind and neither of them ending the way he wanted them to.

They stared at each other in the little light left of the day, strangely mimicking the changing landscape between them right now.

"I can't believe this is happening." In his disbelief, he paced up and down trying to digest the disconcerting news.

She was leaving.

In all the days gone by, he hadn't prepared himself for this. He got caught up in the presence of Iylah; it didn't occur to him it was all a temporary situation. The strength in his legs threatened to give out at the very thought of something happening to her. Sitting himself down, he took in breaths, holding his head in his hands, the known tightening of his chest he'd learnt to be wary of, approaching.

She said nothing further—her muffled sniffles said it all. He didn't trust himself to say anything that wouldn't blow them out of the water—measuring his words as he measured his breath. He recalled the many times he had wanted things to be different for her. To cast off all restraint and simply have the life she deserved—a free life. She wanted to take a shot at it, but he didn't like it. Did he think he would be the one to save her? The one to give her that life?

You need to let her do this.

That utterance halted every other loud voice. Wiping the mixture of anger and panic from his eyes, he stood up again, this time taking her hands into his. The impending darkness hid the details of their features.

"I desperately wish I could swap places with you." He confessed.

"I wouldn't ever ask you to do that."

Jeb scoffed, watching her hands in his, safety within reach. "I would still do it, anyway."

It no longer came as a shock how solid his care for her towered. He accepted it for what it was—the hurdle being presented now wasn't an unfamiliar one. Watching someone he cared about risk their life and there being nothing he could do about it. The recurring theme was not lost on him.

"I can't stop you from doing this, can I?"

Iylah shook her head, sorrow spread across her striking features matching what pumped through his distraught body.

He needed to let her go.

God, if you're still listening, would you keep her? You're better at this than I am.

twenty-three

Lylah

Kathy and Iylah stood side by side at the entrance of the Chapel. Their eyes roamed across it, up and down from floor to ceiling—taking in the finished work of Iylah's creative and expensive vision. The many hands who volunteered their hours and ears to instruction were no longer there as the day approached the night. The Astons and Iylah the only ones left picking up any remnants of flowers or invisible string ahead of tomorrow night.

"My goodness!" Kathy's eyes widened in sheer amazement at what she beheld.

The entire Chapel space flowed with an array of various colors of Zinnias arranged in whatever manner the frame they were on dictated. From the entrance where they stood, on either side of them—nine foot metal frames rose from the floor towards the ceiling, curving overhead, covered in Scarlet Flame, Zinderella Peach and White Zinnia's intermingled with lush green foliage of the Ruscus Israeli variety, sprinkled with some Babies-breath.

Iylah humbly admitted her limitations when it came to the floral arrange-
ments. As it turned out, one of her nemeses knew a thing or two about them,
proceeding to give Iylah and fifteen other ladies from the church an impromptu
workshop. The result came with lots of laughs when clumsy fingers struggled,
the final product of it all was what she and Kathy were taking in now.

A Garden of Hope of their own.

Frames upon frames she'd spent blistering hot days toiling over were covered
in vibrant and bountiful blooms, placed strategically in spaces where their natural
beauty shone. Surprisingly, the frames held up well—her grip on things, not so
much.

Iylah was silently positive she had given herself arthritis in her right hand. It
was entirely worth it to see the glistening in Kathy's ocean blue eyes.

"I don't know how you pulled it off, but you did." The smile that spread on
Kathy's face was unmatched, filling Iylah's heart with a rich satisfaction.

It felt good to do things for others. It felt even better to have people to do
things for. A pang of remorse dug its sharp arrowhead in, with the epiphany of
how selfishly she lived. She didn't want to go back to that—couldn't go back to
that. She didn't want to go back to being so isolated. Without hesitation, Iylah
put her arm around Kathy's shoulders, drawing herself in for a side embrace. She
most definitely was going to miss this.

"I'm going to miss you, Kathy." She confessed, the realisation creeping in, no
matter how viciously she fought against it.

Her mother was irreplaceable, but Kathy did a marvelous job of guiding Iylah's
Bambi-esque steps, and that was often.

"As am I, gorgeous girl." She squeezed Iylah's side, causing a teetering tear to
slide discreetly down Iylah's face. She swiped it away efficiently.

Iylah didn't count on her decision two weeks ago after a desperate prayer,
to rip at her heart so much. Not because of what lay ahead, but what she left
behind.

The morning smell of freshly brewed coffee each day awaited her rising on
the bedside table. The leisurely mid-mornings spent in one of the lawn chairs in
the backyard. Laughter abounded at the dinner table from whatever story told
to embarrass Jeb. Sunday mornings sitting on the cushion-lined pews while her
heart learnt new things and questioned what it knew. The conversation of a
ten-year-old filled with the most intriguing questions. The safety of being cared
for with no conditions to meet. The intent eyes of a man that bore to her core

with their tenderness towards her. The certainty she would ever experience these things again was slim and close to none, but she thanked God she had.

She couldn't avoid what needed to be done. Lena called it irresponsible and a trauma response—she really enjoyed throwing that around. Eric Mane called it a risky plan that could yield final justice or a problematic end. And Iylah? She called it a step of faith and courage, invoked by reading her mother's most recent journal entry and the assurance that if death were to be her end, she wasn't afraid. If it were to end in Stefan not seeing another inch of America ever again, and her breath to fully be released, she would not wait.

Living in captivity boded far more treacherously than losing the breath in her lungs. Each night as she wrote her solemn fears and offered them up to God, her memory jogged back to the Good Shepherd, and she clung onto beckoning hope, they would be side by side as the valley approached.

"Everything okay?" Frank's voice from behind drew them both out of their emotional appreciation of a newly formed bond, causing them both to turn around.

"Yes, dear. We're merely taking in the fruit of everyone's labor." Kathy beamed up at her husband of forty-eight years.

When Jeb mentioned how long his parents had been wed, her disbelief didn't hide itself. Jeb responded by saying that people to genuinely falling in love and staying in love for the rest of their lives was not an impossible task. He said he still believed it to be true despite his own life experience. Iylah wondered quietly how things between them would have played out if ex-wives and criminal ex-boyfriends were nonexistent. Which led to her own introspective question—did she share the sentiment?

Her relationships never stood stable enough to warrant the thought of a lifelong commitment such as marriage. Falling in love only happened to those who had their lives sorted out and in place, she thought. That was until the man staring back at her found himself in her Manhattan townhouse one early summer's day.

"You have done an amazing job, Iylah." Frank's aged gray eyes turned to her. "We could never thank you enough for this. This was definitely not in our humble budget."

Not knowing quite what to do with all this praise, Iylah clasped her hands over her chest, hoping the spotlight on her would soon dissipate. She caught Jeb's slight smirk before he averted his gaze to the car keys in his hand. The small smirk released relief in her. The first time today she witnessed any form of a smile on him. He wore a serious expression and a dent in his dipped brow each time she saw him, since the river.

She ruminated about what was on his mind. Dare she ask. She couldn't—scared of what he shared shredding at her heart once again, like his response did last night.

"I'm gonna go pick up the pizza for dinner." Jeb craned his neck, searching around for his mini-me, who spent most of his free time attached to his Nintendo Switch, undisturbed for the day. "Tylor! Let's go, buddy." On cue, Tylor popped out of somewhere still glued to his gaming. "I'll meet you guys back at the house."

And they were off.

Iylah's shoulders dropped along with her heart. The distance between them being intentional—it stung regardless of Iylah's knowledge of the necessity behind it. She left the day after tomorrow with no assurance of anything remaining the same and every indication her life would change further.

Maybe they were simply a summer thing born from proximity, shared struggles and nothing better to do.

She cleared her throat. "I'll go grab my bag." Excusing herself, she scurried off, a familiar tug gripping her chest.

Recalling the last time she experienced a panic attack—just before the plane took off from New York on their way to Clovis. Jeb hadn't noticed because she sat as far away from him as possible. She hadn't wanted him to see how broken she was.

Turns out she was still broken, just not as hopeless.

❧ ☙

The muffled sound of her phone ringing forced Iylah's head out from under the covers. The dimly lit room made it hard to see through half-closed eyes. Slight hints of the sunrise painted the walls through the drawn curtains. Purely by instinct, she searched for her phone on the bedside table. Grabbing it and struggling to see the name on the screen, she answered it, barely getting the words out.

"Yes?" Her sleep-drenched voice forwent pleasantries.

"Good morning to you too, sleepyhead." Her chirpiness caused Iylah to wince. "Why are you still in bed?"

"Because it is—" Iylah adjusted her eyes to read the time on her phone, "5:40. Lena. You're three hours ahead, remember?" She groaned, pulling the covers over her, the fan in the room doing its utmost to cool her exposed feet.

"Have you packed yet? Your flight leaves at midday tomorrow, right?" Lena's morning coffee had clearly kicked in.

"No, I have not packed yet." She half mumbled, "And I don't know, I'll have to check my emails."

"Yes, your flight is at midday. I checked it this morning." Lena stated with no room for argument. "I've spoken to Dad. He won't be home when you arrive, and he's been warned not to push you. When do you plan on telling him what's going on?"

"Never." Iylah tried to swallow away the taste of sleep in her mouth. She made a mental note to put an end to Lena's managing of her life. They were only three years apart—Lena with all her accolades and maturity wore those three years like they were ten.

"Iylah!"

"I'm joking. I'm joking." Now fully conscious, she propped herself upright in the bed, adjusting the fine strap of her yellow silk pajama top. "I'll tell him when I get the chance." No promises. "How are the girls?"

"Driving me nuts!" Lena confessed through a hushed tone. "Were we this terrible to Mom? The hormones, the drama, the judgment. It never ends!"

A sleepy, fond smile roused on Iylah's face. "I was. You were little Miss Perfect." And annoyingly so too.

"Then why am I getting your payback?"

"I don't have kids yet—"

"Yet? This is a new development." Lena's interest piqued at the revelation that tumbled out.

Throughout her twenties, Iylah vocally took a stand to disclose that kids were simply not on her agenda. Now, her twenties were close to ending, and her perspective changed.

The doorknob on Iylah's door turned ever so subtly. Iylah pulled the covers up to her chest, aware of her braless state. The door opened and in popped Kathy, robed up with curlers in her ash gray hair and a cup of coffee in hand.

"Only me." She whispered, tiptoeing in as if not to disrupt the way of things.

Iylah mouthed a thank you and watched her tiptoe out, just as quickly as she came.

Jeb sent Kathy in.

Iylah rubbed her eyes with a frown, pinching the bridge of her nose, a foreboding sitting in her empty stomach.

"Lena, I'll call you back. I've gotta go. Thanks for the stupidly early morning call."

"Start packing." She ordered, saying her goodbyes. "Call me before your flight tomorrow."

"I will not miss it—"

"Just call me. Love you. Bye." And she hung up.

Iylah scanned the steaming cup of coffee on the bedside table. Throwing herself back into the pillow, she prayed the day would go quickly.

Can you please make this easier, Jesus?

✄ ໑

Iylah adjusted the translucent, skinny glass vase standing tall and centre stage on one of the many tables strewn across the floor of the Chapel. She experimented with the minimal stems of Zinnias to make them not look so organized—naturally placed is what she went for. This being vase number sixty-seven, she adjusted.

Stepping away from the table, taking one last look over before guests arrived. She surveyed the ceiling where singular stems hung from invisible string, creating the desired effect of blooms raining down. Her stomach loose with nerves, hankering for a cigarette. The strongest one yet since the fateful night she lapsed.

I need to find my purse.

Unsure of the whereabouts of her purse, she scoured the tables within her proximity. Suddenly feeling self-conscious, she smoothed over the front of her dress, pacing in circles in her crystal-bowed black pumps. For whatever reason, she packed the impractical pair of heels while on the run from New York. Iylah now thanked herself for the foolish addition to her luggage. The dress she wore, a new purchase that arrived the week of the gala.

She opted for a navy blue off the shoulder gown, with ruche detailing draped from one end of her shoulder to the other. The belt accentuated her slim waistline and the curves of her hips, courtesy of all the ice cream she consumed over the summer. Its length grazed her heels, while each stride revealed just enough leg through the front slit. Her mother taught her how to dress for fundraisers—like a lady with a hint of spark and fire. Iylah always went for the fire, but now she understood the lady element of a woman's dress. Even if it cost more than most guests at this gala made in a month's wages.

There it is!

Iylah scurried towards her bordeaux patent leather clutch, sitting unattended next to the live band's instruments. A swift memory cruised to the forefront of her mind. This all felt familiar.

The need for things to go perfectly. The desire to be perfect. The notion that perfect was the only option. At every single prestigious event she attended since her pre-teen years with her parents, the unspoken but heavily implied rule of high society was perfection at all costs. Her mother chased after it at the prompting of her father, and soon enough Iylah caught wind of being part of the chase. Until she could no longer keep up. She could never keep up. She guessed that's when rebellion set in.

Blindly, her hands searched for the nicotine gum she had packed last minute, striding within her best current ability towards the ladies' bathroom. Thankfully, everyone was too busy laying out the buffet, rearranging the chairs or simply having a chat to notice her slowly losing the battle of her nerves.

She pushed the swinging door to reveal the empty ladies' bathroom. Throwing her clutch on the countertop, she gnawed away at the gum attempting to do her breath work, both hands now on her hips. Exhaling through her nose, inhaling through her mouth, Iylah's reflection stared back at her.

She couldn't remember when she had last taken a proper look at herself in the mirror. A timidity always present about what she would see back. The same image of an anxiety riddled, confused and angry woman would face her every time. This time a small gasp involuntarily escaped her.

Her recently salon-tended curls sat in an updo, with two tailored strands falling at each side of her face like a parted waterfall framing its best features. It framed her face and softened her striking eyes. Eyes that looked alive, not sunken despite the waves of anxiety she rode right now. She looked healthy, high cheekbones and all. In the afternoon, a makeup artist came by the house to spruce up her and Kathy's faces—Iylah's little treat for Kathy. Along with the tidy sum, she planned on donating anonymously tonight for the church's missionary funds.

I have not been given a spirit of fear or timidity; but I have been given a spirit of power, love and self-control.

Iylah practiced what Kathy taught her to do when the mind ran stories with intent for chaos. She repeated the verse a dozen times until vomiting wasn't a threat anymore.

Life was evolving, and she prayed going back to Seattle would not hinder that.

Jeb

The smooth jazz played above the buzz of conversation, laughter and enjoyment filling the place. The finger food overflowed, as did the non-alcoholic drinks. He was nothing short of impressed by his parents' efforts to fundraise, let alone how it all turned out. Every single person in the room dressed up in their finest. It certainly wasn't every day the sleepy town of Clovis hosted this caliber of an event—even for a small church. Pride rebounded within him, not just for his parents but for Iylah. Her hand in this, subtly seen from the color and vibrancy in every corner.

Traits of hers he enjoyed seeing rub off on anyone close enough—including himself. Reminding those who forgot that life was meant for living and not spectating.

Jeb sipped his fruity punch, his other hand in the pocket of his black suit pants. His version of dressing up, toned down in a simple white collared dress shirt with long cuffed sleeves, black dress pants and dress shoes. His untrimmed long hair slicked back in a low bun, and his face was clean shaven. That was the extent he was willing to go. Dressing up was not something he did often—it made him feel like a phony.

Many of the faces in this room he could trace back to his younger years, when his parents first took on running the church. Families and couples who remained steadfast over time and the seasons it brought—much like his mom and Dad. New, younger faces were present. A handful of single women who all at some point in the night found Jeb for conversation, young couples too. One expecting their first child, and a few who were more than happy to have a Saturday night away from bedtime duties. He glanced over at his own bedtime duty, looking disinterested in everything going on around him, stuck in his own inner world.

Jeb's disconsolate heart sank even further at this sight. They spent the afternoon together, going from one house viewing to another hoping to find their new home. Meanwhile, he was acutely aware that without a job, few realtors would touch him with a rental lease agreement. His savings and the additional money from the property Dawn and him owned in Phoenix—thanks to some inheritance money from his grandfather—was sold in the divorce. Even after using his share of it to pay for Dawn's rehabilitation treatment, he considered himself lucky not to be broke.

The unlucky part of it all was dealing with the fallout and carnage of self-negligence, dating many years back, and the dread of failing Tylor.

How is one to know the right way to move on from a former life, taking care of a cheating, reckless addict? How is he supposed to have any meaningful relationship with another woman, while this wound gaped open and any attempts to trust were proving rather fatal?

Instinctively, his vision roamed the room looking for her. His efforts in distance were turning out to be a lot harder than he thought. He needed time to think without her breathtaking jade eyes torching everything inside of him. Or wanting to reach for her, seeking a taste of her lips again. He wasn't ready for this, and neither was Tylor.

Jeb's eyes settled back on his son, reluctantly joining his Gammy on the makeshift dance floor. A young boy his age shouldn't have to deal with what he's dealt with.

The days and nights Dawn didn't come home, Tylor wouldn't eat well until she returned, and each time Jeb took her back because he saw the relief in his son's eyes. Never mind the soul numbing days Jeb endured in the aftermath. Never mind the ways in which Dawn played with his earnest heart, counting on his kindness to forgive her sleeping around. Never mind that the remnants of his relationship with his family still required him to pick them up. Never mind that a wildly ravishing woman waltzed into the faculty lounge one day, only to occupy a massive space in his charred heart. Yet he couldn't bring himself to fully believe they could have a future. Oh, and the added twist of her leaving tomorrow. Jeb didn't know if he would see her again, nor hear from her.

Did he care? He absolutely did.

Roaming around once again, he couldn't spot her. Putting his finished glass of punch on the nearest table, he cut across the room seeking her presence out.

Where could she be?

Making his way out of the Chapel through a back hallway leading to the office, the kitchen, the counseling room and the courtyard. He glimpsed light coming from the courtyard through the kitchen window, where a team of caterers worked seamlessly.

There she sat, leaning against one of the high concrete garden beds lining the outskirts of the courtyard. The hanging lights twinkled above the courtyard like carefully placed bright stars lighting up the night. The melodic sound of the jazz band drifted effortlessly through, providing a soundtrack. Her head hung low, her arms bracing herself where she stood. And the dress she wore made it hard for him not to ache for her in an embrace.

Upon seeing her, Jeb realized his breath held hostage in his throat. Words always escaped him in her presence.

Ever so aware, she noticed him standing at the entrance of the courtyard. Not a single sound left her mouth, not a smile pulled at her lips. Just her stare pulling him in closer to where she emanated. Where they both now stood, eyes wandering over each other, and silence weaving through the background noise of the jubilance inside.

What else was there to say that could possibly make them feel better?

Listening to the pounding of his heart, Jeb retrieved his hand from the pocket of his pants extending it to Iylah, palm turned upwards ready to receive hers. With no questions asked, eyeing him through her eyelashes, she took his extended hand. Jeb pulled her up and tugged her close, feeling his entire body stiffen at her proximity. He silenced the alarm, Iylah's hand landing on his chest while the other remained tucked in his. With precision, his other hand found her lower back. He swore she shuddered at this innocent touch. He could hear her charged breath close to his ear as he led them in a gentle sway. No one around, just the balmy summer night's air surrounding them, accompanied by the underlying sounds of the gala's auction beginning.

The scent she wore ingrained itself once again in his memory—a scent he ascertained would fill all he remembered of his summer. Under his grasp, she felt like the breeze whispering around them—refreshing to his heart and electricity to his bones. He couldn't think about tomorrow; he didn't want to. Despite its waiting to be acknowledged by him and he hated it. She was still here.

He pushed aside the need to shield himself from the brutal awakening awaiting them tomorrow and chose these present moments to mark and seal what they would remember of each other. He rested his face against her curls, allowing himself to bask in what she did to him, embracing the terror and the hope.

Is it even possible for me to be her friend? Face it—you're screwed!

"Is this our last dance scene, you know, like in those cliché movies?" Iylah pulled her head back, taking him in, slight teasing written on her face. "Also, where did you learn to dance like this?"

He smiled, his attentive interest mapping her face. The eyes he daydreamed about, the cheekbones sharp at a glance but soft under his thumb, her nose that crinkled with every laugh, and the lips he dared to invite himself to the afternoon he lost his battle against restraint. He was going to miss her.

"Mexico, when I was twenty-one. A friend of mine roped his mom into giving me impromptu lessons."

There were friendships he let slip away over the years. Maybe it was time to revisit them. Along with interests to aid him on his journey back to a normal life. A few things needed revisiting in this new portion of life he found himself in.

"So are you saying you can salsa too?" Her eyes widened under the dim light guiding them. " 'Cause that I would really love to see."

Jeb chuckled at her enthusiasm. "Maybe one day."

If he got himself together after picking up the shattered pieces of his exploded life. He wondered soundlessly whether she would stick around on the periphery until then. Or was it simply wishful thinking and this would fizzle out into a distant friendship of sorts?

Involuntarily, his brow furrowed, betraying his inner thoughts.

"What's wrong?" Iylah noticed and asked her question gently.

She had a way of carefully prying open his muddled self until he couldn't resist but expose his inner workings, as dire as they currently were.

"Can I call you?" He managed the words out past the newfound grief of hopes dashed, swallowing down the uncertainty never worked.

The hesitation showed in Iylah, breaking their eye contact to look away at nothing in particular.

"Jeb, I can't do this hot and cold thing, where we get so close and it scares us, then we pull away to our separate corners. Will you be calling as a friend—I just—I don't want to be strung along or string you along for that matter."

She spoke the truth. It's how things played out over the last couple of weeks. He stopped swaying, not letting her go, dancing merely an excuse to hold her.

"You're right." He whispered, tilting her chin up so he could see her face. "I'm sorry for my part in that. You deserve better than lousy half attempts." The affection in her eyes towards him put a boldness in his speech and chest. "But I will call you. If you pick up is up to you. I don't know if I have it in me to just be your friend, Iylah, but if that's all we become—I still wanna know what your voice sounds like when life stops being a jerk."

Even if we don't know what lies on the opposite end of this calculated risk, you're taking.

He kept that part to himself. "I'll take the risk with you."

Jeb shared the tired conclusion he came to last night—laying awake with too much to decide to go to sleep. Beyond today his wildly hopeful desire was to have Iylah in his life, no matter what it looked like, as long as she was in it.

Iylah's hand dropped from his chest to rest on his bicep, while she traced his face with roaming eyes. "Okay."

He smiled, his stomach a flurry of wild butterflies. "Okay."

My God! She is beautiful!

"Can we go back to you showing me your salsa?" A cheeky grin spread across her face.

Jeb threw his head back, a genuine laugh filling the space of the courtyard.

Life became significantly better with her in it. He didn't desire to find out what it would be like without her. Now only if she remained alive for him to enjoy even a sliver of her laughter on his mind swirling days.

twenty-four

"For I know the plans I have for you', declares the Lord, 'Plans to prosper you and not to harm you, plans to give you hope and a future. Then you will call on me and come and pray to me, and I will listen. You will seek me and find me when you seek me with all your heart. I will be found by you'. Declares the Lord—"

Jeremiah 29v11

I needed this. I'm struggling to see past what it feels like I'm losing, in order to gain greater freedom. The Bible says my freedom is found in Jesus. I'm understanding this, but I'm also believing that this truth should affect every area in my life. If You are to be the center of my life, as I've heard Frank say many Sundays past—then I ought to live like it. So even if my heart is torn leaving not only the safety of the Aston's, but the unconditional love, kindness and understanding they have shown me, I am going to trust (well try to) that you do have plans for me. That my future will be better than what was. That I will no longer be a nomad hopping from one place to the next in search of refuge and home. I want to seek You with all my heart, I'm going to need your help on that. There is currently another that has weaseled his way into my heart. Jeb has captured my heart, and it doesn't feel like I'm getting it back anytime soon. If he is part of Your plans and future for me, please make it easier on the both of us. Please let him find You too. Or You find him since it's what You're great at. Whatever harm awaits me in this risky kinda stupid next step, please keep me from it.

Iylah

Lylah

TWENTY-FOUR

Scrolling through the images of lives she knew from a distance now, Iylah let her thumb drag along blindly on the screen of her phone—browsing the feed of people she followed on Instagram.

Along with saying goodbye to the habit of smoking, she replaced the habit of scrolling with Bible reading, painting, chats with Kathy, gazing upon Jeb, board games with Tylor and the odd conversation with Frank. Needless to say, the desire to keep up with her high-society pals' perception of her own life no longer existed. A world she'd been removed from for a while now, but a world she needed to re-enter if their devised plan had a shining chance of working. According to Eric Mane, the more Iylah appeared active—out and about, the greater the likelihood of luring Stefan's attention.

The irony didn't fall short on her.

For all the months spent running away from the past reality of him, she presently attempted to reel him back in hoping to get rid of him for good. As terrible of an idea as it seemed, it was an idea that came to her after a desperate prayer.

She took it as a sign—one she hoped she read right.

The latest notification from her most recent post grabbed her attention.

Out of the disdain of the goodbye's she shared earlier with the Aston's, she slouched on the chartered plane reliving her time in Clovis through the many photos she captured on her phone. Inwardly admitting to herself how Jeb-centric they were. Anyone looking through them would assume they were together, from the way her face lit up in the photos of them together, to the way he stood protectively close and not for the purpose of getting in frame.

One particular snap prodded at the gap forming since her departure—the one from the church courtyard last night. His broad shoulders turned to the camera, walking ahead of her, one hand in the pocket of his pants, the other carrying her clutch, while the strung lights covered the courtyard in a moody ethereal feel. The fondness of the memory taking over, she posted it to her Instagram. She didn't tag him, just left him as a mystery to most and protected close to her heart. She hoped he wouldn't mind.

Though she revelled in the newfound experience of caring about him as intensely as she did, she trod with shackled feet unable to do the full sprint in the glory of new love like she wanted to. The shackles needed to come off her feet and back onto Stefan's wrists.

Iylah clicked on the notification button to see five hundred of them. It appeared five hundred of her ten thousand and two hundred followers took a keen interest in the mystery man suddenly on her grid. The only man on her grid.

Welcome back to the world of the phony.

She sighed, averting her eyes out the window of her father's town car, cruising steadily along the express highway. The last time she graced Seattle with her presence was three years ago, her father's nuptials to the pint-sized Kendra taking place then—before the family jet-setted off to Lake Como where the wedding was lavishly held. The glitz and the glam of the wedding itself a far cry away from what she saw of her parents' wedding photos.

Her mother's youth beamed through those early photos—it always made Iylah aware of the life and vibrancy that ran in her mother's veins. Her father's now tailored edges were far more soft back then, as he drank in his new bride. Being a young girl, she flipped through those photo albums in admiration of their love—it proved to be a different story as she grew older and her father changed. The harder he worked, the more money he amassed—the more money he amassed the more he wanted. It didn't seem to end until most nights his presence was missing from the dinner table and her Mother's excuses for him turned into less believable ones. From reading her Mother's journals, she learned more about the inklings she picked up on as an adolescent.

The town car turned off the highway into the road heading down towards the floating bridge separating the peaceful, rather sleepy neighborhood of Medina from that of Montlake. Tucked in the peninsula coming off Lake Washington, the streets of Medina boasted lush greenery lining its roadsides. Homes ranging from middle class American to we-bathe-in-money-everyday houses, barely occupied during the winter days when their millionaire—or billionaire—owners were jet setting wherever summer called. Her father was the latter.

This dozy pocket of Seattle a haven away from the bustle of the rest of the county. If you had a hankering for fast food, there would be nothing fast about it. The best food available to you needed a drive over to neighboring Bellevue. Iylah figured she would find herself there later today.

The roof of her father's waterfront property came into view against the vibrant blue sky—Leyland Cypress trees in its foreground. The town car slid into the street that accommodated a few gated residences who took their privacy and security seriously. The perfect place to be for someone being hunted down, like her. Despite the surveillance cameras lining the street, her heart somewhat counted the Aston's being a safer refuge—next to the six foot two, blonde-haired, silver-eyed man who'd cemented himself as a pillar of calm for her.

The low lying sadness in the pit of her stomach remained since Jeb drove her to the airport earlier that morning. Iylah's goodbyes were not perfected. She hated them, particularly the ones where her words got choked up and her insides felt heavy from already missing someone. Few people in her life made her despise goodbyes. The Aston's quickly climbed on the list. Kathy's parting words ensured Iylah knew she was now inscribed as part of their family, not making it at all easier.

Neither did Jeb's firm hand holding when she reached for his hand, nervously calculating the cost of what she was doing. No turning back. Jeb was stoically quiet the entire drive, the only sign of an internal struggle being the tension riddling his jaw.

Her awareness of how he didn't agree with what she was doing, sat between them like a stow away. He knew he couldn't stop her.

In parting ways Iylah blurted out, "Please don't hate me for this."

To which Jeb responded with a distant smile, evading reaching his concerned eyes, saying that not a single part of his heart hated her. He didn't say much else, she read it all in the affection chiselled in detail across his face.

With a kiss on his cheek and a prolonged embrace, she vowed to pick up when he called. He pressed her close, she could feel the thumping of his heart reverberating through his body.

The gates to the property opened up wide as they pulled up to the front of the driveway. Everything remained as it had been on her last visit. The meticulously kept lawns on either side of the driveway were being showered by the sprinkler system in place. The town car crawled up the winding driveway bringing the concrete facade of the two-story house in sight.

Iylah never was a fan of the brutalist architecture, and that probably explained why she didn't visit regularly—it didn't feel like a home. A trophy? Yes.

The car came to a halt outside the wide double garage housing at least four of her father's favorite toys.

Releasing a rattled sigh, Iylah grabbed the strap of her rucksack, leaning into the car door to push it open, not waiting for the driver. Stepping out onto the concrete paved driveway, Clovis became far.

"Thank you." She half muttered to her driver, who placed the rest of her luggage next to her.

Through the corner of her eye she caught the shadow of a figure approaching her from the main entrance of the house.

Maria.

The five-foot nothing, dark-haired, Greek firecracker employed by her father to manage the house, came to greet Iylah with her always endearing smile.

"Welcome back Ms. Iylah." Before she reached for Iylah's luggage, she gave her customary double kiss on her cheeks, tip toeing to reach even after Iylah had bent down.

"C'mon Maria, you know better than that." Iylah protested the title attached to her name, slinging her rucksack over her shoulder and following Maria, now already five steps ahead with Iylah's luggage in tow.

"No, no, no." She waved her hand in the air silencing Iylah's protest, "Mr Fredrick pay my bills, I show you respect. It how it work in my country."

A country Maria could afford to visit every year for the last seven years because Iylah's father did in fact pay all her bills, on top of her already substantial salary.

Some would call it generous, Iylah learned it was how he bought loyalty.

The vast foyer of the building with its vaulted double height ceiling, made the house appear sterile and clean with little to no character. A nonsensical giant artwork hung right across from the front door, adding to the lack of character.

Maria climbed up the floating staircase with glass panels alongside it, Iylah's luggage in tow.

"I take your bags to your room Ms. Iylah. Chef made lunch for you. Go eat."

"Maria, these bags are heavier than you. Let me take them." Iylah picked up her duffel bag, trotting up the stairs to catch her.

Maria let out a hearty chuckle, completely ignoring her. "I stronger than you Ms. Iylah. You break. But you got big bum now, maybe no break."

Iylah laughed at the cheek of unfiltered Maria. She led her down the lengthy hallway, yet again strewn with muted artworks making Iylah to pull a face at each one she walked past.

Seriously. Who chose these?

Maria entered one of the guest bedrooms, with its vast view of the lake as part of the backyard. Iylah instinctively inched towards the view, distracted throwing her bag on the plush rug. Drawing the glass door to the balcony open, the summer air wafted in the room. Standing with her arms over her chest, she inhaled the memories Seattle air always brought back—the woodsy pine tree aroma triggering them.

Fond memories. Childhood memories. Memories of her Mother. A heaviness wedged itself in her chest. Was this what she had been running from?

Maria excused herself, but Iylah didn't take notice in her preoccupied state. She scoped the expanse of the lake. A boat docked by the property's private jetty, bobbed in place under the current of the lake. Like many properties along this waterfront, a boat was necessary to enjoy summer here. Come Labor Day tomorrow, there would be plenty of activity happening on this lake and the greater area of Seattle.

Taking out her phone from her pocket, she captured a short video of her view, captioning it 'Seattle summers', before uploading it to her Instagram. As forced as it felt, she stuck with the program.

Her phone dinged with a new message.

Jeb Aston

> Four things·
> Do you know anything about the
> mysterious $75k donated last night?
> Do you also know anything about this
> Bible I found on my bed?
> Is there a reason why the back of my head
> Is on your Instagram?
> And did you get to your Dad's okay? ☺

Amused by all three questions, Iylah smirked making her way back inside, her fingers glided across the phone screen, a response to Jeb imminent. She threw herself on the king sized bed with its luxurious bedding and multitudes of pillows.

I don't know anything about the first two! But as far as the back of your head on my instagram... would you have preferred the one of you half dead from a hike? Got here safe and sound under the watchful eyes of my personal bodyguards

There was absolutely nothing normal about having personal FBI agents assigned to you on watchful duty. The threat level of it all not lost on her. Out of the haven of Clovis, the reality of her life's current standings weighed on her like a bag of wet concrete, more than she expected. The possibility of not knowing whether this would end in an assured result of safety, or the menacing outcome of death, felt delusional to cling onto a positive hope. Stefan's plans for her would surely be ones to ensure she paid for her betrayal. Loyalty, as poisoned and twisted as it came, was one of his slightly endearing traits—until he caught a whiff of someone breaching it.

She tried not to ponder on it much on the plane. Knowing the way her ex operated, made the worry win. Walking through the valley of the shadow of death took a realistic meaning right now.

Exhaling, in an effort to remove the weight of mingled emotions sitting on her chest, she watched as the typing dots appeared in the message thread with Jeb. She couldn't decipher whether her stomach housed butterflies or small knots in anticipation of his response. Frankly, it began to feel near impossible to keep on top of the typhoon. She didn't know which emotion to tend to right now. Inhaling, she leaned in to not trying to understand it all.

You've got a plan, right God?

Her phone dinged twice.

Right. Must be some other trust funded woman then 👀
Honestly, I would have picked this pic. It says a lot

She snorted a laugh. His preferred photo showing his thumb up accompanied by the widest grin on his face, while Iylah hunched over in the background, fighting for air in between holding back the urge to vomit. It was from the one morning Iylah made the dire mistake of asking Jeb if she could join him on his morning run, in a ploy to throw off his lady-fan who persisted in watering her garden every morning, to catch a curious glimpse of Jeb's shirtless exercise. Six miles later, Iylah's legs turned to Jell-O, her lungs scratched for any oxygen available and her stomach reminded her how coffee on empty, never won battles. It was the last time she ever volunteered herself up for a brutal morning start.

Some more typing dots appeared, before quickly making an exit, and popping back up again.

This place isn't the same without you...

You're not helping.

A twinge of regret struck her heart at his words. His honest words. Jeb wasn't one to shy away from sticky conversations and whatever they brought. A trait she admired, yet it also frightened her—it meant she too had to be honest and look how far it got her. Nine hundred and fifteen miles away from the person who occupied most of her thoughts.

I need some air.

Suddenly feeling trapped beneath it all, Iylah got off her bed choosing to forgo lunch for a drive instead.

∾ ∾

The engine of her father's Mercedes AMG coupe purred a throaty rumble, sitting in the parking lot with Iylah behind the wheel. In a bid to put to rest the bubbling angst in her, she ripped through the quiet streets of Medina, the power of the V8 engine causing her to grip the wheel ever so firm.

She hadn't foreseen herself driving to the place where people were literally put to rest. More specifically where her mother laid to rest. Picking up flowers was not an option—Iylah blindly drove to the cemetery. The years accumulated since her last visit. The number of them present in the way she didn't dare set foot out of the car.

The timid urge for a cigarette sprung up—quietly suggestive. Her fingers gently drumming against her full bottom lip, betraying the humming anxiety in the background of her body. She flashed a quick look in her rearview mirror to see if she could spot the undercover car of the agents. They drove following behind her upon exiting the gates of the property, but since then no sight of them. Her gaze turned back out of the windscreen towards the many tombstones erected across Lake View private Cemetery.

Help me, please. This is harder than I thought.

Taking the bravest breath she could muster in all its shakiness, Iylah opened the door stepping out into the quiet surrounding the cemetery. The stillness caused her to defensively cross her arms over her body, hugging herself for needed strength.. Each step she took towards her Mother's tombstone, making the edges of her tightly wrapped grief unravel. It felt as though someone intentionally took the time to undo each seam holding in everything she hemmed shut, keeping it from encompassing her life more than it already had. Her knees buckled the moment she stood before her Mother's tombstone, meeting the soft grass surrounding it.. The threatening tears no longer listening to her powerful will, making themselves known in streams cascading forcefully. A booming gutted wail rose through her ribs, up and out of her throat. In shock of the foreign sound leaving her body, Iylah clutched at her mouth, hands shaking and shoulders heaving. The mental images of the gradual deterioration of her Mother's health found themselves and reminded her they were there. She keeled over, sinking further into the manicured grass, losing the fight for any composure.

The neurological disease stole parts of her mother one ability at a time, over the course of two years. The woman who abounded in vitality, reduced to eating from a feeding tube in her last few months. Here and there Iylah caught glimpses of her mother's truest self in her deep brown eyes. Those moments were fleeting and they stole any hope Iylah clung to of her getting better. Naively at eighteen she believed it so, no matter what the doctors said, until the morning her mother chose to rest from her ordeal. Since the heart piercing morning, Iylah made her own choice of running hard and far away, not turning back in the slightest.

Iylah's head pounded. Unable to stop it all from coming out, she hunched over rocking, her sight blinded by the burning relentless tears. It all caught up. The sobs came one after the other causing her stomach to ache from the tension coursing through her body. No words could come out. Neither did her thoughts set themselves straight. Exactly what she feared happened—answering for the years she neglected to acknowledge the pain and the gashing hole death left in its wake.

The warmth of a hand fell on her shoulder, causing her to startle looking around in search of its owner. Upon her arrival the cemetery was empty of life, and it remained that way. Not a single person in sight. Wiping the tears and snot from her face with the back of her hand, she craned her neck but still found no one.

The Lord is near to the brokenhearted and saves those crushed in spirit.

The words tumbled around within her, finding a place to land amidst the pain of loss—being a balm to an ailed heart.

Her body hiccuped in response to the avalanche unleashed. Once again a warmth settled on her body, covering her gently but firmly—a foreign experience for her. A hush lulled her sobbing allowing her to ease in what felt like an embrace of comfort.

Jesus?

twenty-five

Jeb

Jeb took a sip of his neat whisky, its bite warming the back of his throat. His eyes scanned the bar bustling with bodies, laughter and loud conversation. A part of him found it all too busy and over stimulating to his senses. He wondered if his age showed and considered the perfect timing of quitting his job at The Dead Pony. Maybe quiet spaces with ambient music were now his type of scene. He scoffed inwardly.

Highly unlikely.

He concluded the lack of sleep running around and tearing his nerves apart is what made him sensitive to such an environment.

The nights were becoming longer than he remembered them ever being—his brain more active than it needed to be until the glimpses of daylight and birdsong showed. When sleep ran from him, he resorted to doodling sketches in one of the pads he bought for Iylah—the subject of his sketches not surprising him. His attention always strayed to the gifted Bible, untouched and unopened next to his bed. The courage to open it wasn't there, instead he reserved that courage for simply getting through the days.

"Mate, you are lookin' absolutely miserable." Clint positioned himself across from Jeb, returning with two more glasses of whisky for them both. "Ain't no chance of any lass coming to chat with ya."

Jeb half heartedly smiled. "Was that the plan? Find a couple of women to sort out this newly single guy? I could have saved you the plane ride and told you over the phone it would not work." He shot back the remaining whisky in his glass before reaching for another.

His always single friend turned up at the front door of his parents' house, bearing gifts for his godson and extending an invitation for a night on the town to his newly divorced friend of fifteen years. Clint, consistently loyal, made the stopover to Clovis in the middle of one of his many business trips to Los Angeles. A year and a bit had gone by since they'd last seen each other—phone calls and text messages kept this friendship fuelled.

Clint shrugged. "You would've deprived me of seeing your handsome face." He reached over to give Jeb's stubbled cheek a teasing stroke.

Jeb drew his head back, away from Clint's hand with a grin at his friend's taunting. "Stop. Why are your hands so soft, man? You've been sitting behind a desk for too long."

Clint slicked his graying hair back, "Ladies love soft hands mate."

"No, they love your money and your gifts. Aren't you getting too old for all of this sleeping around?" Jeb turned the central focus on Clint's own state of affairs.

Never one to settle down or even desire to, a man of many women, choosing to have his options—albeit younger options, for however long they suited him. Which wasn't very long. Clint got away with it, he could get away with it. Only a head shorter than Jeb, his English charm and preppy look seemed to be irresistible to many, along with his blue eyes and six-figure wallet—-he had no trouble getting attention.

Their first interaction, many years ago at a pub in the East of London where Jeb worked to pay for the next leg of his backpacking across Spain. Clint—intrigued by this American getting equal amounts of attention from the female patrons as him—jeered at Jeb across the noise of the full pub—

"Are you my competition?"

To which Jeb responded—"Only if you like making enemies."

And a friendship struck up.

"And what's the other alternative?" Clint shot Jeb a trying look. "Settle down and have my tail handed to me, only to be alone again when she's had enough? I think not, mate."

Jeb didn't take his friend's words to heart. Truth be told it wasn't a lie. Yet despite his own exploded version of settling down, he still believed two people could commit themselves to each other in honesty and devotion. He just didn't know if the energy to ever try again lay within him.

He took a sip from his fresh drink, to drown the image of Iylah surfacing once again. Four days went by painstakingly since she left and since he'd heard from her. His mother let slip about her recent phone call with Iylah two days ago. From what Jeb gathered the memories of her mother and the grief they brought were doing a number on her. She didn't respond to his messages checking on her, making him restless not knowing if she was okay. As the days went on, he couldn't bring himself to pick up his phone and call, despite desperately wanting to.

The abrupt revelation of her missing presence, created a vacuum threatening to suck him into a state of despair he knew would be waiting for him down the line.

"You hear from that school?" Clint filled the silence between them, inviting Jeb's mind back to the present.

Jeb stared down into the woody amber hues of his drink, taking another sip.

"Yeah, I did. I start on Monday." He didn't hide his lack of enthusiasm about it.

Teaching art to high schoolers wasn't on the table for how he saw the rest of the year going. Though thankful for the job because it meant stability for him and Tylor—mixed emotions showed themselves. The starting over aspect of it drained the remnants of life out of him.

"At least now I won't get turned down by every real estate agent in this city."

"Hey given the circumstances, you ain't doin' too bad."

Jeb scoffed, not entirely believing Clint's words, locking eyes with him he said dryly, "Thanks for the vote in confidence. But really how does a nearly forty-year-old, divorced, single parent with a ten-year-old son, who spent the last seven years of his life chasing after an addict start his life all over again?" Jeb's frustration showed as he rubbed his brow roughly. "I spent all my energy and time wasting it on a dysfunctional marriage. I'm tired man. I've got a son to take care off and I can't screw that up Clint." He shook his head the truth of it all spiralling in him. "And to top it off, I've gone and caught feelings for a woman who could very well get hurt at the hands of a psychopath ex."

Clint sucked on the back of his teeth, tending to his words carefully—a rare thing for him.

"Out of all of this muck there still is good in it, mate. For starters you're no longer responsible for that wench of an ex. You get to build a different life for your boy now—a new life. And from the state of you, it's a miracle that young, perky lass can even stand ya."

Jeb chortled at Clint's last words.

"I know you're tired, but don't give up on things before you've given 'em a fair go."

"I need to stop drinking 'cause you're making a lot of sense." Jeb swirled his whisky in the glass.

"Of course I'm making sense." Clint motioned to his brain. "Not just good looks and a fat wallet, ya' know?"

"Tell that to the lady over there." Jeb motioned to the leggy blonde a couple of tables away from them, who spent most of the evening eyeing them up, along with her brunette friend—walking past every so often to make sure she went noticed.

Jeb made brief eye contact with her, Clint turning his head in her direction.

True to his womanizing form, Clint extended a friendly small wave of interest piquing her curiosity further—she ushered herself out of her seat.

"When in America, hey." Clint shot Jeb a wink, and that felt like his cue to leave.

Jeb tipped back the rest of his drink—patting Clint on the back he stood up from his seat ready to leave. "Let me know how it goes. Or don't, actually. I'm gonna go for a walk."

"Just remember you're single now mate." Clint called after Jeb, the eager blonde arriving at his table.

The night air blew awareness into Jeb's slightly swimming head. He wasn't a man who drank much, but with Clint he could be persuaded otherwise and his current mind-space held things he would rather drown out.

He pulled his phone out of the pocket of his jeans checking the time, to see how wise a decision walking back home was. Squinting his eyes at the blaring light of his phone rendering him half blind, finding two messages from Iylah awaiting him. He paused his walking to open them undistracted.

Why is she sending me a link to a house? That's how she wants to start a conversation?

IylahTrustfund Dawson

> A realtor should drop by tomorrow
> morning with the keys. Consider me your
> new landlord! (You don't actually have to
> pay me rent thought) ☺

What?

Without a second thought, he called her disregarding the time and everything else stopping him from calling her. On the fourth ring, she picked up.

"Hey Jeb," her voice involuntarily brought the recollection of her nestled against his chest, bidding him to come out of hiding.

Would he dare deny the hold she had on him?

Fighting the overwhelming urge to spit out how he missed her, he dealt with the matter at hand. "Iylah you can't randomly just buy houses for people."

"I didn't. I put a lot of thought to it—did my research and bought an investment property in Clovis to start my portfolio. So it's not random and you're not just people—you're Jeb." Her points sounded well rehearsed and somewhat convincing.

Bewildered by this gesture, Jeb searched for what to say. "You don't have to do this to get my attention—"

"Jeb, this is not for your attention. I care about you and whatever I can do to lighten your load I will do. In this case, you need a place to live, I need an investment property. Don't make a big deal of it." She dismissed his mild protests. "Also, where are you? Is that music in the background?"

"A buddy of mine is in town, we went out for a couple of whiskies." Jeb kicked a loose stone off the sidewalk deciding then it wasn't a good idea to walk. More than a couple of whiskies tilted his system.

"I like this newly single Jeb, strutting his stuff out on the town."

"We both know it's not like that, for very obvious reasons." Jeb scoured up and down the road, willing for a taxi to drive by to his aid.

You are the obvious reason.

"Iylah, thank you. From the bottom of my heart." Though the reality of her grand gesture hadn't registered in his foggy brain, there was no denying how light the load would soon become with house hunting taken off his hands.

Another crack appeared in his fortified wall. Her concern for him calling this wall's bluff for being foolish for attempting to keep her out.

"You're welcome, Jeb."

"Are you doing okay?" His voice softened, inquiring of the woman he couldn't stop thinking about.

He leisurely paced a small distance, in no hurry to be anywhere but here.

"I am now." Though he couldn't see her face, he sensed her smile through her words. "I'm sorry for my radio silence for the last few days. It's been a lot being back here. Are you okay?"

"I am now." He grinned sheepishly.

How she had the innate ability to bring a refreshing calm to his tumultuous mind, he didn't know—he was thankful for a reprieve.

A silent pause sat comfortably in their phone call.

"Is it too cliche and out of bounds to say I miss you?" Iylah confessed.

"Not if it's the truth." The dormant firecrackers in his stomach set off again. "I miss you—a lot."

Clint was right. Jeb couldn't go giving up on the good things out of his weariness. She was a good thing during his hugely unrecognizable life and he saw why.

His heart was curious if anything lay beyond this thing they labeled as a friendship. Now if only they could fast forward past this part.

∽ ৹

Jeb stood in the middle of what he assumed to be the living room—daylight bouncing off the Oak hardwood flooring of the two bedroomed bungalow.

With no furnishings, it looked more spacious than the clapboarded gray-beige exterior presumed. The white accents of the door frames, built-ins and windows aided in ushering in more light into the house. A hint of the smell of fresh paint hung in the air. Jeb's fingers brushed against the white dune walls in search of any wet paint spots.

His eyes were on the lookout for any flaws visible. As much as he wouldn't verbally admit, all this felt too good to be true. A recently renovated house in a gated community, where Tylor and he could settle in. Stuff like this didn't happen to people like him.

Upon arriving his first critique was the lock on the front door feeling a bit shaky and probably needing replacement. His second critique being the iridescence of the lights emitting a sterile glow. By the third thing—being one of the two bathrooms located too close to the kitchen—he discovered he was trying to find any reason to not be blown away by this act of kindness towards him.

Miserably aware how deep the wounds obtained from his failed marriage ran, he chastised himself. They were deep enough for him to feel like a fish out of water upon being on the receiving end of care.

Apart from his parents, a very brief message from his older brother Ezra, Laura's spontaneous and short visit to check on him, coupled with Clint's rendezvous—which ended with a blonde who turned out to be a poor decision on Clint's part—the attentiveness of Iylah to his life and current needs spun his head.

"Cool!" Tylor zoomed in and out of various rooms, exploring them the only way a boy his age could do. "This place is huge, Dad!" His beaming face popped up in the open-plan kitchen where Jeb was.

Jeb grinned at the sight of the smile on his son's face. Life brought little to be excited about for both of them. Jeb had an inkling his own state of disarray proved to be something Tylor picked up on.

"Well, it's a lot bigger than our old home in New York that's for sure." Jeb stuck his hands in the pocket of his relaxed denim shorts, taking it all in—unsure what to make of all this.

"Not as big as Iylah's house though." Tylor slid across the floors, testing out their reliability in providing efficient skids.

Jeb jeered. "Nothing is as big as that. C'mon, let's go check out the backyard."

Nor as empty.

He remembered thinking how lonely it must be for Iylah, living in all that townhouse and how quickly he learned she was accustomed to such a loneliness—it no longer bothered her and she didn't take much notice of it.

When she left for Seattle, he sensed she counted the cost of walking away from what she gained being around his family. Certain things she said gave the impression his family operated differently from hers. His impression rang true. She disclosed in their conversation last night after Jeb asked, her dad kept his distance even with her arrival at his home. He opted to stay at his inner city penthouse with his disgustingly young wife, as Iylah put it. Jeb refrained from pointing out their own obvious age gap. He let her get the point across.

Their conversation spanned over four hours and through the various motions of him finding a cab, making himself a grilled cheese when he got to his parents, to when the whisky's downed pulled him into sleep a lot quicker than he desired. He pondered their conversation this morning, a coffee in the mug he always served hers in, lessening his drowsy state.

He'd asked her what it felt like being in Seattle after so long, to which she responded it didn't feel like home anymore. She briefly mentioned a trip to her mom's graveside, quickly diving for another topic of choice. He wouldn't let her. He expertly probed—entirely taught to him by his mother—compelling her to share the truth of her jagged grief pouring out, followed by an encounter that aided in mending the irritated wound. She said she was sure of it—Jesus met her on her knees in the cemetery. Nervously laughing she promised she wasn't going crazy. Jeb told her he believed her, and he did. He too once knew what it was like. When she pried for more information, he sensed another part of his heart clench in hesitance to acknowledge his dwindled belief.

No amount of resistance could undo the things he found to be true of the God who kept his eyes on him. Jeb just didn't need a reminder of how far he'd wandered, though his life screamed it out.

He questioned if God thought he deserved a second chance, or third, make that a fourth for that matter. Jeb feared the answer, and so the Bible Iylah gifted him remained closed.

The backyard with its patch of partially dry grass, and concrete paving extending as a patio from the house, looked easy enough to maintain without too much fuss. Right now that was the capacity Jeb currently held, one that could handle less fuss.

They would officially move in a week from now. He spent most of the morning arranging their furniture and belongings to be sent from New York to Clovis. The earliest it could happen being Thursday next week. He settled for that.

Mapping out what the days coming looked like for both him and Tylor, the twinge of anxiety reminded him it lurked in the background of his life—a new unwelcome camper. He looked over at his son kicking away at some bits of dead grass. Though Tylor didn't voice his fears, Jeb witnessed them running through his mind whenever Tylor drifted off into silent thought. They were the same in that regard.

The depth of their thoughts encompassing every outcome, yet never hoping for the best. Life always handed out in bucket loads the things that made hope feel expensive. Maybe the time came for them to get help for the weights they both carried.

"Hey buddy, come here for a sec." Jeb called Tylor over to him, popping a squat to get a better view of his son's eyes.

Tylor obediently went to his dad.

"Listen," Jeb pushed long strands of hair away from Tylor's downcast eyes, his smile long gone and forgotten. He tilted Tylor's chin upwards so his eyes could rest on his own. "You and I are gonna have a big few first's in the coming days. It's okay to be nervous and scared. I'm nervous and scared too—"

"Really?" Tylor searched Jeb's eyes for confirmation.

"Mhmm." Jeb nodded, "You start school on Monday, I start my new job on Monday too. You're gonna make new friends, so am I. We'll be living in a new house and a new area. I know it's a lot, but we can do it—together. I need you to do something for me though?"

"What?"

"Every time it gets hard, I want you to write a letter—"

"To who?"

"To whom it may concern. That's who you write it to. Now when it gets hard write that letter saying what's bothering you and what's happened. We'll find a special spot in the house to put all our letters and at the end of each week I'll post them." Jeb saw a glint of confusion run across his son's face with the crinkling of his nose. He stifled a laugh.

"But who's gonna read them?" Tylor shifted his weight from one foot to the other.

"I won't read them, but someone who loves the both of us very much will." In his sleepless nights and the dark of his room, Jeb dove into numerous articles online about the effects of divorce on children. Along with how children in families with an addict parent struggle to find normalcy after living in perpetual dysfunction.

The guilt festered in Jeb with each article he read. Why had he stayed so long? What did it say about his own dysfunction?

"Okay." Tylor shrugged his approval of the idea.

"Awesome." Jeb stood up ruffling Tylor's hair a shade lighter than his. He made a mental note to inform his mom of her new role.

"Mom says she still loves you."

Once in a while these rogue reminders would spill from Tylor's lips, courtesy of the weekly phone call he got with Dawn as part of Jeb's mercy to her. Full custody of Tylor had been awarded to Jeb, with no visitation rights for Dawn until she managed to get clean for a year.

Jeb's fury simmered progressively in him every time Dawn planted her seeds of chaos and manipulation in Tylor as she always did. The leash on this liberty needed to be tightened.

Jeb chose his words amongst the sea of angry slurs in his mind.

"Of course she still loves you. She just needs to get better."

"She asked me if you like Iylah? I told her maybe."

For crying out loud!

Jeb put his hand on Tylor's shoulder, approaching the matter the best way he could think of. "Next time Mom asks you anything about Iylah, tell her to ask me, okay, buddy?"

"Okay."

"Iylah and I are just friends." A statement he hated for its truth, but understanding how necessary it was for the sake of his ten-year-old processing the remnants of an old life, with the merging of a new one.

Any glimpses of being more with Iylah were becoming more of a blurry horizon. Not enough though to put an end to the yearning, almost burdensome desire to be with her.

> Hey can I call you tonight? I promise I won't keep you up past your bed time 🙂

He tucked his phone back in his pocket, a brooding cloud of restlessness showing itself.

Does this get better?

twenty-six

09/05/2019

'Taste and see that the Lord is good; blessed is the one who takes refuge in him. Fear the Lord, you holy people, for those who fear him; lack nothing. The lions may grow weak and hungry, but those who seek the Lord lack no good thing. '

Psalm 34v8

I've been learning just how interested you are in my day-to-day Jesus. It doesn't feel like You are off at a distance, just waiting for me to screw up so you can come clean my mess begrudgingly. I make a lot of messes and will probably make some more. But to know that You are so close and near, near enough to cloak me with what feels like a thick blanket of comfort—it's blown my mind and my heart to say the least. Are You always this good? Are You always this loving? I've done nothing that makes me a worthy candidate for getting to know You like this. You can ask my father, he's got a long list of things that disqualify me ten times over. I want to see how good You are; I want to taste more of what it means to know You. I don't want to know you from a distance, because You drew close enough to meet me on my knees and in pain. I want to know You up close, despite my fears of the future and my weakness in shame. I want the good thing You offer so I can lack nothing. If I'm being honest, I don't know what's better than You. You are the good thing to me.

Iylah

She pulled herself out of the lake's fresh water, up onto the jetty she dived off twenty minutes ago. The Seattle sun lured her out of the house for a swim—her first swim since her arrival five days ago. Slicking her wet curls back, she squeezed the water out of them, causing it to slide down her arms. Self consciously she smoothed over her red swimsuit with its round scoop neck, fitting a bit more snug than she recalled.

Is this the beginning of the end for my body? I need to lay off the ice-cream for a bit.

The fable of bodies changing once you were ushered into your thirties, showed its head, waiting to be proven true. Her thirties were fast approaching, peeking over the next two weeks. And what did she have to show for it? Besides a passport full of stamps and an ex hunting her down.

Reaching for her towel, she dried her face and neck, followed by her arms, her legs still dangling in the water over the jetty's edge. The sour words of her father remained lingering in the back of her mind from their brief encounter this morning.

Four days ago, she disclosed to him her current situation and why she retreated to the shores of Seattle. Her father deemed it unsafe for him and Kendra to stay at the house. He didn't consider asking his youngest daughter if she was okay. Or if he could help her in any way. He simply shook his head and walked away with packed bags, Kendra in tow—giving further instruction to Maria stating if she felt unsafe she was welcome to take a leave of absence with pay. Naturally with Maria's loyalty bought, she took the offer willingly leaving Iylah to fend for herself in this six bedroomed house.

Iylah didn't hear from her father until this morning, in a fury of accusations telling her to get her act together—the alternative of removing access to the Trust would be his forced hand. All tipped off by him finding out about her recent purchase of real estate. She didn't retaliate as per the norm. She didn't ask the questions she harbored of what her father did to her mother. The peace she gained since the undoing of her grief at her mother's graveside, made it hard to be upset. After all, her father had a point. She figured her last act before she potentially lost access to his money would be to help Jeb.

Instinctively the thought of Jeb made her pick up her phone, to find a message from him, sending her insides in a flutter.

Yeah sure. I'm having dinner with my
father, I can call you after?
Ha! Says the one who fell asleep mid
sentence 😴

Tossing the phone onto her piled towel, she focused on the expanse of the lake. The earthy green hues reflecting the greenery surrounding it, acting as a mirror to what lay beneath it. She swayed her feet slowly in the water, watching the surface of it disperse at the motion. She grasped at her phone to take a photo of the traces of splendor catching her intrigue in this simple occurrence. Inclined to keep her new capture to herself, she did as instructed by posting it up on her Instagram, captioned 'Lake days'.

Eric Mane confirmed her pre-empted visibility online, did work in their favor of bringing Stefan out of hiding, after what seemed to be a few weeks of no sighting of him. He appeared to have left the streets of New York, taking to Los Angeles. Eric Mane made the point of noting how Stefan traced Iylah's steps, staying far enough to look like he wasn't. He reckoned soon enough Stefan would make his way to Washington State.

Waiting to be found by someone void of a single good intention towards you held an odd feeling.

Iylah recalled the days of the court trial, sitting up on the witness stand testifying against him. Stefan himself in no way ever physically harmed her—his words did most of the harm—yet the chilling stare he kept on her as she spoke, made her believe if he ever got the opportunity to in the future, he would take great pleasure in making good on his reputation of intolerance towards disloyalty. The same pleasure he took in ending the lives of seven men as she watched on.

What if he does actually kill me? Or kidnap me? Am I prepared for the worst to happen? How much can the FBI really keep me from harm?

Her pulse increased, the questions piling on trying to pull her under. She recognized how it worked now. The moment she believed a single fear, the floodgates would prove flimsy and open up every other persistent fear.

Inhaling pensively, taking in the earthy scent of the lake's surroundings, she shut her eyes, raising her head to the sky, allowing the sun to radiate upon her with its warmth.

Jesus you know what's going to happen. I know you love me and I know you're here with me.

She rolled her shoulders back, the faint image of her dream from two nights ago returning uninvited. In place of the searing nightmares occupying most of her nights, new dreams were sprouting—planting seeds of hope instead of dread. This dream watered the seed in her heart. The seed of affection towards Jeb.

Dressed in a white linen sundress, barefoot in a backyard garden, she stood. A bunch of Zinnias in her hand, as she continued to pick some more from an endless bed of them. In the dream's background, laughter filled the space—the laughter belonged to three people; a little girl, a young boy, and a man. The flowers in hand, Iylah found herself at a dining table brimming with food, like a banquet. She propped the flowers in a long yellow vase. The three people flanked close to the table, the little girl nestled up to Iylah's hip, light curls flowing from her head and bright eyes staring up at Iylah. The boy, who looked like a teenager—and awfully similar to Tylor—sat across from where Iylah stood, smiling at her reaching for food. A pair of arms hugged her waist from behind, catching her by surprise. She turned to find out who they belonged to, only to come face to face with Jeb. It was their home. It was their laughter. It was their love.

Iylah woke up from the dream, her face teary, a wistful hope capturing her. She kept this dream close since then, with no desire to tell anyone—earnestly praying her mind wasn't insistent on playing tricks. She wrote it down in her journal, praying one day if she had a daughter, she would witness it too. Then she bought a house nearly identical to the one in the dream, Jeb remaining none the wiser.

Her phone dinged with a message.

Jeb Aston

Donel Looking forward to hearing your voice.
In my defence, it was the whiskies that took me out.
Clint's left so no bad influences for that tonight.
I hope dinner with your dad isn't too bad.
Sidenote - the house is incredible. Again, we will
name it in your honour. The Manor of Iylah.

Her grin matched the state of her heart.

Even in the mess, if this is what falling in love entailed, she wished the mess would soon clear, allowing her to experience it with no restraints.

"And we will have a bottle of your Nebbiolo." Her father handed the gloved waiter the menu, along with a nod dismissing him..

He commanded attention wherever he went and if he didn't gain it, he sure never went back there again. Sitting across from him at a prized table in The George, Iylah witnessed why he was described as an enigma in many of his circles. He ran his businesses with a firm hand and a no nonsense demeanor to match. Some would say such a manner is the reason his wealth increased yearly—they weren't onlookers at the cost of his family he so willingly paid.

His eyes darted across the grandeur of the restaurant, scanning faces, avoiding the one in front him. The one which craved his validation since the tender age of ten, but never received it.

Placidity sat as another guest at their table. Iylah's fingers traced the stitching of the napkin impeccably placed on the right corner of her portion of the table. Jitters found their way to the forefront of her functioning. Conversation wasn't their strong suit, still Iylah's questions needed answers when her father wasn't tearing down her life choices—so she tried.

"What are you currently working on?" Iylah cleared her throat, breaking through the deafening silence between them.

"Nothing you would be interested in." His cool blue eyes rested on the presence of the waiter returning with a bottle of their most expensive red wine—pouring it in the manner they were vigilantly taught to. Her father shut down her feigned interest in his work.

"Thank you." She threw a polite smile towards the waiter pouring into her glass.

Taking a tentative sip of from her glass, her taste buds embraced the fruity flavours of cranberries and a hint of raspberries.

"You quit your job in New York because of this—" He waved a hand in the air, unsure of what to call her troubles, "What now? What happens after this?"

"If I don't wind up dead?" She held his scrutinizing gaze, watching the corners of his mouth twitch in an effort to refrain from saying whatever tickled the tip of his tongue. "Well, the only thing I'm okay at is art—"

"You're not just 'okay' at art Iylah, your taste and skill-set is impeccable."

Though he spoke encouragement, his expression sat stern and unsoftening.

She ignored the wonky compliment like she did with most. "I want to start up my studio. Create, sell and exhibit there."

An idea mulled over by her in the recent days, during her time spent alone with nothing but her classical music friends in the morbid house. She occupied whatever vast room invited the most natural light in on any day—a technical pencil and pad in hand bringing her imaginings to life on paper. One desire she earnestly prayed she would have the breath in her body to see materialise.

"You would need a bit of a following to even consider opening one up to make a profit." He swirled the wine in his glass, his interest keen at the sound of a potentially profitable business idea.

"I'm aware. It's a long-term idea." She smoothed over her slicked back hair, the rest of her curls held up by a claw clip, spilling over in density.

Her father was the first person whom she shared her fleeting idea with—unsure now if it was smart to do so.

"And if it doesn't pan out the way you think it will?"

"I will go back to teaching somewhere." She took another sip of her wine, thankful for its warmth down her throat—just about the only warm thing in this conversation.

Between her and Lena, their father held a more invested interest in Lena's life. After all, having a prominent lawyer for a daughter amongst those in high places, boded well for his own reputation. Iylah merely remained the pretty one to display—nothing about her life showed itself as worth boasting to anyone. All of it a mashup of haphazard decisions and big purchases.

"Are we going to purchase another house wherever this somewhere you end up is?" He leaned in, elbows on the table, hands clasped showcasing his Rolex Day-Date catching the light from overhead, its gold bracelet gleaming.

"Depends—can I add them to my new portfolio of properties?" She raised an eyebrow, meeting his sarcasm with her own cheek. This is how it went with the father-daughter duo.

He sniggered, the bitter tones revealing disapproval. "If you intend to make money from it, buy property where people actually want to live. Not Clovis."

"What's wrong with Clovis?"

"Let's just say the demographics there don't really make the place worth going to." The ugly head of pride reared in him.

"Of all the things I know you to be, a bigot is a new shameful color on you." Her words weren't minced, nor were they hiding her disgust at his statement.

"Young lady, the world isn't the rose scented fantasy you like to think it is." His voice deepened and lowered. "The sooner you open your eyes to see it the better. College dropouts thrive in places like Clovis."

"Well, college-dropouts seem to be better men than you." Iylah's subdued rage towards him quickened with each passing minute she sat across from him.

Seeing him tonight was regrettably her idea. A way to have an honest conversation about the past. About her mother. Not a single intention from Iylah to tear her father down. It appeared the years apart did not make him a better man.

"What happened between you and Mom?"

Her question drained the color from his face, quicker than a response could come from him. He averted his eyes, leaning back in his seat, bringing a hand up to rub his forehead. His blindsided reaction suggested a story lay beneath the uncovered surface. No words came forth from him.

"What did you do to my Mother?" A foreshadowing pit formed in her stomach.

From experience, her father was quite apt at provoking pain in an offhanded manner. Growing up, her parents marriage glowed as the picture of dinner parties, extravagant holidays, laughter tickling the ears but not hit the heart. Had she taken the time to question its depth, she would find things were swept under the rare vintage oriental rug—often.

"It was a long time ago Iylah—" shame washed over him, his shoulders sinking into a hunch. A screaming difference from the astute manner he portrayed in two minutes ago.

"I don't care how long it was, I want to know what happened." The words came from her dry mouth.

He sighed, closing and opening his mouth, but failing to get the truth out. Iylah waited with trapped breath.

"It was after the miscarriage—"

"What?" Iylah muttered the question, the news of her mother enduring a miscarriage rendering her stunned.

"Your mother wasn't the same anymore. She became despondent—wouldn't look at me, wouldn't let me touch her. The woman I'd married was gone." He rubbed his mouth, followed by another weighty sigh, "I'm not proud of what I did—"

"What did you do?" She asked firmly, afraid of the unveiling to come.

He peered up to meet her baffled gaze. Was that regret she saw? Surely not. The man before her stayed hardly capable of emoting remorse.

"I had a year-long affair, and she found out."

Iylah reeled back in her cushioned seat, holding on to the armrests trying not to sink further into the overwhelming disbelief of the truth told to her. An obstructing weight lodged in her chest, anchoring her in place.

He continued, "She forgave me because that's who Lillian was. The most tenderhearted, gracious soul who didn't deserve to die the way she did. When you were born, it was like she caught a second wind of joy. I believe she loved you more than she did me." Disdain tinted his last words. "So much so, that on your thirtieth birthday half of my company's shares are being signed over to you as a shareholder. The half that was hers when we first started out. In the event that I die, Lena gets my half of the shareholding stakes. It was that or an impending divorce."

Iylah shook her head, hearing the words but not willing to accept them as reality. Nowhere in her entire existence had there been mention of what her father disclosed now. How he kept her at arm's length, funding her life into oblivion without so much as an interest in her wellbeing, made heartbreaking sense.

"I loved your mother, Iylah." His voice faltered, "I just didn't deserve her, and I knew it. Hell—everybody knew it, except her."

"Do you love me?" A sliding tear proved the hurt dealt to her heart.

The question digging up her deep seated need for his approval. Despite spending her younger years fighting against it, it still hung around like a ghost terrorizing an empty home.

I love you. I do.

The words thumped around inside of her, rendering whatever her father said next irrelevant.

Before he could speak, Iylah snatched her purse, pushed her chair back and walked away from the tattered remains of their relationship. He didn't call back for her. He didn't go after her.

The answer to her question lay in his remaining seated.

She tugged the cashmere throw closer around her body, the night breeze calmly whipping around her on the balcony next to her room. The gaslit outdoor fire pit, giving her surroundings an amber glow from its flames. A restless sigh escaped from her body, as she blankly stared towards the city lights glinting far ahead.

Life's habit of throwing flaming hot curve balls to see if she could catch them, wore down her new found resolve of hope.

Her brow furrowed contemplating the pain her mother must have endured upon losing a child. Followed by the injury of betrayal by someone she loved. How on earth did she keep that infectious smile on her face? The joy she exuded showed no signs of this profound heartbreak. Iylah turned her sights to the journals sitting next to her.

To Jesus her mother turned. Jotting words of prayer, grief, lament, joy, thanksgiving and everything in between. He held it all for her and didn't let up in holding her til her dying breath. The same Jesus who Iylah experienced in the days gone by and the days to come—she was sure of it.

Grappling for her phone, she opted to video call the only person she desired to talk to with the ability to still her racing mind.

He picked up, laying against the bedframe of the bed he perched on, biting the end of a pencil, his bare broad shoulders on display with his hair lazily tossed to one side.

"There she is."

Her lips spread in a robust smile at the sight of Jeb. "Hey—"

"This is what we're doing now? If I knew video calling would be on the agenda tonight, I definitely would have done something about the bags under my eyes. I look like hell." He ruffled his hair, rolling over onto his side, using his free hand to support his head.

"You look fine." She assured him with her slight giggle, fine being an understatement to how he truly looked. "If anything my bags are outdoing yours."

"You look stunning, bags or not. I refuse to believe you can look terrible."

Heat traveled to her cheeks each time he complimented her and he was well aware of the effect it had on her. The smirk on his face said it all.

"How was dinner with your dad?"

Iylah sighed, fighting the distraction his flexed bicep brought to the conversation. She recalled the safety wrapping around her the times his brawny arms held her in an embrace. It didn't happen often but when it did, it left a pining imprint in her.

"Hmm—let's just say my relationship with him is hanging on by a very thin, invisible thread."

What remained of it was already in question, Iylah unsure how to move forward with him.

"Wanna tell me about it?"

"It's a lot Jeb honestly—" The thought of it made her shoulders sag in exhaustion.

"Perfect. A lot seems to be the general rate at which we both do life at the moment, so it fits right in there."

Iylah laughed, "You're not wrong. Don't say I didn't give you a warning to opt out."

"I would never opt out of anything to do with you. I'm ready when you are."

Even through the screen of her phone, his unmoving focus soaked her up leaving no part of her feeling unseen.

She retold the revelations of her father, the struggles of her mother and the suspicions uncovered from reading her mother's journals. All the while Jeb listened intently, quietly, paying every ounce of attention to her. By the time her recap of night ended, her strength gave out, a torrent of weariness setting in.

"Holy smokes!" Jeb changed his position, sitting up as though too astounded by the news to comprehend it laying down.

Iylah caught a flash of his sculpted shirtless torso—she averted her eyes, hoping he hadn't caught her lingering.

"Are you okay? I mean, that's a whole new dump truck of stuff to add—"

"To my already chaotic life?" Iylah pulled the claw clip open, her curls cascading down around her face. She ruffled them, dispersing their volume, til they sat unhindered, nice and full. "Yes, I am aware. Don't they say it gets worse before it gets better?"

"I don't know who 'they' are, but 'they' need to stop talking for the sake of all of us out here trying our best."

Laughter rolled out of Iylah, amusement parting the proverbial clouds.

"Bright side is you get to call yourself a business woman once you turn thirty, thanks to your mom." Jeb said. "When is your birthday?"

"In two weeks."

Lena promised to come for it, to help Iylah usher in her thirties. And if Iylah were honest with herself, she hadn't been looking forward to spending it alone despite accepting that it might be the case.

"Care for some company on your birthday?" He twirled a pencil between his fingers revealing a well-mastered habit of his. "I've been trying to come up with an excuse to come see you, this one sounds as good as any."

"The threat of a dangerous crime lord on the loose doesn't scare you away?" She tested, allowing the rising temperature in the pit of her stomach to spread to the rest of her limbs.

Jeb chewed on the corner of his lip before responding, "I'll take my chances."

Playing around with her curls, Iylah allowed her swooning to settle. To deny the existing pull to each other would be denying themselves a way back to an actual connection with someone where plenty of others failed between them.

"Hey Jeb, is it easy for you to trust me?" A question nibbling away at her since their conversations last night. Her curiosity let the question be heard.

The small screen made it hard to read his expression, she was sure he drew a long breath before answering.

"It's not a simple answer." He scratched his head, "It's not personal. There's—it's just—I have years of broken trust telling me not to trust you." He scoffed hindsight giving him vision, "But you being you is making me question why on earth I shouldn't trust you. I'm coming up short on reasons not to." The faintest smile took the place of the pained scowl across his face.

Taking his confession to heart and treading diligently around the scraggy edges of his broken heart, she said, "I guess that's what ten years married to Dawn did?"

Jeb combed his fingers through his hair, looking away again.

"It was supposed to end as a three-month fling on holiday in Bali, then she got pregnant. The religious part of me then rushed to do the decent thing. She wasn't ready for marriage, I probably wasn't either. But we had this beautiful baby boy who completely stole my heart—I wanted him to have a mom and dad who loved each other. Turns out there wasn't any love and God had other plans." He clenched his jaw, Iylah seeing the anger stored away in the wounded parts of him.

"Are you angry with God, Jeb?" Her prickly question came out timidly.

Silence came from his end, taking in everything else but her. He rolled his shoulders back with a slight wince of pain. His eyes finally rested on her, not hiding the truth, "I guess I am. Does that change what you think of me?"

She shook her head, "No. It helps me understand you."

They stared, allowing space for the broken pieces of their lives not to scare them, but to see what could be made of it.

"Right." Jeb cleared his throat. "We should probably get some sleep."

"Mhmm." Iylah sensed her quizzing and response hit a point of weakness in Jeb. She wouldn't dare ask further than she already had. "Goodnight Jeb."

He pondered on something unsaid before finding his words again, "Goodnight Iylah Jane." A sad smile danced on the edges of his lips, tugging at her own misery—resonating with how he felt.

With a small wave and a tender smile of her own, Iylah ended the call.

She sank back into the outdoor cushioned seat, unsure the well of her being smitten had an end. She couldn't run from it, being taken under by it the only course going forward. This man had the ability to open her up out of herself and stir a flame up with his sterling intensity. Being brave enough, she'd describe it as a magnificent unfolding—just maybe it would be enough to dull the jagged edges of life.

Perhaps the purpose of finding love in this lifetime was necessary to bring out the abounding colors of ordinary days, through the careful unrelenting pursuit of another flawed human being.

Her phone rang, scattering her thoughts.

"Jeb?" She answered.

"I'm falling in love with you, Iylah." His voice cut through every other sound in the night, as she zoned into it—his profession causing the well of affection to spill over. "Your emerald eyes, your curls, the way your skin feels under my fingertips. Your laugh that comes from the deepest part of you, the way you find beauty in the most mundane things. The way you move, your curiosity for new things, how generous you are—even how you are with my Mom. My God, your lips! All of it keeps me up at night and runs rings around me during the day. I—" He exhaled in surrender to it, "I just need you to be patient with me while I figure this out, because it's not just me—"

"It's Tylor too." Her voice came softly, "I know Jeb."

"So don't die on me anytime soon, please?" The plea tugged at her.

"Okay." She half whispered, emotion grabbing hold of her throat

"Promise?"

"Promise."

"Goodnight Iylah."

"Night Jeb."

The phone slid away from her ear, an avalanche of relief and awe following. Displacing the rejection she sunk in earlier in the evening, she laid herself across the seat, hugging the throw. No longer feeling the dread of spending her days alone. In the place of dread, now sat a new friend who had never walked these parts of her heart—the desire to be someone's forever.

twenty-seven

09/07/2019

'Therefore, since we are surrounded by so great a cloud of witnesses, let us lay aside every weight, and sin which clings so closely, and let us run with endurance the race that is set before us.'

Hebrews 12v1

I find myself getting increasingly discouraged, mad and sad. It all comes in waves that don't seem to let up. The current wave that's settled in my stomach is anger. The recklessness of my father with the hearts and people given to him to protect makes me so mad. I always thought a father and husband were the protector of his wife and children, I see none of that in him. I see selfish ambition; I see controlling others by trying to buy their loyalty. While he has profited from it and succeeded in business by being like that, I don't know if I want to be part of the way he does things. My mother obviously had a reason to sign over her shares to me, I don't currently see it but I guess that's where trusting you comes in. You have seen behind the scenes, the motives and the methods, so tell me what I should do. The other wave that keeps crashing over me is the reality of my past—there are so many things I wish to have not done. I keep remembering them all, struggling to put them to rest once and for all. The habits, the anxiety that used to pop up every time something major happened have started to knock at the door again. Help me Jesus not to turn back to them for comfort. Help me resist the urge to slip into

old ways just because I'm angry or sad. If this cloud of witnesses is truly watching, I
hope my mother gets to see what you're doing with my life.
  Iylah

Iylah

The old brick building attracted her to this church, thanks to a quick Google search. It held similar characteristics as Frank and Kathy's church—the main one being how it stood as a staple in the community surrounding it.

The older the church building, the older the church and the less clutter of the unnecessary, Iylah thought. At least that's what the images from different churches on Google displayed. Their inclination for fancy lights and smoke machines didn't grab her. She just wanted a church like Living River, with people like Frank and Kathy, even the two Sour Sisters for variety. She missed them.

Sipping from a recyclable cup of weak coffee in the church's refreshments area, at the back of the hall—she put calling them on her to do list. Including Jeb, of course.

An enamored smile crept up on her face, the thought of him sending quick and short vaults through her.

Two nights ago, she learned about the withholding of love by the man she called father and the accepting, unconditional love of Another who proved to be a better lover than the rest. Not forgetting—the confession of a man whose past didn't cause her to feel afraid in his admission of falling in love with her. No wonder the sensation of being all over the place clouded her weekend.

Until this morning, singing along to an old hymn urging everyone to turn their eyes upon Jesus. The tears sprung, the words sinking deeper into the tepid cracks of her heart, acting as a balm and reminder to her tired mind. Overwhelmed by the new reality of not walking this treacherous road alone, Iylah perched in her seat. A new way of life she wasn't quite used to yet—the roads she travelled always used to have just her.

Her eyes flitted around the dispersing—mostly older—congregation of the church.

Do young people not go to church anymore?

Her presence stood out more than she anticipated. Leaving the house, she considered herself underdressed in high-waisted flared jeans, paired with a ribbed silk, camel brown v-neck jumper. The black and gold charm detailed stiletto boots she found in the back of the wardrobe came in handy.

Aware of the awkwardness of her standing alone while others chattered, she slipped a hand in her back pocket, finding solace in it

Maybe I should just go? Yep. I should.

Taking a gulp full of coffee, she emptied her cup ready to toss it in the strategically placed recycling bin.

"Excuse me?"

Iylah spun around, taken by surprise at someone's attempt to talk to her. An older woman with peppered gray hair stood before her, a red lipstick painted smile welcoming her to conversation. Iylah guessed the woman's age to be around her mother's age, coupled with a rather youthful glint in her eye. A similar glint to the one Kathy always had—an all-knowing expression. She was a foot shorter than Iylah but held the stature of a six-foot something giant. A quiet confidence oozed out of her.

"Sorry to disturb you, but you look awfully familiar." The woman clutched at her string of well-kept pearls.

"I do?" Iylah quizzed, dusting off her hands from nothing in particular.

"Yes. You look like the spitting image of a friend of mine who used to come to this church, actually. She went to be with Jesus a few years ago." The woman studied her face, probably trying to trace it to her old friend.

"I'm sorry to hear that. She must have been a special lady." Iylah offered some comfort in her words.

"Oh that she was." She chuckled gracefully, "But when the Lord called her home, Lillian had to go—"

Lillian? The name tingled in Iylah's ears, arresting her full attention. She probed further. "Wh—what was Lillian's last name?"

"Dawson. Lillian Dawson." As she said the name, a dawning came over the woman, watching Iylah's hand come up to her face, shock overtaking her eyes.

Holy cow! How did I wind up here?

"That's—um—she's my mother." Iylah rested a hand on her chest, this new piece of information becoming too much for her to wrap her tired mind around.

Thanks to a five-minute Google search, she chose to come to her mother's old church. Really?

"My name is Iylah. Iylah Dawson."

The woman's eyes glistened with recognition and tears, taking in Iylah up and down, before she leapt forward, embracing Iylah like she'd known her all her life. Iylah received her hug, restraining against the urge to fall into a puddled mess.

Most of her mother's friends were nowhere to be found after her death. It all but confirmed the frailty and vapidness of friendships she herself was acquainted with amongst those with affluence. To now be found in the arms of another person who seemed to value her mother, meant more than she thought it would.

"We used to pray for you." Her words came out in a hushed tone of awe as she held on to Iylah. "We used to pray that Jesus would find you."

Iylah succumbed to the tears. The reassurance of not being alone coming in quickly and fast.

◌ ◌

Jeb

He pulled the door shut delicately behind him, walking soft-footed down the hallway out into the living room, where his dad reclined watching replays of a basketball game.

For the longest time before moving out of home at eighteen, this time on a Sunday evening held fond memories. It used to be the only time he caught his dad unconsumed by other people's matters—done for the day after hours spent at the church earlier, and without the inquisitive ears of his mom who usually found herself buried in some historical fiction novel. These were the ways his otherwise frequently occupied parents wound down before a new week came in. Now at thirty-eight, Jeb counted this as the opportune time to bring his own matters to his dad.

"Who's playing?" He balanced himself on the edge of one of the mustard armchairs, the wide-screen television displaying its vibrant colors across the dimly lit room.

"Pelicans against the Warriors." Frank never really supported a team. His busy days didn't allow time to follow the sport with intention. "Did Tylor go down alright?"

Jeb nodded, taking in the athleticism of the two teams playing—searching for the right words to express the weight on his mind, "Yeah. Once his nerves settled, he got to sleep pretty quickly."

Jeb kept Tylor company, striking up a conversation to take his mind off his first day at a new school tomorrow. Tylor didn't express his nerves, but Jeb studied the sullen mood he wore all day, despite spending their afternoon skating. No amount of assuring could settle the scared thoughts of a ten-year-old boy starting middle school with no friends and no familiar comforts to aid him. Jeb resorted to talking much about nothing until Tylor's eyes drowsily shut.

Now that his son was taken care of, he could feel his own nerves bubbling to the surface. His new job at the local arts high school being one primary cause, the other causes revolved around a particular woman he couldn't get enough of, and another he needed to vigorously wash out of his system.

"Hey Dad, I'm—uh—I'm thinking about seeing someone, professionally, for Tylor and myself." The words came out in staccato, stiffly and awkwardly, with the admission of weakness seeking counsel. "I can't move past the anger clogged up in my chest—" meeting his dad's curious eyes proved too hard, Jeb honed in on his wringing hands. "And I'm afraid it's gonna turn me into someone I can't recognise and won't like."

Humility told him to seek the wisdom of his dad, when insecurity screamed out the unsavoury lies claiming no one could help him—it'd gotten harder to subdue the shouting.

Frank switched off the heightening game to hear his son out and steer him in a direction away from destruction. "Neil."

"Grumpy old man Neil?" Jeb puzzled by his suggestion of the man known to have the longest standing record of attendance at Living River. "I thought he retired?"

"Not entirely. He only sees people I recommend to him. I'll give him a call, see if he will meet with you both." Frank read the uncertainty on Jeb and added, "He's helped a lot of people navigate all kinds of situations. His methods are direct and somewhat effective—"

"Somewhat?"

"Yeah—depends on how the person received his methods. I'll call him tomorrow for you. So?" A coy smile rode over Frank's brow.

"What?"

"Are you and the young lady—whose name we won't mention because your mom is still awake—are you dating? Do they still call it dating these days? Can never keep track."

Jeb rejected the notion of him dating with a grunt.

His track record before Dawn couldn't be classified as dating, probably more close to the sleeping around he ratted Clint out for regularly. Those days youth flowed in abundance, fueled by the burning coals of doing everything his upbringing forbade him to. Before Tylor, before an ex-wife, serious relationships made him uneasy and stifled, much like the Christian faith he once professed. Now? Well now, the hint of embarking on the unknown grounds of dating didn't have a daunting air because of Iylah. Simultaneously, it also brought its own new challenges, because of Iylah and because of Tylor.

"I have a few things to get over before I can even consider it. I wouldn't be any good for her right now." The truth he ruminated over couldn't be dismissed.

It pained him to acknowledge it, despite having lost pieces of his heart to her already.

"That's not what I saw when she was here." Frank mulled over his words, processing them before they came. "When was the last time you were intimate with Dawn?"

Dumbfounded by the intrusive and blunt exposition, he obliged his dad still and answered, "Over two years ago—maybe more, actually."

The desire to be intimate with Dawn got snuffed out entirely after she turned up at the bar while he worked one night, barraging him for free drinks. Tylor remained at home unfed and all alone. Hastily telling Marcus that he needed to leave, he witnessed Dawn flirt successfully before he grabbed her by the arm, dragging her unwillingly home.

The constant humiliation always bore a hole of regret in him.

"When did you realise it was the end?"

"You're not going to charge me for this riveting counselling session, are you?" Jeb's endeavor to make light of the way the lingering memories poked at his bruised ego didn't fool his dad, who shot him a raised eyebrow. "Alright. About the same time I met Iylah. But what does that have to do with anything?"

"Son–" Frank shifted in his own armchair to face him. "Why did you stay as long as you did?"

"That's the million-dollar question." Jeb's fingers scratched at his head, glancing down at the mushroomy colored rug beneath his feet. He shrugged, daring to sift through the crevices of his life to find an answer. "I guess I was holding on to doing things right—"

"Right by whom? It did you and Tylor no good to put yourselves in that position."

"Don't you think I know that now?" Agitation showed itself in his voice. Jeb raked through his loose hair, a pricking uncomfortable heat invading the corners of his chest. "I didn't want to fail Tylor or Dawn, so I stayed. I thought I could fix her, but I couldn't."

"And you think you can fix Iylah?" Never one to beat around the bush, Frank sought the truth from Jeb.

"That's the thing, Dad—she doesn't need me to fix her. With the threat of death at her doorstep, she's handling it far better than anyone should. I'm the one who needs fixing." He admitted what he suspected of himself. He couldn't afford to be unaware of his wounds—a luxury out of his realm of expenses. "She asked me if I was mad at God, and I told her I was."

"Well, are you Jeb? Are you angry with God?"

He sneered, his gaze taken up by his hands. "Honestly—it feels like I'm being punished for—" He struggled to bring himself to confess the hammering thought assaulting his conscience daily, "Punished for walking away from what I used to believe. Any god who punishes for the exercising of free will—which he gave, by the way—I'm not sure I can feel anything but mad towards him." Jeb's chest rose and fell with increased breaths.

"I hate to sound like the one bearing the obvious, but son—it is that free will you exercised in choosing to stay in a marriage of dysfunction and turmoil. God didn't make you do that—maybe a misinformed idea you have of Him, sure. Jeb, He gave you free will because He doesn't want passive slaves. He wants you to freely, willingly come to Him. You're not being punished by Him—it's the consequences of choices and actions done outside of what God calls good. Our version of good is completely out of order—it's sin-filled. What you're going through now is because of that."

It didn't matter how his dad framed it—everything within Jeb disagreed. From where he sat, it definitely felt like a stern, unrelenting judgement. Not wanting to disclose anymore, he angled the conversation in a different direction, standing to leave for his room.

"Let me know about Neil." The rigidity of tension stiffening his body added an involuntary clenching of his fists.

"Sure, son." His dad didn't push any further.

Grateful that he didn't, Jeb trudged away, exhausted by it all.

Will it get better?

twenty-eight

Jeb

His knuckles rapped sharply on the painted green wood of the front door of Neil Garret's house. The ball of nerves circulating in his midsection orbited any courage left in him.

This doesn't feel like courage.

It felt strongly like defeat. The entire week felt and looked defeated. Fresh starts ought to come with clear yellow-taped warnings of just how insufferable and soul-crushing they can be.

Jeb ran his listless hand through his new short tresses, agitation slightly rising at how long it took for this door to be answered.

To mark the beginning of a clean slate, Jeb headed to the barber after his first day teaching art to less than enthusiastic high schoolers whose minds darted everywhere, except at his instructions. He recalled the last time he wore his hair this short—when his family returned from the last missionary trip he would ever go on in Peru. Since then, his hair ran long and annoyingly luscious, according to Dawn. His way of setting himself apart from teenage Jeb, marking the beginning of his descent from everything he grew up knowing.

He counted on this new short mullet trim to serve as a physical reminder that life needed to change.

He scratched the short beard around his jawline offhandedly, the sound of footsteps approaching did nothing to settle the humming anxiety in him. The door opened, revealing Nerelle Garrett in all her colorful splendor. No surprise his mom and her got along like a house on fire.

"Jebby," the name she fondly called him since the age of eight when she taught Sunday School all those years ago, seemed to have stuck. "Come on in." She waved him through their front door enthusiastically.

Hands now hidden in the pockets of his jeans, Jeb meekly entered their rather large home housing just Neil and her—no kids or grandkids anywhere in sight.

"Hey Mrs G." Suddenly feeling like the little boy who eagerly answered every question right under her watchful tutoring.

"Neil's out the back reading one of his heady books again." Nerelle led him through a long hallway, the passing front rooms filled with the orange-tinted light from the ending day. "I'll get an earful about whatever he reads later. Gosh, that man's memory capacity is like a modern day computer." Her jovial laughter filled the spaces his conversation lacked.

How on earth is she married to Grumpy Garrett?

Nothing about Neil exuded jovial, and this remained the sole reason Jeb's nerves probably wouldn't ease up.

His first therapy session with the guy who once told him God didn't like people who stared, after he caught young Jeb ogling at him hobbling down the footpath with his cane. The man never smiled.

Sitting astutely in his lustrous green backyard under the shade of a Sycamore—the withering heat no match for their sprinkler system—not a single line on his face pointed towards smile lines. His focus buried in the book Nerelle mentioned, glasses tittered right at the pointy edge of his nose.

"Good luck." Nerelle encouraged in a hush, motioning Jeb through the open floor to ceiling glass doors leading to the backyard. She knew her husband and his ways—that didn't bring any comfort to Jeb.

As Jeb moved through the doors, Neil raised his line of vision slightly, only to return to whatever he read. Jeb hovered next to the empty wooden lawn chair beside Neil, unsure how to greet the man.

"Jeb." Neil beat him to it, placing a bookmark in his pages, before closing his book, revealing how thick of a read it was.

"Neil." Jeb mirrored his less than cordial demeanor, the need to turn back and retrace his steps out of their well-kept home increasing.

"Take a seat." Neil signaled to the empty chair, taking off his glasses and placing them on top of the book disposed on a side table nearby.

"Nerelle says you're reading another one of your heady books—anything I've ever read?"

Neil jeered. "If by heady she means intellectual, then yes I am. Don't be fooled, she reads way more 'heady' books than both of us sitting here." He used air quotes for his wife's description of his reading habits.

Apart from the walking cane and the limp, not much about Neil implied his older age of sixty-nine. His hair always remained a pristine chestnut color—Jeb wouldn't be fooled into thinking it wasn't from a bottle of hair dye. When Neil spoke, he did so with eminent authority. You couldn't dare question anything he said because he knew almost everything about everything. Quick with his wit too.

"Well, that's one more book than I've ever read." Jeb dug the heels of his Converse's into the tuft green grass.

"I highly recommend it—reading that is. It relaxes the mind when we're preoccupied trying to comprehend new information in written form."

"Is this psychologically proven?" Jeb tested, knowing full well Neil never divulged incorrect information.

"What do you think? You know what, never mind—how can I help you today, Jeb?" Neil dismissed the small talk Jeb attempted to make, wanting to get to the bottom of Jeb's spiralling life.

"Well—" unsure where to begin, Jeb leaned forward in his seat, clasping his hands. "Um—I'm not sure what Dad told you?"

"Nothing. Just that you wanted to see me."

"Right." The task of catching Neil up on his life is not one he would enjoy doing.

"Let's start here—to what do we owe the pleasure of your being back in Clovis?"

A rough sigh escaped his body, preparing to retell the last two months. "My son and I have moved from New York after my recent divorce. We needed a fresh start, and I wanted him to grow up around my family."

"How recent is this divorce? And the cause of it? Was it a mutual decision?" His tone of voice remained level, not giving away any hint of shock or sympathy—steady and even as he spoke.

"My divorce got finalized about three weeks ago. I have full custody of my son. And no, the decision wasn't mutual. I filed for divorce."

"And the reason behind your decision?" Neil probed for what Jeb left out.

"She cheated multiple times over the course of our marriage, and she has a drug habit. It was tearing us apart." Jeb's clenched fist revealed how much it still tore him apart.

"How many times did she cheat? And how did you find out?"

The skittish energy in his stomach found its way up to his shoulders, where it usually visited. Under close observance of Neil, he restrained himself from rolling them back as was habit.

"Um—about six times. The first guy was a one night stand, a regular at the bar I used to work at. He came and told me because, apparently, Dawn stole money from him. After the fourth one night stand, I kind of knew the signs and figured it out on my own. By the sixth guy, they were no longer one night stands. When she got served with the divorce papers, she was at the guy's house."

His throat tightened, remembering the sharp jolts of devastation rippling through his body the day his lawyer told him. That day held two distinct recollections—the nail in the coffin between him and Dawn, and the open door extended by Iylah for no reason other than she could.

Guilt showed its face at the thought of Iylah.

In the centre of a rather trying week, which involved Tylor's complete meltdown after a hard third day at school and Jeb's sweat-soaked nights from terror waking up in a state of panic—he created distance from Iylah.

With the recent days further cementing the surfacing belief, he simply could not offer her anything good. Never mind his confession of every single one of his affections towards her growing. Affections no switch could turn off, the way his body reacted to any thought of her, betrayed him. All he offered right now were barbed pieces of a heart tired and bitter.

"Do you recall what went through your mind and emotions when you found out the first time?" Neil stole Jeb back into the present, away from his guilt-driven meandering mind.

Jeb cleared his throat, resting a hand behind his neck, beginning to feel exposed with each question Neil asked.

"Hurt. Angry. Worthless—like I wasn't good enough for her." He stole a glance back over his shoulder where Neil sat unmoved and inquiring. "It felt like I drove her into another guy's arms—"

"So you took her back?"

He nodded silently, shame loudly clamming up in his bones, feeling stupid and used.

"It's easy to turn that anger onto ourselves when we've been wronged. We may even believe that we deserved it, leading us to make a misjudgment. Did she ever apologise?"

"She always did." Jeb's gaze penetrated a single white Zinnia standing unassuming in the garden before him.

"Did you believe her?"

"After the second time, no. But I still stayed." He sneered at his own foolishness.

"Why do you think you stayed, Jeb? She gave you every reason to leave. Were you hoping she'd change?"

He shrugged, the question he had asked countless times coming up short with a reasonable answer. All the answers made him sound weak and deluded. "I was trying to do the right thing. Growing up, that's all I'd ever heard. Get married, have children, in that order because that's how God designed it. She got pregnant after we'd been fooling around for three months, and I had this urge to mend it by creating a family—I knew she wasn't ready for that, I wasn't ready for it. But I had Tylor to think about, and her."

"You didn't want to fail." Neil put words to the urge he felt so many years ago—even now.

"I guess I didn't."

I didn't want to add it to the list of things I didn't do right.

Small fragmented pieces of the past displayed themselves across his mind. Moments he deemed failures. Not going to college. Walking away from a faith he knew worked. Spending his years building nothing but collecting cheap thrills. Raising Tylor in a loveless marriage. Staying with a woman who didn't care if he went for a run in the morning. The threat of failure appeared to be keeping him in a chokehold, one he didn't know existed around his neck.

"Let's start there. Why is failure something you fear?"

For all his grumpy quirks, Jeb admitted to himself, Neil dug and sifted through the whirlwind of Jeb's life quicker than he could have done himself lying awake in his bedroom.

Maybe this is why Nerelle kept Neil by her side—his skilled manner of tending to broken lives.

And Jeb's life shone as a picture next to the word 'broken' for anyone who needed an example.

Jeb kicked the upturned corner of the rug under his bare feet in the garage. The space once served as Iylah's studio, now unused, all things untouched as she left them.

The nights she spent here, tending away at a painting she'd dreamt up, were his favourite. Only because they served as an excuse to come and simply be in her presence with small talk. He missed those. He missed her tremendously.

She picked up on the fourth ring. "He lives. It's an actual miracle." Her voice on the other end of the line was enough to pull him out of the misery of the days gone by.

"Hi Iylah." The grin on his face gave way to the pleasant buzzing travelling around in him. "Sorry, I know it's really late, I just—I needed to hear your voice." He placed himself on the stool she always propped herself in, allowing the truth of his 10pm phone call to be known.

"Are you okay? I haven't heard from you in a bit. I was starting to feel some sort of way about it. After ten unread messages, y'know a girl can only keep it together for so long." No sign of accusation in her voice. Though her words were true, she delivered them teasing and not scolding.

"I know." The heel of his palm rubbed across his brow. "It's been a predictably terrible week so far. Needed to process it. I'm sorry, I should have called." He added that mistake to the list of things he can't get right.

"That bad, huh? Jeb, you can call me even when there's stuff happening and you're not okay. You don't need to be okay all the time to call me, I'd actually prefer that you called on the days you're not okay—" her request bore witness to the care she displayed for him. "That's what friends are for."

Somehow the use of the label struck a nerve and continued plucking on it, the term echoing its finality. He didn't like it. Not one bit. Reality reminded him he had no choice in the matter and that's how it needed to stay—especially since Neil disclosed his professional opinion on what Jeb faced. Making Jeb feel weaker than he did before seeing Neil.

"Okay." He responded drily, not having the energy to fight off the friend zone they both initiated.

"I thought you were avoiding me, 'cause of our last conversation—I mean, I get it—"

"Wait—wh—why would I avoid you because of that?" His brow dipped into a frown, realising how his silence affected her more than he'd considered.

"I don't know—maybe you didn't mean to say it? Or you decided you wanted nothing to do with me since, y'know—since nothing can really happen." She sounded uncertain, and it triggered his own uncertainty.

He wanted to silence the lies she spoke of and offer her reassurance that he did in fact fully mean what he confessed, more so now as the days without her continued. Jeb craved her physical presence, yearned to re-do their last week before she left and couldn't for the life of him shake off the way she felt under his touch penetrated into the cracks of his bleeding heart. He couldn't say all that.

Instead, he said—

"Well, Iylah, it's not like anything I said was reciprocated back. As far as I can see, this all could be entirely one-sided." The familiar simmering anger rose above reason, boiling over before he could attempt to put a lid on it. "*I kissed you*—"

"I kissed you back—" she retorted at his insinuation.

"You left—" the hurt spewed out in all its black gunk, his anger taking no notice of who its target was.

"I had no choice, Jeb! Are you kidding me? You ignored me for days, then you get angry at me for telling you how it made me feel? Maybe being friends is a better option for us. You clearly didn't read any of the messages I—forget it. It doesn't matter. Call me when you've figured out what you want. Or don't call me. Whatever." Silence replaced her voice after she hung up.

Leaving Jeb sitting in a heap of rage, shame and fear. His insides burning up, making him restless. His breathing increased, his vision narrowing until he couldn't focus on a single thing anymore. A slight ringing took over his ears, dread filled his chest, aware of the impending panic coming in. The leather of the stool suddenly felt hot to the touch in the vice grip of his hand, as he tried steadying himself on it. Shutting his eyes in a grimace, he did as Neil had instructed him to do earlier. He just didn't think he'd be putting it into practice so soon.

Maybe medication wasn't such a bad idea.

Iylah

Iylah threw her sketchbook onto the empty couch space next to her. Her mind was far too frazzled to even contemplate finishing the mock-up of her next creative project. A project she hoped would get her foot in the door as an exhibiting artist. Right now though, such a desire ran far from her priorities.

She gazed around the living room she sat in, alone. Except this time, she sat alone and mad. Perhaps confused too.

Jesus, what is going on? I thought loving someone was supposed to be simple. This is definitely not it.

She rubbed her face, desperate to re-do the phone call with Jeb from thirty minutes ago. Her week of tossing and turning from his silence, made worse by Kathy's confirmation two days ago—Jeb wasn't doing too well. Iylah resorted to calling his mother when her calls and messages were being dodged. When loving someone meant more to her than she thought it would, it took constant self-assurance to confirm she in fact cared seriously for Jeb.

Care in the form of a love unfamiliar to her. Never having been on the receiving end of it, she resolved to be the person who loved wholly and with no reservation—in case she only got one shot at it.

Now she sulked, unsure what she ought to do after her unexpected fight with Jeb.

I need to rinse off this yuck feeling.

She got up, ready to shower and call it a night. Maybe this would resolve all on its own? Should she call him back?

No.

She frowned, placing her empty glass of water into the sink. She wished he would just tell her what's really going on.

The ringing of her phone and the name running across her screen intensified her frown.

"Yes?" The word slipped out aggressively, greeting Jeb visible on her screen.

Immediately her tongue regretted its utterance of annoyance at the sight of him.

His eyes were sullen, weariness etched in their corners, no sign of the smile that did things to her. His new haircut, enough to tug at her lips in the faintest of smiles. It suited him. In fact, it emphasized the strength of his jawline more, even with the fresh beard running around it. Her stance softened.

He cleared his throat to speak. His mouth opened and shut, showing the struggle happening within him. A bit of terror travelled along Iylah's spine, while butterflies fluttered one wing at a time, rapidly. She waited for whatever he had to say.

"I'm not that great at showing anyone when I'm not okay. It's not something I'm used to." His voice sounded withdrawn, like something grabbed a hold of his throat, making it difficult to speak.

Recognition of his weathered appearance, sunk her heart heavier than an anchor ever could.

"Jeb, did you have a panic attack?" She spoke softly, treading carefully, wanting to tend to his fragile state.

A shaky hand came up to his forehead, partially shielding his gaze from her, betraying how uncomfortable he felt. Iylah lowered herself down onto one of the kitchen stools close by, glumness washing over her seeing him like this.

"I've been getting them a lot. Sometimes in the middle of my sleep."

She experienced the same terrors—ones that came at full force in the night all too often. Though they seldom came now, though. Her shoulders crumpled at the knowledge of the giant Jeb faced. She still clung to her sword from slaying her own giants, in anticipation of another one to come.

Pity is not what he needed. She definitely didn't need it when she fell endlessly through the void of despair. She hesitated to say anything, knowing men like Jeb operated on stoicism when they were afraid. Stoicism isn't what she saw before her. He was choosing to let her in, past the rugged exterior and hardened shell of the heart beating in his chest.

She allowed him the space to tell her what ate away at him.

"I had my first therapy session today," he sniffled away the emotion drenching him, "With the grumpiest old man this side of California." The lightest wry smile pulled the corner of his lips upwards, not fully reaching a grin.

Ease settled over her strained shoulders at the news of his new grumpy therapist. "How did it go?"

His hand hid his piercing eyes, dropped from its place as a shield. He looked at her now, bloodshot eyes and all. The totality of her wanted to wrap her arms around him to bring him comfort. The screen between them made that obviously difficult.

"Turns out, I'm experiencing post traumatic stress symptoms from everything. Along with an underlying fear of failing that seems to be a running thread throughout my life since I was a teenager." He cleared his throat, scratching away at his head. "So much so that everything I attempt to do is motivated and informed by that fear. He recommends I go on medication to help me cope with anxiety."

Oh Jesus. Please give him a break. He needs it.

"And how do you feel about everything he said?" Iylah kept her responses short and question-led.

His jaw worked before he spoke. "It makes me feel weak." His features crumpled into a scowl, clouding over him. "How am I supposed to take care of Tylor like this? How do I move on from this without falling apart?"

"Same way you have been all these years. You're not in the slightest weak." Iylah shook her head, the tears of compassion for his brokenness lining her throat, reaching her eyes. "I've seen you show up for people even with all that's going on. That doesn't change just because you need a break from carrying the weight of your world." The frenzy building in her to relieve him of such a weight grew with each second her eyes took him in. He didn't deserve this.

As the pair of them watched each other, she saw his chest rise and fall slowly and intentionally, leading himself out of a state of apprehension. It became apparent Jeb hardly believed any kind words about himself—it wouldn't stop her from saying them. He needed to hear it.

"You took care of me." She pulled on the sleeves of the crewneck sweater she wore, feeling flushed in remembering the attention he always gave her.

The morning coffees, the makeshift art studio he appeared to be sitting in right now, the comfort when things got a little too confusing—down to his bewildered response when she told him her plan to trap Stefan. It all spoke of care.

"You took care of Dawn. Frankly, I don't know any divorced man who would take time out of his day to physically take his ex-wife to a rehab centre. You're taking care of Tylor." A slow, controlled breath released from her. "It's time to take care of you."

"I read your messages—" The expression across his face shifted, making him unreadable. "Iylah, I've got nothing to give you that isn't messy or complicated. And I can't do that to you—"

"I don't mean to compare cards here but—um—I'm currently being watched by FBI agents, who are listening in to this phone call, and I'm pretty certain my ex wants to kill me." She tucked a stray curl behind her ear. "I can do messy and complicated. That doesn't scare me." She swallowed, sifting through what truly sent her heart barreling for cover. "What scares me is you telling me you've fallen in love with me and then disappearing for a few days without a heads up."

His fingers ran through his trimmed tresses, the last traces of his guard falling away before her. "I'm sorry about before. You're the polar opposite of what I'm used to—"

"You mean to tell me you don't know any other spoiled, trust-funded women?" She teased lightly.

Jeb's shoulders lowered, showing signs of relaxing his posture along with another faint smirk. "There's that. Iylah, I've been married for ten years to a woman whose idea of caring about me included telling me I wasn't the man she thought I was, while she spent days on benders with random men." The muscles around his mouth tensed. "I don't know how long it's going to take me to get over that. I don't want to hurt you. Exhibit A literally happened forty-five minutes ago. You're the good thing. The good thing I don't want to fail at."

A dipping descent overrode in her, knowing the signs of where the conversation headed.

Bravo Iylah. You scared him off with your messages.

Logically, her brain ticked over with the reality of where they both stood in these woods. Surrounded by the dense vegetation threatening to strangle their very beings before they could even reach the uncharted road on the other side, which also held uncertainty. The besotted part of her convinced her not to allow him to make a decision that could seal the end of the beginning.

He'd been right. She left Clovis to tend to her thicket of life. Who was she to deny him his space to deal with his own thicket?

"You want space?" She wavered, clinging to all hope she misread the route this started going on.

He shook his head, sparking further hope in her. "I don't want it, but I think I need it."

And that hope took a nosedive.

Iylah swallowed back the tears waiting on the side of the stage, ready for their performance. A fog setting over her, she nodded emphatically, a forced tight-lipped version of a smile trying its best to be convincing that she was okay with this.

"Sure."

Too late. A tear found its way centre stage. She promptly swiped it out of existence, hoping he didn't see it. Jeb's crumbling face and glistening eyes proved he already had.

"You're right—I left. I guess it's your turn. Um—"

"Iylah—"

"I'm gonna go, Jeb—" The downpour imminent, she needed a quick escape, "I hope you make your way out of this. I mean it. Please take care of yourself."

With one small smile and a timid wave, she ended the video call.

In time for loneliness and rejection to greet her, bowling over her last reserves of hope. She was alone again.

twenty-nine

Jeh

Iylah Trustfund Dawson

> Hey, I've been trying to call, but I guess you're busy?
>
> Hope your week of first's is starting out okay--for you and Tylor. Thinking of you both.
>
> Call me when you can

> I wanted to tell you this in person (well over the phone)...I guess this will have to do...
>
> I'm in love with you too. It's the scariest thing to admit because I know a lot is going on, but I can't help it. It's you and I want it to be you. All of you. Not for what you give me, but for who you are. I see you and its made me a better person. I don't want to know what life is like without you or Tylor.
>
> Talk soon? ❤

> Please return my calls

> I hope you're okay xx

His phone lay open on the white speckled bench-top—the sixth time he'd reread these messages since their last phone call. The familiar tugging in his chest surfaced as it did each time his mind wandered to the call. Watching his words cause her to pretend she was okay with what he requested haunted him.

Space.

He said he needed it. At the time, yes, his mind needed a reprieve from the constant badgering of the ways in which he failed, and Iylah sitting every inch in her good looks bore a striking resemblance to something he could fail at. Five days later, the space he'd requested felt more like a wet blanket—meant to give him warmth and protection, but making him increasingly aware it kept out the warmth she exuded.

"Hey Dad, what time is Mom going to call?" Tylor made his way into the kitchen, an empty plate of pizza in hand.

They'd been eating Pizza for dinner and lunch for the last two days since moving into their new home and once his mom's home-cooked meals ran out. The smallest part of Jeb felt irresponsible for the lack of nutritious meals they'd eaten. The smile each night on Tylor's face when they picked up the pizza sliced Jeb's guilt in half. The last box of belongings unpacked, everything they owned occupied their new places, a modest amount of relief hunkered on his shoulders—it was probably time to lay off the pizza.

He glanced at the time on his phone screen, dreading the nearing minute in which Dawn called. Same time every Tuesday night his phone would ring with the designated line in-patients used at the rehabilitation centre. Apart from last week, her calls were a weekly thing. Today's call however held a different air to it. Jeb tossed up what he needed to say to her that determined how often she could have access to Tylor. The things he never got the chance to say the entirety of their marriage because the gloom he lived under made it hard to breathe.

And now?

His second visit to the Garrett's house today after work proved less daunting than the first. For starters, he had an idea of what he got himself into—secondly, he needed to get everything off his chest and wiped off his shoulders. Tonight, Neil's advice at the forefront of his mind, meant there were certain issues he needed to lay to rest in their grave once and for all—if he wanted to ever have a chance of starting over.

"In ten minutes. Don't forget to—"

"Wash my plate. I know Dad, you've only told me to do it ten thousand times." His more than observant ten-year-old, dutifully followed the protocol in their new home.

Jeb grinned at the cheek of him, ruffling Tylor's hair as he walked past, headed towards the kitchen sink with a window overlooking their backyard. He turned his sights back to his phone, willing it to ring, not from Dawn's call but from Iylah.

Despite being the one broaching for space between them, he inadvertently waited for her call. She took heed to his request and didn't send so much as a message. Why would she?

Multiple times a day, while he babysit a class of teenagers without the keenest interest in art, he'd push the thought away—

What if I never hear from her again?

It twisted his stomach in knots, the sheer possibility of his fear driving her away, while he searched for his personal self-preservation. All he saw this act of self-protection doing was keeping him from seeking what he really wanted—a new life. Neil agreed.

In the shortest space of time, Neil's insight became valuable to him. He saw right through Jeb and didn't hesitate in straightening his footing on reality and the possibility of changing it—starting with himself.

His mom came first in that category, however.

After unpacking the last few boxes she turned to her son with the ever-present smile on her face and kindly pointed out that if Jeb still thought God was punishing him, then having a new home to live in, a new job to provide for his son and the prospect of starting over with people who cared for him, seemed like a rather generous punishment. Her parting words before she embraced him, toppled the last foundational piece of his walls. Maybe he needed to stop punishing himself. Only time would determine how well he did that.

Subconsciously he opened up the portal to everyone else's lives. Instagram. The interest in what everyone did with their day to day didn't appeal to him—his time spent on it minimal. Until a certain green eyed, caramel skinned, curly haired woman hooked him—all of him. His fingers tapped on her recently posted image.

An original watercolor painting of hers. The water depicted green and blue in its hues, with vibrant colored droplets surrounding submerged legs, like diving into a colorful new world only seen in the motion of moving. Her page displayed more of her impressive artwork over the last week. She'd probably needed the distraction after he pushed her away.

Jeb scrolled through the next few posts, back again to the one stroking an unfamiliar color of jealousy in him. He told himself how stupid it was to feel this way, but no rationale subsided the inkling of jealousy.

Iylah sat all smiles at some outdoor restaurant, next to a dark-skinned, young, chiseled version of Superman—his arm around her back rather comfortably, smouldering for whoever took the photo of them. She leant into him, obviously relaxed enough to do so. Captioned—The troublemakers. Class of '07.

Insecurity knocked on his door again.

Cut it out Jeb! C'mon!

Just as he swiped out of Instagram, fed up with their distance, his phone rang. Dawn.

"Hey Ty, get changed into your pj's while I talk to Mom for a bit." He prompted Tylor playing on his Nintendo, as he sat on the new Chesterfield couch—courtesy of Clint, a housewarming present of sorts.

Tylor didn't make a motion to move.

"Now please."

The second prompting pulling him out of his immersion and off to his room.

Jeb swiped to answer the call, making his way out of the kitchen, directing his feet through the door out to the backyard where the evening balmy air met him.

"Hey Dawn, how are you?" He always kept it civil. He hoped it would stay that way.

"Jeb, I'm doing okay. Being locked up in here is driving me stir crazy. How are my boys?"

A flare of well suppressed anger leapt up, threatening to derail the call at her term of endearment. He rolled with it and keep it short. "Good. Listen—I just wanted to talk to you before I put Tylor on—"

"Is everything okay?" Her voice piqued at his statement.

He couldn't answer that just yet, so he cut to the chase. "Tylor tells me you keep asking him about Iylah and me?"

"Is there an 'Iylah and you'?" Her question proved why this very conversation was necessary.

"Dawn, we're not married anymore and we aren't getting back together after you complete your treatment. I need you to know that and come to terms with it. What happens in my personal life no longer matters to you—not that it ever did." He chastised himself inwardly for letting a hurt slip through. "Who I choose to start a new life with is none of your concern, and you shouldn't be digging for information from our ten-year-old son. Is that clear?" His tone remained neutral but firm, making no mistake in portraying exactly what he meant. "If it continues, I'll be forced to minimize your contact with Tylor."

"Is that it?" The moment the edge in her voice appeared, Jeb rendered the end of this conversation unredeemable. "After ten years of marriage, you now suddenly have your own personal life? Don't forget I gave you Tylor after you begged me not to get an—"

"It's not suddenly Dawn. You lost your right to be a part of our lives the second you cheated and didn't get help for your addiction." Irritation itched away at him, he told it to cool down. He would not be the one to burn the bridge—for Tylor's sake.

"She's at least fifteen years younger than you, Jeb. It's not going to last. She's going to get sick of you and I don't want my son around her little s—"

"I forgive you Dawn."

The words stopped the venom spewing further from her mouth.

He said it again so there would be no mistake, though he hadn't planned on saying it. Something in him told him it was true. He'd forgiven her. "I forgive you, because I will not let what happened between us stop me from loving someone else." The cool wetness of a tear found its way down his stubbled cheek.

He swiped at the tear, stunned by its appearance.

He loved her.

"You love her?" Dawn's question barely making it out.

"I do." His admission making his heart proud for finally being forthcoming about it—the strain coursing through it unclogging itself from his inner workings.

Without another word, she ended the call leaving Jeb standing in his dimly lit back yard, phone in hand and a new sense of what needed to be done next.

He dialled his mom's number.

thirty

09/17/2019

'Trust in the Lord with all your heart, and do not lean on your own understanding. In all your ways acknowledge him and he will make straight your paths.'

Proverbs 3:5

I've read mom's journals enough to know that none of this is meant to be easy. I never assumed it would be, but she taught me how you meet people in the very sucky parts of following you. Well, Jesus I've hit a very sucky part. My heart is so bothered by it all, it's clouded some of the hope you've given me. It's made me fearful about what my future really looks like and who is going to be in my future. I seem to lose people at a very frequent rate. The rejection from it all keeps knocking loudly and persistently it's hard not to answer the door. Help me believe fully how much you love me, and can it replace every other love I chase that could never equate to yours. Tell me what to do with my father. Tell me what to do with Jeb. I can't shake the feeling that there is more to come, that it's not as simple as walking away. My heart tells me it's not, but my mind screams he doesn't want this. Whatever the case, keep him. Call him back. Shut stupid fear and anxiety up so he's not plagued by it. You're doing it for me, so you can do it for him. Make his path straight. Make my path straight. Make our path straight, even when I don't understand how you could possibly do it. I know you're good at it.

Iylah

Lylah

She clicked the car remote twice to open the trunk of the AMG coupe, hoping the space was enough to fit her art supply restock. The shop assistant from Arts & Craftsman Supply quickly in tow, holding two more larger sized bags. He dumped them into her trunk, wide eyed, mouth ajar taking in the car.

She didn't blame him—the car is a guy magnet. The wrong type of guys ironically. Men like her father. Interested in fast cars, how they looked and having the right woman on their arm to elevate their appearance. Solely an appearances car. She liked it for its speed.

"Nice ride." The barely twenty something old guy commented.

"Thanks." She slammed the trunk shut, "Belongs to the most bigoted man in Seattle."

He didn't know what to do with her specific piece of information, only offering an uncomfortable chuckle, before turning around to head back to his underpaid job with a tepid pursed smile.

I need to let that go. Actually, I have a few things to let go.

Rubbing her lips together from the exasperation of the week, Iylah slid herself into the red leather seats, pressing the ignition button bringing the thunderous engine to life.

For all the angst the past seven days carried to her front door, there were subtle whispers of promise shaking her out from the cusp of discouragement. During the moments rejection threatened to topple her over—first from her father and then a shocking hit from Jeb—she put herself under a spotlight, asking the age-old question of what she wanted from this life? More so now, what did the breath in her lungs serve purpose for?

A glimmer of an answer came one evening. A soundtrack of old hymns she happened across filled the silent pockets of the much too vast house, while she water-colored a scene of Cadmium yellow and orange, Alizarin Crimson to show off the sky and its reflections of the sunset, over a Cobalt Green and Ultramarine Blue mixture depicting the lake. Each gradient seamlessly blending into the next. As she'd sunk into the expensive couch unsuitable for painting activities, she welcomed the distraction from thinking about Jeb to thinking about her own future.

Her desire to put down roots stoked questions needing resolved answers. How would she set about starting her career as an artist once all this city-hopping drama ended? If it ended well. Where would she stay? Would Jeb call her again?

The questions tumbled around her that night, doing more robbing of her peace than she desired. She sent out a silent prayer of help, not expecting how quick the response would be. The next day she tested the answer, getting in touch with an old high school classmate, Jase. His parents kept ties to most of the Seattle art precinct and from memory they loved her. They didn't love the trouble her and Jase got into every so often. Still, a soft spot for the girl who turned down dating their adolescent son developed somehow.

Jase was right in the convenient middle of establishing his own gallery space—with a 'modern relevant twist'. If working at the König taught her anything, it'd be that modern art trailblazed at a rate no-one older past millennial years had seen before. Her skillset being classic and fine art didn't stop her taste venturing into more modern attempts of art.

Whatever Jase devised with his team, she wanted to be part of and she mentioned it to him, not in the slightest aware that by the end of their lunch date, she'd be walking away commissioned by him to be one of the opening exhibiting artists once the gallery's doors became known. Right now, said doors were still being installed.

The answer to a half mumbled prayer proved Jesus to be a great listener and planner. Now to wait for the rest of her heartfelt prayers to find their place and form.

Jeb being the main prayer.

The car throttled under her guidance through the inner city streets of Seattle. Her eyes darted to the rearview mirror to look out for the commonplace Ford SUV tracing her every move like she had a tail. They went everywhere with her, their names only divulged to her the night she ordered them dinner. A simple thank you for guarding her while her ex gallivanted across America in search of her whereabouts.

Funny that. Stefan doing everything he could to find her, while the man she actually wanted, and dare she say out loud, the man she loved kept his distance for the last week.

Iylah didn't know how much longer she could maintain this silence from him. More than once, she typed up a message to send to Jeb, quickly tapping the arrowed x on her phone, shushing away the impatient side of her who needed to know where they stood. His presence in her life no longer an acquainted one, but rather a desired one.

She kicked herself at how she ended the conversation. Running away from the uncomfortableness of him needing space and failing to recognise why he was doing so.

Hadn't she done the same thing plenty of times?

Only the ones she pushed away didn't care marginally enough to stick around. She didn't know how to correct it and she hoped the days weren't wasting away an opportunity to fix it. She wanted him in her life and she wanted to be in his. That she was certain of with no reservations.

Did he?

Jesus I really hope he's okay. I miss him and I want to talk to him, but y'know do what you gotta do. I guess.

Her mind wandered to the first piece she intended to start on for Gallery Modern Art—not what Jase called it but a nonsensical name she came up with. The booming ringing of an incoming call vibrated its way out of the car speakers, amplified in the less than spacious ride. Her gaze flicked to the touch screen display to her right, a gasp leaving her at the name scrolling across it. Feeling an urgency she jammed on the answer option, not allowing it to ring any longer.

"Jeb!" The relief in her was not hidden, and she didn't intend to hide it. She didn't care what he called for, the utmost important thing was him calling.

"Hi Iylah, quick question—"

No 'how are you', no 'let's talk'.

Her mouth went dry awaiting the first question he'd ask her in a week. His voice alerted the longing in her gut, reminding her once again how she missed him.

"Yes?"

"Uh—are you at home by any chance?"

"Wh—um—what do you—no I'm not." Her face wore a frown of puzzlement, unsure what type of phone call this was, "Why? Also, how are you? I mean—"

Jeb's amused laugh travelled throughout the car, triggering another motion in her stomach, of butterflies this time. "I'm kinda at your house right now."

"I'm sorry," She shook her head, not comprehending what exactly he meant, "What do you mean kinda?"

"I'm standing outside this ridiculously larger-than-life gate—"

"I am beyond confused right now. Are you in Seattle?" She could feel her eyes widen at this possibility.

"I said I'd come for your birthday, so here I am."

"Are you joking? No, seriously?"

He laughed again through his words, "Are you home or not?"

"Oh my gosh, you're not joking!" Without meaning too, her foot stepped heavier on the accelerator sending the car streaking down the highway. "I'm driving on the highway, fifteen minutes away. Do not move. Do not go back to Clovis."

"Iylah, I'm not going anywhere. I'll see you soon."

"No, don't hang up. I literally haven't spoken to you all week," Excitement rippled around in her, the magnitude of seeing him in person shocking to her system in more ways than one.

"I'd rather you kept your attention on the road than talking to me. I'll see you when you get here."

"Okay." Her grin no match for everything else leaping inside of her, "See you soon."

The call ended just as all her questions started. How did he know the address to her father's house? After days of no contact with his sudden presence for her birthday tomorrow unbefitting of where they'd left off. He sounded better, almost happy. Had something changed?

God do you really work this fast?

Try as she did to keep under the speed limit, her foot made other plans. Plans to see Jeb and figure out what was going on. Surely it was a good sign of him turning up unannounced at the house.

The assumptions and questions rolled through her mind, not relenting the closer she got. By the time she pulled up into her father's street, the thumping of her heart rip-roared over the niggling probes.

The moment her eyes took him in, leaning against one column framing the iron gates, a duffel bag at his Converse clad feet, any doubt of his impromptu visit disintegrated rapidly.

At the sight of the car coming to a halt in front of the gate, he straightened himself up tucking his phone in the back pocket of his slouching style jeans. He looked leaner than she remembered, the new haircut framing every feature on his face.

Iylah flung her door open, desperate to give the man standing there wearing a satisfied smirk a hug she'd been dying to all week. And she did just that. Words being completely insufficient to greet him with. He received her, their bodies pressing against each other in a tight squeezing embrace, hiding his face in her neck. They both held on a little longer.

Tears formed, his scent and nearness overwhelming her, the safety she'd always found in his arms still there.

She needed to see the eyes she missed stealing looks into. Pulling back to take him in, her hand rested along the line of his jaw. The weariness she remembered sitting around his eyes, no longer there. In them she saw relief. "I thought—"

When his plush lips found hers, they silenced whatever she thought, stealing her breath into his. His hand gripped the small of her back, while the other slid up her neck under her flowing curls, his fingers hidden in them. Pulling her closer by the waist, the taste of him making the darkness behind Iylah's closed eyes spin in a dizzying whirl. Her lips tingled from the electric current he imparted.

Jeb pulled back from her lips. She steadied herself from the whiplash, placing a hand on his chest. His nose grazed the tip of hers.

"I missed you." His breath marked her lips as he spoke in a close hush that sent her spine crackling in response.

"I can't believe you're here." Was all she said, fighting the temptation to say more.

She hoped this meant a start of what she prayed earnestly for.

Jeb

He withdrew his hand from her reach, for the second time away from the bags full of art supplies he'd grabbed from the luxuriously expensive looking Mercedes she drove.

"I've got it, Iylah." He juggled his duffel back over his shoulder, while the other hand held the contents of some art store she bought out, "Are you planning on opening up your own art supply store, or?"

Iylah pushed open with great effort the wide and towering solid wood door, revealing a foyer holding a solid wall in its midst, a floating staircase led upstairs lined with glass panels next to it. A striking edgy chandelier hung from the high vaulted ceiling emphasising the extravagance of the house. The polished light authentic Maplewood floors sprawled out to other parts of the house on the lower floor hidden behind the marble wall.

Jeb's mouth gawked at the scale of wealth displayed around him, stopping in his steps, head craning around to take it in.

"What is it your dad does again? I'm in the wrong profession."

"Investment banker. Him and my Mother started up a few minor companies back in the day in finance and they got bigger over the years." Iylah walked ahead of him, leaving Jeb to follow along astounded at all he was seeing.

"Just how big did they get?"

He found himself in the open-plan kitchen with a sprawling dark marble island in the middle. The only indication it was a kitchen being the range hood where he supposed a stove was. All appliances were hidden in plain sight.

"Big enough. Do you want some water?"

His awe of this place increased as he surveyed the large living space across from the kitchen—another chandelier and a wall of glass doors revealing an outdoor patio complete with a built-in cooking area. Beyond it sprawled a backyard with private access to a lake.

"Um—yeah sure. Thanks."

He spotted a boat docked further down but the jetty.

"Right, just casually have a lake with a boat in your backyard." He muttered under his breath, lowering his bag to the floor and her supplies up on the kitchen island.

A bottle of Spring Water appeared in front of his face, snapping him out of his impressed daze, his attention back on the woman he hadn't seen or spoken to in what felt like an eternally long time.

Taking the bottle from her hand, he simultaneously grabbed a hold of her wrist keeping her in place next to him. He turned his body to face her, the tang of her lips still on his. Eye to eye, with little space between them, he recalled how much he enjoyed being this close to her.

"I have so many questions about how rich your dad is, but—" he reached for strands of her curls, pushing them aside to reveal more of her angular high cheekbone. She visibly sucked in her breath at his touch. "I need to let you know—"

"Iylah!" A third person made themselves known in the house.

Both their heads snapped toward the front door, where the voice boomed from. A silver-haired man, olive skinned and clean shaven, made his way through the foyer. He strode in like he owned the place, or multiple places like this judging by the gleaming of his gold watch. A smug expression on his face at the sight of Jeb and Iylah.

"Am I interrupting?" He tossed two large envelopes on the kitchen island walking around it to get to the fridge.

"What are you doing here?" Iylah stepped back from Jeb, her arms crossed over her chest.

Jeb did a double take at the tension laced in her firmly shut jaw. It hadn't been there a few seconds ago.

"You're not going to introduce us?" The smugness didn't leave the man's face. An air of confidence and arrogance across his brow, as he leaned against the island a bottle of water in one hand.

Iylah's searing gaze didn't leave the man's sight. Jeb swore contempt lasered from her eyes.

"Jeb, this is my father, Fredrick Dawson."

The introduction made Jeb awfully aware of the resemblance between Fredrick and his daughter. Their eyes shaped the same, though different colors. The same set tensed jaw displaying the state of their relationship. The way the corners of her mouth pulled upwards as she pursed her lips, just like he was doing right now. She was her father's daughter.

"Welcome Jeb." Fredrick's icy blue eyes darted from Iylah to Jeb, not a single trace of sincerity in sight.

The man definitely had enemies.

Jeb gave a curt nod, not inclined to say anything beyond that.

"Again, what are you doing here?" Any affection Iylah held towards her father didn't make an appearance.

Her defensive posture and words, all the evidence Jeb needed to evaluate where father and daughter ranged in the scale of civility.

Instinctively, he gravitated closer to her, an impulse of protectiveness sweeping through him. Fredrick noticed.

"Your birthday present, from your Mother." Fredrick motioned towards the two envelopes sprawled on the bench top. "Have your lawyer look it over. I'll send someone to pick up my signed copy. Please don't take too long with it," He made his way out of the kitchen retracing his steps back out, pausing just as he got to Iylah, "And oh—enjoy your new place." He motioned to the house they all stood in.

"My new place?" Her face still stone in expression, "What are you talking about?"

"My birthday gift to you. Title deeds are in the other envelope." He leaned in giving his daughter a cold kiss on the cheek, catching Jeb catching a whiff of his rather fruity cologne. "Happy birthday darling daughter."

Like the enigma he appeared to be, Fredrick slinked his way to the foyer, leaving Iylah and Jeb motionless from their encounter with him.

"I don't want it!" Iylah called out to him, a vein vividly popping through the skin of her throat, dropping her arms to her side fists clenched.

"Yet you have no problem taking half my companies!" A tinge of anger sounded in Fredrick's voice, the front door slamming shut marking his exit.

Tension hung in the air, reaching the high ceilings, suppressed words lingering around them. Jeb examined Iylah, her chest rising and falling faster than it ought to, worked up by the four minutes her father entered and left.

He reached for her clenched hand, gently prying it open. "Hey, hey—" he spoke tenderly, "Iylah, look at me." He touched her chin, coaxing her head to turn to him.

When she did, the sadness laying in her emerald eyes stirred his own anger. Not just at her dad, but at himself for the terrible week he must have put her through. She didn't need any of it.

Stepping in closer towards her, his chest grazed against hers, eyes tracing the scowl etched in her face settling finally on her penetrating gaze. "I'm sorry. He sounds like a piece of work, and I've been one too. I shouldn't have left you hanging like I did. It hurt you and I hate myself for it."

"Why did you?" She asked so quietly, Jeb certain it was one she replayed in her mind the last few days.

"I was scared." He gulped the fear down even then. "Scared, I couldn't measure up to what you needed. Scared of the chaos from my past and messing up any future I had with you. I'm still scared. Now I'm more scared of not getting to love you at all. Can you forgive me?"

The dull ache of guilt he carried around, needed her forgiveness.

"What?" She whispered.

"Can you forgive me?" He repeated.

"No, not that. Of course I forgive you—you love me?" Her brow dipped inquiring of his affections towards her.

The corner of his lips pitched upwards, "Yeah, I do. I love you."

Tears wet her smiling eyes observing him, his skin littered with cool goose-bumps from the adoration in them. "That's a relief because I love you too."

Wrapping her up, Jeb left no space for distance between them—they'd had enough of that. Her face nestled in the cradle of his neck, the heat of her breath against his skin flaring up desire she alone stirred in him.

Mom was right. Maybe God sent her to me.

Iylah

The lake's cool water pooled around her calves, as she swivelled her ankles in circles submerged beneath the water's surface—the length of her dress hiked up just above her knees. The full moon hanging over them lit up the rippling motion of the lake, bouncing its luminosity off the roofs of neighbouring houses in their grandeur.

Iylah leaned back on her arm, her other hand toying around with the stem of a wine glass housing the remains of the 1995 Domaine Leroy Pinot she took a fancy to from her father's cellar. Technically now her cellar, according to the documents sitting unmoved on the kitchen island.

Upon pouring Jeb a glass while he expertly prepared their dinner of a Spanish Paella, he remarked he felt somewhat unworthy of drinking a wine worth enough to buy a house. She tucked his comment away, to bring up at a later time with a question attached to it.

"I don't know where you learned to cook like you're a Spaniard, but my stomach is very much impressed." She threw her head back, searching the deep night sky with the twinkling stars as its companion.

"An old lady who owned a hostel I was staying at in Spain made it for me once. Paid her in garden work so she could show me how to make it." He chuckled, the memory drawing a fondness. "Took me a week. I only planned on staying there for three weeks—it ended up being four."

After the emotional highs and lows the morning brought, they spent the early portion of their afternoon sourcing ingredients from Pike Place Market. Jeb's insistence on cooking for her tonight winning her curiosity. His habit of feeding her over the course of them knowing each other stuck, and she didn't mind it one bit.

Her efficiency in a kitchen sat awfully far down the spectrum of inadequacy, and it showed when she attempted to dice some onion, nearly severing a thumb off, leaving Jeb dumbfounded at her technique. She pouted stating there were many other things she excelled at. He teased and said he didn't mind being her personal chef going forward.

Once they finished meandering through the market with two bags full of fresh ingredients, coy gazes exchanged and the intentional brushing past the other, the next order of the day was a late picnic lunch. A picnic lunch that could only be experienced on the grass of Gasworks Park, Lake Union dazzling its onlookers gathered there—displaying the cityscape of Seattle.

The place Iylah experienced her first drag of a cigarette at seventeen, before taking it up seriously two years later after her Mother's death.

Jeb being privy to parts and areas of Iylah's growing up spiked a low dose of forced vulnerability in her bones. No man possessed such a keen interest in her like he did. The reality of falling in love with one so attentive to her as Jeb, caused her to worry about him witnessing parts of her he may not like. Her weaknesses beyond what he already experienced. The parts of herself she didn't like. Yet she couldn't help but unfold in his presence. Opening up her world usually stowed away from anyone's grasp or eyes.

"Will you take me to see your Mom tomorrow?" Jeb moved his feet around in the water, the sleeves of his jeans rolled up.

Iylah's head shot around to look at him, the question warming her heart but making her feel more fragile in his hands. "Um—sure, if you want me to."

"I do." He nodded emphasising his desire. "She was important to you and you're important to me. Besides, I'm not entirely convinced I'm the type of guy your Dad approves of. I have a feeling your Mom would love me."

Her thumped whenever he mentioned how he felt about her. At no point did she get used to it, and she hoped she never would, no matter how much it scared her.

"She would've loved you, and probably would've given you a play-by-play on me." She confessed, a grin spreading, her focus not wavering from him.

"You mean like the way my Mom is with you?" Jeb quizzed, raising a glass of her father's favourite whisky to his lips. She sensed a teasing in his words. "She told me how many times you called during the week to check on me. She also told me I was being a coward and being mad at God who sent you to me, was the dumbest thing I could ever do."

"Wow. Kathy did not pull any punches." Iylah giggled. "I was worried about you. Short of blowing up your phone like a stalker, she became my best sane option."

Iylah remembered the back and forth she had with herself before deciding to call Kathy. Caring enough to do so—not caring too much about how it made her look.

"Meddling mother's, huh." He huffed, "She's right though, on all fronts. I do think God sent you to me." Sincerity dripped in his voice, sending a tug through Iylah's middle. "In what world would our paths have ever crossed? I've never believed in coincidence or luck. I'm still working out where I stand when it comes to my faith. Some things though, are making it extremely hard to be mad at a God who made you."

His arm slid around her waist, making sure not a single inch of space was left between them sitting side by side.

A shimmer of heat travelled around her, rising to fill her cheeks when his lips pressed against her forehead. She laid her head upon his shoulder and its strength.

"Seems he did the same for me." She inhaled, peeling back another layer for him to see.

"Promise me you won't hide the parts you think would scare me?" His leg moved around in circular patterns in the water, brushing against her heel as it did so. "I want to see you for all you are, even those parts."

"I don't think our lives are giving us a choice of hiding the worst parts, anyway." Her head rose to find him watching her under the crisp moonlight. "I mean, you saw the way I decimated that onion."

His laugh wrapped itself around her heart, making it leap in bounds. The timbre of his laughter bounced along the surface of the water as it petered out, leaving the soundtrack of the night to fill its space.

"The way you look at me, makes up for it."

In the darkness around them acting like a cloak keeping them hidden in its fabric, Iylah's skin lit up in goosebumps. Jeb's hand found stray strands of curls hanging over Iylah's face. He twirled one around his finger gently, releasing it to bounce in place.

Each time they touched, it elicited a chain reaction of flurry, warmth and the buzzing of a mild obsession brewing in her towards him. The sensation far better than any cigarette or any high out there.

"Did you decide if you're going to take the medication for anxiety?"

Jeb turned away, casting his eyes out onto the water and its rolling tides. Apprehension settled over him like a fog. She noticed it in the creases taking over the corner of his eyes.

"I've got them with me. Never taken them. It's weird thinking about relying on a small pill to make you feel better." He took a breath in.

"Yeah it is. I didn't quite like how they made me feel, but I also didn't like not being in control when the panic hit."

"You don't get panic attacks anymore?"

She shook her head, struggling to remember when the last time was. "I think my last one was on the flight to Clovis from New York. The nightmares stopped too."

"You've never mentioned nightmares before. Were they bad?" Concern laced his words. His care unrelentingly sweet.

"Oh, yeah." She blew air out of her lungs. "I used to get them a lot in New York and in Germany after it happened. The scene from that night replayed repeatedly on loop each night."

The sting of the dreadful fear they used to induce, no longer hitting her in the parts it used to. In its place, a weighty assurance of being kept made itself at home.

"The nightmares stopped the day you told me about Jesus out in the backyard under the tree." She smiled reminiscently, marking the road she once travelled on unknowingly.

"Really? I didn't know that." He cleared his throat.

Iylah continued, grabbing a hold of his hand. "And then you gave me your Bible. Jeb, you introduced me to Jesus, and it changed my life." She squeezed his hand, "He's not punishing you, y'know—he's been waiting for you." Her furrowed brow exposed how out of the blue those words came from to her.

Iylah heard him attempt to sniff away whatever her statement conjured up. He brought up his free hand wiping the tears she couldn't see with the heel of his palm. His grip in hers tightened, unshed tears tensing his. She didn't dare say another word, acutely aware of a similar moment she had with him, sitting side by side in lawn chairs, while her insides caught on fire that didn't burn her down, bringing her back to life from a dreary gray washed existence.

He gave a soft singular tearful chuckle. "You're good at this."

"Nope, just telling the truth." She enveloped her arms around his neck, planting a tender kiss on the side of his head.

There they sat, two bodies, the moon their beacon of light, the gentle lapping of the lake against their legs the only sound they could hear, lulled with the rhythmic breathing of the other. Two lives attempting to rebuild from the rubble with new pieces. She hoped they would build something that lasted. He was becoming important to her too and no amount of self control could stop it.

thirty-one

Jeb

He plated the scrambled eggs on top of the lightly toasted slices of sourdough bread.

The morning sun streamed through the lake facing windows of the kitchen, lighting up the breakfast he prepared, while Iylah remained asleep on the couch in front of the larger-than-life television screen, where they spent the night watching a heart wrenching movie of loss and loneliness.

As the movie progressed, Iylah inched closer to Jeb for comfort and it was then he understood the shelter he brought her. It was in the way she curled her feet underneath her, leaning in towards him, laying her head on his shoulder.

What once struck him as a manageable fire, turned into an engulfing, ferocious flame of an earnest love for her. One he didn't go searching for, yet presented itself and held him hostage for an answer and to be acknowledged with purposeful intention.

With it came the timid trepidation of jumping ahead of himself, but seeing her response to his presence, the fear dissipated and gave in to a blooming hunger for her to be his and his alone. Sitting there, the weight of her impressing into his side, he'd fought his overwhelming urge to smother her in delicate kisses.

After their night sitting out on the jetty, certainty grabbed a hold of him, showing the evidence of her being a light at the end of an extremely dark and withered life. Any resistance he held towards the God he didn't frequently acknowledge, she chipped away at it by her mere existence.

Jeb witnessed bits of the woman she'd been and now he watched with marvelled eyes whom she continued becoming. Then why did he hesitate, when he felt the gentle pull towards finally giving in to the God who could change an entire person's heart? He held onto something else other than surrendering.

"Birthday girl! Where are you?"

The sound of a woman hollering through the house, caused Jeb to drop a well-charred cherry tomato onto the pristine marbled gray stone tiles where he stood.

"Crap!" He muttered under his breath, reaching for the cloth he found lying around in the butlers kitchen, erasing the red stain away from sight.

"Iylah!" The voice drew nearer to the kitchen, the sound of heels striking the very tiled floor he was wiping.

He straightened up from his cleaning errand to face the woman standing at the entrance of the kitchen, a leather brown suitcase in tow beside her.

"Hi." He self-consciously waved, the evidence of his cherry tomato incident in one hand, suddenly feeling like an intruder.

The woman every bit a replica of Iylah, only with straight blown out hair, light brown eyes, a head shorter and built a bit more sturdy than Iylah's slender figure. They both had the same dark caramel hues in their skin. She appeared more put together and practical in her dress sense. Shown by the light washed jeans she wore paired with a linen blouse and those quarter heeled shoes women couldn't stop wearing since 2007 in their varying styles.

"You must be Jeb?" She offered an introduction, placing her handbag on the brass cushioned kitchen stools lining the other side of the kitchen island.

"That's me. And you must be Lena?" He made his hands free to extend a friendly handshake across the depth of the kitchen island.

"The one and only." She shook it, firmer than most. "And where is the birthday girl?"

"Knocked out on the couch. Fell asleep after watching the saddest movie known to man."

Lena grunted, sitting herself down.

"Are you hungry? I've just finished making breakfast, and I was about to make coffee too." He turned his back to access another plate to dish out his offering of morning sustenance.

"I would be lying if I said what you've made there isn't making me hungry."

"Great! I'll plate you up some." And that's what he did.

"Do you make a habit of this? Making breakfast for Iylah?"

Unsure whether Lena was impressed or simply testing what kind of man he was, he made light of her question.

"I've seen how Iylah cuts onions and honestly it would be irresponsible of me to allow her anywhere near a stove." He sliced through the loaf of sourdough bread, before travelling to one end of the kitchen to dip it into the toaster.

Lena laughed at his observation. A measured laugh, nothing like the full-bodied, head throwing laughter of her younger sister.

"What's so funny?" Iylah made her half asleep presence known, shuffling her feet through the kitchen to Lena's side, a yawn escaping her mouth.

"How you're no good in the kitchen." Lena stood up, enclosing Iylah in a hug, "Happy birthday little sister."

Iylah received the hug somewhat awkwardly, it made Jeb smirk. Iylah never one to enjoy being the centre of attention. He tucked away this endearing trait of hers in the new space she occupied in him.

"How was your flight?" Iylah staved off the hug, wriggling herself out of Lena's reach.

Lena shot Iylah a quizzical look, her eyes running up and down her sister with a raised eyebrow. "Are you pregnant?"

Iylah trudged over to the fridge, opening it to retrieve something. Jeb kept his head down on the food he prepared for the two sisters, hiding his intrigue to Iylah's incoming response.

"Lena, how? How could I be pregnant? I haven't—" Her sentence trailed off causing Jeb to raise his head curiously the piece of information he had no business asking but danced around his brain at least once a week.

No fire outside the fireplace.

Or so he'd grown up being told—the fire being sex and the fireplace being marriage. Maybe if he listened to the carefully crafted anecdote, the bitterness of life's lemons would have tasted less bitter. He harbored no intention of asking about the men of her past. The knowledge of Stefan was enough.

"I'm not pregnant. Just constantly hungry thanks to not smoking. So yes, my butt is bigger—Maria pointed that out hilariously." A carton of orange juice was in Iylah's hand, as Jeb struggled not to make eye contact that would betray him.

"So birthday girl," He placed two made plates of breakfast before each woman, willing to change the subject past the focus on Iylah's anatomy, "What is it you want to do today?"

"First, I take up your offer to be my private chef going forward, 'cause wow!" Iylah's eyes widened at the meal before her.

"If you got this every day—" Lena speared her folk through the fluffy eggs, tasting them with closed eyes, "I understand the bigger butt."

"You made the eggs the same way Kathy does." A fond smile covered Iylah's face, "I've never cried over eggs before, but I think I just might."

"You sir, need to meet my husband and teach him how to do all of this, okay?" Lena motioned to her plate.

Jeb, satisfied with their reaction, said, "I'm afraid my Mom swore me to secrecy."

That she did. The five times he hounded her in the last week desperate to know how to make Iylah's proclaimed favourite eggs.

As he made the coffees, the order of the day was discussed, while the fleeting emotion of happiness seemed to stay put in him for longer than it usually did. He was thankful for its company. The task at hand now remained not to succumb to the notion of how quickly this happiness could end. He would instruct his mind to be present and behave.

At least try to.

Iylah

"Thank you."

Iylah's stomach responded in a mild rumble at the sight of the Firefly Squid and Rapini Salad placed in front of her by the waiter. Her sharpened chopsticks already in hand, but doing the courteous thing of waiting until everyone else's meal had been placed before them.

The smell of Jeb's Grilled Seasonal Fish wafted across the table, making her second guess her meal choice. She side-eyed Lena's dish next to her, settling to go after Jebs when she was done.

"So, do you share food Jeb? 'Cause this one has a habit of eating from people's plates." Lena motioned over to Iylah by her side, looking accused of a heinous crime. "Used to drive our mother crazy."

"She never really gives me a choice," He grinned, throwing a subtle wink in Iylah's way.

He was correct in saying so. Since they'd known each other and where food was concerned, he'd witnessed her habit of asking politely before she ate a considerable portion of his food. But he always let her. They'd become quickly comfortable with one another. She rather enjoyed the feeling of having that with someone.

The Japanese restaurant around them bustled with patrons here to enjoy the decadent cuisine on offer. Dimly lit and decorated in a minimal modern Japanese way. Her eyes roamed across the long room, scanning the faces out of a hypervigilant habit.

I need to stop doing that. You're safe, Iylah, relax.

She rolled her shoulders back unknowingly, catching the glance of Jeb quick to notice, giving her own wink.

Their day mainly held stealing looks at Jeb wherever he found himself to be, either by her side or looking onwards at something that caught his attention.

Iylah heeded herself twirling in a bubble of delight, losing count of the number of times she wore a heartfelt smile. Never one to swoon over any man, she did so frequently with him. When he reached for her hand on their hike, not allowing Lena's complaining presence to steal away from their time together. When he stared onwards at her while she snapped away on her camera. When they arrived at the restaurant as they waited to be seated, he stole a kiss and confessed how she made it hard to concentrate on anything else. To the retro film camera he sourced as a gift to her, under the knowledge of her wanting to dabble into fine photography more. It all caused her heart to swim in an ocean of uncharted territory. She observed how easy diving deeper into those new waters with him would be.

The conversation and food continued to come between the three of them, making for a perfect birthday dinner for the woman who rarely celebrated much of her life. Tonight marked the beginnings of a life worth celebrating. In the midst of Lena telling Jeb a long-winded story about the time she went to Spain many moons ago, two dark clothed men pulled her line of vision as they conversed in stealth with the head waitress by the entrance.

Thing One and Thing Two—also known as Mike and Dalton. She'd learned their names after ordering them dinner one night as a simple thank you. Thing One, Mike, presented his identification badge, most likely stating what he needed. Iylah and Dalton exchanged a look—he gave her the smallest nod.

What are they doing in here?

A chill danced across her bare shoulders, through the asymmetrical chocolate brown, form fitting maxi dress.

Something was happening. The head waitress nodded to whatever was being said, directing Mike and Dalton to an empty table in the restaurant's corner. Close to the entrance, accessible enough to see the entire room.

Iylah was familiar with this surveillance tactic—Stefan's bodyguards used to do the same.

Her stomach knotted up.

Something's wrong.

"Iylah?"

Jeb's voice drew her back to their table. His head followed where her gaze once was—the table Mike and Dalton occupied.

"You okay?" His brow crumpled questioningly.

The sound of her phone ringing beat her to answering his puzzled face, startling her into a little jump. Jeb's frown intensified.

"One second, sorry." She rummaged blindly in her clutch, getting a hold of her vibrating and dinging phone.

Eric Mane's name screamed across her phone, yanking her stomach further down.

"Um—I've got to take this. I'll be back."

She got up from her seat, throwing the napkin on her lap into her unfinished plate of food, quickly scanning for the bathroom sign.

She double checked each cubicle, like the cliche she saw in movies, and answered the phone.

"Hey Eric—"

"Iylah sorry to interrupt your birthday dinner—"

"How'd you know it's my birthday?" She realised how dumb the question was as soon as it left her mouth. "Sorry dumb question. Is everything okay?"

"Stefan is in Seattle, as of an hour ago. Now remember we've been prepared for this moment—"

The next sentences that followed from Eric Mane dulled in volume, a whooshing sound entrancing her ears. The onset of panic gripped Iylah's senses, robbing her briefly of any control. It was finally happening. Somehow she deluded herself into thinking this day would never come. A reckoning of sorts.

Why had she been so naïve in thinking so?

"Iylah?"

"Yes, I'm here." Her voice scratched the surface of being audible, restricted by the remaining giant yet to be slain.

"Mike and Dalton have surveyed the restaurant you're at. Five other agents are stationed by your house in varying locations. Our protection surrounds you, when Stefan makes his move towards you. We can't be in the house with you, but rest assured we are there. Is this clear?"

"Yes." Was all she could manage amidst the sinking taking place inside of her. Leaning against the door of a cubicle, she pushed past the tightness of her chest to ask, "What do I do now? And what about my sister and Jeb?"

"You go about your evening as normal. If you wish to tell them you can. I'll be in touch if anything changes. But you have my word, we will do our best to make sure you come out of this unharmed Iylah."

His wasn't the assurance she needed, but she obliged. "Thanks Eric."

He hung up.

All her strength unattainable, Iylah keeled over bracing herself by the knees, her breath shaky. The prickling sweat appeared at the back of her neck. The dress she wore unexpectedly feeling too tight and restricting.

Jesus, help. I need you in this. Show me you're here.

Jeb and Lena.

She straightened up gingerly, remembering where she stood. In the toilet. In a restaurant. Jeb and Lena waiting for her. She couldn't tell them. What good would it do to have them worried and fearful? If the worst came up, she'd put herself in the line of whatever trouble arose. This was Stefan for goodness' sake. Trouble was coming.

It would be okay, right?

Though I walk through the valley of the shadow of death—

Like a lamb to the slaughter?

I will fear no evil—

Even the evil that brings certain death?

Your rod and your staff they comfort me—

But will they protect me?

She needed to get it together. This wasn't the time to fall apart and frazzled at the seams. Shaking her hands out, taking a few inhales and exhales, she dared to believe it would be okay. The other alternative wasn't an option.

Exiting the bathroom, she briefly locked gazes with the two FBI agents assigned to her, turning away just in time for Jeb to witness the exchange again.

"What did I miss?" Iylah cleared her throat, sitting back down in her chair, her appetite nowhere to be found.

She did her best to avoid eye contact with Jeb, he wasn't easy to fool. Lena on the other hand, was at the moment. Lena took advantage of time away from the kids and husband, another drink in hand.

"You missed out on another drink. Jeb here is tapping out and you birthday girl, have only had one sip of your wine. You losing your touch?" Three drinks deep Lena made an appearance, peering at Iylah through her lashes.

"Looks like you've got me covered." Iylah motioned to the drink in her hand, mustering an amused smile.

"Do you know these guys?" Jeb nodded towards Mike and Dalton.

The truth danced on the tip of her tongue, along with knowledge that if Jeb was privy to the situation, the chances stacked pretty high enough he wouldn't go back to Clovis in the morning like his plane ticket dictated. She wouldn't allow it. And Lena would do exactly what she does best—find any means for Iylah to avoid facing this, when she in fact needed to.

The truth needed to be shelved right now, and Iylah's best acting needed to come forward.

"No idea." She shook her head trying to sell the lie. "They keep staring, so I'm just staring back." She shrugged, faking disinterest.

"Right." Jeb stretched out the word as he spoke it, his head tilted watching her.

His foot grazed alongside hers under the table, halting the jittering of her foot exposing the anxiousness travelling through her. The gesture sped up her nerves more.

How was she supposed to keep this from him?

Jeb

The slight sound of the approaching morning, ushered Jeb out of his comfortable sleep. Opening his eyes to the darkness of her room, the electric blinds doing an efficient job of hiding any traces of the risen sun. His body clock told him an estimate of it being 6AM, the time he woke up each morning for a run without fail. This morning, he approached the day differently.

She lay asleep next to him, her body turned in to face him—even in her subconscious she gravitated to him. A sleepy half smile formed on Jeb's face, watching her chest rise and fall through the tank top she wore. The moments of their night together swiftly returned to mind, cementing their reality all over again.

A tug rested in his stomach, prompting him to move closer to her. His eyes making out her silhouette in the absence of daylight. If he reached out and touched her, she was sure to wake up. He resisted the urge and settled for gazing upon her allure.

After dinner they'd arrived back at the house, Iylah being uncharacteristically quiet. Finding a moment to themselves, Lena making an exit for bed, Jeb listened to his suspicions and asked Iylah if there was anything she needed to tell him. From the hawk eyed guys at the restaurant, to the phone call she disappeared for, and the sudden worry written across her face in big uppercase letters.

Iylah brushed it off as tiredness. Jeb lay awake in the bedroom next to hers, unable to shake off the telltale signs of a lie. The way she avoided all eye contact, the nervous tics showing up in various parts of her body. After all, his experience with Dawn taught him the hard way how to spot a lie.

Deciding he needed it resolved at two in the morning, he called her phone to see if she was awake. She answered and invited him to her room.

An uneasy edge developed in his gut, his mind debating whether to probe further when he spotted her bloodshot eyes and a journal next to her on the bed. Wanting to bring her comfort, he carefully hauled her up as close as he could to his chest. In the middle of asking her again what was happening, her kiss silenced him rendering the question forgotten—their hands and bodies moving entangled with one another.

He took heed to the niggling voice telling him to keep his pants on and keep hers on too. He couldn't distinguish whether the early years of his adolescence filled with many warnings and a brief talk with his dad when he ended up lighting a fire outside the fireplace, prompted the niggling. All he deduced it to was the decision to not cross that physical line with her, regardless of how everything in him fought to be close to her in that way.

He confessed long-distance relationships did not appeal to him in the least, but neither did a life where she wasn't in it. So for her, he would go against a shelved preference and pursue a new life with her. Hesitation didn't appear in her words when he brought Tylor up—with the biggest smile she said confidently she would follow their lead. He believed her, her lively eyes unable to hide the depths of her heart, as she fell into a gentle sleep.

The birdsong outside increased, he reached for a stray curl draped across her forehead, pushing it back where the others lay undisturbed. She stirred slowly under his hand, eyes still shut in light sleep.

A foreign dread found space in his chest, the thought of him leaving today the source. Right here is where he wanted to be. Undisturbed by the world calling outside, hidden in the safety of this newfound haven they created between themselves.

"Are you staring at me while I sleep?" Her voice laden with sleep broke through the quiet. She didn't open her eyes, nestling closer to him, her head on his bare chest, the curls he stroked rushing against his chin.

"Is it creepy if I was?" His hand at home in the dip of her waist as she lay on her side, turning on his.

"If you deny it, yes it is." She draped her own arm over him, showing no signs of getting up.

"How do you not have bad morning breath?" He teased, pushing himself up to get a better look at her. He leaned against his propped arm. "Did you get up early and brush your teeth?"

"I don't know whether or not to be offended. Did you just assume I would have bad morning breath?" She moved back, tilting her head upwards to look up at him.

He grinned, more than content to spend his morning skipping a run. The little light peering in acted as his torch, revealing her freshly woken up, not a trace of makeup—barefaced and beautiful. "My God, you are breathtaking."

"Nice rescue." Her art of deflecting compliments showed itself, nestling her head back into the nearness of his chest.

"Why can't you take compliments? I've never seen anyone swipe them so far out of existence every time they get one, like you."

"'Cause for most of my life, I've felt like a fraud. Compliments didn't make that any better. What time is your flight?"

"Eleven thirty." He lowered himself to reach her eye level. Bright eyed and fully awake. "But that's a few hours away, so let's not worry about it right now." He traced the outline of her full lips, plump and soft, with his thumb—inviting him once again.

Shattering their hideaway's illusion, the bedroom door flung open, carrying with it a stream of light and Lena.

"Here we go." Iylah muttered under her breath for Jeb's ears.

"Good morning, folks." Lena pressed whatever it was to open the automatic blinds, "I thought I would find you in here." She motioned towards him, striding in across the room full of energy making Jeb whimper.

Iylah noticed, stifling her giggle, rolling over away from Jeb. His hopes for more time alone with her slipping with every curtain Lena opened. He empathised with her husband, she definitely wore the pants.

"I made a reservation for us for breakfast on the way to the airport. We leave in forty-five minutes." Just as quickly as she appeared, she was gone again, the same way she came in—striding.

Jeb pushed himself up to sit, Iylah hopping off the bed revealing her long legs, accentuated by the satin shorts she slipped into last night. His mind wandered, so did his eyes.

"This is what she's like with no kids or husband to boss around. Basically runs your life."

"Sounds like Lauren." Removing himself from the bed, he met Iylah halfway around it. Hindering her path forward, Jeb picked her up in a hug, allowing her body to imprint into his.

Not a single part of him wanted to let go, nor did he want this weekend to end. He fought hard to shake the dipping sensation in his gut. Still no word as to what caused the weight still resting on her.

Iylah noticed worry overcoming his expression when he put her down.

"What's wrong?" A concerned fold chiseled itself on her brow, observing him.

His face softened into a small smile, "Nothing. Not the greatest at good-bye's—hate them." He shrugged, losing at removing the sinking sand in him.

"You make it sound like it's a forever goodbye. It's not." Her hand stroked the center of his chest.

The strong need to protect her sat alongside the uneasiness in him. The world he desired to hide away from came knocking with its reminders.

"I know. I just—I want to make sure you're okay and doing that from a thousand miles away doesn't seem like enough."

"It's not forever." The gentleness in her voice usually worked as solid reassurance. This time it didn't. "Remember, I've got armed FBI agents watching my every move. I wouldn't be surprised if they were using binoculars right now staring at your very taut back muscles."

He succumbed to a grin.

"Besides, once this is over, I'm moving to Clovis." She nonchalantly added a new piece to the equation which they had not discussed in all their interrupted conversation last night.

Iylah strolled away into the walk-in wardrobe, leaving him with hands on his hips, digesting this news.

"When did you decide that?" Unable to explain why he wore a frown on his face instead of a more pleased variation of expression.

"Last night." She called back.

"Are you sure?" An unworthiness crept into him., starting from the shoulders down.

To have someone willing to upend their lives and follow his own, was a foreign thing for Jeb. Iylah pushed on the wound caused by careless hands, offering to help it heal.

She popped back out from her cave of clothes, grasping some in her arms, stopping a short distance from him. "Jeb Aston, I would do anything for you."

He believed her. Her resolve with such a statement dispersed the lingering uneasiness in him.

"Now go take a shower before she comes back and puts us both in time out." Her eyes gleamed with mischief and sincerity all at once.

Lips parting into a smile, he shook his head, not entirely sure what he had done correctly to deserve her.

"Yes, ma'am." Taking his marching orders.

∽ ∾

Iylah

Iylah flicked her loose curls over her shoulder, tilting her head at an angle giving her hair permission to stay, as she bit into her breakfast taco.

"You could use the fork and knife you've been given. It will be a whole lot cleaner." Lena surveyed her digging in with both hands, the way a taco should be eaten. "All that sauce all over your fingers." The disapproval continued, Lena tinkering away at her three scrambled eggs, served with hash browns and toast.

Iylah shook her head in protest, chewing diligently, deciding it best not to choke on the mouthful.

"Fork and knife with tacos? Nah. You gotta get in there." Jeb got it.

"This is unsanitary, Jeb." Lena pointed at Iylah with her knife, "Wait til she touches you with those fingers."

Jeb half-choked, half chuckled at the truth Lena presented.

"It's like you didn't eat dinner last night? Dang Iylah." Lena's running commentary unceasing.

Swallowing the last bit of her food, the opportunity to defend herself arose.

"Food tastes so much better. I'll wash my hands if it bothers you that much." Iylah inhaled a breath from her efforts, scanning the tables seated with people at the cafe she frequented as a teenager.

Besides the new furnishings and the layout, not much changed over time in Hudson's. The menu remained the same. The breakfast tacos were deliciously the same as she remembered. She wasn't the same. Life for her somersaulted in changes and she preempted more were to come.

Eyeing Jeb beside her, he pulled on his Brisket Omelette apart with a fork. He was part of the changing, regardless if the past came barreling down towards her. The kinks in her stomach she'd spent all night trying to untie, reminded her of it.

"Honestly, I don't think I've ever seen you wash your hands." Jeb jumped on the train of commentary with Lena as the driver.

Feigning offence, Iylah's mouth gaped. "Whose side are you on? I wash my hands, thank you very much."

"Prove it." He winked, taking a sip from his cup of coffee.

"I like you. You are good for her unsanitary behind." Lena approved of his cheeky quip.

Any hope of defeating the allegations against her were lost, she conceded relishing the company she was in—uncertain of the day she'd experience this again. She needed to make sure they departed the streets of Seattle as swiftly as she could hurry them up. Her mind showed no signs of resting until then.

Instinctively she scoured the seats around her again, searching for any sign of trouble.

None had come last night, giving her a false sense of security. Eric Mane's instruction to keep herself close to home once Jeb and Lena left, shattered the notion of being out of harm's way once and for all.

She thanked Jesus silently for the way He worked in this life of hers. Hoping and a praying to witness more of His wonderful ways past the here and now.

Jeb

He swung his duffel bag into the trunk of the town car. The assigned driver for them, shutting its hood behind Jeb. He thanked the driver before retracing his steps back to Iylah and Lena mid-goodbye in front of the Maserati Levante Iylah drove them in.

To say the wealth of her family did not astound him would be lying. Knowing she now owned a third of that wealth made him wonder how their newfound relationship would be affected by it. He wouldn't—couldn't allow her to do anymore than she'd already done for his parents, for him and Tylor.

The sisters said their goodbyes, Jeb getting closer to the least favourite part of his weekend in Seattle. Lena made her way over to the town car waiting to take them to their separate flights at the airport—leaving Jeb and Iylah to reconcile the bittersweet emotions of parting.

He stepped closer to his awaiting girlfriend in all her wild maned glory, a coy satisfaction on her face. His arms encompassed her waist, her green eyes displaying love for him. It caught him off guard and he confessed it.

"I don't think I will ever get used to those eyes looking at me."

He brushed dark locs of curls away from her face, resting his hand in the crook of her neck. Leaning in, her familiar scent awoke his insatiable desire for her, meeting her cushiony full lips with a wistful kiss—followed by another more firm, more fervent. Her hands tugged at the bottom of his shirt, clutching at it, setting his body alight in response to the bliss it was kissing her.

He pulled back ever so slightly, another kiss still in reach. "I hope you washed your hands."

She giggled, "I did." She bit her bottom lip. "I love you, Jeb."

"I love you." The words nudged his heart over the cliff, ready to freefall into whatever came next for them. "I'll see you soon, okay?"

She nodded, arms wrapping around his neck, steering him close to her. "Thank you for coming."

"I'd do anything for you." He didn't let go, the plunging pit finding its way to the surface again. Burying his face in her shoulder, he planted a simple kiss before retreating, his arms unravelling from around her. "I'll call you when I get home."

She backed away, blowing kisses as she did.

He didn't dare say it aloud risking being labelled insane, but everything within him told him she would be his wife one day. He watched her jump into the car, the throaty rumble of its engine stirring with her behind the wheel. Waving at him, she pulled out of the parking lot, turning into the main road.

His fingers traced her lingering kiss on his lips, as he turned towards the waiting town car, the fire running through him simmering down.

The screeching of car tires, accompanied by an eardrum bursting sound of steel crashing into steel broke his stride. Shattering glass hit the gravel of the road, quickening his steps to a light jog towards the exit of the car park. The smell of burning rubber engulfing his nose. Another bang resounded as an engine revved. His arms fell limp by his side. A little further down the road, a black Ram with its crumpled front repeatedly drove into the side of what once was the passenger door of a Maserati Levante, tossing it around.

Sharp, loud ringing overtook Jeb's ears. Instant sweat breaking out over his body. The hammering of his heart drowned out the sound of his voice yelling out her name. The scratching of his throat the only indication of the force behind his calling out. He compelled his legs to run toward the catastrophe. Two hefty brooding men hopped out of the beaten RAM. Handguns extended towards her car, the resounding piercing of bullets overshadowed the ringing in his ear. Someone screamed in the background. Arms appeared tackling him from running further—two, three bulletproof vest wearing men attempted to stand in his way. Three others swarmed in where the two mangled cars rocked. Jeb's clenched fist swung at the nearest guy restraining him, causing the man to stumble to the ground with the crackling of his jaw. Still, Jeb couldn't get past the two others blocking his way to her.

"We can't let you go there." Someone beside him repeated the words over and over.

Gasping for air to get to his lungs, his chest heaved, the blood in his veins running like lead, while he helplessly watched gun wielding men surround the scene of the wreckage, their weapons aimed at the two culprits forced to the ground.

A woman wailed in between shrieks, throttling out her name. "Iylah!"

His knees hit the gravel beneath his feet. Head pounding. Commotion surrounding his torn apart world. Grabbing at the strained breath struggling to find its way out.

"Oh, my God! Oh my God!" Hot tears stung his face, his vision blurring.

In a matter of minutes the end to a perfect weekend, threatened to unravel the entirety of his life some more.

thirty-two

Jeb

Leaning against the gray-washed wall of the waiting room, his foot tapped warily—exposing the worry running through his body. Jeb held his phone to his ear waiting for her to pick up on the other end. His bandaged hand wiped gruffly at his running nose. His hand the only broken part of his body, which didn't explain how everything else hurt. All heavy and in pain.

"Hey darling," His mother answered his call with her sunshine disposition.

"Hey Mom." He turned around to face the wall, tucking his throbbing hand under his elbow, across his ribs.

"How's Seattle and our gorgeous girl? Staying out of mischief?"

"Um—" Jeb's voice threatened to crack.

The images of Iylah's lifeless, blood covered, mangled body being removed out of a destroyed car by firefighters, tormented him. He shut his eyes tightly, pleading for them to go away.

"She—um—" nothing came out. He tried again. "She's been in an accident, Mom. It's terrible—" A shaky breath left his body, the pressure on his chest increasing.

"Oh, Jeb. What happened?"

"He got to her. He got to Iylah." Repeating the gut stomping truth made it harder for him to stand straight. The pain of it cinching his insides together. "We're just waiting for the doctor to get back to us. What if she doesn't make it?" His shaking hand came up to his mouth, covering it before the fear riddling him escaped. "I can't lose her—I can't."

"Jeb, listen to me. You don't know that right now, okay? Wait to hear what the doctor says. In the meantime honey, you need to reacquaint yourself with the Lord in prayer."

The ground swayed beneath him, unsure where to begin with such a task.

An hour and a half passed since their frantic arrival at Overlake Medical Centre. Iylah being whisked in on a stretcher, multiple machines already attached to her from the ambulance ride. Neither Jeb nor Lena was allowed to ride with her, under the strict instructions of an FBI agent—instead assigning one of his armed men the task of protecting her. Jeb fought back on that instruction, not trusting their already foiled efforts of protection over her, only to be apprehended firmly and escorted in a siren wielding SUV with Lena curled in disbelief.

Lena's efficiency went missing as she struggled to articulate to her husband what happened on the phone, breaking out into a body rocking sob—leaving Jeb to fill in the blanks for her husband whilst steadying a falling apart Lena with one able arm.

It was only at this moment, his Mom on the other end of the line, that the third wave of shock attacked him aggressively.

"Can you do it for me?" He sniffed the tears back weakly, "Can you pray for her?"

'Of course. We will pray for you both, honey."

"Thanks. I'll let you know if we hear anything."

"Who are you with?"

Jeb turned back around to face the rest of the waiting room littered with people, all in for their varying reasons.

"Her sister. Her dad's out of the country. So it's just us."

He didn't add the bit where Lena berated her dad on the call for caring very little about her sister. If he turned up, Jeb wasn't sure he wouldn't do the same to him.

"I'll speak to you soon. Tell Tylor I love him, will you?"

He said goodbye and headed back to his seat next to a detached Lena. They slouched despondently, the rest of the hospital buzzing with activity. He didn't have the energy for small talk. Most of it was consumed trying not to explode into shattered bits of anxiety. He sensed it knocking, waiting for acknowledgement.

Dancing around at the centre of his focus, conflicting images of Iylah brought on a vibrating headache. Her blowing kisses at him. The destroyed Maserati's alarm sounding with her still in it. Her body pressed against his so firmly the fullness of her chest engraved against his. Her face swollen, blood hiding the beauty of her. His hand engulfing hers securely as they walked hand in hand surrounded by lush nature. The sound of her hearty laugh that always caused her eyes to light up with unadulterated joy. Sirens bleeding over the wails of her sister. The agony in waiting for them to cut her out of the car, while she remained in it alone for twenty minutes. Him sitting on the curbside too crushed to do anything, also fighting the urge to do everything.

He leaned forward in the hospital chair, cradling his head, struggling to think about anything else but her.

"Are you Iylah Dawson's family?"

Jeb lifted his head to identify the voice. A man dressed in scrubs and a lab coat, an iPad in hand and tired eyes, stood before them.

Lena stood up, Jeb followed suit.

"Yes, I'm her sister, Lena and this is Jeb, her boyfriend." She introduced them, her voice raspy, a reminder of the ordeal they were currently living.

"Lena, Jeb. I'm Doctor Moore—" He tapped the ID attached to the pocket of his lab coat, "I am the doctor attending to Iylah." His gaze did not meet theirs, intently consumed on whatever news awaited them on the iPad.

"How is she?" Jeb braced himself for what would come.

"She sustained severe injuries to her body from the accident, including bullet wounds to her arm. For her level of injuries it was best to put her in a medically induced coma—"

"What are her injuries?" Agitation tickled Jeb's impatience. He just wanted to know if she would survive.

"Brain swelling, cerebral edema, hence a medically induced coma and ventilator to ensure enough oxygen is getting to the brain while we wait for the swelling to go down. She sustained a pelvic fracture from the impact. We've scheduled a surgery to do an internal reduction. Basically, we are inserting metal plates and screws to stabilize her pelvis. Her right leg will require a cast for six months for the upper leg fracture. The bullets in her right arm have been removed and we will monitor them for any complications or infections." He ended the list, lifting his gaze up to finally rest on them. "She is extremely lucky to be alive, given the impact of the accident. It will be a long road to recovery for her, but right now our focus is decreasing the brain swelling. Bones and fractures heal over time—a brain injury like hers, if not recovered well can jeopardise any hope of a full recovery."

"Jesus!" Lena exclaimed, her eyes widening at the diagnosis.

"What's the worst outcome?" The realist in him wanted to be prepared, but even as he asked he wasn't certain what sort of preparation he could do.

"Like I said, the fractures are fixable and with rehabilitation and physical therapy after surgery, she will be able to have movement. With the brain swelling, if it increases we'll have to go the surgery route to help ease the pressure on the skull from the lack of room. The longer she's in the medical coma, the slimmer the chances of her not ending up in a vegetative state. Our goal is to do what we can to eliminate those chances."

Vegetative state?

Jeb ran a hand through his hair, the remaining hope in him deflating, each diagnosis doing its best to remind him there was no controlling the outcome. "When can we see her?"

"She's just been sedated in the intensive care unit, I would say—" he glanced at the watch on his wrist, "In the next hour, a nurse will come get you and escort you to her room."

"Thank you, Doctor Moore." Lena thanked him for doing his job, as he dismissed himself with a nod.

Feeling queasy, the whisperings of anxiety leaning close, Jeb decided he needed some fresh air.

"Um—Lena I'm gonna go for a walk. Need some air."

He didn't wait for a response from her, his legs led him away from the waiting room in haste, the fingers of panic beginning to sink their nails in his chest. His head hung low, no idea what direction he went in, anticipating what was coming next, terror traveled through his system. He bumped into a shoulder clumsily. Deciding to make the most of this incident he asked the nurse, now rubbing her hit shoulder, where the hospital chapel was.

Two seconds of brief instructions found him in a room with a few rows of chairs facing nothing—confusing him. No cross. Green plants sparked a bit of life to the room that could otherwise take on the impression of a small meeting room. The automatic sliding door shut behind him doing a sufficient job of separating the bustle of hospital corridors, from the serene essential oil smelling room. A low soundtrack of some ambient instrumental lulled the room to mimic peace. Not a single soul sat in there. That suited him just fine. Jeb beelined for a seat in the middle.

His back pressed into the chair, eyes shut, and jaw set. The breaths he took were getting less shallow and more even, slowly driving his galloping heart down to a steady pace.

It's been so long.

The reality of it washed over him. His mind contemplating the idea of reopening a proper conversation line beyond half mumbled sentences for prayer. He ran long enough and hard enough to finally conclude—God wasn't the one who had changed, it was him. He created as much distance as possible from ever allowing his heart to believe in the goodness of who God was.

"It's been a long time and this feels hard." His utterances started coming out in a whisper barely audible to anyone else. "I know you can hear me. I know I'm the one who ran away, turned my back on everything you are and that's worked out as bad as expected." Jeb rubbed his face, catching the silent tears falling, "I really love her Jesus. I don't deserve it, but I'm asking you to bring her back to me, please?" His chest tightened with grief and desperation. "Every part of her that's been messed up, heal her. I've seen you do it more than I would like to remember, so I know you can do it. I'll quit being angry, I'll quit running—her life for my life."

෴

"She can hear you if you talk to her. She won't respond, but stories about your lives together, experiences. They all help." The young nurse walked Jeb and Lena through a list of ways they could participate in helping Iylah while sedated.

He couldn't look away from her. She lay there unmoving, tubes going in and out of her body, hooked up to their corresponding machines detailing her body's efforts and sustaining it where she couldn't.

Unrecognisable in her features, only by her curls surrounding the pillow her head lay on. A heaviness overtook Jeb's stomach like a set of bricks. He mustered enough courage to not give in to the anguish of seeing her like this.

Lena battled tears, losing to their sheer force. His arm across her shoulders, Jeb attempted to provide some relief from the harsh reality in front of them.

"Can—" he cleared his clogged up throat, "We read to her? She—um—she reads her Bible every morning." Jeb motioned to the Bible he gifted her, now in his possession.

Along with the rest of her belongings, Eric came bearing some good news and remnants of the ordeal.

"She does?" Lena asked.

"Yep," A pained smile on his face, "Every morning with a cup of coffee." The memory of the coffees he placed by her bedside for over a month vividly made a return, saving him from the edge of hopelessness.

"You sure can. It helps with brain stimulation." The nurse's chirpy demeanor felt out of place, but needed for someone who probably dealt with a dozen cases like this one.

"And music?" He added.

"Yes. As long as the volume is at a low decibel and not too violent or offensive." She continued to oblige Jeb's inquiries.

He chuckled softly, "Oh, she's got the music taste of a sixty-year-old woman. No violence and offensiveness. Just old and—" he trailed off, leaving out the brutal word on the tip of his tongue, unspoken.

Lena scoffed in the background. Turning, he watched the frown on her face deepen in a similar manner Iylah's did.

"I've spent so long trying to protect her, ordering her around, I don't think I took the time to just know who she evolved into. I don't even know what music she listens to, Jeb."

"I'm sure once she's recovered she will be happy to fill you in. Meanwhile, I'm looking forward to you filling me in on what she was like growing up." His voice held an air of confidence he couldn't quite convince himself he had. He hoped she would buy it.

A phone rang requiring attention from one of them in the room. It was Lena's.

"Sorry, I gotta take this. It's my assistant." She turned away to answer it, "Hey Kenzy—"

Jeb returned his sights back to a motionless Iylah, all the adventure and vibrancy she oozed on a current leave of absence. He inched closer to her bedside, plopping the Bible down on a vacant seat as he did so. Reaching for her still, cold hand, a foggy gloom overcame him, pondering on how fast it all happened. His head spun over it if he pondered on it too long.

"Excuse me, does this television work?"

"It should."

A conversation happened in the background between Lena and the nurse. All Jeb could do in that moment to hold himself together was lean in, planting a kiss atop of Iylah's head.

"You're safe now. It's gonna be okay." He whispered sentiments of hope over her.

"Iylah Dawson, the socialite and daughter of business tycoon, multimillionaire and local Seattle resident, Frederick Dawson, has been involved in what eye witnesses are calling a brutal attack—"

Jeb's attentiveness snatched away from Iylah to the television displaying the local news being reported.

"Ms Dawson was seen earlier today by an eye witness having breakfast this morning here at Hudson's with her sister, a prominent lawyer Lena Dawson-Williams, and a male companion, Jeb Aston, who many are speculating is her current boyfriend—"

An image of Jeb sitting on the curbside, head held in his hands, surrounded by two armed agents popped up on the screen. The image tightened his chest, the despair he felt then making its way back up now.

How did they get these images?

"Local authorities believe Ms Dawson was on the run from her ex-boyfriend, a German convicted felon and drug syndicate boss, Stefan Hartmann, who was known to the CIA and FBI. Hartmann had been released early from prison whilst serving a thirty-five-year sentence. It is unknown what his basis of release was—"

The news station displayed an image of Stefan and Iylah together. Iylah's face sullen with a discrete smile, leaning against the shoulders of a serious faced, buzz cut Stefan looking directly at the camera, his stare speaking volumes of his recent actions. The image dated February last year.

The lump in Jeb's throat turned into budding anger, forcing him to look away from the screen any longer.

"Hartmann is claimed to have orchestrated the brutal attack against Ms Dawson, before being found later himself castrated in a dumpster of a local diner in Spokane.

Police are investigating the circumstances behind the death of Hartmann. Ms Dawson is currently in critical condition at a private hospital here in Seattle—"

The screen went black, Lena being the source of it turning off, her face in a scowl.

"Those snakes. Who gave them all this information?" She tapped away at her phone screen, barely averting her eyes from it as she addressed him, "Sorry Jeb, I've got to get on top of this before it spreads. Welcome to the family." A small sarcastic smile tried itself on her face before fleeting away at the sound of her phone ringing again. She answered it, turning to leave the room. "Yes dad, I'm on it." And she was gone, attending to whatever ensued.

"If there's anything you need please don't hesitate to come find me." The young nurse took her opportunity to relieve herself from their presence.

Jeb nodded with a grave smile, "Thanks."

A foreign wave of tiredness zapped Jeb. The nurse leaving the room, he seated himself in the only chair available, carrying his old worn Bible on his lap. Not thinking much of it, fingers thumbed through the delicate pages he once poured over eagerly, using every color pen under the sun to underline what spoke to him in his young years.

A fond smile of remembrance crept up. The days of spending a couple of hours at a time reading through the words spurring him forward and invigorating him with an other-worldly hope, surpassing anything he was yet to experience further on in this life.

It became clear what he traded that in for. The days he lived after letting go of all he knew and experienced, brought a numbing diluted version of what was real.

My life for her life.

He didn't know if God would take him up on his offer, but he certainly knew he'd been heard.

His fingers rested on the page he searched for. The words on it tumbling out in a weary mutter, loud enough for him and his sleeping love to hear.

"The Lord is my shepherd; I shall not want—"

thirty-three

Iylah

    She sat on the hill's edge, a quiet breeze nipping away at her loose curls and the hem of her long white garment. The garment like silky butter against her skin. Her skin radiating the warmth of the light surrounding her. A light bigger in magnitude, far more vast than that of the sun. Everything it touched didn't have an ounce of darkness upon it. It felt familiar. Iylah slid flying curls behind her ear with a slight annoyance at their straying. The meadows before her rolled on in their expanse, the grass whipping around her under the breeze's gentle command. In the distance a bubbling of water sounded, drawing her up on her feet to follow its whisperings. She found a brook tucked beneath the cusp of a hill—crystal clear, flowing from one stretched end to another. Bending low, revealing her reflection, that of a fleecy sheep. Forgoing her hands, she drank straight from the water, tasting the brooks sweet refreshing.

    Iylah!

A commanding, pleasant voice beckoned her. Though its sound didn't touch her ears, her heart reverberated its calling.

Iylah!

It called again and again, til her bare feet hit the ground running in search of it—yearning to be near its owner. The breeze grew stronger and gripping as she pushed through up and down the hills, chest burning in search of more air, she kept going. The further she found herself, the grip of darkness crept up behind her, in front of her, surrounding her. An invitation to fear came, the pace of her feet slowing to a halt. Without the light's warmth, a chill climbed her spine. Out of breath and confused, she craned her head around in search.

Iylah!

Another stood beside her, the One whom the voice belonged to. His presence brought a delightful comfort dispersing away the tip toeing fear. He glowed iridescent and ever bright, from head to toe. Her heart told itself she was known by Him and He was known by her. He held her hand as they traversed side by side, each step they took darkness seemed to retreat without a fight. Even as it clutched at her trailing garment, her eyes were set on His hand engulfing hers in protection. She leaned her head upon His shoulder, the warmth of His nearness setting her heart ablaze.

They continued onwards.

Jeb

That was a weird experience.

Jeb chucked the duffel bag in the back seat of his car parked under the shelter of the Fresno International Airport carpark. Despite the shade, the heat inside his car blasted his skin as he turned the key in the ignition, his back already perspiring. With summer on its way out, the heat did not relent.

His journey in and through Customs went rather quickly comparatively to what he experienced to be normal. The other half of money and luxury lived their lives on expedition, having no time to waste. Particularly not in a Customs line at an airport. Hopping off the private jet afforded to him by Iylah's family, he sure became aware yet again of the vast difference in ways of life.

At Lena's insistence, he gracefully accepted the offer of having a private jet available at his beck and call to transport him back and forth from Seattle to Fresno, Fresno to Seattle. Along with a hotel room at the Hilton within walking distance of the hospital, temporarily under his name for whatever foreseeable future Iylah spent in the hospital's sterility and the life-sucking grasp of a coma. If his way was given to him, the chair next to her bed sufficed for sleeping in. Lena, in all her efficiency, scheduled them both to take shifts of care.

While one sat talking, reading, playing music, hand holding—in his case praying, sketching much of nothing—the other recuperated in a place of solitude, away from beeping life-giving and monitoring machines.

Away from Iylah.

No matter how many times his head hit a pillow to find sleep, it never came. All it brought were figments of the attack, the news reports doing their rounds, and the constant fielding off a barrage of missed calls and texts from siblings, friends and Dawn.

Driving the familiar streets allowed his mind to wander off back to where she lay. The scenes around him whirled past in a haze, much like everything else over the two days gone. His head swam every hour, like a lucid dream, unshakeable and keeping him trapped in its semi-reality. Except reality remained whether or not he woke up from it.

The sting of tears spiked behind his eyes. Tears for her, tears for his son, whose life didn't show signs of getting easier.

On a tearful call last night, Tylor told his father how he missed him and how he hated school. Jeb's mom elaborated on a fight that took place between Tylor and a classmate for reasons neither child wanted to share.

The cracks were showing in an unignorable manner.

Jeb dragged himself onto the jet this morning, his body aching, mind hazy and heart in two places at once. Nothing in him wanted to leave Iylah's side, with minimal signs of progress made in her recovery, a surgery completed on her pelvis, a cast applied on the broken leg and pain medication to stave off any inkling of pain despite her sedated state. He recalled after the surgery, her body convulsing from a seizure, an onslaught of the medical staff on duty rushing through the door. He cowered by watching helplessly like a scene from a heart-wrenching movie playing out before him, his character being one of the main ones.

The doctor implied the seizure revealed the severity of her brain swelling, and prepared both he and Lena for the approaching possibility of another surgery to be performed on Iylah, when a neurosurgeon arrived.

That night, Jeb allowed the sobs to rock him and rob him of breath, his head submerged under the rushing pressure of the shower in his lonely hotel room. He begged God to do something, the plea barely able to leave his lips, ripping his heart beyond what he could physically bear. Two hours later, giving him a break from the tossing and turning, Lena called him with the news.

Prior to the operation on her skull to relieve the pressure, a cautionary CT scan had been taken of Iylah's brain, leaving the neurosurgeon puzzled and questioning why the operation was needed. The swelling showed itself decreased significantly beyond anything deemed normal. Another CT scan proved the miracle to be true.

Never an unbeliever of miracles, Jeb saw God's listening ear clearly—his unbelief put on trial. He sensed it when he read the Bible to Iylah. The ancient text stirring his present heart, knocking gently. He contemplatively wondered if unbelief would answer the door? Or if the glimmer of hope he sensed could fling it wide open?

Pulling up into his parents' driveway, a breath of relief involuntarily left him. Taking a moment to bring himself back to the present reality, he sat behind the wheel while the engine of his car settled.

The front door of his parents' house opened, the figure of his five foot five mom standing in its frame—waiting for him eagerly to hop out of the car.

He moved prudently, a promising headache starting at the back of his head, taking himself out of the car and towards his mom. The compassionate smile on her face, coupled with the worry filling her eyes, a familiar look he saw growing up and one that brought him an odd sense of comfort. Comfort in the knowledge of someone caring enough to be worried about him.

"Hi Mom." He cleared his throat, the sediment of the days gone by like sandpaper to it.

"Hi son," She opened up her arms, inviting him into her ready embrace.

Without any hesitation, he walked into them, feeling no shame in needing it. She rubbed his back, soothing the weight strewn across his shoulders and back.

He hoped Tylor would always call him a safe space the way his parents felt to him—no matter how far he ran and how many years it took to come back.

They headed into the house where a homemade jug of lemonade was waiting to quench whomever thirsted, along with an open ear to whoever needed to be heard. A common posture Kathy kept for many, only this time this posture was to Jeb's benefit.

Sitting at the kitchen table, they exchanged stories of the last few days, and the heartbreak they brought. Jeb struggled to bring the adequate words forward to describe the whirlwind of it all, but settled on a few things he was certain of. His love for Iylah and his need to be with her no matter what it looked like. His concern for his son and commitment to building a life safe for him.

"And how about you, Jeb? What do you need for yourself?" Kathy inquired of her son the way she always did. Not pushing, not prying but lovingly creating a path to revelation.

His response whispered itself within him, stunning him to a pause of silence, mulling over what it meant. Feeling the weariness in his soul, his body carrying signs of the bashing of life's waves, his admission came in between the choking emotion constricted in his throat.

"I think I need Jesus."

Everything in him agreed with that undeniable truth.

∾ ∾

"When can I talk to Mom again?" Tylor wriggled his body down in his bed, Jeb pulling the planet-adorned bed covers over him, tucking the corners in, creating a cocoon of comfort for him.

Jeb kicked over a stray football displaced on the floor, among other items. Tylor really settled into their new residence, going as far as officially calling it home and treating it like such—hence the messy room. Jeb sat himself down in the space he cleared, bringing his knees up to his chest.

"It will be a while, buddy." He searched for the words to share the nature of Dawn to a son who adored her. "Mom needs to get better. Until then, it's tricky to have her in our lives."

"Why is it tricky?"

"Well, sometimes people have a hard time thinking about others. They don't know how to treat other people properly, and they end up hurting them, so it makes it hard for anyone to be friends with them or have them in their lives."

"Did Mom hurt you, Dad?" The questions of a ten-year-old knew no bounds. Jeb ironically admired that about Tylor.

"Yeah, she did son, and Dad has forgiven her. But for now, until Mom gets better, I'm afraid we won't be calling her. I want you to know that none of this is your fault and you're not being punished for anything. I'm just trying to keep you safe." Jeb reached over, giving his son a stroke across his forehead. "Now, do you want to tell me what happened at school a few days ago? The fight?"

Tylor shook his head timidly.

"Tylor?"

"He said you didn't care about me and that's why you left." An angry pout formed on Tylor's face.

"What? How?"

"His mom saw you on the news with Iylah and said you were being the opposite of responsible."

A pang of anger simmered in his chest. "Tylor, I would never abandon you, okay? I went to visit Iylah, and then something happened to her, so I stayed to make sure she was okay. But I would never choose someone else over you. I love you and always will be here."

"Is she okay?" Tylor avoided his dad's eyes, pulling at the corner of his pillow.

"I hope so." A genuine hope, one he clung to whenever anxiety showed its face once every hour.

"I know you like her."

Jeb smiled gently at his son's observant ways. "I do like her—a lot." To put it simply.

"Does she make you happy?"

His smile grew at Tylor's interrogation, but also at the answer behind the question. "Yes, she makes me happy, son. Very happy."

Tylor seemed to ponder his response before saying, "I like her too 'cause she makes you happy."

Jeb laughed, rising from his sitting position to give Tylor a kiss on the head. "Get some sleep, buddy. I'll see you in the morning."

Jeb's phone dinged in the pocket of his shorts, notifying him of a new message. Closing Tylor's door behind him, he checked his phone to see a message from Lena instructing him to call her as soon as he could.

He dialled her number, making his way down his short hallway into the living room area.

"Hey Jeb," Lena answered her phone on the second ring.

"Lena, is everything okay?" He sank into the new leather of the armchair, ignoring the noise it made as he did so.

"Yes, everything's okay. I just thought you would want to know—they are going to start waking Iylah up from the coma. The doctors are satisfied with the recovery of the brain swelling and want to reduce the medication for her sedation."

"That's great!" The news dispersed energy into his worn-out body. "How long does it usually take for this sort of process?"

"A few days, he said, until she gains consciousness. There may be potential side effects from the withdrawal process that we need to be prepared for." Lena's voice trailed off, triggering the dread sitting in his stomach. "She could be completely delirious when she wakes up, not knowing what happened, not knowing who we are. They'll only find out the extent of how much the trauma to the brain has affected her when she is conscious."

"So you're saying that coming out of the coma is only half of her recovery?" He swallowed hard, the possibility of what could go wrong looming right in front of him.

"Yeah." A detached, tired sigh came from Lena.

Jeb frowned at Lena's words. "Right. I guess we'll wait and see."

He rubbed his face with his free hand, still trying to compute this news, both in its good forms and complicated forms.

They were going to wake her up—that was good. No one knew the extent the accident affected her brain yet, leaving the worst open for possibility—that's complicated.

"I'll be back on Friday. I just need a couple of days to sort things out with my family. Keep me updated."

"I understand if it is all too much for you, Jeb. You've got your own life to live and priorities beyond my sister—"

Jeb wouldn't allow Lena to finish, creating an excuse for him to bail. "Iylah's important to me. No matter how all of this pans out, I'm not going anywhere. I love your sister, Lena. I'm in this for the long haul."

Even if it continued to be super messy, one day it wouldn't be that way anymore. That's the day he was holding out for—with her.

"You're a better man than most, Jeb."

"I don't know about that. I'll see you in a couple of days. Thanks for keeping me updated."

They said their courteous goodbyes, leaving him dumbfounded in his seat.

You've gotta help me with this, Jesus. Whatever the worst outcome of this may be, work it out to be good.

He blew air forcefully out of his mouth, attempting to relieve the accumulating pressure in his chest. His fingers danced across the screen of his phone, trying to find answers on the internet to piece it all together.

Nothing surprised him anymore, and he resolved to take it as it came. The wise words given to him by his mom became a new way of practice for him.

thirty-four

Lylah

"Is my husband here yet?"

Her throat felt like blunt razor blades tumbling around, eyes fluttering half open as best as she could keep them open. The cloud of heavy fog around the front of her head did nothing to jog along her thoughts.

The same woman's voice sounded in the distance, despite her proximity. "Iylah, sweetie, you don't have a husband."

Why does she keep saying that?

"Why do you—" She swallowed the collection of saliva welling up in her mouth, "Keep saying that? You're lying. Why are you lying?" Those few words withdrew more energy than she'd counted on from her drug-worn body.

"Shhh." A hand covered her limp hand beside her. "Get some rest, okay?"

"I don't like you." Iylah turned to address the figure standing next to her bedside, unable to quite make out a face. "You're bossy and you lie."

Struggling to maintain consciousness, she fell back into a groggy sleep.

I just want Jeb here.

∾ ৹৴৹

"What is your name?"

The doctor she'd seen weaving in and out of her room in between her bouts of dazed consciousness stood at the foot of the hospital bed charting notes on the iPad in hand.

A nurse at her bedside recorded the information displayed on the monitoring machines attached to Iylah's chest, hand and finger. The woman, who had not left her side since she awoke, wore the heaviest frown on her face.

Iylah couldn't remember who she said she was.

"My name is Iylah Aston." She said timidly, fiddling with the edge of the hospital grade sheet covering her.

"Who is the current President of the United States?"

The questions kept coming, sprouting agitation in her, thinking hard about the answers.

Shaking her head, she dropped her gaze away from those before her. "I don't know."

"Do you know what day it is today?"

A pounding sensation took over her temples. She shut her eyes—the pain travelling down to the base of her neck. "No."

"Alright." Doctor Long Nose scribbled something on his electronic device.

Her penchant for forgetting names resulted in her naming people by their most prominent feature. The nurse beside her dubbed Nurse Blondie and the woman at her beck and call since awaking, she called Miss Bossy.

Out of all the faces coming and going, the one she desired to see most didn't make an appearance.

Where was he? Tending to the kids, probably. She wanted to see them too. To look into the sparkling eyes of her little girl and at the soft smile of her tall boy. Oh, and the need to feel the lips of her man again, she couldn't wait for that.

Her head sunk back into the pillow, her eyes cast up to the ceiling after Doctor Long Nose and Miss Bossy exited the room. No doubt to talk about her.

"Would you like some water, Iylah?" Nurse Blondie flashed her a sympathetic smile.

Iylah nodded, not trusting her words, a dam of tears threatening to burst down the walls keeping them away.

"I'll be back soon." With a gentle tap on Iylah's hand, she walked off to her water fetching errand.

Shutting her eyes once more, battling the tears and the fog swirling her into confusion, Iylah hummed a tune sounding out in her tired brain, the words to it not quite coming around—lulling herself into a short sleep.

Fingers intertwined with hers, a hand stroking hair away from her cold forehead. The hands felt masculine, yet tender in their dealing with her. She tried to squeeze the fingers nestling with hers, traces of a sleepy smile drawing across her face. Resisting the sleep that kept calling, Iylah pried her eyes open to find intense sterling silver eyes delicately taking her in, tiredness brimming in the skin under them.

"You look tired." Her voice came out strained and croaky, morphed by the painkillers given to her.

"You look beautiful." He perched himself on the edge of the hospital bed, leaning closer to kiss her on the forehead.

She reached up to grab the material of his t-shirt, keeping him close—her fisted hand trembling at the motion of it. The tears she'd kept for him, slid freely and silently, his scent comforting her. Pine and mint.

"I missed you."

"Not nearly as much as I have missed you." He took both her hands in his, sitting back down, pecking each knuckle of hers.

Through heavy eyelids, she watched him. The dark blonde hair showed streaks of gray, his clean-shaven, tanned face displayed the strong edges of his jaw, his soft gray eyes and shoulders that sat wide and lean through his clothes.

"Wow. You are hot. How did I get you?"

"That's a story for another time." He chuckled, revealing the smile she probably fell in love with. "Get some rest , I'll be right here."

"Promise?" Her eyes shut involuntarily.

"Promise."

"I can't wait to see the kids. I miss them." Satisfied with seeing the face of her husband, she drifted back into sleep that snatched for her.

Jeb

Shutting the door quietly behind him, Jeb entered the corridor of the hospital where Lena and Doctor Moore awaited him.

"Well?" Lena stood, arms crossed, the lack of sleep around her eyes betraying the worry stewing in her from the last six days.

"Um." Jeb tried to gather his dismembered thoughts.

Iylah was awake, that's all that mattered to him. In and out of sleep, sure, but she could talk, she could smile, she recognised him. The only problem being, her memory placed him beyond what they were.

Jeb stuck his hands into the pockets of his charcoal cargo trousers, not sure what else to do with them or the situation at hand.

"She definitely remembers me. She definitely thinks we have kids." Even as he said the word aloud, he struggled to understand where her version of events came from.

He'd arrived back in Seattle today, after three days in Clovis tending to Tylor and informing his new job of what was taking place in his world. Surprisingly,

Ned, the principal, understood far more than Jeb initially gave him credit for—telling Jeb how much the students were enjoying his art class. He found himself with the flexibility to work four days of the week, making him available to fly back to Seattle over the weekend.

Jeb chalked it up to a prayer he'd said the night before his meeting with Ned.

A lot of those were spurting from his lips spontaneously these days. Hand in hand with making use of the Bible, Iylah gifted him.

"It's been three days, Doctor Moore. Are we sure her memories are going to right themselves?" The desperation in Lena boiled over.

Her sister had forgotten who she was, but remembered a man she'd only known for the last six months. Jeb understood her frustration. He hadn't foreseen himself being the one Iylah clung to in her state. Nights away from her were spent fretting over his being erased entirely from her memories. The opposite had clearly happened.

"The last thing she remembers is the night before the accident." Doctor Moore's eyes couldn't meet Jeb's, not for lack of trying. "In great detail, she remembers her time with Jeb." A pinkish hue coloured Doctor Moore's neck, betraying the sort of details likely divulged.

Despite the conversation at hand, Jeb curbed his mind from wandering back to the memories she disclosed, stifling a baffled smirk.

"She remembers nothing about Stefan." Lena added.

"Which is common. The brain does like to blot out traumatic memories. In this case, I think that is highly likely. We'll keep monitoring her over the next few days. The thing with post-traumatic amnesia is, it could last anywhere from a couple of days to months or years. So you need to be prepared for when it lifts, which means preparing her for the true reality of what her life was before the accident. If she brings up another misconstrued memory, gently but firmly correct her. Answer as many questions as she asks. When she gets agitated, try to divert her attention away to something else. Okay?"

Lena and Jeb both nodded silently, each trying to come to terms with it all.

"I'll consult the hospital's physiotherapist about starting her rehabilitation process. She's going to need to relearn most of her motor skills."

Jeb could feel his heart sink as the doctor rattled off the normal day-to-day things Iylah needed to learn to do again.

Her life had truly changed—he couldn't say it was for the better. The man who terrorised her last few months was buried six feet underground, unable to harm her anymore, but he'd left one heck of a scar. Jeb counted it a mercy that she didn't remember it all.

"Thank you, Doc." Lena expressed her gratitude, Doctor Moore leaving to tend to others on his probably long list.

The immensity of what lay ahead for Iylah's recovery caused him to lean against the wall. Still, his decision remained. His mind made up, he wasn't going anywhere.

"Did you guys talk about marriage the night before the accident?" Lena attempted to do her own piecing together.

Jeb shook his head. "We didn't." Not a whole lot of talking had been done in those early hours of the morning. "I don't know. Maybe it was on her mind before the accident, but she never shared it."

It had been on his mind before the very moment that landed her in the hospital bed behind the door next to him.

Clint's statement rang true. Regardless of his last marriage leaving burn holes in his heart, the hopeful romantic in him fell deeply in love with Iylah. Enough to help him move past the blows dealt to him by another. Now what was he to do with those desires?

Take it a day at a time.

～～

Iylah

She tried to chew the mushy food in her mouth that tasted oddly like meat, minus the texture of it. Scrunching her face at it, she swallowed out of obligation.

Jeb laughed, holding the next spoonful for her to suffer through. "Is it that bad?"

"It's horrendous, babe." She swallowed again, trying to cleanse out her mouth, watching the smile on his face slowly taper down to a small upturn of the lip. "This stuff should be illegal."

Her eyes, less heavy now, allowed her to be awake longer than her five-minute stints of consciousness. She looked around the sterile hospital room. A wall of flowers in one corner and nothing much else to brighten up this dreary room—just her and Jeb in it.

"Where's Ms. Bossy?"

"Who?" Amusement danced across Jeb's raised brows. "Do you mean Lena?"

"Yeah her. Is she a friend? Family friend? Some random lady who won't leave me alone?" She took another bite of the mushy meat.

Jeb paused in his feeding efforts. "Lena's your sister. Older sister. Your only sibling."

"Really?" Her own brow rose.

"Really."

"Parents?"

Jeb set aside the plate of whatever he spoon-fed her, a certain seriousness taking over his mesmerising eyes.

"Um—your mom died when you were nineteen. Your dad's still alive."

She saw the tensing of his jaw as he spoke of her dad.

"You don't like my dad?" She rested her head back on the propped pillow behind her neck.

"I've only met him once, so I can't judge the guy, but it was definitely a memorable experience." Even as he said so, disdain laced the way he spoke about him. "Let's just say, his not being here says a lot."

"So I don't have a good relationship with him?"

Jeb cocked his head to the side, finding the words to say what she was piecing together. "Not from what you've said or what I've seen—no."

"How long have we been married?" Her eyes glanced at the tan line around his ring finger where one once sat.

Why wasn't he wearing it?

Again, avoiding her eyes, he took hold of her hand, opening his mouth to say something only to shut it again.

"Jeb?" A lump lodged itself in her throat. She hoped it wasn't the food coming back up. "Tell me the truth."

"We're not married, Iylah." His simple answer, holding her confused stare.

"Are you married to someone else?" She pointed to the sign that a ring once sat on his finger, feeling the sadness of a reality she thought was true fall away.

He scoffed, looking at his hand she'd now retracted hers from. "No, I'm not. I'm divorced from someone else."

"So we don't have children?" Her question went against the ingrained reality she woke up with.

He shook his head almost in regret.

"Are we even friends?" She chuckled in disbelief.

"Yeah, we are. More than friends." There was tenderness in the way he said it. It stirred something familiar in her.

"You love me, don't you?" She witnessed it in his attentiveness, his nearness and his touch.

"With absolutely every part of me, I do." He abashedly grinned, the glistening wet in his eyes not going unnoticed by her, evoking her own tears.

She reached for his hand again. "Good. 'Cause you feel like home."

epilogue

THE SKIN UNDER HIS right eye pulsed with heat, swelling up and feeling tender to the touch. The cross punch staggered him back in a blinking frenzy, attempting to dissipate the stinging of the ruptured blood vessels making his vision cloudy. The sour combination of blood and sweat swam around in his eye as he shut and opened it, his ribs sucking in from the effort needed to defend himself from the onslaught of punches delivered to his body.

Fumbling with the straps of the gloves he wore on his hands, Jeb spat out the mouthguard and its metallic taste from his mouth. Taking a knee, pain seared through the right side of his face.

"Dude, are you okay?" Danny's feet came into Jeb's blurred view. Next to him, another pair of sneakered feet stood. Probably Mo's.

"Water—" Jeb's breath came in short desperate stints, his lungs burning with each deep inhale, "Please."

He straightened himself up, standing and disposing of the gloves rather gruffly.

When Neil suggested an outlet for Jeb, he probably hadn't meant one that would bring constant injury to Jeb's physique week in and week out. But this seemed to have stuck, and it did what he needed to rid his system of any outlying anger and stress. God knows his life was never short of it. That and the shallow brownie points it won him with Tylor always helped.

"Head back." Mo came to his aid, tilting Jeb's head and expertly prying the wounded eye open before a squirt of water flushed out traces of the blood he could somehow taste in his mouth.

"Is it gonna be alright?" The concern in Danny's twenty-something voice rang genuine.

Mo inspected the eye Jeb could barely see out of—the puffy skin around it preventing him from doing so.

How was he going to explain this to the nosy adolescent and reluctant artists he taught tomorrow? This particular injury would prove hard to hide—unlike his bruised back and sides courtesy of shielding himself from multiple jab kicks. Although five months in his skill in preventing such injuries had increased, enough to find in himself the confidence to spar a baby-faced guy like Danny, with energy and agility to boot.

"Yeah, an ice pack and some eyedrops will do you some good." Mo placed a cold compress on the eye, taking Jeb's hand to hold it in place.

Great! I need to get better at dodging those crosses.

Jeb held the compress in place, bending over to retrieve his discarded gloves. Danny rushed to pick them up for him, extending the olive branch for his precise hit.

"Sorry, man."

"Danny, it's kickboxing. That's what we were doing." Jeb shrugged his sweat-drenched shoulder, receiving the gloves back from Danny. "I'll be alright. You may not be next time." He ribbed him in the side, making his way across the ring to leave.

"Alright, old man. Let's not get too carried away now. This crosshook is lethal, sir." Danny called after Jeb.

"Don't I know it." He half chuckled to himself, navigating his way to the locker rooms partially blind.

This was his new normal.

Thursday evening after dismissing his last class for the day at the local arts high school, Jeb found nailing hooks and roundhouse kicks into punching bags and pads for the better part of the last five months. Monday and Tuesday nights were much the same. On those nights Tylor had football practice after school. Jeb always made a point to be present at least twenty minutes before the end to watch his nearly eleven-year-old son find joy in a sport Jeb never really understood the appeal of. Tylor gravitated towards it and prided himself on becoming the best running back in the Fresno middle school district. Each time Jeb witnessed the sheer determination across Tylor's face with every play and instruction, he couldn't hold back from muttering a quick prayer of thanks. Thanks for his son being spared the worst of a tumultuous upbringing, they were both once stuck in.

The guilt subsided with the passing days, and the forgiveness towards himself came along with daily practice. One day he could say he'd completely forgiven himself for staying far too long in a marriage that bore an expiration date. He'd be able to put to bed the little niggling reminders of what a crushed spirit and trampled heart felt like.

Right now, one foot in front of the other seemed to do the job. Reforming his life as a thirty-nine-year-old single dad held far more complexities than he cared for coming down his path.

Jeb threw his gym bag blindly into the back seat of his Ford SUV, one hand still clutching onto the cold compress doing what it needed to over his eye. Driving with one capable eye would prove to be a better test of his memory than his vision. He knew these Clovis roads like the back of his slightly throbbing hand.

Another injury to add to the list. This should be fun.

Taking his phone from the pockets of his California State hooded sweatshirt, he shot a quick message to Tylor.

> Ten minutes away. Please be ready. Don't make me talk to Ethan's mom please!!

She meant well, but her knack for trying to set Jeb up with every single woman in the town started to wear thin. The temptation to make up a fake relationship just to get her off his back enticed him more times than it should have.

Out of habit, he traced back through his past text messages as he sat idly in the parking space of Muscle Kickboxing Gym. The familiar way his chest ached every time he read the messages showed itself with no mercy to his pounding eye.

Four months. Exactly four months to the date, he'd read the last words of communication she would send him.

'I need some space to figure things out,' it read.

Not a phone call. No explanation—just the simple, blunt request. He saw it coming. Worse still, he understood why she needed the space she requested.

How did you tell the person you loved, whose life had been upended, that you didn't want to give them space because you were afraid. Afraid that space would prove you didn't belong in their life. He couldn't, so he obliged even when it punctured his already perforated heart.

> How's she doing this week??

He threw his phone over to the passenger seat after sending the text. His only lifeline to her. One he was thankful for.

The engine came to life as he turned the key, preparing himself for the handicap drive ahead. The pinging of his phone halted the movement of his car before he could pull out. He retrieved it without a moment to waste.

Lena D.W

> Hey Jeb, Iylah's getting there. She's a lot more mobile this week, still in pain and still trying to hide it. Have you heard from her yet? Can I tempt you in a surprise visit? We'll be back in Seattle at the start of March.
> Her stubbornness is the one thing the accident didn't take away, but I think it would actually do her some good seeing you. Forget space—space is overrated right now. Blame the painkillers!

His heart drummed at an increased rate, the sheer thought of seeing her pouring relief onto his already tethered restraint. All he needed was this invitation—granted it didn't come directly from Iylah. Her sister, Lena, was as good as any authority to receive it from. Now how on earth would he last an entire month, the reality of seeing her drawing closer yet distant all at once. And if she rejected him, what then?

Be patient.

For her, anything!

Author's Note

Oh man! This story has lived on my heart for more than I would have liked it to. By God's grace, it now lives in these pages you have just poured over.

My desire in telling the story of Jeb and Iylah is to reveal the constant hand of a God who cares enough to meet us in our muck and mire. When every thing points to a constant state of hopelessness, there is a Hope that beckons beyond the dark and illuminates the very spaces we tend to hide in. This is true for Jeb and Iylah. I know it's true for me.

I hope as you read this story, you were reminded of the astonishing miracle salvation is. The beautiful gift we get to live out within us.

With that being said, my thanks go highly and supremely to my Jesus. The One who loved me back to life. The One who shows his faithfulness even when life hits hard. The One who calls me His own. Without Him none of this is even remotely possible.

To my darling loves—my husband Benjamin, my womb fruit Victor and Aneesa—thank you for releasing me to do this. Thank you for being a part of God's plan with me for the generations to come. He has truly blessed us.

To my mother, Patricia Saunyama—your example is one I thank God for. The way you live for God and are submitted to Him, is the way I desire to be one day. I love you mummy. Thank you for EVERYTHING.

To the friends and family that have encouraged me through this journey of becoming an author—thank you a thousand times over.

To my hype team—Dad, Ruwa, Ruvimbo, Tino WE DID IT!

A special mention to these lovely ladies—Savannah Sullivan, Bailey Kelsen, Ruwa Saunyama, Ruvimbo Saunyama. Your feedback brought this story to life and helped shape it in a way I wouldn't have been able to do alone. Thank you for your time and efforts!

To the reader—thank you for taking a chance on the beginning of this story. I hope you will follow along as the story of the Aston family continues. Like many of us, God is not done with them yet.

All glory to God.

www.ingramcontent.com/pod-product-compliance
Lightning Source LLC
Chambersburg PA
CBHW011917130726
47904CB00015B/2654